CAPTAIN PANTOJA
AND THE SPECIAL SERVICE

CAPTAIN PANTOJA

Mario Vargas Llosa

AND THE
SPECIAL SERVICE

Translated from the Spanish by GREGORY KOLOVAKOS
and RONALD CHRIST

HARPER & ROW, PUBLISHERS
NEW YORK, HAGERSTOWN, SAN FRANCISCO, LONDON

Library of Congress Cataloging in Publication Data

Vargas Llosa, Mario, 1936–
 Captain Pantoja and the special service.
 Translation of Pantaleon y las visitadoras.
 I. Title.
PZ4.V297Cap [PQ8498.32.A65] 863 76–26380
ISBN 0–06–014494–7

78 79 80 81 82 10 9 8 7 6 5 4 3 2 1

To José María Gutiérrez

Il y a des hommes n'ayant
pour mission parmi les autres
que de servir d'intermédiaires; on
les franchit comme des ponts,
et l'on va plus loin.

<div align="right">

FLAUBERT,
L'éducation sentimentale

</div>

CAPTAIN PANTOJA
AND THE SPECIAL SERVICE

1

"Wake up, Panta!" Pochita is saying. "It's eight o'clock already. Panta, Pantita."

"Eight already? God, I'm tired," yawns Pantita. "Did you sew on my new stripe?"

"Yes, Lieutenant, sir," Pochita stands at attention. "Oh, excuse me, Captain, sir. Until I get used to it, honey, you're going to continue being my little lieutenant. Yes, it looks just fine. But get up now—don't you have an appointment?"

"Yes, at nine," Pantita is lathering his face. "Where will they send us, Pocha? Hand me the towel, please. Hey, where do you think?"

"Here, in Lima," Pochita is looking out at the gray sky, the terraces, the cars, the pedestrians. "Oh, it just makes my mouth water: Lima, Lima, Lima."

"Don't be a dreamer. It'll never be Lima. What a pipe dream," Panta looks at himself in the mirror, knots his tie. "If it's only some city like Trujillo or Tacna I'll be happy."

"How funny this item in *El Comercio* is," Pochita is making a face. "In Leticia some guy crucified himself to announce the end of the world. They put him in a nuthouse but people took him out by force because they think he's a saint. Leticia's in the Colombian part of the jungle, isn't it?"

"How handsome you are dressed up as a captain, my son," Mother Leonor puts the marmalade, bread and milk on the table.

"Now it's Colombia; before it was Peru. They took it away from

1

us," Panta spreads butter on a piece of toast. "Give me a little more coffee, Mama."

"I wish they'd send us to Chiclayo again," Mother Leonor brushes the crumbs onto a plate and removes the tablecloth. "After all, we were so well off there, isn't that so? To me, the main thing is that they don't make us move too far from the coast. Get going, boy. Good luck. You have my blessing."

"In the name of the Father and the Holy Ghost and the Son WHO DIED ON THE CROSS," Brother Francisco raises his eyes to the night, lowers his eyes to the torches. "My hands are tied, the wood is an offering, make the sign of the cross for me."

"Colonel López López is waiting for me, miss," says Captain Pantaleón Pantoja.

"And also two generals," she gives him a funny look. "Just go in, Captain. Yes, that one, the brown door."

"Here's our man," Colonel López López stands up. "Come in, Pantoja. Congratulations on that new stripe."

"The highest grade on your promotion exam and by unanimous decision of the judges," General Victoria stretches out a hand, claps him on the shoulder. "Bravo, Captain. That's how you serve career and country."

"Sit down, Pantoja," General Collazos is motioning to a sofa. "Make yourself comfortable and hold on tight, so you can hear what you're about to hear."

"Don't scare him, Tiger," General Victoria is waving his hands. "He's going to think we're sending him to the slaughterhouse."

"The heads of the quartermaster unit have come in person to notify you of your new assignment. That should tell you it's got its problems," Colonel López López adopts a grave expression. "Yes, Pantoja, it's a rather delicate matter."

"The presence of these chiefs is an honor for me," Captain Pantoja clicks his heels. "Hell, Colonel, you're really intriguing me."

"Want a cigarette?" Tiger Collazos takes out a cigarette, a lighter. "But don't just stand there—sit down. What, you don't smoke?"

"You see—for once the Intelligence Service was right," Colonel

2

López López pats a photocopy. "Just like it says: not a smoker, not a drinker, no wandering eye."

"An officer without vices," General Victoria marvels. "Now we have someone to represent the military in Paradise, next to Santa Rosa and San Martín de Porres."

"Don't exaggerate," Captain Pantoja blushes. "I've got to have some vices you don't know about."

"We know you better than you know yourself," Tiger Collazos lifts a folder and puts it down on the table again. "Your eyes would pop if you knew the hours we've spent studying your life. We know what you did, what you didn't do, and even what you will do, Captain."

"We can recite your service record from memory," General Victoria opens the folder, shuffles note cards and forms. "Not even one punishment as an officer and barely half a dozen demerits as a cadet. That's why you've been selected, Pantoja."

"From among almost eighty officers in the division—no fewer," Colonel López López raises an eyebrow. "Now you can puff up like a peacock."

"I'm grateful to you for the high opinion you have of me," Captain Pantoja's vision blurs. "I will do everything I can to live up to that confidence, Colonel."

"Captain Pantaleón Pantoja?" General Scavino is shaking the telephone. "I can hardly hear you. You're sending him to me for what, Tiger?"

"You made a fine record for yourself in Chiclayo," General Victoria is leafing through a report. "Colonel Montes was desperate to hold on to you. It seems the district ran like a watch, thanks to you."

" 'Born organizer, mathematical sense of order, executive capacity,' " Tiger Collazos reads. " 'He conducted the administration of the regiment with efficiency and real inspiration.' My God, that half-breed Montes fell in love with you."

"So much praise mixes me up," Captain Pantoja lowers his head. "I've always tried to do my duty, nothing more."

"What service?" General Scavino lets out a horse laugh. "Look, Tiger, neither you nor Victoria can pull my leg. I'm no fool."

"O.K., let's take the bull by the horns," General Victoria seals his lips with a finger. "This business demands the utmost secrecy. I'm talking about the mission that's going to be entrusted to you, Captain. All right, let the cat out of the bag, Tiger."

"In brief, the troops in the jungle are screwing the local women," Tiger Collazos takes a breath, blinks and coughs. "There are rapes all over the place and the courts can't handle them all. The entire Amazon District is up in arms."

"They bombard us daily with dispatches and accusations," General Victoria is plucking at his beard. "And protest committees arrive from even the most out-of-the-way little towns."

"Your soldiers are dishonoring our women," Mayor Paiva Runhuí squeezes his hat and loses his voice. "Just a few months ago they molested my dear sister-in-law and last week they almost raped my own wife."

"No, not my soldiers—the country's soldiers," General Victoria is making pacifying gestures. "Calm down, calm down, Mr. Mayor. The Army sincerely regrets your sister-in-law's misfortune and will do what it can to compensate her."

"And do they call rape a 'misfortune' nowadays?" Father Beltrán gets rattled. "Because that's what it was: rape."

"Two uniformed men grabbed Florcita as she was coming from the farm and they mounted her right there in the middle of the road," Mayor Teófilo Morey bites his nails and hops up and down in place. "With such good aim that now she's pregnant, General."

"Miss Dorotea, you're going to identify those criminals for me," growls Colonel Peter Casahuanqui. "No crying, no crying; you'll see how I'm going to fix this."

"You think I'm going to go outside?" sobs Dorotea. "Me, all alone, in front of all those soldiers?"

"They're going to march right by here, in front of the guardhouse," Colonel Máximo Dávila is hiding behind the iron railing. "You're going to peek out at them through the window and as soon as you spot the brutes, you're going to point them out to me, Miss Jesús."

"Brutes?" Father Beltrán spits. "Wretches, curs, imbeciles, I'd say. To subject Mrs. Asunta to such infamy! To tarnish the uniform that way!"

4

"My servant, Luisa Cánepa, was violated by a sergeant, and then by a corporal and later by a private," Lieutenant Bacacorzo is cleaning his glasses. "She must have liked it or something, Commander, but one thing we can be sure of now is that she's turned into a prostitute by the name of Knockers and has some queer they call Chameleon for a pimp."

"Now point out to me, Miss Dolores, which of these men you want to marry," Colonel Augusto Valdés is pacing in front of the three recruits. "And the chaplain will marry you this instant. Choose, choose. Which of these do you prefer as the father of your future baby?"

"They surprised my wife right in the church," the carpenter Adriano Lharque is sitting stiffly on the edge of his chair. "Not the cathedral, but the Church of Santo Cristo de Bagazán, sir."

"That's how it is, dear listeners," bellows Sinchi. "Neither fear of God nor respect for His sacred house nor the noble gray hairs of that dignified matron, who has already given two generations to Loreto, were able to restrain those sacrilegious, those lustful men."

"They began to tug at me, oh, my God, they wanted to throw me on the ground," cries Mrs. Cristina. "They were falling-down drunk and you should have heard the obscenities they were saying. In front of the main altar, I swear to you."

"The most charitable soul in all Loreto, General," thunders Father Beltrán. "They violated her five times!"

"And also her little daughter and her little niece and her little adopted daughter—I know it all already, Scavino," Tiger Collazos is blowing the dandruff off his epaulets. "But that priest Beltrán, is he for us or against us? Is he or isn't he the Army chaplain?"

"I protest, both as a priest and as a soldier, General," Father Beltrán sucks in his stomach, sticks out his chest. "Because these abuses do as much damage to the Army as to the victims."

"Of course, what the recruits tried to do to the lady is very wrong," General Victoria hedges, smiles, salutes. "But her relatives almost beat them to death; don't forget that. I have the medical report here: broken ribs, contusions, shredded ears. In this case it was a tie, my dear doctor."

"To Iquitos?" Pochita stops sprinkling the shirt and holds up the

iron. "Oh, how far away they're sending us, Panta."

"With wood you make the fire that cooks your food, with wood you build the house where you live, the bed where you sleep and the raft on which you cross the river," Brother Francisco is suspended above the forest of unmoving heads, anxious faces and open arms. "With wood you make the harpoon that catches the fish, the spear that hunts the warthog and the coffin in which you bury the dead. Sisters! Brothers! Kneel down for me!"

"It's one hell of a problem, Pantoja," Colonel López López is shaking his head. "In Contamana the mayor issued an order telling the residents to lock their women up at home when the troops are on leave."

"And especially so far away from the water," Mother Leonor drops the needle, ties off the thread and cuts it with her teeth. "Are there many mosquitoes up there in the jungle? You know how they bother me."

"Take a look at this list," Tiger Collazos is scratching his forehead. "Forty-three pregnancies in less than a year. The chaplains under Father Beltrán married about twenty women, but of course, this depravity requires more radical measures than forced marriages. Up till now punishments and warnings have not changed the picture: a soldier arrives in the jungle and turns into a prick gone crazy."

"But you're the one who seems least excited about the place, dear," Pochita goes around opening and dusting off suitcases. "Why, Panta?"

"It has to be the heat, the climate, don't you think?" Tiger Collazos gets excited.

"Very likely, General," stammers Captain Pantoja.

"The warm humidity, that excess of nature," Tiger Collazos passes his tongue over his lips. "It always happens to me: I get to the jungle and I start breathing fire—I feel like my blood is boiling."

"If your wife hears you"—General Victoria laughs—"watch out for her claws, Tiger."

"At first we thought it was the diet," General Collazos slaps his belly. "That the garrisons used a lot of spices, something that made the men's sexual appetites worse."

6

"We consulted specialists, even a Swiss doctor who cost a pile of money," Colonel López López is rubbing two fingers together. "A dietitian loaded with titles."

"Pas d'inconvénient," notes Professor Bernard Lahoe in a little book. "We will prepare a diet that, without diminishing the necessary proteins, will weaken the libido of the soldiers by eighty-five percent."

"Don't go overboard," mumbles Tiger Collazos. "We don't want a troop of eunuchs either, Doctor."

"Horcones to Iquitos, Horcones to Iquitos," Second Lieutenant Santana is getting impatient. "Yes, very important, top priority. We have not obtained the expected results with Operation Swiss Ration. My men are dying of hunger, of tuberculosis. Today another two fainted during inspection, Commander."

"No joking, Scavino," Tiger Collazos is wedging the telephone between his ear and his shoulder while he lights a cigarette. "We've gone over and over it and this is the only solution. I'm sending Pantoja to you, with his mother and his wife. Have a good time."

"Pochita and I already got used to the idea and we're glad about going to Iquitos," Mother Leonor is folding handkerchiefs, sorting skirts, packing shoes. "But you're still down in the mouth. What's the matter with you, son?"

"You're the man, Pantoja," Colonel López López stands up and grabs him by the arms. "You're going to put an end to this headache."

"After all, it *is* a city, Panta, and it seems nice," Pochita is throwing rags into the garbage, tying knots, closing her pocketbooks. "Don't make such a face. Wouldn't the mountains be worse?"

"To tell you the truth, Colonel, I can't see how," Captain Pantoja swallows. "But sure, I'll do what I'm ordered."

"For the time being, you'll go to the jungle," Colonel López López grabs a pointer and marks a spot on the map. "Your center of operations will be Iquitos."

"We're going to get to the root of this problem and nip it in the bud," General Victoria strikes his open hand with his fist. "Be-

cause, as you must've guessed, Pantoja, the problem isn't just women being molested."

"But also recruits condemned to living like monks in all that wicked heat," clucks Tiger Collazos. "Serving in the jungle is very tough, Pantoja, very brave."

"Every skirt is spoken for in the Amazon settlements," Colonel López López is gesturing. "There's no red-light district, no loose women or anything like that."

"The men spend all week locked up, carrying out details in the mountains, dreaming about their day off," General Victoria imagines. "They walk miles to the nearest town. And what happens when they get there?"

"Nothing. Because of the damned lack of females," Tiger Collazos shrugs. "And then the ones who don't get laid lose control after the first glass of anisette and jump like panthers on whatever walks by."

"They've reported cases of buggery and even bestiality," Colonel López López states precisely. "Would you believe that a corporal in Horcones was taken by surprise while carrying on like a newlywed with a monkey?"

"The monkey answers to the absurd name of Milkmaid of the Fifth Barracks," Second Lieutenant Santana is choking on his laughter. "Or rather *answered*, because I killed her with a single shot. The degenerate is in the guardhouse, Colonel."

"In short, abstinence makes for a hell of a lot of corruption," says General Victoria. "And demoralization, nervousness, apathy."

"We've got to give these starving men something to eat, Pantoja," Tiger Collazos is looking him solemnly in the eyes. "Here's where you come into the picture, here's where we're going to use your organizing brain."

"Panta, why are you sitting there so quiet and mixed up?" Pochita puts the ticket in her wallet and asks where the gate to the plane is. "There'll be a big river. We can go swimming, take walks to see the Indians. Cheer up, honey."

"Son, what's making you act so strange?" Mother Leonor is watching the clouds, the propellers, the trees. "You haven't opened your mouth the whole trip. What's bothering you so much?"

8

"Nothing, Mama. Nothing, Pochita," Panta is fastening his seat belt. "I'm all right, nothing's the matter. Look, we're landing. Isn't that the Amazon?"

"All this time you've been acting like a dumbbell," Pochita is putting on her sunglasses, taking off her coat. "You haven't said a word, you sleep with your eyes open. God, how hot it is. I've never seen you so changed, Panta."

"I was a little worried about my new assignment, but that's all over with now," Panta takes out his wallet and hands a few bills to the driver. "Yes, that's right—number 549, Hotel Lima. Wait, Mama—I'll help you get out."

"You're an officer, aren't you?" Pochita throws her travel bag on a chair, takes off her shoes. "You knew they could send you anywhere. Iquitos isn't bad, Panta—can't you see it looks like a nice place?"

"You're right. I've been acting like a dumbbell," Panta opens the closet, hangs up a uniform and a suit. "Maybe I'd grown fond of Chiclayo. I promise that's all over. All right, let's unpack. Can you believe this heat, babe?"

"As for me, I could live here in the hotel for the rest of my life," Pochita is lying on her back on the bed, stretching out. "They do everything for you. You don't have to worry about anything."

"And would it be right to have Cadet Pantoja in a cheap hotel?" Panta is taking off his tie, his shirt.

"Cadet Pantoja?" Pochita opens her eyes, unbuttons her blouse, leans an elbow on the pillow. "Really? Can we take care of that now?"

"Didn't I promise you we would once I got my third stripe?" Panta shakes his trousers, folds and hangs them up. "He'll come from Loreto—how does that strike you?"

"Great, Panta," Pochita is laughing, clapping, bouncing up and down on the mattress. "Whee, I'm happy—the little cadet, Pantita Junior."

"We have to take care of this right away," Panta opens his hands, comes closer. "So he gets here soon. Come over here, babe—where are you running to?"

"Hey, what's wrong with you?" Pochita jumps from the bed, runs toward the bathroom. "Have you gone crazy?"

9

"C'mon, c'mon, for Pantita's sake," Panta stumbles over a suit-case, knocks over a chair. "Let's take care of it right now. C'mon, Pochita."

"But it's eleven in the morning. We just got here," Pochita spars, pulls back, shoves, gets mad. "Let go; your mother's going to hear us, Panta."

"To break in Iquitos, to break in the hotel." Pantita pants, fights, embraces, slips. "Come here, beautiful."

"Now you see what's been gained by so many threats and dis-patches," General Scavino is brandishing a written communiqué covered with stamps and signatures. "You're also to blame for this, Commander Beltrán. Look at what this guy's beginning to orga-nize in Iquitos."

"You're going to tear my skirt," Pochita hides behind the ward-robe, throws a pillow, begs for a truce. "Panta, I don't recognize you. You're always so . . . so formal; what's happening to you? Let go—I'll take it off myself."

"I wanted to cure a disease, not cause one," Commander Beltrán reads and rereads General Scavino's flushed face. "I never imag-ined the medicine would be worse than the sickness, General. Unthinkable, terrible. Are you going to permit this atrocity?"

"The bra, the stockings," Pantita perspires, throws himself down, leans back, stretches out. "Tiger was right: in this humidity, you breathe fire, your blood boils. C'mon, nibble me where I like it. The ear, Pocha."

"I'm embarrassed in the daytime, Panta," Pochita complains, wraps herself in the bedspread, sighs. "You're going to fall asleep. Don't you have to be at headquarters at three? You always do."

"I'll take a shower," Pantita kneels, bends over, straightens up. "Don't talk to me, don't distract me. Nibble my ear. Like that, just like that. Ahh, I already feel like I'm coming. Oh, babe, I can't tell who I am."

"I know very well who you are and why you've come to Iquitos," mutters General Roger Scavino. "And straight off I'll tell you that your presence in this city doesn't please me one bit. Let's get things clear from the start, Captain."

"Excuse me, General," Captain Pantoja stammers. "There must be some misunderstanding."

10

"I'm not in favor of this Special Service you've come to orga-
nize," General Scavino moves his bald head nearer the fan and
closes his eyes for a moment. "I was opposed from the beginning
and I still think it's an outrage."

"And above all, an unspeakable act of immorality," Father Bel-
trán is fanning himself furiously.

"The commander and I have kept silent because our superiors
are the ones who give the orders," General Scavino unfolds his
handkerchief and wipes the sweat from his forehead, temples,
neck. "But they haven't convinced us, Captain."

"I didn't have anything to do with this project, General," Pan-
toja, motionless, perspires. "It was the surprise of my life when
they told me about it, Father."

"Commander," Father Beltrán corrects him. "Can't you count
stripes?"

"Excuse me, Commander," Pantoja lightly clicks his heels. "I
didn't have anything to do with it, I promise you."

"Aren't you one of the brains in the quartermaster unit who
thought up this nonsense?" General Scavino grabs the fan, puts it
in front of his face, his skull, and clears his throat. "Anyway, there
are some things that have to be understood from the start. There's
no way I can stop this from happening, but I'll see to it that this
touches the armed forces as little as possible. No one is going to
spoil the image the Army has won for itself in Loreto since I've
been in charge of the Fifth Region."

"That's what I want too," Pantoja is looking over the general's
shoulder at the muddy water of the river, at a barge filled with
bananas, at the blue sky, at the fiery sun. "I'm ready to do what
I can."

"Because if the news leaked, there'd be an ugly mess," General
Scavino raises his voice, stands up, rests his hands on the window
sill. "The strategists in Lima calmly plan dirty tricks at their desks,
because it's General Scavino who'll have to weather the storm if
the thing becomes public."

"I agree with you, you have to believe me," Captain Pantoja
sweats, sees the sleeves of his uniform getting wet, implores. "I
never would've asked for this assignment. It's something so differ-

11

ent from my usual work, I don't even know if I'll be able to carry it out."

"Your father and your mother came together on wood to make you, and the woman who carried you struggled and opened her legs to give birth to you on wood," Brother Francisco is screeching and thundering up there in the darkness. "The wood felt HIS body, grew red with HIS blood, received HIS tears, grew moist with HIS sweat. The wood is sacred, the plank brings health. Sisters! Brothers! Open your arms to me!"

"Dozens of people will march through that door. This office will be filled with protests, with signed documents, with anonymous letters," Father Beltrán gets agitated, takes a few steps, comes back, opens and shuts his fan. "All the Amazon District will raise the roof and think the mastermind of the scandal is General Scavino."

"I can already hear that demagogue Sinchi vomiting out his slander against me on the radio," General Scavino turns, is suddenly disturbed.

"My instructions are for the Special Service to function with the greatest secrecy," Captain Pantoja dares to take off his kepi, to rub a handkerchief across his forehead, to wipe his eyes. "I'll keep those orders very much in mind at every moment, General."

"And what the hell could I invent to placate the people?" General Scavino shouts, goes around the desk. "Have they given any thought in Lima to the role I'll have to play?"

"If you'd rather, I can ask for my transfer today," Captain Pantoja grows pale. "To prove to you that I have no interest in the Special Service."

"What a euphemism these geniuses have thought up," Father Beltrán taps his heels, his back turned, looking at the glistening river, the cabañas, the level stretch of trees. "Special Service . . . Special Service."

"Nothing doing with transfers; they'd send me another officer in a week," General Scavino sits down again, fans himself, wiping his bald pate. "It's up to you whether this hurts the Army or not. You've got a responsibility on your shoulders as big as a volcano."

"You can sleep peacefully, General," Captain Pantoja stiffens,

12

throws back his shoulders, looks straight ahead. "The Army is what I respect and love most in life."

"The best way you can serve it now is to keep far away from it," General Scavino softens his tone and attempts a friendly expression. "While you're in command of that Service, at least."

"I'm sorry," blinks Captain Pantoja. "What are you saying?"

"I don't want you ever to set foot in the quartermaster's or in the barracks at Iquitos," General Scavino turns the palms and backs of his hands to the humming, invisible blades of the fan. "You're excused from attending all official functions, parades, Te Deums. Also from wearing a uniform. You'll dress only in civilian clothes."

"I even have to come to work in mufti?" Captain Pantoja continues to blink.

"Your work is going to be very far away from the quartermaster's," observes General Scavino with misgiving, with consternation, with piety. "Don't be naïve, man. Do you think that I'd be able to open an office for you here—for the traffic you're going to organize? I've arranged for a depot on the outskirts of Iquitos, by the river. Always dress as a civilian. No one must find out that that place has any connection with the Army. Understand?"

"Yes, General," the astonished Captain Pantoja is nodding. "Only . . . well, I wasn't expecting anything like this. It's going to be—I don't know—like changing my personality."

"Remember that you've been assigned to the Intelligence Service"—Commander Beltrán comes away from the window, approaches him, gives him a benevolent smile—"and that your life depends on your ability to go unnoticed."

"I'll try to adapt, General," stammers Captain Pantoja.

"Nor is it advisable for you to live on the army base, so go look for a small house in the city," General Scavino is mopping a handkerchief over his eyebrows, ears, lips and nose. "And I want you to have no relations with the officers."

"You mean friendly relations, General?" Captain Pantoja chokes.

"They're not going to be amorous," Father Beltrán laughs or grunts or chokes.

13

"I know it's difficult, that it's going to be hard on you," General Scavino agrees in a friendly way. "But there's no other way, Pantoja. Your mission will place you in contact with all kinds of people in the Amazon District. The only way to avoid any reflection on the Army is by sacrificing you."

"In short, I must conceal my position as an officer," Captain Pantoja sees in the distance a naked boy climbing a tree, a lame pink heron, a horizon of burning underbrush. "Dress as a civilian, mix with civilians, work as a civilian."

"But always think as an officer," General Scavino is banging on the table. "I've appointed a lieutenant who will serve as a liaison between us. You'll see each other once a week and through him you'll give me an account of your activities."

"Don't worry at all. I'll be quiet as a tomb," Lieutenant Bacacorzo raises the glass of beer and toasts the other's health. "I'm on top of it all, Captain. Is it all right if we meet on Tuesdays? I thought the meeting place should always be bars and brothels. You'll have to hang out a lot in those places now, won't you?"

"He made me feel like a delinquent, some kind of leper," Captain Pantoja is examining the stuffed monkeys, parrots and birds, the men who drink standing at the bar. "How the hell am I going to start working if even General Scavino is sabotaging me? If my own superior starts out by discouraging me, by asking me to disguise myself, by not letting me be seen."

"You went to headquarters so happy and you come home again with that dumb face on," Pochita stands on tiptoe and kisses him on the cheek. "What happened, Panta? Did you get there late and get hollered at by General Scavino?"

"I'll help you as much as I can, Captain," Lieutenant Bacacorzo offers him potato chips. "I'm not an expert, but I'll do what I can. Don't complain; a lot of officers would give anything to be in your shoes. Think what freedom you're going to have. You'll choose your own hours, your own schedule. Besides all the other tidbits —eh, Captain?"

"We are going to live *here*, in this ugly place?" Mother Leonor is looking at the peeling walls, the dirty floors, the cobwebs on the ceiling. "Why didn't they give you one of those pretty houses on the army base? Once again, Panta, you're not enough of a man."

14

"Don't think I'm becoming a defeatist, Bacacorzo; it's just that I'm really at a loss," Captain Pantoja tastes, chews, swallows, mumbles delicious. "I'm a good administrator, sure. But they've taken me out of my depth and now I don't know my ass from a hole in the ground."

"Did you take a look at your center of operations yet?" Lieutenant Bacacorzo is filling the glasses again. "General Scavino has sent around an order: no officer in Iquitos can go near that warehouse on the Itaya River, under penalty of thirty days hard labor."

"Not yet. I'll go tomorrow, early," Captain Pantoja drinks, wipes his mouth, holds back a burp. "Because let's be frank: to do this the way they're asking, you'd need some experience in the business. Know the night world, have been a little wild."

"Are you going to the quartermaster's like that, Panta?" Pochita comes near him, touches the sleeveless shirt, sniffs at the blue pants, the little jockey cap. "What about your uniform?"

"Unfortunately, that's not my case," Captain Pantoja grows sad, sketches an embarrassed gesture. "I never was wild. Not even when I was a kid."

"We can't get together with the officers' families?" Mother Leonor flourishes the feather duster, the broom, a bucket, dusts, cleans, scrubs, becomes frightened. "We have to live as if we're civilians?"

"Just think—when I was a cadet, I chose to stay in school studying on the days when we had leave," Captain Pantoja is remembering nostalgically. "Grinding away at math, most of all, is what I like best. I never went out to parties. Though maybe it sounds like a story to you, I only learned the easiest dances: the bolero and the waltz."

"Not even the neighbors can know you're a captain?" Pochita wipes windows, scrubs floors, paints walls, gets scared.

"So what's happening to me is awful," Pantoja looks around distrustfully, speaks into the man's ear. "How can someone who's never had any contact with 'specialists' like them organize a Special Service, Bacacorzo?"

"A special assignment?" Pochita waxes doors, papers cupboards, hangs paintings. "You're going to work in the Intelligence Service? Well, now I'm beginning to get all the mystery, Panta."

15

"I picture the thousands of soldiers who are waiting, who are counting on me," Captain Pantoja examines the bottles, gets emotional, dreams. "Who tick off days and think they're already on their way, they're going to get here, and my hair stands up on end, Bacacorzo."

"I don't give a damn about military secrets," Mother Leonor puts closets in order, sews curtains, dusts screens, plugs in lamps. "Secrets from your mother? Tell me, tell me."

"I don't want to cheat them," Captain Pantoja is getting upset. "But where am I going to start?"

"If you don't tell me, you're going to wind up being sorry," Pochita makes beds, puts down throw rugs, varnishes furniture, arranges glasses, plates and napkins in the cabinet. "No more little pinches wherever you like, no more nips on the ear. You choose, sonny boy."

"To start with, Captain"—Lieutenant Bacacorzo cheers him on with a smile and a toast—"if the Special Service doesn't come to Captain Pantoja, Captain Pantoja must go to them. It's the simplest way, it seems to me."

"As a spy, Panta?" Pochita rubs her hands together, looks around the room, mutters how much we've improved this pig sty —right, Mother Leonor? "Like in the movies? Oh, sweetheart, how exciting."

"Take a little stroll this evening through the red-light districts of Iquitos," Lieutenant Bacacorzo scribbles addresses on the napkin. "The Mau Mau, the 007, The One-Eyed Cat, the Little San Juan. To familiarize yourself with the atmosphere. I'd be happy to go with you, but Scavino's instructions are final, you know."

"Where are you going in that outfit?" Mother Leonor answers yes, no one would recognize it, Pochita; we should get a prize. "My God, how dressed up you are. A tie, even. You're going to roast in this heat. A top-level meeting? At night? How funny that you're a secret agent, Panta. Yes, I know. Shh, shh—I'll be quiet."

"Ask in any of those places for Chino Porfirio," Lieutenant Bacacorzo folds the napkin and puts it in his pocket. "He's someone who can help you. He procures 'washerwomen' at home. You know what they are, don't you?"

"For this reason HE did not die by drowning, by burning, by

16

hanging or by flogging," Brother Francisco is moaning and shouting above the sputtering of the torches and the murmuring of the prayers. "For this reason HE was nailed to a piece of wood, for this reason HE chose the cross. Let him who wants to listen, listen; let him who wants to understand, understand. Sisters! Brothers! Beat your breast three times for me!"

"Ahem . . . I mean hello," Pantaleón Pantoja blows his nose, sits on the stool, leans on the bar. "Yeah, a beer, please. I just got to Iquitos, I'm taking a look around town. They call this place the Mau Mau? Oh, because of the arrows, the totems. I get it now."

"Here you go, ice cold," the bartender serves the beer, dries the glass, points to the dance floor. "Almost nobody's here 'cause it's Monday."

"Uh, I want to find out something . . . umm, ah"—Pantaleón Pantoja clears his throat—"if it's possible. Just for the information."

"Where can you find chicks?" The bartender makes a circle with his thumb and index finger. "Right here, but today they all went to hear Brother Francisco, the saint of the cross. They say he came all the way from Brazil on foot and that he can perform miracles. But look who's coming in. Hey, Porfirio, over here. I want to introduce you to this gentleman. He's interested in a little tourist information."

"Blothels and dames?" Chino Porfirio winks at him, bows, shakes his hand. "Of coulse, mistel. With pleasule; I tell you what's goin' on in two minutes. It not goin' to cost you much mole than a beel. Cheap, light?"

"Glad to meet you," Pantaleón Pantoja motions him to sit down on the next stool. "Yeah, sure, a beer. Now don't get the wrong idea—I don't have any personal interest in this myself, just a technical one."

"Technical?" The bartender turns up his nose. "You're no stool pigeon, are you, mister?"

"Blothels, thele ale vely few," Chino Porfirio holds up three fingers. "Youl health and a good life. Two decent ones and a leally foul one, fol beggals. And thele ale also the wholes that go house to house on theil own. You know, the washelwomen?"

"Oh, really? Very interesting," Pantaleón Pantoja is urging him

17

on with smiles. "Just curious. I don't frequent those spots. You got connections? I mean friends, contacts in those places?"

"The Chink's in his glory when it comes to whores," the bartender laughs. "They call him the Fu Manchu of Bethlehem, the floating house district, the Venice of the Amazon District. You get down there yet?"

"I done evelythin' in my life and I no leglet it, mistel," Chino Porfirio blows off the foam and takes a swig. "I got no money but I sule got expelience. Ticket sellel fol a movie house, pilot on a balge, snake huntel fol expolt."

"And they kicked you outta all those jobs for bein' a whoring old asshole, brother," the bartender lights a cigarette for him. "Tell the man what your mama predicted about you."

> *"A Chinaman who's boln pool*
> *Dies a pimp, thief ol fool."*

Chino Porfirio sings and recites with horse laughs. "God, my pletty little mothel in holy heaven. Since we only live once, we got to live it up, light? We tly a second cool dlink, mistel?"

"Sure, but . . . ahhh, hmmm," blushes Pantaleón Pantoja. "I have a better idea. Why don't we go someplace else, friend?"

"Mr. Pantoja?" Madame Chuchupe breathes honey. "So very pleased to meet you, and come in, make yourself at home. We treat everyone well here, except for those crooked soldiers who want a discount. Hello, my little Chinese bandit."

"Mistel Pantoja come flom Lima and he fliend," Chino Porfirio kisses her on the cheek, pinches her backside. "He going to open a business hele. You know, Chuchupe, luxuly selvice. This dwalf's name Fleckle, leal name Juan Chupito Civela, and he mascot of the place, mistel."

"Better if you said foreman, bartender and bodyguard, motherfucker," Freckle reaches for bottles, picks up glasses, collects tabs, turns on the record player, herds women onto the dance floor. "Or is this the first time you've come to Casa Chuchupe? It won't be the last, you'll see. There aren't many girls because they've gone to see Brother Francisco, that guy who put up that big cross next to Lake Morona."

18

"I was thele too and thele was lotta people, and the tlinket vendols must be laking it in," Chino Porfirio delivers his goodbyes. "Fantastic speakel, that blothel. You not understand him vely good, but he stilling up the people."

"Everything that you nail to wood is an offering, everything that ends up on wood rises and HE WHO DIED ON THE CROSS receives it," chants Brother Francisco monotonously. "The many-colored butterfly that gladdens the morning, the rose that perfumes the air, the bat with little eyes that glow in the dark and even the chigger encrusted under your fingernail. Sisters! Brothers! Erect crosses for me!"

"What a long face, but you can't be *so* serious if you're running around with this Chinaman," Chuchupe cleans off a table with her arm, pulls up chairs, loosens up. "Let's see, Freckle, a bottle of beer and three glasses. The first round's on the house."

"Know what a *chuchupe* is?" Chino Porfirio is whistling, showing the tip of his tongue. "Most poisonous snake in Amazon. You can imagine things this woman says about people to get nickname like that."

"Be quiet, you bum," Chuchupe shuts him up, sets out the glasses, smiles. "To your health, Mr. Pantoja. Welcome to Iquitos."

"Poisonous tongue," Chino Porfirio points to the Chinese decorations on the walls, the scarred mirror, the red screens, the dancing fringes of the mottled armchair. "Just that she good fliend and this house, though it seen its yeals, is best in Iquitos."

"Take a look at what's left of the goods, if nothing else," Freckle is pointing: little half-breeds, whites, Japanese, even an albino. "It took a good eye on Chuchupe's part to choose her women, mister."

"Good music, makes you wanna dance," Chino Porfirio gets up, grabs the arm of a woman, drags her to the dance floor, dances. "A *pemisito* to shake up youl bones. C'me hele, fatty. C'me hele."

"Can I buy you another beer, Madame Chuchupe?" Pantaleón Pantoja coaxes an uneasy smile and whispers, "I'd like to ask you for a few facts, if it's no trouble."

"What a friendly devil that Chino is. He never has any money but how he livens up an evening," Chuchupe folds a piece of

19

paper, throws it at Porfirio's head, hits the target. "I don't know what they see in him. They're all dying for him. Look at him going nuts."

"Matters related to your—you know—to your business," insists Pantaleón Pantoja.

"Sure, happy to," Chuchupe gets serious, agrees, autopsies him with her stare. "Though I didn't think you came to talk about business but for something else, Mr. Pantoja."

"My head is killing me," Pantita curls up, covers himself with the sheets. "My body is falling to pieces, I got the shivers."

"Why wouldn't it kill you, why wouldn't you have, and what's more, it makes me glad," Pochita taps her heels. "You went to bed around four and you came in falling-down drunk, you idiot."

"You've vomited three times," Mother Leonor goes back and forth between kettles, washbasins and towels. "You've left the room stinking, son."

"You're going to explain what all this means, Panta," Pochita approaches the bed, eyes blazing.

"I already told you, sweetheart—it's got to do with work," complains Pantita from between the pillows. "You know only too well I don't drink, how I hate keeping late hours. It's torture for me to do those things, dear."

"You mean to tell me you're going to go on doing them?" Pochita grimaces, screws up her face. "Going to bed at dawn, getting drunk? Oh, no you're not, Panta—I promise you you're not."

"Come on, don't fight," Mother Leonor is carefully balancing the glass, the pitcher, the tray. "Come, child, put on these cold towels and take this Alka-Seltzer. Quick, with the little bubbles."

"It's my work, it's the assignment they've given me," Pantita despairs, fades, loses his voice. "I hate all this—you've got to believe me. But I can't tell you anything. Don't make me talk; it'd be very bad for my career. Have faith in me, Pocha."

"You've been with women," Pochita breaks out sobbing. "Men don't get drunk until dawn without women. I'm sure you were, Panta."

"Pocha, Pochita, my head is splitting, my back is hurting me," Pantita places a cloth on his forehead, reaches under the bed, pulls out a chamber pot, spits saliva and bile. "Don't cry. You make me

20

feel like a criminal and I'm not, I swear to you I'm not."

"Close your eyes and open your yap," Mother Leonor holds out a steaming cup, puckers her mouth. "And now this little cup of very hot coffee, my little boy."

2

SSGFRI

Dispatch Number One

GENERAL SUBJECT: Special Service for Garrisons, Frontier and
 Related Installations
SPECIFIC SUBJECT: Preparation of command post and evaluation
 of possible enlistment sites
CLASSIFICATION: Top Secret
PLACE AND DATE: Iquitos, 12 August 1956

The undersigned, Capt. (Quartermaster) Pantaleón Pantoja,
Peruvian Army, commissioned to organize and put into operation
a Special Service for Garrisons, Frontier and Related Installations
(SSGFRI) for the entire Amazon region, respectfully presents him-
self to Gen. Felipe Collazos, Chief of Administration, Supply and
Logistics of the Army, salutes him and reports:

1. (a) That as soon as he arrived in Iquitos, he presented him-
self to the Command of Region V (Amazon) in order to greet Gen.
Roger Scavino, commander in chief, who, after receiving him in
a friendly and cordial way, proceeded to communicate to him
some of the measures taken for putting into operation in the most
efficacious manner possible the mission that has been entrusted to
him—namely, that in the interests of protecting the good name of
the military, it is advisable that the undersigned never appear in
person at headquarters or in the barracks of this city, that he not
dress in uniform, that he not reside in military housing, that he not

fraternize with the officers of the base, which is to say that he should act at all times as a civilian, because the persons and areas that he will have to frequent (the society of brothels, slums) are not appropriate as anticipated acquaintances for a captain of the armed forces. (b) That he must act strictly in accordance with these arrangements, despite the distress that may result from the effect of his having to conceal his position as an officer in our country's Army, of which he is very proud, and that he must keep himself apart from his companions in arms, whom he considers his brothers, despite the delicate family situation that this creates for him, since he is also obliged to maintain with his mother and with his own wife the most absolute secrecy; and, consequently, that he must nearly always fail to tell the truth for the sake of family harmony and the proper fulfillment of his assignment. (c) That he accept these sacrifices, conscious of the undeferable nature of the operation his superiors have entrusted to him and of the interests of our soldiers who serve the Nation in the most remote regions of the jungle.

2. (a) That he has already taken possession of the site located on the banks of the Itaya River assigned by headquarters of Region V as a command post and quartermaster's depot (for recruitment/provisioning) for the Special Service. (b) That the soldiers detailed to the Service answering to the names of Sinforoso Caiguas and Palomino Rioalto have already been placed under his command and have been chosen by their superiors and according to strict standards for their virtues of outstanding conduct, tractability and a certain indifference toward persons of the opposite sex, since, in contrast, the type of work they will perform and the peculiarities of the environment in which they will be placed would be likely to arouse temptations in them and cause subsequent problems for the Service. The undersigned wants to make clear that the site where the command post and quartermaster's depot are located possesses the best qualities: first of all, size and proximity to means of transportation (the Itaya River); second, protection from accidental discovery since the city is located quite far away and the closest inhabited spot, the Garote rice mill, is situated on the opposite shore. (There is no bridge.) On the other hand, it enjoys good topographical possibilities for the installation

23

of a small dock, so that after the Special Service has established its circulatory system, all shipping and receiving can be carried out under the direct supervision of the command post.

3. (a) That during the first week, the undersigned had to concentrate all his time and efforts on cleaning and improving the premises, a semi-quadrilateral 1,323 meters square (a quarter of whose surface is roofed over with corrugated tin), enclosed by thin wooden partitions and having two large doors, one opening on the trail to Iquitos and one on the river. The area of the roofed section is 327 meters square and is paved; it consists of two floors, the higher one being only a wooden platform with a railing that leads to a little fire stairway. On this floor the undersigned has installed his command post, private office, files and records. In the lower part—which can be observed at all times from the command post —hammocks for Sinforoso Caiguas and Palomino Rioalto have been hung, and a crudely constructed toilet has been installed. The unroofed part of this site is a large unsurfaced yard that still has some trees in it.

(b) That a week for the preparation of the site might seem excessive—symptomatic of a lack of discipline or laziness—but the truth is that the location was not in usable condition and was, excusing myself for using the word, filthy, for the reasons stated here: due to the fact that the Army had abandoned it, this depot had come to be used for miscellaneous and illegal practices. Hence it had been taken possession of by some followers of an individual of foreign origin, Brother Francisco, founder of a new religion and a supposed performer of miracles, who travels the Brazilian, Colombian, Ecuadorian and Peruvian Amazon region on foot and by raft, erecting crosses in the towns he passes through and having himself crucified, in order to preach in that preposterous pose, in either the Portuguese, Spanish or Indian languages. He is in the habit of announcing catastrophes and he exhorts his devoted followers (who are countless—despite the hostility that the Catholic Church and the Protestants profess toward him—due to the individual's charisma, which is, without doubt, very great, since his preaching has a great effect not only on simple and uncultured people, but also on educated persons, as has unfortunately taken place, for example, with the undersigned's own mother) to divest

themselves of their material goods and to build wooden crosses and offer sacrifices for the time when the end of the world will come, which he promises will be very soon. Here in Iquitos, where Brother Francisco has spent the past few days, there are numerous "arks" (that is what they call the temples of the sect created by this individual, in whom, if headquarters deems it appropriate, the Intelligence Service should perhaps take an interest), and a group of "brothers" and "sisters," as they call each other, had converted this depot into an "ark." They had installed a cross for their unsanitary and cruel ceremonies, which consist of crucifying all sorts of animals in order to have the victims' blood bathe the addicts kneeling at the foot of the cross. Consequently, the undersigned found countless carcasses of monkeys, dogs, wildcats and even parrots and herons on the premises, as well as grease spots and bloodstains all over and, undoubtedly, swarms of infectious germs. On the day on which the undersigned occupied the premises he had to call in the police in order to dislodge the Brothers of the Ark, just as they were preparing to nail up a lizard, which was confiscated and handed over to the Military Storehouse for Region V.

(c) That previously, this unlucky site had been used by a sorcerer or witch doctor, Master Poncio, who the "brothers" expelled by force, and who celebrated nighttime ceremonies here by preparing a concoction of *ayahuasca* stems, which, it seems, cures illnesses and provokes hallucinations, but also, unfortunately, immediate physical disorders, such as an excess of saliva, overflowing of urine and massive diarrhea, excretions that, along with the dead bodies of the animals later sacrificed and the many turkey buzzards and predatory animals attracted here by the leavings and the carcasses, had turned this place into a veritable hell for your eyes and nose. The undersigned had Sinforoso Caiguas and Palomino Rioalto procure shovels, rakes, brooms and buckets (see receipts 1, 2 and 3) so that, working diligently under his supervision, they could burn the garbage, wash down the floor and walls and disinfect everything with creosote. Later it was necessary to insert poison and plug up holes as well as to spread traps to halt the invasion of rodents, so abundant and brazen that, although it sounds like an exaggeration, they came out and walked contemp-

25

tuously before the undersigned's eyes and even bumped into his feet. The whitewashing and painting of the walls was attended to, which persistently called attention to the shameful writings and drawings (the spot must have concealed illicit lovemaking as well) and the little crosses of the "brothers" that show through. At the same time, it has been necessary to acquire in the Bethlehem Market, at bargain prices, some office furniture such as a desk, chair, table and filing cabinet for the command post (receipts 4, 5, 6 and 7).

(d) That in regard to the open ground (where many objects such as tin cans and broken-down engines can still be seen, which were left behind by the Army from the time when it used the site as a depot and which the Special Service has not wanted to destroy while awaiting further orders), it has been swept up and duly cleaned. (Even a dead snake was found, under a pile of branches.) The undersigned has the honor of reporting that in one week— by imposing details of ten and even twelve hours, of course—he has succeeded with all of the above actions in converting the indescribable dung heap that was turned over to him into a habitable site: simple but orderly, clean and even pleasant, such as befits all branches of our Army—even clandestine ones, as in the present case.

4. (a) That once the site was prepared, the undersigned proceeded to draw up various maps and charts to demark with the greatest exactitude the potential number of users, the area that SSGFRI will cover and the routes its convoys will follow. (b) That the following figures summarize the preliminary topographical evaluation: the Special Service will cover an area of approximately 400,000 square kilometers, which includes 8 garrisons, 26 posts and 45 encampments as potential utilization centers, toward which the primary means of communication from the command post and logistics center are the aerial and river routes (see map number 1), although in some exceptional cases transportation can be effected by land (in the vicinity of Iquitos, Yurimaguas, Contamana and Pucallpa). (c) That in order to determine the potential number of users of the Special Service, he was allowed to send (with the authorization of the commander in chief of Region V) the following questionnaire of his own devising to all the Garri-

sons, Frontier and Related Installations, so that it could be administered by the company leaders or, in their absence, by the group commander:

1. *How many* unmarried *recruits and soldiers are under your command? Before responding, consider that for its purposes, this questionnaire groups among the* married men *not only the recruits and soldiers joined in marriage by the Church or State but also all those who have common-law wives, and includes those who, in an irregular or sporadic manner, maintain some sort of intimate cohabitation in the vicinity where they serve.*

NOTE: *The questionnaire is aimed at establishing, with the greatest precision, the number of men under its administration* who do not maintain any form, permanent or temporary, of marital life.

2. *Once having ascertained with the greatest exactitude the number of* unmarried men *under your command (in the sense established by the questionnaire), proceed to subtract from this sum all recruits and soldiers who for one reason or another could be classified as incapacitated for the realization of intimate activities of a normal marital sort—that is, those who are inverts, inveterate onanists, impotent and/or sexually apathetic.*

NOTE: *Taking into consideration the natural concern of each individual for what others might say, for human prejudices, as well as the logical fear of being the butt of jokes on the part of anyone who might recognize himself among these exceptions, the supervising officer is advised how risky it would be, in order to complete this statistical elimination, to rely exclusively on the testimony of each recruit or soldier. Therefore, in order to answer this part of the questionnaire, it is recommended that the officer combine the facts obtained from his personal interrogation with the testimony of others (friends' and companions' confidential information concerning the subject), his own observations or some clever and daring subterfuge.*

3. *Having performed this subtraction and having established the number of recruits and soldiers,* UNMARRIED WITH MARITAL CAPABILITY, *under your command, proceed with cunning and discretion to verify among those who compose this group the number of marital services each subject calculates or knows he will require monthly in order to satisfy the requirements of his virility.*

NOTE: *The questionnaire attempts to establish a tabulation of minimum and maximum aspiration, according to this example:*

> *Maximum aspirations per month: 30*
>
> Subject X
>
> *Minimum aspirations per month: 4*

4. *Having established the preceding tabulation, attempt to determine among the same group of* unmarried men with marital capability *under your command, by means of the same technique of indirect soundings, seemingly casual questions, etc., how much time the subject calculates or positively knows the marital service will last in his case (from the preliminaries to its full conclusion), according to the same maximum/minimum scheme:*

> *Maximum aspiration per service: 2 hours*
>
> Subject X
>
> *Minimum aspiration per service: 10 minutes*

NOTE: *Compute the averages for sections 3 and 4 of the questionnaire separately and relay these figures without particularizing the information. The questionnaire intends to establish the desired normal monthly average of services necessary to the virility of the recruits and soldiers under your command, as well as the desired normal mean time for each service.*

(d) That the undersigned desires to give evidence of the enthusiasm, the speed and the efficiency with which the officers of the garrisons, posts and encampments have responded to the questionnaire at hand (only one-fifteenth of the posts could not be

consulted because of obstacles to communication due to imperfections in the transmitting apparatus, bad weather, etc.), which has warranted the drawing up of the following table:

Potential number of users of the Special Service:
 8,726 (eight thousand seven hundred and twenty-six)
Number of monthly services (average aspired to per user):
 12 (twelve)
Time of individual use (average time aspired to):
 30 (thirty) minutes

All of which means that in order to fully accomplish its mission, the Special Service would have to be in a position to guarantee to all the Garrisons, Frontier and Related Installations of Region V (Amazon) a monthly average of 104,712 (one hundred four thousand seven hundred and twelve) services, an objective obviously far beyond the present potential.

(e) That the undersigned is conscious of the obligation to initiate the Service, establishing modest and attainable goals, keeping in mind the truth and wisdom concealed in sayings such as "Haste makes waste" and "The early bird catches the worm."

5. That it is necessary to know if the intermediate ranks should be included among the potential users of the Special Service. The undersigned requests a rapid clarification on this matter, because if the superiors' answer is affirmative, the estimates obtained will alter considerably. Keeping in mind the already elevated number of potential users and the increased number of aspirations they indicate, the undersigned takes the liberty of suggesting that, at least in the first stage of its operation, the Special Service *not include* the intermediate ranks of officers.

6. (a) That he also proceeded to establish the first contacts for the purpose of recruitment. Thanks to the cooperation of an individual answering to the name of Porfirio Wong, alias the Chink, whom he met by chance in the nightclub designated the Mau Mau (260 Pebas St.), he made a nighttime visit to a place of entertainment, located on the highway to Nanay Beach, that is administered by Madame Leonor Curinchila, alias Chuchupe, and frequented by loose women. Since the said Leonor Curinchila is a friend of Porfirio Wong, the latter was able to introduce her to the

undersigned, who, for his purposes, was able to pass himself off as a businessman (import/export), having recently settled in Iquitos and being in search of recreation. The above-mentioned Leonor Curinchila showed herself to be cooperative and the undersigned —there being no other way out than to drink a lot (receipt 8)— succeeded in gathering valuable data related to the work system and the habits of the establishment's personnel. Thus in Casa Chuchupe some 16 women form what might be called the permanent stable, because there are others—about 15 or 20—who work irregularly, coming some days, missing others, for reasons ranging anywhere from venereal diseases (e.g., gonorrhea or chancres), contracted in the offering of their services, to transitory concubinage or short-term contracts (e.g., accompanying a lumberjack on a week's trip to the mountains), which temporarily take them away from their place of business. In brief, the entire staff of Casa Chuchupe, both fixed and fluctuating, is some 30 prostitutes, although the actual (but rotating) stable each night is only half that. On the day when the undersigned carried out his inspection, he recorded only eight present, but there was a special reason: the arrival in Iquitos of the aforementioned Brother Francisco. Most of these eight must be more than twenty-five years old, although this calculation is uncertain, since in the Amazon the women age prematurely, it not being uncommon to meet on the street very seductive-looking women with developed hips, firm breasts and an insinuating walk who, judging by the standards of the coast, are assumed to be twenty or twenty-two and then turn out to be thirteen or fourteen. Besides, the undersigned conducted his observations half in the dark, Casa Chuchupe being poorly lighted, because there are not enough electrical outlets, or maybe on account of lasciviousness, since darkness is more seductive than light and, if I may be permitted a joke, since "all cats look gray in the dark." Pushing thirty, then, the majority are average-looking from a good distance, if evaluated by a functional criterion and without going into fine points. That is, they have attractive and rounded bodies, especially in the hips and the breasts—parts that tend to be generous in this corner of our country—and presentable faces, although at close range it is possible to confirm more defects, the result not so much of being born ugly but rather of acne, smallpox

30

and the loss of teeth—the latter a fairly frequent mishap in the Amazon because of the debilitating climate and inadequate diet. Among the eight women present, those with white skin and native jungle features predominated; next came the mulattoes and finally those of an Oriental type. The average height is short rather than tall and the vitality and the joy typical of this country is a common characteristic of the personnel. During his stay on the premises, the undersigned saw that when they were not offering their services, the prostitutes danced and sang enthusiastically, making a racket without giving any signs of fatigue or dampened spirits, and often breaking out with jokes and brashness of the shameful nature only to be expected in this sort of establishment. But, at the same time, they did not have a troublemaking nature, although judging from the jokes that escaped from Madame Leonor's and Porfirio Wong's lips, bloody accidents and incidents do sometimes occur.

Furthermore, the undersigned states: (b) That he was also able to verify, thanks to the aforementioned Chuchupe, that rates for services vary and that only two thirds revert to whoever performs the service, the remaining third going to the house. (c) That the difference in rates has to do with the greater or lesser physical attractiveness of the prostitute; with the duration of the service (the client who wants to be serviced several times or to sleep with whoever has attended him naturally pays more than someone who is content with an expeditious and merely physiological service); and also, and above all, with the level of the prostitute's specialization and tolerance. Madame Curinchila explained to the undersigned that very much to the contrary of what the latter had innocently suspected, it is not a majority but rather a small minority of clients who are content with a simple and normal service (rate: 50 soles; duration: 15 to 20 minutes), most clients demanding a series of variations, elaborations, additions, distortions and complications that fall under what has come to be called "sexual aberrations." (d) That among the full gamut of services offered are those ranging from simple masturbation performed by the prostitute (manual: 50 soles; oral or "blow job": 200 soles) to the act of sodomy (in vulgar terms: "up the chocolate chute" or "browning": 250 soles) or 69 (200 soles), Sapphic spectacles or "bumping pussy"

31

(200 soles per person), or more infrequent cases such as those of clients who demand to whip or be whipped, to put on or view costumes and be admired, humiliated and even defecated upon, extravagances whose rates fluctuate between 300 and 600 soles.

(e) That keeping in mind the dominant sexual ethic in this country and the reduced budget of the SSGFRI, the undersigned has reached the decision to limit the services that may be requested of his co-workers, and consequently to what the users may aspire, to *simple and normal service,* excluding all the enumerated deviations and those related in spirit. (f) That as a function of this premise the Special Service will establish the recruitment and will fix the duration and price per service. Which will not prevent the Service, when it has come to fully satisfy the demand in quantitative terms—if its finances increase—from considering the suitability of initiating qualitative diversification of its services in order to take care of particular cases, fantasies or necessities (if the superiors so permit and authorize).

(g) That the undersigned was unable to establish precisely what the calculation of probabilities and the sales figures (marketing) would indicate is the daily average of services that a prostitute renders or is prepared to render, in order to have a tentative idea, first, of her monthly earnings and, second, of her operational capacity; because, apparently, the most extraordinary arbitrariness reigns in this field. Thus in one week a prostitute can earn what she will later not be able to collect in two months, all depending on many factors, among which are, possibly, the climate and even the stars (astral influence on glands and male sex drives), which are not worth determining. (h) That the undersigned was at least able to ascertain, chiefly by means of jokes and tricky questions, that the most attractive and efficient of them can in a good night's work (Saturday or the eve of a holiday) perform some twenty services without being left excessively exhausted, which authorizes the following formulation: a convoy of ten specialists chosen from among those with the greatest output would be in the position to provide 4,800 simple and normal services per month (a six-day work week), working full time and without accident. Which means that in order to meet the maximum desired objective of 104,712 monthly services, a permanent corps of 2,115 specialists in the

maximum category would be required. A fantastically high figure at this time, of course.

Furthermore, he states: (i) That apart from the prostitutes who work in establishments (in this city, besides Casa Chuchupe there are two others of the same sort, although, apparently, of an inferior class), there is in Iquitos a large number of women nicknamed "washerwomen," who lead a loose life in an ambulatory manner, offering their services from house to house —by preference at dusk and at dawn, since these are the hours of least police vigilance—or stationing themselves at different spots, such as the Plaza of 28 July and the environs of the cemetery, in search of customers. For this reason it seems obvious that the SSGFRI will not have any difficulty in recruiting personnel since the native work force is more than sufficient for our moderate initial potential.

(j) That the female personnel of Casa Chuchupe, like that of similar places, as well as the "washerwomen" who operate on their own, have male protectors (gigolos or pimps), generally individuals from a bad background, some having debts to settle with the law, to whom the women are obliged (many do it voluntarily) to hand over all or part of their wages. This aspect of the matter— the existence of gigolos and pimps—will have to be kept in mind by the Special Service at the time of personnel recruitment, since these individuals unquestionably could become a source of problems. But from his unforgettable days as a cadet, the undersigned knows well that there is no mission without its difficulties and that there are no difficulties that cannot be conquered by energy, will power and work.

(k) That the management and maintenance of Casa Chuchupe seems to be conducted successfully only due to the efforts of two people: the owner, Leonor Curinchila, and, performing duties that range anywhere from bartender to janitor, a little man of very short stature, almost a dwarf, of undefinable age and mestizo background, Juan Rivera, nicknamed Freckle, who jokes familiarly with the personnel and who is obeyed by them with speed and respect and who is also popular with the clientele. Which makes the undersigned think that, following the above-mentioned example, the Special Service would be able to function with a minimum

33

of administrative personnel, provided that it is properly structured.

(l) That his reconnaissance of a possible place for intercourse has served the undersigned to form a general idea of the environment in which he must necessarily work and to conceive some immediate plans, which, once worked out, he will submit to his superiors for their approval, revision or rejection.

7. (a) That in his desire to acquire broader scientific knowledge giving him better control of the goal to be attained and the means by which to attain it, the undersigned attempted to obtain in the libraries and bookstores of Iquitos a stock of books, pamphlets and magazines related to the topic of the services which the SSGFRI should offer. Unfortunately, he must communicate to his superiors that his efforts have been nearly fruitless, because in the two libraries of Iquitos—the Municipal Library and that of the College of St. Augustine—he found no text, neither general nor specialized, specifically devoted to the subject which interested him (sex and related matters). Instead, he experienced some rather embarrassing moments inquiring about the subject, since he obtained curt answers from the employees, and, in the St. Augustine library, a priest allowed himself to go so far as to even insult him by calling him immoral. Nor in the three bookstores of the city, the Lux, the Rodríguez and the Mesía (there is a fourth, that of the Seventh-Day Adventists, where it was not worthwhile to attempt an inquiry), could the undersigned find any first-rate material. To make matters worse, he only obtained, at high prices (receipts 9 and 10), some insignificant and cheap manuals bearing the titles *How to Develop the Male Drive, Aphrodisiacs and Other Secrets of Love, All About Sex in Twenty Lessons,* with which he has modestly inaugurated the library of the SSGFRI. (b) That he requests his superiors, if they see fit, to send him from Lima a selection of specialized works on everything related to sexual activity, masculine and feminine, in theory and in practice, and especially documentation on matters of basic interest like venereal diseases, sexual prophylaxis, perversions, etc., which undoubtedly will have a beneficial effect on the Special Service.

8. (a) That to conclude with a rather humorous personal anecdote and in order to alleviate the indecent subject matter of this

34

dispatch, the undersigned takes the liberty to recount that his visit to Casa Chuchupe lasted until nearly four in the morning and caused a serious gastric disturbance, resulting from the copious libations he had to imbibe and to which he is little accustomed because of his nonexistent taste for liquor and his doctor's proscription (some hemorrhoids, fortunately already eradicated). (b) That he had to recover by resorting to a civilian doctor so as not to avail himself of the military clinic in conformance with the instructions received (receipt 11), and not a few domestic difficulties caught up with him when he returned home at those hours and in that improper condition.

God bless you.
[Signed]
CAPT. (QUARTERMASTER) PANTALEÓN PANTOJA, PA

cc: Gen. Roger Scavino, Commander in Chief of Region V (Amazon)

encl: 11 receipts and 1 map

Night of August 16–17, 1956

Under a blazing sun, the bugle for reveille begins the day in the barracks of Chiclayo: buzzing commotion in the barracks, shouts of joy in the yards, cottony smoke from the kitchen chimneys. In a few seconds everybody has awakened and everywhere there reigns a warm, benevolent, stimulating atmosphere of alert readiness and lively abundance. But, meticulous, uncorruptible, punctual, Lieutenant Pantoja is crossing the open area—the taste of coffee with boiled goat's milk and toast with preserved eggfruit still in his mouth—where the band practices for the National Holidays parade. The columns of one company are marching up and down in straight lines and high spirits. But, rigid, Lieutenant Pantoja is now overseeing the distribution of breakfast to the soldiers: his lips are silently counting and, prophetically, when he mutely reaches 120, the mess sergeant serves the last drop of coffee and

hands out piece of bread number 120 as well as the 120th orange. But now Lieutenant Pantoja, standing still as a statue, watches how some soldiers are unloading sacks of provisions from the truck: his fingers follow the rhythm of the unloading like a conductor following the measures of a symphony. Behind him, a firm voice, with an almost imperceptibly masculine depth to it that only an ear as sharp as a scalpel could detect, Colonel Montes paternally asserts: "Better food than Chiclayo's? Gentlemen, neither the Chinese nor the French have anything to compare with seventeen varieties of duck with rice." But now Lieutenant Pantoja is carefully tasting the contents of the kitchen kettles without moving one facial muscle. The mulatto Chanfaina, the head cook, has his eyes fixed on the officer, and the sweat on his forehead and the quivering of his lips reveal anxiety and panic. But now Lieutenant Pantoja, in the same meticulous and inexpressive way, is examining the clothes the laundry returned, which two privates are stuffing into plastic bags. But now, in reverent gestures, Lieutenant Pantoja is presiding over the distribution of boots to the recently weighed-in recruits. But now Lieutenant Pantoja, with an expression—yes, now he is animated and almost loving—is pinning little flags onto some charts, correcting the statistical curves on a blackboard, adding a figure to a logistics chart. The company band is playing a lively folk dance.

A humid nostalgia has saturated the air, clouded the sun, silenced the bugles, the cymbals and the bass drum—a sensation of water trickling between the fingers, of spit swallowing up the sand, of burning lips that turn gangrenous when they brush a cheek—a feeling of a balloon that has burst, of a movie that has ended, of a sadness that is suddenly frightening: hear how the trumpet (for reveille? for mess? for taps?) again tears the warm air (of morning? of afternoon? of night?). But now a growing tingling has sprouted in his right ear and rapidly spreads throughout the entire lobe and then infects his neck, encircles it and scales his left ear: deep within, it too has started to tremble—shaking its invisible fuzz, opening its innumerable thirsty pores in search of, asking for . . . and now the disobedient nostalgia, the fierce melancholy, have been replaced by a secret fever, a diffuse apprehension, an uneasiness that takes a pyramidal shape like a meringue, a corrosive fear.

36

But Lieutenant Pantoja's face does not reveal it; one by one he scrutinizes the soldiers who are getting ready to enter the clothing storeroom in an orderly manner. But something provokes discreet laughter from those parade uniforms looking down from way up there, where the roof of the storeroom ought to be but where the reviewing stand of the National Holidays is instead. Is Colonel Montes present? Yes. Tiger Collazos? Yes. General Victoria? Yes. Colonel López López? Yes. They have begun to smile timidly, concealing their mouths with their maroon leather gloves, turning their heads a little to one side, whispering? But Lieutenant Pantoja knows how, what, why. He does not want to look at the soldiers who await the whistle to enter, collect their new clothes and turn in the old, because he suspects, knows or guesses that when he looks, confirms and positively knows, Mother Leonor will know and Pochita will too. But his eyes suddenly switch their look and examine the military formation: ha ha, how funny—oh, what a disgrace. Yes, that's how it happened. As thick as blood, the anguish flows under his skin. While he watches, a prisoner of icy terror, fighting to hide his feelings, he looks at how they're done up, they're filling out the recruits' uniforms in the chest, in the shoulders, in the hips, in the thighs, their hair is flowing from under their caps, their features have grown smooth, sweet and blushing, the masculine stares grow tender, ironic and mischievous. The panic has been replaced by rebellious and sarcastic ridicule. He makes the abrupt decision to put all his eggs in one basket, and sticking his chest out a little, he orders: "Unbutton your shirts, damn it!" But already they are passing under his eyes, the buttons undone, the buttonholes empty, the backstitched edges of their shirts swaying, the flitting, erect nipples of the recruits, the wobbling and alabaster, the delicate and earthy breasts swinging to the beat of the march. But Lieutenant Pantoja is already leading the company, his sword raised, his profile severe, his forehead noble, his eyes clear, stamping the asphalt decisively: one-two, one-two. No one knows how he curses his luck. His suffering is profound, his humiliation great, his shame infinite because behind him, marking time without any martial rhythm, blandly, like mares in the mud, come the recently inducted recruits, who did not know enough to bind their breasts, to wear deceptive

37

shirts, to trim their hair to the five centimeters prescribed by regulations and to cut their nails. He senses them marching behind him and guesses they are not trying to imitate masculine expressions; they are aggressively exhibiting their feminine qualities: they stick out their busts, grind their hips, wiggle their backsides and shake their long hair. (A shudder: he is about to pee in his pants. Mother Leonor would find out when she irons his uniform, Pochita would laugh when she sews on his new stripe.) But now it is necessary to concentrate chicken-heartedly on the parade because they are crossing in front of the reviewing stand. Tiger Collazos remains solemn, General Victoria hides a yawn, Colonel López López assents understandably and even gaily. The poison would not be so hard to swallow if, off in one corner, rebuking him with sadness, anger and disappointment, there were not also the gray eyes of General Scavino.

Now it does not matter so much to him anymore: the ticking in the ears has flared up violently and he, ready to risk everything, orders the company: "On the double! March!" and sets the example. He moves at a rapid and harmonious cadence, followed by soft, warm and inviting footsteps, while he feels a warmness up and down his spine like the steam from a pot of duck and rice just taken off the stove. But now Lieutenant Pantoja has stopped dead in his tracks, with the disorderly company right behind him. With a slight blush on his cheeks, he makes a rather unclear gesture, which, nevertheless, everyone understands. The machinery has been set in motion, the awaited ceremony has begun. The first section marches in front of him and it is annoying that the standard-bearer, Porfirio Wong, wears his uniform so sloppily. He manages to think: "He'll need a reprimand and training in the use of uniforms," but the recruits have already begun, while passing in front of him—as he stands motionless and expressionless—to unbutton their jackets rapidly, to show their hot breasts, to stretch out their hands to lovingly pinch his neck, ear lobes, upper lip, and then, advancing—one after another, one after another—his head (he makes it easy for them by bending), to enticingly nibble the tips of his ears. Sensations of eager pleasure, of animal satisfaction, of maddening and far-reaching happiness, erase the fear, the nostalgia, the ridicule, while the recruits pinch, caress and nibble

38

Lieutenant Pantoja's ears. But among the recruits, some familiar faces blow cold gusts over his happiness, stabbing him with uneasiness: unhorsed and grotesque in her uniform, Leonor Curinchila passes by, and hoisting the standard with the quartermaster's insignia, comes Freckle; and now, closing up the final section—anguish that gushes like a jet of oil and soaks Lieutenant Pantoja's body and spirit—a still indistinct soldier: but he knows—the suffocating fear, the tormenting ridicule, the intoxicating melancholy have returned—that under the insignia, the cap, the baggy pants and thin drill shirt a very sad Pochita is sobbing. The bugle sounds loudly and Mother Leonor is whispering to him: "Pantita, your duck and rice is ready."

S S G F R I

<div align="right">Dispatch Number Two</div>

GENERAL SUBJECT: Special Service for Garrisons, Frontier and Related Installations
SPECIFIC SUBJECT: Correction of estimates, first recruiting and specifications of the SSGFRI
CLASSIFICATION: Top Secret
PLACE AND DATE: Iquitos, 22 August 1956

The undersigned, Capt. (Quartermaster) Pantaleón Pantoja, PA, officer in charge of the SSGFRI, respectfully presents himself to Gen. Felipe Collazos, Chief of Administration, Supply and Logistics of the Army, salutes him and reports:

1. (a) That in Dispatch Number 1, of 12 August, in the section relating to the number of women the SSGFRI would require in order to meet the demand for 104,712 monthly services—a sum obtained by rough calculation of the first market estimate (permission is hereby requested of the administration to use this technical term)—the undersigned calculated that number to be "a permanent corps of 2,115 specialists in the maximum category [20 daily services], working full time and without accident."

<div align="right">3 9</div>

(b) That this calculation suffers from a grave error—for which the only person responsible is the undersigned—due to a masculine view of duty that inexcusably caused him to forget certain personal problems of the female sex, said problems demanding in this instance clear correction of the estimate, unfortunately with an unfavorable result for the SSGFRI. Thus the undersigned forgot to deduct from the specialists' number of workdays the five or six days per month when they are menstruating ("that time of month" or "period"), during which time they can be considered incapacitated to offer their services—as much because of the widespread masculine custom of not having carnal relations with women during their menstruation as because of the myth, taboo or scientific anomaly, which is firmly rooted in this section of the country, that to have intimate contact with a bleeding woman produces impotence. All of which clearly invalidates the earlier estimate.

(c) That taking this factor into account and fixing an approximate monthly average of 22 functional days per specialist (excluding five for menstruation and only three Sundays, since it is not extravagant to suppose that one Sunday in each month will coincide with the menstrual cycle), the SSGFRI would require a staff of 2,271 specialists in the maximum category, operating full time and without accident—that is, 156 more than the earlier dispatch had incorrectly calculated.

2. (a) That he has proceeded to recruit his first civilian co-workers in the aforementioned persons of Dispatch Number 1: Porfirio Wong, alias the Chink; Leonor Curinchila, alias Chuchupe; and Juan Chupito Rivera, alias Freckle. (b) That the first of the aforementioned will receive a basic wage of 2,000 (two thousand) soles per month and a bonus of 300 (three hundred) soles for each field mission and will fulfill the duties of a recruiting officer (for which he has been prepared by his many dealings on behalf of women with a dissipated way of life—both in "houses" and as "washerwomen") and chief of convoy in charge of the protection and control of the shipment of specialists to utilization centers.

(c) That the hiring of Leonor Curinchila and of the person living with her (which is Freckle's connection to her) turned out to be

easier than the undersigned had supposed when he proposed collaboration with the Special Service during their time off. Thus, with a friendly atmosphere of trust created on the second visit paid by the undersigned to Casa Chuchupe, the aforementioned Leonor Curinchila revealed to him that she was at the point of closing down and that she had been considering selling her establishment for some time. Not because of a lack of clientele, since the number of people visiting the premises increases daily, but due to weighty obligations of various kinds that inevitably siphoned off her income into protection by the police and the auxiliary forces. Thus, for example, in order to obtain annual renewal of her operating permit, for which she applies at Police Headquarters, Leonor Curinchila has to put up, in addition to legal fees, large sums in the form of gifts to the chiefs of Lenocinios and Bares districts. Beyond that, the members of the city's Police Bureau of Investigation (PBI), who number more than thirty, as well as a large number of police officers, have taken to demanding free service at Casa Chuchupe, in regard to both alcoholic beverages and women, under threat of filing a report on the place accusing it of being a public nuisance, which is grounds for closing it at once. In addition to this persistent economic bleeding, Leonor Curinchila has had to resign herself to their geometrically raising the rent on her place (whose owner is none other than the chief of police) under penalty of eviction. And, finally, Leonor Curinchila found herself already worn out by the intense devotion and the feverish, irregular pace demanded by her work—bad nights, foul air, threat of quarrels, swindle and blackmail, lack of vacation or a day of rest on Sundays—without any of these sacrifices resulting in appreciable gains. For all these reasons she gladly accepted the offer to collaborate in the Special Service, taking upon herself the initiative for proposing not a contingent work schedule, but an exclusive and permanent one, and demonstrating great interest and enthusiasm when she was informed of the nature of the SSGFRI.

(d) That Leonor Curinchila, who has already reached an agreement with Humberto Sipa, alias Snotnose, the owner of a pleasure house in the district of Punchana, to transfer Casa Chuchupe to

41

him, will work in the Special Service on the following conditions: 4,000 (four thousand) soles in wages plus 300 (three hundred) soles as a bonus for field work, and the right to collect a percentage no greater than 3 percent, for a period not to exceed one year, on the wages of the specialists contracted through her mediation. Her functions will be those of chief of personnel for the SSGFRI, taking charge of recruiting, fixing schedules, shifts and staff members of the convoys, controlling operations and maintaining general supervision over the female element.

(e) That Freckle will receive a basic wage of 2,000 (two thousand) soles plus 300 (three hundred) soles per assignment in the field, and will be expedition leader and be responsible for maintaining the logistics center (with two associates: Sinforoso Caiguas and Palomino Rioalto). These three collaborators have joined the SSGFRI as of Monday, 20 August, at 0800 hours.

3. (a) That wanting to give a suitable and distinctive look to the SSGFRI and to provide it with symbolic badges that, without announcing its activities to the outside world, would at least permit those who serve in it to recognize each other as well as permit those whom it will serve to identify its members, locations, vehicles and property, the undersigned has proceeded to designate green and red as the emblematic colors of the Special Service, with the following symbolism:

(1) green for the lush and beautiful countryside of the Amazon Region, where the Service is going to forge its destiny, and
(2) red for the virile ardor of our recruits and soldiers, which the Service will help to appease.

(b) That he has already given orders that both the command post and the transport teams of the Special Service display their emblematic colors and that for the sum of 185 soles (receipt attached) he has ordered The Tin Paradise to make two dozen small red-and-green badges (without any inscription, of course), insignia that can be worn in men's buttonholes or on women's blouses or dresses and, without breaking with the discretionary norms required of the SSGFRI, will substitute for the uniform and letter of

42

credentials of those who have and will have the honor of forming this Service.

God bless you.
[Signed]
CAPT. (QUARTERMASTER) PANTALEÓN PANTOJA, PA

cc: Gen. Roger Scavino, Commander in Chief of Region V (Amazon)

encl: 1 receipt

3

Dear Chichi,

Sorry I haven't written in so long. You must be really annoyed
with your sister who loves you so much, and talking yourself
hoarse asking why that silly Pocha doesn't tell me how things are
going for her out there and what the Amazon is like. But honest,
Chichita, even though I've thought about you a lot since I got here
and missed you terribly, I didn't have time to write or the desire
either. (Don't get mad, O.K.?) And now I'll tell you why. It turns
out that Iquitos hasn't been very good to your sister, Chichi. I'm
not so happy with the move, things are not coming along very
good and they're funny. I don't mean that this city is uglier than
Chiclayo—just the opposite. Although it's small, it's cheerful and
friendly, and the nicest thing of all, of course, is the jungle and the
huge Amazon River that you've always heard is as enormous as the
ocean, so you can't see the other side and a thousand other things,
but really, you can't imagine it till you see it up close: it's so pretty.
Let me tell you, we've made a couple of trips in a glider (that's
what they call the small launches here), one Sunday as far as
Tamshiyaco, a little town upstream, and another to a town with
such a charming name, San Juan de Munich, and another as far as
Indiana, a little town downstream, where practically everything
was built by some Canadian priests and nuns, isn't that terrific?
That they'd come from so far away to this lonely place and all this
heat to civilize the wild jungle Indians. We went with my mother-
in-law, but we'll never take her on a glider again, because all three

44

times she spent the trip scared to death, hanging on to Panta, whining that we were going to turn over, you'll save yourselves by swimming, but I'll drown and the piranhas will eat me. (I wish it was true, Chichita, but the poor piranhas would get poisoned.) And later, coming back, complaining about the bites, because, I'm telling you, Chichita, one of the terrible things here are the mosquitoes and the sand fleas (mosquitoes that hide in the grass), they're after you all day long, covering you with bumps, and you spraying on repellents and scratching yourself. So now you see, dear, the disadvantages of having fair skin and blue blood that stir up the little pests to bite you (ha, ha).

What's for sure is that if coming to Iquitos hasn't been great for me, it's been fatal for my mother-in-law. Because she was happy there in Chiclayo. You know how sociable she is, having her clubby life with the old fossils on the army base, playing canasta every afternoon, crying like Mary Magdalene at her soap operas and giving her little teas. But here, everything she liked so much, everything that made her stop calling it "her life in the convent" (oh, Chichi, it kills me just to think of Chiclayo), here she hasn't got all that, so she's taken up religion to console herself, but really it's witchcraft, you better believe it. Because—this'll kill you—that was the first slap in the face I got: we're not going to be able to live on the army base or get together with the officers' families. That's all there is to it. And it's terrible for Mother Leonor, who came here with great illusions of becoming an inseparable friend of the wife of the Commander of Region V and putting on airs like she did in Chiclayo because she was an intimate friend of Colonel Montes's wife and the only thing the two of them hadn't done was get into bed together (to gossip and chatter under the sheets—don't think dirty thoughts). Listen, do you remember that joke? Joey asks Charlie, Do you want my grandmother to act like a wolf? Yeah, sure. Grandma, how long has it been since you did anything with Grandpa? Ou-*o-o-o!*

The simple truth is that with that order, the Army's put us in a real mess, Chichi, because the only modern, comfortable houses in Iquitos are on the army base, or the navy or air force base. The houses in this city are very old, very ugly, very uncomfortable. We've taken one on Sergeant Lores Street, one of the ones they

built at the turn of the century, during the rubber boom, the most picturesque ones with their tiles from Portugal on the front and their wooden balconies. It's large and from one window you can see the river, but it certainly doesn't compare at all to the poorest house on the base. What makes me really mad is that we can't even swim in the Army pool or in the Navy or the Air Force's either, and there's only one pool in Iquitos, the municipal pool, a horrible place where everybody and their brother goes. I went once and there must've been a thousand people, how disgusting, lots of men just waiting around like vultures for the women to get into the water so they could pretend to be jamming in together and you can just imagine what. Never again, Chichi; the shower's better. How furious I am when I think that the wife of any little lieutenant can be at the pool on the army base this very minute, sunbathing, listening to her radio and taking a dip, and here I am glued to the fan so I won't roast: I swear I'd cut off General Scavino's you-know-what (ha ha). Because besides, it turns out I can't even do my household shopping at the PX, where everything's half as expensive. Instead I have to shop in the town stores, just like everybody else. And that's not all—we have to live just as if Panta was a civilian. They've given him a two thousand soles raise as a bonus, but that doesn't make up for anything. As you can see, Chichi, for money for food, poor Pochita is screwed. (That came out like a poem. It can't be so bad if I haven't lost my sense of humor, right?)

Imagine, they have Panta dressed up like a civilian day and night, while the uniforms he likes so much are being eaten by the moths in a trunk and he'll never get to put them on. And we have to make everybody believe that Panta's a merchant who's come to Iquitos on business. The funny thing is that some awful mix-ups come up with the neighbors and my mother-in-law and me because sometimes we invent one thing for them and at other times another, and suddenly some military memories of Chiclayo slip out that must just intrigue them, and all over the neighborhood we already have the reputation for being an odd, rather suspicious family. I can see you bouncing up and down on your bed asking what's going on with this idiot that she just doesn't tell me right away why there's so much mystery. But it turns out, Chichi, that I can't tell you a thing, it's a military secret, and so secret that if

they found out that Panta had said anything, they'd court-martial him for treason against the country. Just think, Chichita, they've given him a very important mission in the Intelligence Service, a dangerous assignment and so nobody is supposed to know that he's a captain. Oh, what a dope I am, I already told you the secret and I'm too lazy to tear up this letter and start over. Swear to me, Chichita, that you're not going to say one word to anyone, because I'll kill you, and besides, you wouldn't want them to put your brother-in-law in the guardhouse or shoot him because of you, would you? So keep quiet and don't run around telling the story to your gossipy Santana friends. Isn't it funny that Panta's turned into a secret agent? Let me tell you that Mother Leonor and I are dying of curiosity to know what he's spying on here in Iquitos, and we're eating him up with questions and we try to get it out of him but he wouldn't let one syllable escape even if he was going to be killed. We'll have to see about that, your sister is as stubborn as a mule, so we'll see who wins. I'm only warning you that when I find out what Panta's mixed up in, I don't plan to tattle to you even if you're wetting your pants with curiosity.

It'll be very exciting now the Army's given him this assignment in the Intelligence Service, Chichita, and maybe it'll help his career a lot, but I tell you I'm not one bit happy with this business. In the first place because I hardly ever see him. You know how reliable and fanatic Panta is about his work, he takes everything they give him so seriously that he doesn't sleep or eat or live until he's finished with it, but at least in Chiclayo he had his duties on a regular schedule and I knew when he was coming and going. But here he spends his life outside the house, you never know what time he's coming in and (this will knock you off your feet) not even in what condition. I'm telling you, I'm not used to seeing him as a civilian, wearing sport shirts and blue jeans and the little jockey cap they've given him, it seems to me I've switched husbands and not just because of that. (Oh, I'm so embarrassed, Chichi, so much I really wouldn't dare tell you.) If only he worked during the day I'd be happy. But he also has to go out at night, sometimes till very late, and he's shown up three times falling-over drunk, he had to be helped out of his clothes and the next day his mama had to put compresses on his forehead and make tea for him. Yes, Chichi, I

47

can see the surprised look on your face, even though you don't believe it, Panta the teetotaler, who only drank pasteurized milk ever since he got hemorrhoids—falling-down drunk and with a thick tongue. Now it makes me laugh because I can remember how funny it was to see him stumbling over things and hear him complain, but at the same time I was in such a fit I wanted to cut off *his* you-know-what too. (No, I'd be cutting off my nose to spite my face, ha ha.) He swears to me and double swears that he has to go out at night on account of his assignment, that he has to search for some guys who only live in the bars, who make their appointments there to throw you off the track, and maybe it's the truth. (Just like the spy movies, right?) But listen, would you be so calm if your husband spent the night in bars? No, well, my dear, not even if I was fool enough to believe you can only see men in bars. There have to be women there who come up to him and start conversations and God only knows what else. I've made a few terrible scenes, and he's promised me not to go out at night anymore except when it's a case of life or death. I've gone through all his pockets and shirts and underwear with a fine-tooth comb, because let me tell you if I find a shred of proof that he's been with women, poor Panta. It's not so bad because his mama helps me with all this, she's horrified at his going out at night and his binges —her little boy, who she always thought was a church saint and who it now turns out isn't quite that. (Oh, Chichi, you'd die if I told you.)

And besides, because of that damned mission, he has to get together with people who'd make your hair stand on end. Just imagine, the other afternoon I'd gone to the matinee with a neighbor I've become friendly with, Alicia, married to a boy who works for the Bank of the Amazon, a very nice woman from Loreto who helped us a lot with the moving. We went to the Excelsior to see a Rock Hudson movie (hold me up while I pass out), and after getting out we were taking a little walk in the fresh air, when passing by a bar called the Camu Camu I see Panta at a table in the corner and what a pair he's with! I nearly had a stroke, Chichi, the woman so covered with make-up there wasn't room for a drop more, not even on her ears, with such tits and an ass spilling over the chair, and the guy was a little half-pint, so short his feet didn't

reach the floor, and what's more, with an incredible ladykiller look. And Panta between the two of them, talking as lively as could be, as if they had been friends all their life. I said to Alicia, look, my husband, and then she grabbed me by the arm, very nervous, come on, Pocha, let's go, you can't go in there. So we left. Who do you think that pair was? The woman decked out like a parrot has the worst reputation in all Iquitos, Enemy Number One of home life, they call her Chuchupe and she has a brothel on the road to Nanay, and her lover, the dwarf, it's enough to make you break out laughing, imagining her making it with that clown, she's depraved and he's worse. What do you think? Later I mentioned it to Panta, to see what his reaction would be, and of course, he choked on that bone so much he started to stammer. But he didn't dare deny it to me, he admitted that this pair lead a bad life. And that he had to go find them for his assignment, that I should never go up to him if I see him with them and his mother even less so. I told him right then and there you can get mixed up with whoever you want to but if I ever find out you went to the parrot's house in Nanay, your marriage is in trouble, Panta. So, my dear, imagine the reputation we're going to get here if Panta begins to be seen on the streets with those people.

Another of his pals is a Chink. I always thought that all Chinks were very delicate, but this one's Frankenstein, even if Alicia does think he's very handsome; these people in Loreto have cockeyed taste. I caught him one day when I went to visit the Moronacocha aquarium, to see the tropical fish (very pretty, let me tell you, but I thought I'd touch an eel and he let out with an electric shock from his tail that nearly knocked me over), and Mother Leonor has also caught Panta in a restaurant with the Chink, and Alicia spied them walking across the Army Plaza and from her I found out that the Chink is well known as a big hood. He exploits women and he's a parasite and a bum. Imagine your dear brother-in-law's friendships. I've put it to him squarely and Mother Leonor more than me, because her son's bad companions make her sicker than they make me, especially now that she believes the end of the world is near. Panta has promised her he won't be seen on the streets anymore with either the woman or the dwarf or the Chink, but he'll have to go on seeing them on the sly because it turns out

that's part of his work. I don't know where it's all going to lead with this assignment and with that sort of connections, Chichita, you'll understand my nerves are upset and I'm very jumpy.

Even though I really shouldn't be like this, I mean about tomcatting and cheating, because—should I tell you, Sis?—you can't imagine how Panta's changed in regard to such things, the intimate ones. Do you remember how he's always been so formal ever since we got married so you always joked a lot and told me I'm sure with Panta you must be doing without, Pocha? Well, you can't laugh at your brother-in-law anymore in that respect, you badmouth, because since he stepped foot in Iquitos he's become a savage. Something terrible, Chichi, at times I get scared and wonder if it isn't an illness, because imagine that before, I've told you, I only got him to tend to his business once every ten or fifteen days (how embarrassing to talk to you about this, Chichi) and now the little bandit's excited every two, three days and I have to put the brakes on his passion, because it isn't right, no, really, with this heat and sticky humidity. Besides, it occurred to me it could hurt him, it seems it affects the brain. Didn't everybody say that Pulpito Carrasco's husband went out of his head from doing it so often with her? Panta says the climate's to blame, a general already warned him back in Lima that the jungle turns men into blowtorches. I have to tell you it makes me laugh seeing your little brother-in-law so horny. Sometimes he's itching to do a little business during the daytime, right after lunch, with the siesta as an excuse, but of course I don't let him, and sometimes he wakes me at dawn with that craziness. Picture this, the other night I caught him with a stopwatch timing how long our business took us. I asked him about it and he got very confused. Later he confessed to me he had to know how long a little business like that took for a normal couple. Do you think he's turning into a pervert? Who's going to believe that he has to check that dirty business for his assignment? I tell him I don't recognize you, Panta, you who were so very, very educated, it makes me feel I'm doing it with some other Panta. Well, my dear, enough dirty talk, since you're a little virgin, and I promise you I'll fight with you forever if it gets into your head to mention this to anybody, especially to those crazy Santanas.

Sure, it half calms me down that Panta has gotten to be such a

pest about doing his duty, it means his wife pleases him (ahem, ahem) and he doesn't have to look for excitement out in the street. But after that, nothing doing, Chichi, because here in Iquitos women are taken very, very seriously. Do you know what's the big excuse your brother-in-law has invented for doing a little business whenever he's horny? Pantita Junior! Yes, Chichi, you heard right, at last he's eager for us to have a baby. He promised me we would as soon as he got his third stripe and he's keeping his promise, but now with this change in temperament, I don't know anymore if doing our business morning and afternoon is to please me or just him. I tell you it's enough to make you die laughing, he comes off the street like a little wind-up mouse and he circles and circles around me until he dares, can we take care of the little cadet tonight, Pocha? Ha ha, isn't that cute? I adore him, Chichi. (Listen, I don't know how I can tell you all these dirty things when you're single.) Up till now, don't breathe a word, Skinny, in spite of working at it, just yesterday my period came, what a pain, I thought this month for sure. Will you come take care of your sister when she's got a big belly, Chichi? Oh, if only it was tomorrow you'd come, what a pleasure to have you here to gossip as much as we want. Of course, you'll wear a dress for the men in Loreto, to find a handsome guy you have to search for him like a needle in a haystack, I'll start giving anyone who's worth it the once-over so you won't get too bored when you come. (Have you noticed how this letter is pouring out of me by the mile? You'll have to answer with the same number of pages, O.K.?) It's not possible that I can't have babies, is it, Chichi? It scares me so much that every day I ask God for any punishment but that one, I'd die of grief if I couldn't have at least one little boy and one little girl. The doctor says I'm perfectly normal so I'm hoping it'll be next month. Did you know that every time a man does his business *millions* of sperms come out of him and only one gets into the woman's egg and makes the little baby there? I was reading a pamphlet the doctor gave me, explaining everything so well you could go cross-eyed with the miracle of life. If you want me to I'll send it to you, so you'll learn about those things for when you get wise, marry, lose your virginity and learn what a soufflé is, you skinny little kid. I hope I don't get too ugly, Chichi, some women look terrible

when they're pregnant, they puff up like toads, varicose veins pop out, really disgusting. I won't please your horny brother-in-law anymore and when you least expect it he'll be out looking for his fun on the street, I tell you I don't know what I'll do with him. I'll bet with all the heat and humidity here pregnancy must be awful, especially not living on the army base but instead where we unlucky people do. I'm telling you, another worry gives me gray hair, I'm glad to have the baby, but what if on the excuse that I got fat that miserable Panta gets tangled up with some woman in Loreto, especially since now I let him have his way about doing a little business even when I'm asleep? I'm dying of hunger, Chichi, I've been writing you for hours, Mother Leonor's already serving lunch, you can picture to yourself how happy my mother-in-law's going to be with the idea of the grandchild, I'm coming, lunch and later I'll continue, so you don't kill yourself, I'm still not ending, *ciao*, Sis.

I'm back at last, Chichi, I took years, it's nearly six, I had to take a nap because I ate like a boa constrictor. Just think, Alicia made us a present of a plate of *tacacho,* a native dish here. Isn't she friendly? It's better that I've found a friend here in Iquitos. I'd heard so much about this famous *tacacho,* it's mashed green bananas with pork, I had to go to the Bethlehem Market to have some, to a restaurant called Aladdin Panduro's Lamp where there's a great cook, so I pestered Panta until he took us there the other day very early, the market is open at dawn and closes early. Bethlehem is the prettiest place here, you'll see, an entire neighborhood of little wooden houses floating on the river, people get from one side to the other in little boats, I'm telling you, it's so original, they call it the Venice of the Amazon, even though you see a lot of poverty. The market's very good to get to know and to buy fruit, fish or the necklaces and bracelets the Indians make, very pretty, but not to go and eat, Chichi. We nearly died when we entered Aladdin Panduro's, you can't imagine the filth and the hordes of insects. The plates they brought us were black with flies, you frightened them and they came back right away and got in your eyes and mouth. In the end, neither Mother Leonor nor I tasted one mouthful, we were sick to our stomachs, that barbarian Panta ate three platefuls and also the dried meat that Mr. Aladdin in-

sisted he had to have with the *tacacho*. I told Alicia about how disappointed we were and she told me one of these days I'll make you *tacacho* so you can see how good it is and this morning she brought us a platter. Delicious, Sis, it's like a dish of *chifles* from the North, although not quite the same, the banana tastes different here. The only trouble is it's heavy as lead, I had to force myself to get it down, and my mother-in-law is bent over with stomach-aches and gas, green with embarrassment because she can't control herself and little farts keep popping out in front of me, soon she'll explode from it and go straight to heaven once and for all. No, how mean I am, poor Mother Leonor, deep down she's good, the only thing that annoys me is that she treats her son as if he's still a baby and a little saint, isn't she a stupid old thing?

Did I tell you that the poor woman is finding her amusement in superstition? She's turned the house into a garbage dump. Imagine, after we were here only a few days, there was a big commotion in Iquitos over the arrival of Brother Francisco, you've probably heard about him, I hadn't until I got here. In the Amazon he's more famous than Marlon Brando, he's founded a religion that's called the Brothers of the Ark, he goes everywhere on foot and wherever he goes he hangs up an enormous cross and dedicates Arks that are his churches. He has a lot of followers, especially among the working people, and it seems the priests are furious about the competition he's giving them but until now there hasn't been one peep out of them. Well, my mother-in-law and I went to hear him in Moronacocha. There were lots of people and the surprising thing was that he spoke crucified like Christ, believe it or not. He was announcing the end of the world and asking people to make offerings and sacrifices for the Last Judgment. I couldn't understand him very well, he speaks a very difficult Spanish. But the people listened to him hypnotized, the women were crying and got down on their knees. I got caught up with the emotion and even burst out crying, and you can't imagine my mother-in-law, she was sobbing loudly and we couldn't calm her down, the witch-doctor had really gotten to her, Chichi. Later, back at home, she was praising Brother Francisco and the next day she went back to the Ark of Moronacocha to talk with the "brothers" and now it turns out the old lady has become a "sister" too. It's like a bolt out

53

of the blue: she who never paid much attention to true religion ends up a pious follower of heretics. Just imagine, her room is full of little wooden crosses, and if it was only to distract herself, fine, but the dirty part of the business is that this religion has a mania for crucifying animals and I don't like that because every morning I find cockroaches, butterflies, spiders nailed to her little crosses and even a mouse the other day, what a horrifying, disgusting mess. Every time I come across one of those dirty things I throw it into the garbage and we've already gotten into some good fights. It's screwy because as soon as a row breaks out, and there's one every minute here, the old lady starts to tremble thinking it's the end of the world and every day she begs Panta to get a big cross made for the front door. Just look at how many changes in such a short time.

What was I telling you, kid, when I stopped for lunch? Oh, yes, about the people of Loreto. God, Chichi, everything they say was right and a lot more besides. Every day I find out something new, I'm nauseous and keep asking what is this? Iquitos must be the most perverted city in Peru, even worse than Lima. Maybe it's true and the climate has a lot to do with it, I mean about the women being so awful, you can already see how Panta put one foot in the jungle and turned into a volcano. The worst thing is that these floozies are really attractive, the men are so ugly and with no class and the women are so great. I'm not exaggerating, Chichi, I think the most beautiful women in Peru (with the exception of yours truly and her sister, of course) are from Iquitos. All of them, the ones who look decent and the ones from the town and even —I'm telling you—the hookers, maybe they're the best. Some shapes, kid, with a little way of walking so flirty and brazen, moving their backsides with a lot of nerve and throwing their shoulders back so their bust can be seen sticking out. Some pushy ones wear pants that fit like gloves, and do you think they flinch when men say things to them? What a question! They walk a straight line and look them in the eyes so fresh it stirs up some of the men to grab them by their boobs.

I have to tell you something I heard yesterday when I went into the record shop (where they have the four-for-three system, you buy three things and they give you the fourth, fantastic, isn't it?)

54

between two very young girls. One of them asked the other: "Have you ever kissed a soldier?" "No, why're you asking?" "They kiss diviiiiiinely." She made me laugh, she said it with that Loreto accent and in a loud voice, not worrying if everybody heard her. They're just that way, Chichi, as fresh as they come. And do you think they stop at kissing? What a dreamer! According to Alicia, these little devils start getting into big trouble as early as high school and they learn to take care of themselves and everything and when they get married, the really smart ones put on a big act so their husbands believe they're doing it for the first time. Some of them go to those witches who prepare *ayahuasca*—you've heard about it, haven't you? A concoction that makes you dream really wild things—so they'll make them like new again. Just imagine, imagine. I swear to you every time I go out shopping or to the movies with Alicia I come home blushing from the stories she tells me. She says hello to a friend, I ask her who's that, and she tells me some terrible woman, imagine that, who has had at least a couple of lovers, all the married women have gotten involved at some time or other with a soldier, airman or marine, but especially with a soldier, they have great prestige with these floozies. Chichi, it's not so bad for me they don't let Panta wear a uniform. These crazy women take advantage of the husband's smallest slip and Pow! cuckolded. Skinny, it makes you afraid of them. And do you think they do things right, in their own beds and sheets? Alicia said to me, if you want, let's take a walk down to Moronacocha and you'll see all the cars where the couples are carrying on (but really, I mean it) one next to the other, as if nothing was happening.

Just think, they found a woman carrying on with a police lieutenant in the last row of the Bolognesi movie house. They say the film broke, the lights went on and they caught them. Poor people, can you imagine the shock they got when they saw the lights were going on, especially her? They had stretched out, making good use of the benches they have instead of seats and the last row being empty. A tremendous scandal, it seems the lieutenant's wife nearly killed the woman, because an announcer on Radio Amazon who's terrible and gives out all the facts repeated the story in a blow-by-blow description and the lieutenant ended up being removed from Iquitos. I didn't want to believe a story like that but

55

Alicia pointed out the girl to me on the street, a really good-looking brunette, with a face that couldn't hurt a fly. I looked at her and said to Alicia, you're fibbing, they did *business* business in the middle of the movie, so uncomfortable and afraid of being caught? It seems so, they caught the girl without her blouse on and the lieutenant with his little bird up in the air. After Paris, Iquitos is sin city, Skinny. Don't think Alicia is a chatterbox, I worm it out of her, from curiosity and also to be forewarned. My dear, here you have to have four eyes and eight hands to defend yourself from these women of Loreto, you turn your back and they make your husband disappear on you. Even though she's a native, Alicia is *very* serious. Though at times she wears pants that are so tight she has to use a shoehorn to get them on, still she doesn't go around arousing the men, she doesn't give them such fresh looks as the other women in Iquitos.

As to how nervy the women of Loreto are, how stupid I am— I've been forgetting to tell you the funniest and best part (or really the worst). You can't imagine the disaster we had when we were in the middle of getting ourselves settled in this house. Have you heard people talk about the famous "washerwomen" of Iquitos? Everybody's said to me, but where have you been living, Pocha, where did you come from, the whole world knows about the famous "washerwomen" of Iquitos. Well, I must be dumb or wet behind the ears, sister, but never in Chiclayo or in Ica or in Lima did I ever hear people talking about the "washerwomen" of Iquitos. Picture this, we'd been in our little house for a few days, and our bedroom is downstairs, with a window on the street. We still didn't have a maid—now I have one that'd melt your heart, she's so good—and suddenly at the strangest hours there'd be tapping at our window and you'd hear a woman's voice: "Washerwoman! Got any clothes to be washed?" And me, without even opening the window, I'd say no, thanks very much. It never occurred to me to think how strange that there are so many washerwomen out on the streets in Iquitos and on the other hand it's so hard to get a girl, because I put out a little "Girl Wanted" sign and only once in a while did anybody turn up. So one day, it was very early and we were still in bed, I heard this little tap on the window, "Washerwoman! Got any laundry?" and I had let a lot of dirty clothes pile

up on me, because here, let me tell you, with this heat that's so horrible, you sweat terribly and you have to change two and even three times a day. So I thought terrific, she can wash my clothes as long as she doesn't charge too much. I yelled wait a minute, got out of bed in my nightie and went to open the door for her. Right there I should've suspected something funny was going on because she had enough make-up on to be anything but a washerwoman. But me, I'm a dumbbell, off on the moon. The most attractive little thing, cinched in to make her curves stand out, of course, with her fingernails painted and really fixed up. She looked me up and down in the most surprised way and I thought what's wrong with this one, what's wrong with me to make her look at me like that. I told her come in, she came into the house, and before I said anything to her she saw the bedroom door and Panta and Wham! she went right in and planted herself in front of your brother-in-law in a pose that left me cockeyed, her hand on her hip and her legs spread out like a rooster who's going to attack. Panta sat right up in bed, his eyes popping out from the shock of this woman's appearance. And do you know what this thing did before either Panta or I managed to tell her wait outside, what are you doing here in the bedroom? She began talking about her rates, you have to pay me double, that she wasn't used to dealing with women, pointing at me, Skinny, you better believe it, but you really have to turn weird tricks, and I don't know what other vulgarities, and suddenly I realized what the trouble was and my legs began to tremble. Yes, Chichi, she was a w——. A w——! The "washerwomen" of Iquitos are the w——s of Iquitos and they go around from house to house offering their services with that story about laundry. Now you tell me, is Iquitos or isn't it the most immoral city in the world, sister? Panta also realized what was going on and started shouting get out of here, you pig, what are you thinking about, get out right now. The thing had the fright of her life, she caught on to the mix-up and shot out of the house, tripping. Can you picture what a fiasco, Skinny? She thought we were some degenerates, that I had made her come in so the three of us could do a little business together. Who knows, Panta was joking later, maybe it was worth a try, didn't I tell you he's changed a lot? Now it's over I can laugh at myself and make jokes about it but I'm

57

telling you it was really ugly for a little while, I was dying with shame the whole day remembering that little scene. Now you can see what this place is like, sister, a city where the women who aren't w——s try to be and where if you're careless for one second you're left without a husband. Look at what a hole I've fallen into.

Now my hand's fallen asleep on me, Chichi, it's already dark and it's gotten to be very late. I'll have to send you this letter in a trunk so it'll all fit. Let's see if you answer me right away, and as long as mine and with piles of gossip. Are you still going with Roberto or have you switched already? Tell me everything and, honest, in the future I'll write to you right away.

Thousands of kisses, Chichi, from your sister who misses you and loves you,

POCHITA

Night of August 29–30, 1956

Images of humiliation, snapshots of the stinging and inflamed history of the tormenting itch. In the strict, stately Flag Day formation, in front of the monument to Francisco Bolognesi, the cadet Pantaleón Pantoja, in his senior year at Chorrillos Military Academy, while elegantly executing the goose step, is suddenly transported in flesh and spirit to hell, through the conversion of the mouth of his anus and rectum into a wasps' nest: a hundred stingers martyrize the moist, secret wound, while he, grinding his teeth to the point of crumbling them, sweating great, frozen drops of perspiration, marches without losing step; at the gay, sparkling party offered to the Alfonso Ugarte class by Colonel Marcial Gumucio, director of Chorrillos Military Academy, the young, recently commissioned Second Lieutenant Pantaleón Pantoja feels his toenails suddenly freeze when, having barely begun the steps of the waltz with the seasoned wife of Colonel Gumucio, radiant in his arms, the night's dance having recently been opened by him and his vaporous spouse, an incandescent itching, a serpentine swarming, a torture in the form of tiny simultaneous and biting itches widens, swells and irritates the privacy of his rectum and anus: his eyes clotted with tears and without increasing or decreas-

ing his pressure on the plump waist and hand of Colonel Gumucio's wife, Second Lieutenant (Quartermaster) Pantoja, not breathing, not speaking, continues to dance; in the field tent of Regiment 17 of Chiclayo, with the thunder of mortars close by, the ratatatat of grapeshot and the dry belches of the shots from the lead companies which just began the end-of-year maneuvers, Lieutenant Pantoja, standing in front of a blackboard and a map board, explaining to the officers corps in a firm and metallic voice the supplies, system of distribution and the estimates of supplies and provisions, is suddenly and invisibly raised off the ground by a frightening, fiery, effervescent, emulsive and crackling current that burns, stings, exaggerates, multiplies, torments, maddens the anal vestibule and rectal passage and stretches itself out like a spider between his buttocks, but, abruptly livid, suddenly covered with sweat, with an ass secretly puckered by all the stubbornness of a cabbage, his voice hardly blurred by his trembling, he continues to emit numbers, to produce formulas, adding and subtracting. "They'll have to operate on you, Pantita," Mother Leonor murmurs maternally. "Have an operation, dear," Pochita repeats softly. "Get them taken out once and for all, pal," Lieutenant Luis Rengifo Flores echoes. "It's easier than being circumcised, and in a spot that's less dangerous for your manhood." Major Antipa Negrón of the Military Hospital laughs: "I'm going to decapitate these three hemorrhoids with one slash, as if they were the heads on animal crackers, Pantaleón."

Around the operating table, there is a series of moves, splices and grafts that torment him much more than the silent bustle of the doctors and the nurses in their little white shoes, more than the blinding cascades of light that the ceiling mirrors send him. "Is not going to hult you, Mistel Pantoja," encourages Tiger Collazos, who, in addition to the voice, also has the slanted eyes, the quivering hands and the syrupy voice of Porfirio the Chinaman. "Quicker, easier and with fewer complications than the extraction of a tooth, Pantita," he is assured by Mother Leonor, whose hips, double chin and breasts have firmed up and overflowed to the point of intermingling with those of Leonor Curinchila. But there, also bent over the operating table, where they have placed him in a gynecological position—between his legs Dr. Antipa Negrón

59

manipulates scalpels, cotton, scissors, receptacles—are two women as inseparable and opposite as certain couples spinning around in his head now and bringing him back to his infancy, to the beginning of adolescence (Laurel and Hardy, Mandrake and Lothario, Tarzan and Jane): a mountain of fat wrapped in a Spanish mantilla and a child crone, in blue jeans, with bangs and smallpox scars on her face. Not knowing what they are doing there or who they are—but remotely he has the feeling of having once seen them, as if in passing, in a crowd of people—brings an endless agony and, without trying to stop it, he begins to cry: he hears his own deep, loud sobs. "Don't be scared of them, they're the first recruits for the Special Service. Don't you recognize Knockers and Sandra? I already introduced you the other night, at Casa Chuchupe," soothes Juan Rivera, the popular Freckle, who has diminished even more in size and is a little monkey seated on the round, naked, fragile shoulders of Pochita. He feels as though he could die of shame, of anger, of frustration, of rancor. He'd like to shout: "You runt, you abortion, you fetus! How dare you reveal the secret in front of my wife and the widow of my dead father?" But he doesn't open his mouth; he just sweats and suffers. Dr. Negrón has finished his work and stands up with a few bloody pieces dangling from his hands which Panta glimpses for only a second, since he manages to close his eyes in time. Every second he is more pained, offended and shocked. Tiger Collazos laughs. "You've got to face realities and call a spade a spade: the men got to get laid and you either arrange that for them or we shoot you with blasts of semen." "We've chosen the Horcones Post as the pilot project for the Special Service, Pantoja," General Victoria announces cheerfully. And although he is pointing with his eyes and with his hands at Mother Leonor, at the delicate and gaunt Pochita, imploring discretion, reserve, delay, deletion, General Victoria is insisting: "We already know that besides Sandra and Knockers you've enlisted Iris and Lalita. Long live the four musketeers!" He has begun to cry again, at the height of his helplessness.

But now, around the bed of the man who has recently been operated on, Leonor and Pochita watch with love and tenderness and without the least shadow of malice, with an obvious, marvelous, comforting ignorance shining in their eyes: they know noth-

ing. He feels an ironic rejoicing that rises through his body and mocks him: How *could* they know about the Special Service if it still hasn't come into being, if I'm still happy and a lieutenant, if we haven't even left Chiclayo? But Dr. Negrón has just entered, accompanied by a young and smiling nurse (he recognizes her and blushes: Alicia, Pocha's friend!) who cradles an irrigator in her arms like a newborn child. Pochita and Mother Leonor leave the room, giving him a united, almost tragic, farewell from the door. "Knees spread, mouth kissing the mattress, ass up," orders Dr. Antipa Negrón. And he explains: "Twenty-four hours have passed and the time has come to clean out your stomach. These two quarts of salt water will take away all the mortal and venial sins of your life, Lieutenant." Despite its being covered with vaseline and despite the doctor's talent as a magician, the introduction of the irrigator into his rectum tears a shout out of him. But now the liquid is pouring in with a warmth that is no longer painful, pleasant even. For a moment the water pours in, bubbling, swelling his bowels, and meanwhile Lieutenant Pantoja, his eyes closed methodically, thinks: The Special Service? It won't hurt me, it won't hurt me. He lets out another little yell: Dr. Negrón has taken the irrigator out and has placed a wad of cotton between his buttocks. The nurse leaves, carrying the empty irrigator. "Up till now you haven't felt any postoperative pain, right?" the doctor asks. "Right, Major," Lieutenant Pantoja answers, twisting himself with difficulty, sitting up, getting out of bed, a hand squashed against the cotton pinched between his buttocks, and moving toward the toilet, as rigid as a Judas doll, naked from the waist down, on the arm of the doctor, who observes him with kindness and something like piety. A slight warmth has begun to work its way through his rectum and his elephantine bowels now suffer cramps, rapid muscular spasms, and a sudden shudder electrifies his lower back. The doctor helps him to sit on the toilet, pats him on the shoulder and sums up his philosophy: "Console yourself by thinking that after this experience, *everything that happens to you in life will be better.*" He leaves, gently closing the bathroom door. Lieutenant Pantoja now puts a towel between his teeth and bites down on it with all his might. He has closed his eyes, buried his hands between his knees, and two million pores have opened like windows

61

all over his body to vomit out sweat and bile. With all the desperation he is capable of, he repeats to himself: "I will not shit specialists, I will not shit specialists." But the two quarts of water have already begun to descend, to slither, to fall, to burst out, fiery and satanic, pernicious and homicidal, traitorous, dragging solid chunks of fire, knives and awls that scorch, prick, sting, blind. He has let the towel fall from his mouth so he can roar like a lion, grunt like a pig and laugh like a hyena all at once.

4

Rear Adm. Pedro G. Carrillo, Chief of the River Forces of the Amazon,

CONSIDERING:

1. That he has received a request from Capt. (Quartermaster) Pantaleón Pantoja, PA, Chief of the Special Service for Garrisons, Frontier and Related Installations (SSGFRI), recently created by the Army for the purpose of solving a long-standing biological-psychological problem of the noncommissioned officers and soldiers who are serving in remote regions, asking that the River Forces of the Amazon offer him assistance as well as use of their facilities in the organization of the transport system between the command post of the Special Service logistics centers and its utilization centers;

2. That the aforementioned request has the authorization of the Department of Administration, Supply and Logistics of the Army (Gen. Felipe Collazos) and of the Command of Region V (Amazon) (Gen. Roger Scavino);

3. That naval headquarters has considered the request for assistance favorably, at the same time pointing out the suitability of having the SSGFRI extend its services to the Navy bases in the remote regions of the Amazon where the sailors find themselves afflicted with the same necessities and appetites as those of the

Army's noncommissioned officers and soldiers that motivated the creation of the Special Service;

4. That having been consulted in the matter, Capt. (Quartermaster) Pantaleón Pantoja, PA, replied that there are no obstacles to the SSGFRI's acceding to said suggestion, specifying that the River Forces of the Amazon should administer a test of its own devising in the jungle bases for the purpose of ascertaining the potential number of users in the Peruvian Navy (PN) of the SSGFRI, which test, implemented by the officers in charge with all due speed and care, yielded a *potential number of 327 users*, with an *average aspiration per user of 10 monthly services* and an *average duration aspired to of 35 minutes per individual service;*

DECIDES:

1. That the ex-dispensary boat the S.S. *Pachitea,* with a permanent crew of four men under the command of First Subofficer Carlos Rodríguez Saravia, be provisionally assigned to the Special Service as a means of transport on the rivers of the Amazon Basin between its logistics center and its utilization centers;

2. That before leaving Santa Clotilde base, where she has remained after being retired from an uninterrupted half century of navigation in the service of the Navy, a record that began with her outstanding participation in the conflict with Colombia in 1910, the S.S. *Pachitea,* PN, be stripped of flags, insignia and other distinguishing marks that point to her being a ship of the Peruvian Navy, that she be painted the color indicated by Capt. (Quartermaster) Pantaleón Pantoja, PA, provided that it is neither steel gray nor cloud white, which are the colors of the PN boats, and that its original name, S.S. *Pachitea,* on the prow and on the command bridge be replaced with that of *Eve,* which the Special Service has chosen for her;

3. That (a) before assuming their new duties, First Subofficer Carlos Rodríguez Saravia and the crew under his command be duly briefed by their superiors on the delicacy of the mission they are going to execute and the necessity for them to dress as civilians in the performance of same and to hide their status as members of the Navy; (b) they observe maximum restraint in regard to what

64

they see and hear in the course of their deployment and, in general, (c) they avoid the slightest cognizance or disclosure about the nature of the service to which they have been detailed;

4. That the fuel required by the S.S. *Pachitea*, PN, in its new mission be paid for proportionally by the Navy and the Army, according to the respective use of the Special Service, which can be determined by the number of services rendered to each branch per month or by the number of sailings to military garrisons or river bases assigned to the SSGFRI;

5. That because of its confidential nature, this disposition may not be read into the orders of the day, nor posted on the bases, but must be communicated exclusively to the officers who must execute it.

[Signed]

REAR ADM. PEDRO G. CARRILLO
Chief of the River Forces of the Amazon
Santa Clotilde Base, 16 August 1956

cc: Staff of the Peruvian Navy
Department of Administration, Supply and Logistics of the Army
Command of Region V (Amazon)

SSGFRI

Dispatch Number Three

GENERAL SUBJECT: Special Service for Garrisons, Frontier and Related Installations

SPECIFIC SUBJECT: Properties of porpoise oil, *chuchuhuasi, cocobolo, clabohuasca, huacapuruna, ipururo* and *viborachado,* their importance to the SSGFRI, as experienced by the undersigned and suggestions by same

CLASSIFICATION: Top Secret

PLACE AND DATE: Iquitos, 8 September 1956

The undersigned, Capt. (Quartermaster) Pantaleón Pantoja, PA, Chief of the SSGFRI, respectfully presents himself to Gen. Felipe Collazos, Chief of Administration, Supply and Logistics of the Army, salutes him and reports:

1. (a) That in the entire Amazon District there exists the belief that the red species of porpoise (the dolphin of the Amazon rivers) is a creature of considerable sexual potency, which induces it, with the aid of the devil or of evil spirits, to rape as many women as it can in order to satisfy its instincts, and that to accomplish this end it adopts a human form that is so virile and handsome that no female can resist it. (b) That owing to said belief, another belief has become common: porpoise oil increases the sexual drive, making the male irresistible to the female and creating an enormous market for the product in stores and markets. (c) That the undersigned decided to personally carry out an experiment with the purpose of determining in what form this popular belief, superstition or scientific fact could have a bearing on the problem that gave rise to and lies at the foundation of the Special Service. Setting to work with the pretext of a doctor's prescription, he requested his beloved mother and his dear wife to prepare all meals at home with porpoise oil as their basic ingredient, with the results set forth here:

2. (a) That starting with the second day the undersigned experienced a sudden increase in sexual appetite, the abnormality accentuating itself on the following days to the point that on the last two days of the week dirty thoughts and the virile act were the only ideas occupying his mind, as much during the day as at night (dreams, nightmares), with serious detriment to his powers of concentration, his nervous system in general and his effectiveness at work. (b) That he consequently found himself with the need to solicit from his wife and to obtain from her, during the week in question, intimate relations on an average of twice daily, with a resulting irritation and surprise of the same, since the undersigned was in the habit of having relations of an intimate matrimonial nature at a rate of once every ten days before coming to Iquitos and once every three days after arriving, because, undoubtedly due to factors already identified by his superiors (heat, humidity),

the undersigned had registered an increase of the seminal impulse from the very day he set foot on Amazonian ground. (c) That at the same time, he was able to confirm that the aphrodisiacal function of porpoise oil is registered only in the man, although he cannot discount the fact that his spouse, affected by the stimulant in question, disguised it with great fortitude on account of the natural feelings of modesty and decorum in any lady who deserves that name, as the undersigned is proud to say is the case with his good wife;

3. (a) That in his desire to spare no efforts for the optimum completion of the mission that his superiors have entrusted to him and even at a risk to his physical health and family stability, the undersigned likewise decided to personally test some of the recipes that folk wisdom and the lust of the people of Loreto suggest for the restoration or strengthening of virility, vulgarly referred to, forgive the expression, as "raising the dead" or, even worse, "cock cures." The undersigned refers only to *some* recipes, because in this part of the country the preoccupation with everything to do with sex is so keen and diverse that there are literally thousands of compounds of this sort, a fact that makes it impossible, even with the best of intentions, for an isolated individual to exhaust the list even if he is prepared to sacrifice his life for the experiment. (b) That the undersigned feels duty bound to concede that this is a question of folk wisdom and not of superstition: certain types of bark used to prepare infusions drunk with alcohol, like the *chuchuhuasi,* the *cocobolo,* the *clabohuasca* and the *huacapuruna,* produce an immediate and interminable itching that can never be relieved except in the very act of manhood. Particularly effective, because of the almost astronomical speed with which it operates on the generative center, is the mixture of *ipururo* and cheap brandy, which, barely swallowed, caused an unforgivable feverishness in the undersigned, along with an embarrassment that can be imagined, since the experiment was unfortunately not carried out at his own home but in the nightclub The Shadows, in the resort of Nanay. (c) That the potion called *viborachado,* being cheap brandy in which a poisonous snake, preferably a fat one, has been marinated, is even worse and truly fiendish, having an even more cataclysmic effect than the preced-

67

ing infusions, since in this instance it was offered casually to the author of this dispatch at another nightclub in Iquitos called The Jungle and imparted such an urgent and ferocious passion and hardening to him that in order to recover his self-control and peace of mind he had to resort to the solitary vice, which he had believed extinguished in him ever since the days of childhood, in the uncomfortable bathroom of the aforementioned club and with a remorse that has not yet diminished;

4. That for all the above reasons, the undersigned takes the liberty of recommending that his superiors instruct all garrisons, frontier and related installations to categorically forbid the use of red porpoise oil in the preparation of meals for noncommissioned officers as well as its use by individuals among the troops and that the consumption, straight or mixed with other things, in solid or liquid form, of *chuchuhuasi, cocobolo, clabohuasca, huacapuruna, ipuruo* and *viborachado* be immediately prohibited under strict punishment, otherwise the Special Service runs the risk of being bombarded by a demand even greater than the already inflated one it must confront;

5. That he requests the strictest secrecy be maintained in regard to this dispatch (and if possible that it be destroyed once it is read) since it contains extremely intimate disclosures about the family life of the undersigned, who has resigned himself to working with the complex mission that the Army has entrusted to him in mind, but who is uneasy and naturally apprehensive about his fellow officers' jokes, of which he would be the object if this dispatch were disclosed.

God bless you.
[Signed]
CAPT. (QUARTERMASTER) PANTALEÓN PANTOJA, PA

cc: Gen. Roger Scavino, Commander in Chief of Region V (Amazon)

NOTE: *(a) Put Capt. Pantoja's suggestion into effect as a regulation, and, therefore, communicate to all leaders of barracks, encampments and posts in Region V (Amazon) that henceforth the use of*

68

*the ingredients, potions and spices enumerated in the preceding
section is categorically prohibited in the preparation of meals. (b)
In accordance with Capt. Pantoja's request, destroy Dispatch
Number 3 of the SSGFRI by burning since it contains indelicate
revelations concerning the personal and family life of same.*

[*Signed*]
GEN. FELIPE COLLAZOS
*Chief of Administration, Supply and Logistics
Lima, 18 September 1956*

Confidential Decision: PAF Catalina Hydroplane
No. 37, the *Requena*

Col. Andrés Sarmiento Segovia, PAF, Commander of Air Battalion
No. 42 of the Amazon District,

CONSIDERING:

1. That Capt. (Quartermaster) Pantaleón Pantoja, PA, with the
authorization and backing of his Army superiors, has requested
assistance from Air Battalion No. 42 for the continual transfer of
personnel of the recently created Special Service from its logistics
center on the shores of the Itaya to its utilization centers, many of
which are so isolated, especially during the rainy season, that the
only functional means of transport from said points to the logistics
center is by air;

2. That the Command of Administration and Development for
the Staff of the Peruvian Air Force has agreed to accede to the
request in deference to the Army but certifies that it has reserva-
tions concerning the constitution of the Special Service, since it
hardly seems compatible with the natural and proper duties of the
armed forces and dangerous to its good name and prestige—this
being a simple conjecture and by no means an attempt to meddle
in the affairs of the sister institution;

DECIDES:

1. That PAF Catalina Hydroplane No. 37, the *Requena*, be
assigned to the SSGFRI on loan, so that the indicated transport

services may be carried out once the Technical and Mechanical Division of Air Battalion No. 42 of the Amazon District has put the plane in a state that will render it fit to resume flying;

2. That before it is separated from the air base at Moronacocha, PAF Catalina Hydroplane No. 37 be duly camouflaged in such a way that it cannot be recognized at any time as belonging to the Peruvian Air Force while rendering service in the SSGFRI. For this purpose, changes will be made in the color of the fuselage and the wings (from blue to green with red borders) and the name (from *Requena* to *Delilah,* according to Capt. Pantoja's request);

3. That the piloting of Catalina Hydroplane No. 37 be assigned to the subofficer of Air Battalion No. 42 who has had the greatest number of disciplinary actions and reprimands in his service file for the current year;

4. That in view of the state of technical deterioration of PAF Catalina Hydroplane No. 37, due to its many years of service, it be examined weekly by a mechanic of Air Battalion No. 42 of the Amazon District, who will be transported for this purpose, discreetly and in mufti, to the logistics center of the SSGFRI;

5. To earnestly beg Capt. Pantoja that the Special Service take the greatest care and precaution with the Catalina Hydroplane because it is a true historic relic of the PAF, since it was in this noble machine that, on 3 March 1929, Lt. Luis Pedraza Romero linked the cities of Iquitos and Yurimaguas in direct flight for the first time;

6. That the fuel as well as all other expenses that the maintenance and use of the PAF Catalina Hydroplane may incur be the exclusive responsiblity of the SSGFRI itself;

7. (a) That this Decision be communicated only to those it affects or mentions; and (b) that because of its top-secret nature, whoever divulges or shares its contents beyond the mentioned exceptions be punished with sixty days at hard labor.

[Signed]
COL. ANDRÉS SARMIENTO SEGOVIA, PAF
Moronacocha Air Base, 7 August 1956

cc: Command of Administration and Development for the Staff of the Peruvian Air Force
Department of Administration, Supply and Logistics of the Army
Command of Region V (Amazon)

Internal Order of the Medical Corps
of the Vargas Guerra Military Encampment

Commander (Medical Corps) Roberto Quispe Salas, PA, Chief of the Medical Corps of the Vargas Guerra Military Encampment, having inspected the confidential instructions received from the Command of Region V (Amazon), approves the following directives:

1. Major (Medical Corps) Antipa Negrón Azpilcueta, PA, will select from among the corps of male nurses and practical health officers in the Infectious/Contagious Illnesses Section the individual he considers most scientifically and morally trained to fulfill the duties that the instructions from the Command of Region V (Amazon) specify for the future Medical Assistant for the Special Service for Garrisons, Frontier and Related Installations (SSGFRI).

2. In the course of the present week, Major Negrón Azpilcueta will impart to the male nurse or military health officer selected, accelerated theoretical-practical training, with a view toward the duties he will have to discharge in the SSGFRI, which essentially will consist of detecting the infestation of nits, bedbugs, lice, crabs and mites in general as well as venereal diseases and chronic infectious/contagious vulva-vaginal diseases in the female recruits composing the convoys, immediately before their departure to the utilization centers of the SSGFRI.

3. Major Negrón Azpilcueta will supply the Medical Assistant with a first-aid medical kit, including probe, pallet and rubber finger cot for vaginal exploration, two white smocks, two pairs of rubber gloves and an adequate number of notebooks from which the latter must send weekly dispatches to the Medical Corps of the Vargas Guerra Military Encampment on the quantitative and

qualitative operation of the Post of Medical Assistance of the SSGFRI.

4. Communicate this order only to concerned parties and file it with the classification "Secret."

[Signed]
COMMANDER (MEDICAL CORPS) ROBERTO QUISPE SALAS, PA
Vargas Guerra Military Encampment
September 1956

cc: Command of Region V (Amazon)
Capt. (Quartermaster) Pantaleón Pantoja, PA, Chief of the Special Service for Garrisons, Frontier and Related Installations (SSGFRI)

Report of Second Lt. Alberto Santana, PA, to the Command of Region V (Amazon) on the pilot operation carried out by the SSGFRI in the Horcones Post, under his command

In accordance with his received instructions, Second Lt. Alberto Santana has the honor of remitting to the Command of Region V (Amazon) the following report on events that have occurred in the post under his command on the Napo River:

As soon as informed by his superiors that the Horcones Post had been selected as the site for the initial experiment of the Special Service for Garrisons, Frontier and Related Installations, he prepared to put all facilities at the disposal of the operation for its success and radioed Capt. Pantaleón Pantoja to inquire what arrangements should be made in Horcones prior to the pilot project. To which Capt. Pantoja responded by informing him that none was needed because he personally would be transferred to the Napo River to supervise the preparations and the progress of the test.

In fact, on the day of 12 September at approximately 1030 hours, a green hydroplane with the name *Delilah* painted in red letters on the fuselage, piloted by an individual nicknamed

72

"Crazy," landed on the Napo River, carrying as passengers Capt. Pantoja, dressed as a civilian, and a woman named Chuchupe, whom it was necessary to carry off the plane because she had fainted. The reason for her light-headedness was that she had been greatly frightened during the flight from the Itaya River to the Napo River, due to the plane's shaking in the wind and to the pilot, who, according to the assertion of the aforementioned, had performed continual risky and pointless acrobatics, intending to amuse himself by increasing her terror, which her nerves could not withstand. Once the said woman had recovered, she attempted to assault the pilot with words and crude gestures, and it was necessary for Capt. Pantoja to intervene in order to put an end to the incident.

With their nerves calmed down after a quick snack, Capt. Pantoja and his collaborator proceeded to put everything in order for accomplishing the experiment, which was to be observed on the following day, Tuesday, 13 September. The preparations were of two sorts: participational and topographical. In regard to the first, Capt. Pantoja, assisted by the undersigned, established a list of users by asking the twenty-two noncommissioned officers and soldiers of the post one by one—the subofficer was excluded—if they wanted to take advantage of the Special Service, explaining to them for the purposes of this questioning the nature of same. The troops' first reaction was one of incredulity and distrust, and all answered by refusing to participate in the experiment, thinking it had to do with a ruse, as when they are asked for "Volunteers to go to Iquitos" and the ones who step forward are ordered to clean latrines. It was necessary for the aforementioned Chuchupe to appear and speak to the men in gross language so that their suspicion and doubt could be displaced, first by a great hilarity and then by an excitement of such magnitude that it was necessary for the subofficers and the undersigned to act with maximum energy in order to calm them down. Out of twenty-two noncommissioned officers and soldiers, twenty-one registered as candidate-users, the exception being Pvt. Segundo Pachas, who indicated that he was exempting himself because the operation would take place on Tuesday the 13th and that, being superstitious, he was sure it would bring him bad luck if he participated in it. According to the

indication of the male nurse of Horcones, Corp. Urondino Chicote was likewise eliminated from the list of candidate-users because he was afflicted with an eruption of mange, capable of being spread via the respective female recruit to the rest of the unit. Which left a definitively established list of twenty users, who, when consulted, agreed that the fixed price should be deducted from their pay check by the SSGFRI as repayment for the service being offered them.

In regard to the topographical preparations, they consisted basically of preparing four locations assigned to the specialists of the first convoy of the SSGFRI, and these preparations were carried out under the exclusive direction of the so-called Chuchupe. She pointed out that since rain was possible, the sites should have roofs and preferably not be contiguous, in order to avoid auditory interference or emulation, a request that, unfortunately, could not be fully satisfied. Having inspected the roofed installations of the post, which, as the command knows, are few, the provisions storehouse, the radio post and the infirmary were selected as the most suitable locations. Due to its size, the provisions storehouse could be divided into two compartments, using boxes of foodstuffs as a dividing wall. The aforementioned Chuchupe then requested that a bed with its own straw or rubber mattress be placed in each location; or, in its absence, a hammock, with a waterproof oilcloth in order to avoid seepage and the deterioration of the material. They immediately proceeded to transfer four beds (chosen at random) along with their mattresses from the troops' barracks to said locations, but because it was not possible to obtain the requested sheets of oilcloth, tarpaulins used to cover machinery and armaments when it rains were substituted. At the same time, once the mattresses were covered with tarpaulins, mosquito netting was installed so that the insects so abundant at this time of year would not interfere with the utilization activities. It being impossible to provide each location with the chamber pot that Corps Leader Chuchupe requested—since the post did not have even one of said artifacts at its disposal—four feed buckets were provided. There was no difficulty in installing in each location washbasins with their respective buckets of water, nor in providing each site with a chair, a chest or bench on which to place clothes, and two rolls of

74

toilet paper. Seeing how wasteful our female recruits are with this last item—there not being in such an isolated area anything like newspaper or wrapping paper to substitute for it—and how there are case histories of hives and skin irritations among the troops because they have used leaves from trees, the undersigned begs his superiors to be kind enough to order headquarters to replace said items as quickly as possible. The so-called Chuchupe specified at the same time that it was indispensable to hang curtains in the locations that, without leaving them in total darkness, would soften the sunlight and create a certain dimness, which, in her experience, is the most suitable atmosphere for rendering service. The impossibility of obtaining the flowered curtains that Corps Leader Chuchupe suggested was no impediment: First Sgt. Esteban Sandora ingeniously devised a series of curtains from the troops' blankets and greatcoats, which served the purpose rather well, leaving the locations in the necessary half light. Also, in the event that night should fall before the operation was completed, Corps Leader Chuchupe had the light bulbs in the locations covered with pieces of red cloth, because she insisted that the red glow was the most suitable for servicing. Finally, the aforementioned Corps Leader, maintaining that the sites should have a certain feminine touch, proceeded on her own to make little bouquets of flowers, leaves and wild stalks, which she gathered with the aid of two recruits and placed artistically on the headboards of the beds in each location. With which the preparations were concluded and all that remained was to wait for the convoy's arrival.

On the following day, Tuesday, 13 September, at 1415 hours, the first convoy of the SSGFRI anchored broadside on the dock of the Horcones Post. When the transport ship—recently painted green with its name, *Eve,* inscribed in large red letters on the prow—was barely visible, the troops halted their daily tasks, broke out in shouts of enthusiasm and tossed their hats into the air as a sign of welcome. Following Capt. Pantoja's instructions, a guard patrol was immediately set up to prevent any civilian element from approaching the post during the pilot experiment—really a quite unlikely danger if you keep in mind that the closest town to Horcones is a Quechua Indian village two days upstream on the

Napo River. Thanks to the determined collaboration of the female recruits, the disembarking took place with complete regularity. The transport ship *Eve* was commanded by Carlos Rodríguez Saravia (Subofficer in the Marines, camouflaged as a civilian), with a crew of four men, who, under Capt. Pantoja's orders, remained on board during the entire stay of the *Eve* in Horcones. Two of Capt. Pantoja's civilian collaborators presided over the convoy: Porfirio Wong and an individual with the nickname of Freckle. In regard to the four female recruits, whose appearance on the gangplank was greeted with rounds of applause from the troops, they answered to the following names (the four refused to divulge their surnames): Lalita, Iris, Knockers and Sandra. The four were immediately gathered together by the so-called Freckle and Chuchupe in the provisions storehouse in order to rest and receive instruction, while the aforementioned Porfirio Wong stood guard at the door. Keeping in mind the restlessness that their presence provoked in the men of the post, it turned out to be useful to keep the women quartered until the hour fixed for the start of the operation (1700 hours), but it caused a little difficulty within the SSGFRI. Because, after having spent some time recuperating from the fatigue of the journey, the female recruits named above tried to leave the location, alleging that they wanted to get to know the surroundings and stroll around the post. Not being permitted to do so by those in command, they protested loudly with shouts and obscenities and they even attempted to force their way out. In order to keep them secluded, it was necessary for Capt. Pantoja to enter into the provisions storehouse. By way of anecdote, it can be mentioned that soon after the convoy's arrival, Pvt. Segundo Pachas requested to be included among the users, indicating that he was prepared to challenge his bad luck, but he was refused because the list had been drawn up definitively.

At 1655 hours Capt. Pantoja ordered the women to occupy their respective positions, which had been chosen by lot thusly: provisions storehouse, Lalita and Knockers; radio post, Sandra; infirmary, Iris. As supervisers, Capt. Pantoja himself was placed at the door of the provisions storehouse, the undersigned in front of the radio post and Subofficer Marcos Maravilla Ramos in front of the infirmary, each with his own stopwatch. At exactly 1700 hours,

that is to say, when the troops had hardly finished their duties and chores (with the exception of guard duty), the twenty users were ordered into formation and asked to indicate the woman of their choice, thus engendering the first serious difficulty, due to the fact that eighteen of the twenty resolutely indicated their preference for the so-called Knockers and the remaining two for Iris, which left the other two women without candidate-users. In consulting on what decision to take, Capt. Pantoja suggested and the undersigned put into operation the following solution: the five men with the best conduct record for the month, according to service files, were directed to the location of the requested Knockers and the five with the highest number of punishments and reprimands to that of the one named Sandra because she has the most disfigured appearance of the four women (abundant smallpox scars). The others were divided into two groups and directed, by drawing lots, to the respective positions of Iris and Lalita. Once the four groups of five men were formed, it was briefly explained to them that they would not be able to exceed a maximum stay of twenty-five minutes in the location—top time for a normal service according to the regulations of the SSGFRI—and those who waited were ordered to maintain maximum silence and composure in order not to bother their companions in action. The second serious difficulty arose at that moment, since every man fought to be at the head of his respective group in order to be the first to obtain each specialist's services, and this led to shoving and verbal altercations. Once again, it was necessary to impose order and resort to the system of drawing lots to arrange a pecking order in the lines, all of which meant a delay of some fifteen minutes.

At 1715 hours the command to begin was given. It is fitting to state beforehand that, as a whole, the pilot operation was carried out with complete success, more or less within the predicted time periods and with a minimum of mishaps. In regard to the visiting time with a specialist permitted to each user (which Capt. Pantoja had feared would be too short for a satisfactory and complete servicing), it turned out to be excessive. For example, these are the times employed by the five users of Sandra's group, which the undersigned timed: the first, 8 minutes; the second, 12; the third, 16; the fourth, 10; and the fifth, who set the record, 3 minutes. The

men in the other groups registered similar times. In any case, Capt. Pantoja noted that these scores were only relatively valid as a general indication since, due to the isolation of Horcones and to the men's having been quartered here for such long periods (six months for some), they tend to be abnormally fast in being serviced. Taking into account that between one servicing and the next there was a waiting period of some minutes, so that the aforementioned Freckle and Chuchupe could change the water in the containers at each location, it can be concluded that the operation lasted less than two hours from start to finish. Certain incidents arose in the course of the pilot project, but none of a serious nature, some even being amusing and useful in somewhat relaxing the nervous tension of the men who were waiting on line. Thus, for example, due to the carelessness of the post's radio operator, who tunes in daily to Radio Amazon of Iquitos to listen to the program *The Voice of Sinchi,* which we play over the loudspeaker at 1800 hours, the speaker's voice tempestuously broke out over Horcones because the transmitter was on automatic, provoking boisterous laughter and cheerfulness from the men, most of all when they saw the specialist Sandra and First Sgt. Esteban Sandora appear in their underwear, having been very alarmed when the noise broke forth since she was servicing him in the radio post. Another brief incident arose when, making the most of the fact that Knockers and Lalita were operating in neighboring rooms of the provisions storehouse, Pvt. Amelio Sifuentes, in the latter's line of users, maliciously attempted to enter the location of the so-called Knockers, who, as the command will have perceived, was the one who conquered the most affection among the men of Horcones. Capt. Pantoja caught Sifuentes off guard in his rash attempt and severely reprimanded him. In the same provisions storehouse another mishap occurred, which was only discovered by the undersigned after the SSGFRI convoy had departed. During the time devoted to the servicing—or sometime before it— while the women were gathered there, someone took advantage of the situation to open a case of food and take out seven cans of tuna, four boxes of water biscuits and two sodas, without our yet having been able to identify the guilty party or parties. To summarize: with only the exception of these minor incidents, the opera-

tion had ended by 1900 hours with complete success and there reigned in the post a feeling of great satisfaction, peace and happiness among the noncommissioned officers and soldiers. The undersigned neglected to indicate that after being serviced, various users inquired whether it was possible to line up again (in the same or in a different line) to receive a second service. The request was refused by Capt. Pantoja, who explained that the possibility of authorizing a repeat service would be studied when the SSGFRI has reached maximum operational volume.

With the pilot project scarcely finished, the four specialists and their civilian collaborators, Freckle, Chuchupe and Porfirio Wong, embarked on the *Eve* to return to the logistics center on the Itaya River, while Capt. Pantoja left on the *Delilah*. No matter how much the pilot assured the so-called Chuchupe that he would fly the apparatus the way it should be flown and that the incidents of the previous day would not be repeated, she refused to return by plane. Before leaving Horcones, amidst the clapping and the grateful gestures of the noncommissioned officers and soldiers, Capt. Pantoja thanked the undersigned for the facilities put at the disposal of the SSGFRI and for his contribution to its success. Capt. Pantoja indicated to him that this very profitable experience had allowed him to perfect and to outline in complete detail the system of work, control and transfer of the Special Service.

Along with this report, which hopefully will be useful, it only remains to submit for the consideration of the command the request signed by the four lower officers of the Horcones Post that the intermediate command be allowed to be users of the SSGFRI. Due to the good psychological and physical effect that the experience is proving to have had on the noncommissioned officers and soldiers, this petition carries the favorable recommendation of the undersigned.

God bless you.
[Signed]
 SECOND LT. ALBERTO SANTANA, PA
 Chief, Horcones Post (Napo River)
 16 September 1956

ACCOUNTING AND FINANCE SECTION

Confidential Ruling No. 069

The chief officers of the Quartermaster Unit or the subordinate officers placed in charge of said function in the districts, encampments and posts of Military Region V (Amazon) are authorized as of today, 14 September 1956, to deduct from the payrolls of the soldiers' allowances and the noncommissioned officers' wages the remuneration corresponding to the services rendered them by the Special Service for Garrisons, Frontier and Related Installations (SSGFRI). Said deductions must strictly adhere to the following regulations:

1. The rates per service, fixed by the SSGFRI with the approval of its commanding officers, will be of only two types, in all cases and circumstances, namely:

Soldiers: twenty (20) soles per service
Noncommissioned officers (beginning with first sergeant): thirty (30) soles per service

2. The maximum number of permissible monthly services will be eight (8), with no minimum number indicated.

3. The deducted sum will be directed by the commanding officer or the subordinate officer in charge to the SSGFRI, the organization that will remunerate the specialists on a monthly basis in accordance with the number of services they will have performed.

4. For the verification and control of the system, the following procedure will be followed: The commanding officer or the subordinate officer in charge will receive with this Ruling an appropriate number of cardboard coupons of two types, each in one of the symbolic colors of the SSGFRI and with no written markings. Those in red are designated for the soldiers and consequently each

will be worth twenty (20) soles, and those in green for the noncommissioned officers and therefore each will represent thirty (30) soles. On the first day of each month there will be distributed to each noncommissioned officer and soldier of the unit the number of coupons equal to the maximum number of services to which he is entitled, which is to say eight (8). A coupon will be given to the specialist by the user each time he has benefit of service. On the last day of the month the noncommissioned officer or soldier will return the unused coupons to the command, which will at that time make the deduction corresponding to the number of coupons not returned (in case of misplacement or loss of coupons, damages will be indemnified by the specialist, not by the SSGFRI.)

5. Since it is indispensable for reasons of decorum and morality to maintain the maximum discretion regarding the nature of this accounting operation, the deduction for the services of the SSGFRI will appear camouflaged by means of countersigns in the books of the district, encampment or post. For this purpose, the officer or the subordinate officer may use any of the following formulae:

(a) Deduction for cost of uniforms
(b) Deduction for deterioration of arms
(c) Advance for family transfer
(d) Deduction for sports
(e) Deduction for overeating

This Ruling No. 069 will not be posted in the units nor communicated in dispatches or in the orders of the day. The commanding officer or his subordinate in charge will verbally communicate its contents to the soldiers and noncommissioned officers of his unit, instructing them at the same time to maintain the greatest reserve on the subject since it is capable of impugning the reputation or attracting injurious criticism of the military.

[Signed]
COL. EZEQUIEL LÓPEZ LÓPEZ, PA
Chief of Accounting and Finance Section

Approved and distributed:
Gen. Felipe Collazos
Lima, 14 September 1956

Letter from Capt. Avencio P. Rojas, CMC, Chaplain of the Alfonso
Ugarte Cavalry Unit No. 7 of Contamana, to Headquarters of
the Corps of Military Chaplains of Region V (Amazon)

Contamana, 23 November 1956

Commander Godofredo Beltrán Calila, CMC
Iquitos, Loreto

My Commander and Dear Friend:

I am fulfilling my duty in informing you that on two consecutive
occasions in the space of the present month my unit has been
visited by groups of prostitutes—natives of Iquitos—who came
here by boat, were lodged in the barracks and were able to engage
in carnal commerce with the troops in full view and with the
complete approval of the officers. I understand that on both occa-
sions the corps of prostitutes was led by a deformed and dwarfish
individual who, it is said, is known by the alias of Chupo or Pupo
in the brothels of Iquitos. I cannot give you more details concern-
ing this event, which I know about only through hearsay, since on
both occasions I was ordered away beforehand by Major Zegarra
Avalos. The first time, without even taking into consideration that
I was still convalescing from the hepatitis that did so much damage
to my body, as you know only too well, he sent me to administer
the last rites to a supplier of the unit, a fisherman who was sup-
posedly dying, who lives an eight-hour march from here by means
of a trail through pestilent quagmires, and whom I found drunk
and with an almost petty wound on his arm caused by the bite of
a shimbillo monkey. The second time, the major sent me to bless
a field tent—a refuge for explorers—fourteen hours upstream on
the Huallaga, which was an absolutely absurd mission, as you will
comprehend, since never in its entire history has the Army been

82

in the habit of blessing similar installations of such uncertain existence. Both orders were obviously pretexts to prevent my witnessing the conversion of Cavalry Unit No. 7 into a brothel. However, I can assure you that no matter how painful that spectacle would have been for me, it would not have caused me the physical fatigue and psychological frustration that this pair of useless expeditions meant for me.

Once again, I allow myself to beseech you, my dear and respected commander, to be kind enough to support, with all the power of influence that your great prestige has deservedly given you, my request for a transfer to a more tolerable unit where I can execute my mission as a man of God and a shepherd of souls with greater spiritual benefit. At the risk of tiring you, I repeat that there can be no moral fortress or nervous system that bears the unending sneers and constant mockery that I am subject to here, as much from the officers as from the troops. Everyone is apparently convinced that the chaplain is the unit's entertainment and laughingstock, and not a day goes by that they do not make me the victim of some vile trick: at times as irreverent as discovering a mouse in place of the wafers in the ciborium while I am in the middle of celebrating mass; or being the cause of general mockery because an obscene picture has been stuck to my back without my noticing it; or inviting me to drink beer, which then turns out to be urine; and other, even more humiliating things, offensive and even dangerous to my health. My suspicion that Major Zegarra Avalos himself instigates and stirs up these insults against me has already become a certainty.

I place these facts before you, begging you to be kind enough to indicate to me whether a report about the arrival of the prostitutes should not be sent up to the Command of Region V or if it would be convenient for you to take the matter into your own hands; or if, for the sake of higher interests, it is advisable to maintain devout silence on the subject.

Awaiting your eminent advice and offering prayers for your good health and better spirits, an affectionate salute from your subordinate and friend,

[Signed]

CAPT. AVENCIO P. ROJAS, CMC
Chaplain, Alfonso Ugarte Cavalry Unit. No. 7
Contamana, Military Region V (Amazon)

Letter of Commander Godofredo Beltrán Calila, CMC, Chief
of the Corps of Military Chaplains of Region V (Amazon),
to Captain Avencio P. Rojas, Chaplain of the Alfonso Ugarte
Cavalry Unit No. 7, Contamana

Iquitos, 2 December 1956

Captain Avencio P. Rojas, CMC
Contamana, Loreto

Captain:

Once again I must regret your living in such a forsaken spot as
Paita. The female delegations that visited the Alfonso Ugarte Cav-
alry Unit No. 7 belong to the Special Service for Garrisons, Fron-
tier and Related Installations (SSGFRI), an organization created
and administered by the Army and about which you and all the
chaplains under my command were informed by me through Cir-
cular (CMC) No. 04606. The existence of the SSGFRI does not
wholly please the Corps of Military Chaplains and it pleases me
even less, but I do not need to remind you that in our institution
where the general gives orders, the private does not. Conse-
quently, there is nothing to be done but to close your eyes and to
beg God to enlighten our superiors so that they will rectify what,
in the light of the Catholic religion and military ethics, can only
be considered a grave error.

In regard to the complaints that fill the rest of your letter, I must
reprimand you severely. Major Zegarra Avalos is your superior
and it is up to him, not you, to judge the usefulness or the useless-
ness of the missions entrusted to you. Your obligation is to carry
them out with the greatest speed and efficiency possible. With
respect to the jokes of which you are the object, and which, of
course, I deplore, I feel that your lack of character is as much to
blame, and perhaps even more so, as the evil instincts of others.

84

Must I remind you that before anyone else, it is incumbent upon you to see that you are treated with the great deference demanded by your dual position as a priest and a soldier? Only once during these past fifteen years in my life as a chaplain has the respect due to me been lacking, and I assure you that the indecent fool must still be rubbing his face. To wear a cassock is not to wear skirts, Captain Rojas, and in the Army we do not tolerate chaplains with womanish inclinations.

I regret that your poorly understood notion of evangelical meekness, or your mere pusillanimity, causes you to preserve the abject image that says we men of the cloth are not full, red-blooded men, capable of imitating Christ, who with a whip attacked the merchants affronting the Temple.

Greater dignity and greater courage, Captain Rojas!

Your friend,
COMMANDER GODOFREDO BELTRAN CALILA
Chief of the CMC, Military Region V (Amazon)

5

"Wake up, Panta!" Pochita is saying. "Pantita, it's six o'clock already."

"Has our little cadet moved?" Panta is rubbing his eyes. "Let cadet's fathel feel belly."

"Don't talk like an idiot. What's gotten into you, imitating the Chinks?" Pochita makes a gesture of annoyance. "No, he hasn't moved. Touch. Do you feel anything?"

"These crazy 'brothers' have turned into something serious," Bacacorzo is waving the newspaper. "Did you see what they did in Moronacocha? Enough to make you shoot them, damn it. It's good the police are going after them with a clean-up campaign."

"Wake up, little cadet," Panta glues his ear to Pochita's navel. "You no heal leveille? What you waiting fol? Wake up, wake up!"

"I don't like you talking like that. Can't you see how jumpy I am after what happened to that little boy in Moronacocha?" Pochita resists. "Don't push on my belly so hard. You're going to hurt the baby."

"But, sweetheart, I'm just fooling around," Panta is stretching his eyes with two fingers. "I'm hooked on the way one of my aides talks. Are you going to get mad over that stuff? C'mon, gimme a little kiss."

"I'm scared our little cadet's dead," Pochita is kneading her belly. "He didn't move last night, he hasn't moved this morning. Something's wrong with him, Panta."

"Mrs. Pantoja, I've never seen such a normal pregnancy," Dr. Arizmendi soothes her. "Everything's going fine, don't worry. The

86

only thing, take care of your nerves. And for that, you already know: try not to think or talk about the tragedy in Moronacocha."

"Enough. Time to lise and do exelcises, Mistel Pantoja," Panta jumps out of bed. "Uppy! Uppy!"

"I hate you. Drop dead. Why don't you ever try to please me?" Pochita throws a pillow at him. "Panta, don't talk like a Chink."

"I'm just happy, girl, everything's going well," Panta is opening and closing his arms, squatting and jumping up. "I never thought I'd get ahead with the mission the Army gave me. And in just six months I've come so far I'm even surprised myself."

"At first it bothered you to be a spy. You had nightmares and you cried and shouted in your sleep," Pochita sticks out her tongue. "But now I see you love the Intelligence Service."

"Sure I know about that mess," Captain Pantoja agrees. "Just imagine, Bacacorzo, my poor mother got to see that sight. Of course, it made her faint, and she's spent three days in the clinic under medical treatment, with her nerves shot to pieces."

"Didn't you have to leave at six-thirty, son?" Mother Leonor pokes her head in. "Your breakfast's already on the table."

"I take showel in jiffy, Mama," Panta is flexing, shadow-boxing, jumping rope. "Good molning, Mothel Leonol."

"What's wrong with your husband that he's acting like this?" Mother Leonor is astonished. "You and me with our hearts in our mouths with all that's happened in this city and he's happier than a lark."

"The seclet is the Blazilian," Chino Porfirio is whispering. "I sweal to you, Chuchupe. He meet her last night at Aladdin Pandulo's and she knocked him cockeyed. I no pletend, he went closs-eyed with admilation. This time he fell, Chuchupe."

"Is she still as pretty or is she a little run-down?" asks Chuchupe. "I haven't seen her since before she went to Manaos. She didn't call herself the Brazilian then, just Olguita."

"Knockout of a pletty chick and besides hel eyes, tits, legs and all hel life looked like flom a stole window, she splouted a tellific ass," Chino Porfirio whistles, paws the air. "They say two guys died 'cause of hel."

"And what about the student, Mama?" Freckle is wrinkling his nose. "The police chief's son, the guy who hanged himself in

Moronacocha. He also committed suicide over her."

"No, that was an accident," Chuchupe moves his hand away from his nose and gives him a handkerchief. "The kid had already gotten over her. He was coming back again to Casa Chuchupe and chasing our best girls."

"But in bed he made them all call themselves Olguita," Freckle blows his nose and hands back the handkerchief. "Don't you remember how we laughed when we spied on him, Mama? He was kneeling and kissing their feet, imagining they were her. He killed himself for love, I'm sure of it."

"I know why you doubtful, icy lady," Chino Porfirio is pounding his chest. " 'Cause you lack what Chupón and I have too much of: healt."

"Poor thing, I really sympathize with you, Mother Leonor," Pochita shudders. "If I, who only know of the crime from hearing and reading about it, have nightmares and wake up thinking they're crucifying the little cadet, why shouldn't you be half crazy, having seen the child with your own eyes. God, Mother Leonor, I just talk about it and I get goose bumps, I'm telling you."

"Look at Olguita, she's spent her whole life causing trouble," Chuchupe philosophizes. "And she just gets back from Manaos and they catch her working right in the middle of the evening show at the Bolognesi movie house with a police lieutenant. The things she must've done in Brazil!"

"Loud and brassy, just the way I like 'em," Freckle is biting his lips. "Really stacked, here and there, tall as a willow, and she even seems intelligent."

"Want me to drown you in the river, you louse?" Chuchupe shoves him.

"It was just a joke to get you mad, Mama," Freckle jumps up, kisses her, lets out a laugh. "I've got a soft spot only for you. As for the others, I look at them with professional eyes."

"And Mr. Pantoja has already hired her?" asks Chuchupe. "How nice it would be to see him finally fall into a woman's trap: men in love always go soft. He's too straight. It's just what he needs."

"He want to, but no have money," Chino Porfirio is yawning. "Ohhh, I tiled. Only thing I no like about Selvice is this getting up at dawn. Hele come the gils, Chupón."

88

"I should have realized as soon as I got out of the taxi," Mother Leonor is grinding her teeth. "But I didn't, Pochita, in spite of the fact that I noticed how the Ark was fuller than other times and everyone was—I don't know—half hysterical. They were praying, crying out, there were sparks in the air. And to top it all off, that thunder and lightning."

"Good morning, happy and cheerful specialists," Freckle is singing. "Come on, you're going to line up for me, to have your medical examination. First come, first served, and no fighting. Like in the barracks, just the way Pan-Pan likes."

"What eyes flom a lough night, Pichuza," Chino Porfirio pinches her cheek. "We see the Selvice not nuff fol you."

"If you keep working on your own, you're never going to last here," Chuchupe warns. "You've heard it a thousand times from Pan-Pan."

"Being a specialist and a whore—excuse the expression—is incompatible," Pantoja decrees. "You are civilian functionaries of the Army and not traffickers in sex."

"But I haven't done anything, Chuchupe," Pichuza shows her fingernails to Porfirio, slaps her backside and stands her ground. "My face is so bad 'cause I've got the flu and I'm up all night."

"Let's not talk about that, Mother Leonor." Pochita is embracing her, "The doctor has ordered you not to think about that boy, and the same thing for me, remember. My God, the poor child. Are you sure he was already dead when you saw him? Or was he still suffering?"

"I swore I wouldn't go through the medical exam again and I'm not going to, Freckle," Knockers puts her fists on her hips. "That male nurse is a smart aleck. He's never going to lay his hands on me again."

"Then I'll lay mine on you," shouts Freckle. "Have you read that security poster? Read it, read—what the hell does it say?"

" 'Orders are to be obeyed without question or complaint,' " reads Chuchupe.

"You not lead this othel one?" Chino Porfirio shouts. "It hanging hele fol mole than month."

" 'An order can be contested only after it has been carried out,' " reads Chuchupe.

"I haven't read them because I don't know how to read," Knockers laughs. "And I'm proud of it."

"Knockers is right, Chuchupe," Peludita steps forward. "That guy's a bully. The medical exam is his brainstorm for taking advantage of us. With his line about looking for infections, he sticks his hand in up to our tonsils."

"The last time I had to give him a slap," Coca is scratching her back. "He took a bite out of me, right here, just where I get those cramps you know all about."

"Line up, line up, and no complaints—the nurse also has feelings," Chuchupe gives slaps and smiles, prodding them. "Don't be ingrates. What more do you want from the Service that has you examined and always keeps you healthy."

"Line up and get moving, specialists!" orders Freckle. "Pan-Pan wants the convoys ready for departure by the time he gets here."

"Yes, I think he already was. Aren't they saying they nailed him up when the downpour had just begun?" Mother Leonor's voice is trembling. "At least, when I saw him he wasn't moving or crying. And remember, I saw him from very, very close up."

"Did you transmit my request to General Scavino?" Captain Pantoja aims at a heron basking in the sun on the branch of a tree, shoots and misses. "He agrees to see me?"

"He's expecting you at ten in the morning at headquarters," Lieutenant Bacacorzo watches the bird frenetically flapping away over the trees. "But he agreed grudgingly. You know the Special Service has never been able to count on his approval."

"I know it only too well. In seven months I've only been able to see him once," Captain Pantoja raises his rifle again and shoots at an empty tortoise shell, making it jump in the dust. "Do you think that's fair, Bacacorzo? On top of its being a difficult mission, Scavino keeps an eye on me. He thinks I've got a shady character. As if *I* invented the Service."

"You didn't invent it, but you've done miracles with it, Captain," Lieutenant Bacacorzo plugs his ears. "The Special Service is already a reality and in the garrisons it's not only approved of but acclaimed. You should feel proud of your work."

"I still can't—you're wrong," Captain Pantoja throws away the empty shells, wipes his forehead, reloads his rifle and hands it to

90

the lieutenant. "Don't you see? The situation's crucial. At the cost of economizing and great effort, we guarantee five hundred weekly services. And that's like pulling teeth. It leaves us gasping. And do you know the demand we should meet? Ten thousand, Bacacorzo!"

"Little by little," Lieutenant Bacacorzo hardly points toward a tree, shoots and kills a pigeon. "I'm sure with your firmness and your work system, you'll reach those ten thousand lays, Captain."

"Ten thousand weekly?" General Scavino wrinkles his forehead. "It's a raving exaggeration, Pantoja."

"No, General," Captain Pantoja's cheeks are getting red. "A scientific statistic. Look at these charts. It's a question of careful calculation, a conservative one, even. Here, look: ten thousand weekly services correspond to the 'primary psychological-biological need.' If we tried to achieve the 'virile totality' of noncommissioned officers and soldiers, the figure would be 53,200 weekly services."

"Are you sure that the poor tiny angel was still bleeding from his little hands and feet, Mother?" Pochita stammers, opening her eyes, her mouth, wide. "That all the 'brothers' and 'sisters' were soaked with the blood gushing from his body?"

"You're going to give me a fainting fit," Father Beltrán pants. "Who's put this aberration into your noodle? Who said that 'virile totality' is only achieved by fornicating?"

"The most prominent sexologists, biologists and psychologists, Father," Captain Pantoja lowers his eyes.

"I've told you to call me Commander, damn it!" bellows Father Beltrán.

"Excuse me, Commander," Captain Pantoja clicks his heels, becomes confused, opens an attaché case, takes out papers. "I've permitted myself to bring along these reports. They are extracts from works by Freud, Havelock Ellis, Wilhelm Stekel, *Reader's Digest* and Dr. Alberto Seguín, our countryman. If you prefer to consult the books, we have them in the library at the logistics center."

"Because in addition to women, you distribute pornography in the barracks," Father Beltrán is pounding on the table. "I know it very well, Captain Pantoja. In the garrison at Borja your aide the

dwarf handed out this filth: *Two Nights of Pleasure* and *The Life, Passion and Loves of María the Tarantula.*"

"With the purpose of accelerating the men's erections and thereby gaining time, Commander," explains Captain Pantoja. "We do it on a regular basis now. The problem is we don't have enough reading material. They're cheap editions and they fall apart as soon as you open them."

"He had his little eyes closed, his little head fallen over his heart, like a miniature Christ," Mother Leonor folds her hands. "He looked like a baby monkey from a distance, but that white body drew my attention. I approached, went up to the foot of the cross and then I realized. Oh, God, Pochita, when I'm on my deathbed I'll still see that poor little angel."

"In other words, it wasn't just that one time or the initiative of that fiendish dwarf," Father Beltrán wheezes, sweats, chokes. "It's the Special Service itself that gives those books to the soldiers."

"We lend them. There's no budget for giving them away," Captain Pantoja clarifies. "A convoy of three or four specialists has to service fifty, sixty, eighty clients a day. The novels have given good results and so we use them. The soldier who reads those books while waiting in line completes the servicing two or three minutes faster than the soldier who doesn't. It's explained in the Service's reports, Commander."

"My God, I'll have heard of everything before I die," Father Beltrán waves his arms in the cloakroom, grabs his kepi, puts it on and stands at attention. "I never imagined my country's army would ever fall into such decadence. This meeting is very painful for me. I request your permission to leave, General."

"You have my permission to leave, Commander," General Scavino nods at him. "You see what a state that cursed Special Service puts Beltrán in, Pantoja. And of course, with good reason. I request that in the future you spare us the scabrous details of your work."

"How deeply I feel for your mother-in-law, Pochita," Alicia uncovers the saucepan, samples the food with the tip of the spoon, smiles, turns off the burner. "It must have been terrible for her to see that. Is she still a 'sister'? They haven't bothered her? Seems

the police are putting everyone from the Ark under arrest in search of the guilty parties."

"Why have you asked for this meeting? You know I don't want to see you here," General Scavino is checking his watch. "The more to the point and the shorter it is, the better."

"We're completely overextended," Captain Pantoja worries. "We're making superhuman efforts to live up to our responsibilities. But it's impossible. By radio, by telephone, by letter they're overwhelming us with requests we're not in a position to satisfy."

"What is this shit? In three weeks not a single convoy of specialists has come to Borja," Colonel Casahuanqui is becoming infuriated, shaking the receiver, shouting. "You've made my men miserable, Captain Pantoja. I'm going to complain to headquarters."

"I asked for a convoy and they sent me a sample," Colonel Máximo Dávila bites the nail of his little finger, spits, grows indignant. "Does it strike you that two specialists can attend to one hundred thirty soldiers and eighteen noncommissioned officers?"

"And what do you want me to do if I don't have any more girls available?" Chuchupe is shaking her hands, spitting on the radio apparatus. "Lay whores like chickens lay eggs? Besides, we sent you only two, but one was Knockers, who's worth ten. And finally, since when are you so formal with me, Alligator?"

"I am going to complain to the Command of Region V about its discrimination and favoritism, period, end of sentence," Colonel Augusto Valdés is dictating. "The garrison on the Santiago River receives a convoy every week and I get one every month, period. If you think artillery men are less men than infantrymen, comma, I am ready to demonstrate the contrary, comma, Captain Pantoja."

"No, they haven't bothered my mother-in-law, but Panta had to go to the commissioner to explain that Mother Leonor didn't have anything to do with the crime," Pochita also tastes the soup and exclaims it came out fine, Alicia. "And a policeman came to the house to ask questions about what she had seen. You're crazy— she's not a 'sister' anymore. She doesn't want to hear about the

Ark, and as for Brother Francisco, she'd crucify him for the bad time she's had."

"I know all this only too well and it saddens me," General Scavino agrees. "But it doesn't surprise me. When you play with fire, you get burned. People have been corrupted and naturally they want more and more. The mistake was in starting. Now the avalanche can't be stopped. Each day the requests will continue to increase."

"And each day I'm able to service fewer of them, General," grieves Captain Pantoja. "My collaborators are exhausted and I can't demand more from them or I'll run the risk of losing them. It's imperative that the Service be expanded. I'm asking authorization to increase the unit to fifteen specialists."

"As far as I'm concerned, request denied," General Scavino balks, makes a face, rubs his bald head. "Unfortunately, the strategists in Lima have the last word. I'll transmit your request, but with a negative recommendation. Ten prostitutes on the Army's payroll are more than enough."

"I've prepared these reports, evaluations and charts on the expansions," Captain Pantoja is unfolding Bristol boards, pointing, underlining, working hard. "It's a very careful study. It's cost me many sleepless nights. Observe, General: with a budgetary increase of twenty-two percent, we can elevate the operational volume by sixty percent, from five hundred to eight hundred weekly services."

"Granted, Scavino," Tiger Collazos decides. "The investment's worthwhile. It's much cheaper and more effective than the bromide in the food, which never gave any results. The dispatches speak for themselves: since the SSGFRI began operation, incidents in the towns have decreased and the troops are happier. Let him recruit the five specialists."

"But what about the Air Force, Tiger?" General Scavino spins in his chair, gets up, sits down. "Don't you see we have the entire Air Force against us? They've let us know several times they disapprove of the Special Service. And there are officers in the Army and Navy who think this organization is not compatible with the armed forces."

"My poor old lady had grown fond of these crazy people from

94

the Ark, Commissioner," Captain Pantoja is shaking his head with shame. "From time to time she went to Moronacocha to see them and to take some clothes for their children. A strange thing, you know—she never had been very interested in religious things. But this experience has cured her, I promise you."

"Give him the money, you faker, and don't hold back much," Tiger Collazos laughs. "Pantoja is doing all right and we've got to support him. And tell him to choose knockouts for new recruits, don't forget."

"You make me very happy with that news, Bacacorzo," Captain Pantoja takes a deep breath. "Those reinforcements are going to get the Service out of a big fix. We were on the verge of collapse because of overwork."

"See, you got your way. You can contract five more," Lieutenant Bacacorzo hands him a dispatch, makes him sign a receipt. "What does it matter having Scavino and Beltrán against you if the big shots in Lima, like Collazos and Victoria, back you up?"

"Naturally we won't bother your dear mother. Don't worry, Captain," The Commissioner takes him by the arm, accompanies him to the door, shakes his hand. "I confess it's going to be difficult to find the ones who did the crucifying. We've detained one hundred fifty 'sisters' and seventy-six 'brothers' and they're all the same. Do you know who nailed the boy up? Yes. Who? I did. One for all and all for one, like in *The Three Musketeers,* that movie with Cantinflas. Did you see it?"

"Besides, they're going to allow me to make a qualitative change in the Service," Captain Pantoja rereads the dispatch, strokes it with the tips of his fingers, dilates his nostrils. "Up till now I chose the personnel on the basis of functional factors. It was only a question of yield. Now, for the first time, the aesthetic-artistic factor will come into play."

"Hallelujah," applauds Lieutenant Bacacorzo. "You mean they've found a Venus de Milo here in Iquitos?"

"But with both arms and a face good enough to raise the dead," Captain Pantoja coughs, blinks, touches his ear. "Excuse me, I've got to leave. My wife's at the gynecologist's and I want to know how he finds her. It's only two more months until the cadet is born."

"And if instead of a cadet a little specialist is born, Mr. Pantoja?"
Chuchupe starts to laugh, falls silent, is frightened. "Don't get
upset, don't look at me like that. Lord, a person can't even make
jokes with you. You're too serious for a man your age."

"Haven't you read this security motto, you who should be set-
ting the example here?" Mr. Pantoja points at the wall.

" 'No jokes or games during service,' Mama," Freckle reads.

"Why isn't the unit ready for inspection?" Pantoja is looking
right and left, clucking his tongue. "Is the medical examination
over? What are they waiting for to line up and call the roll?"

"Get in line, Specialists!" Freckle forms a loudspeaker with his
hands.

"Get flying, mothels!" choruses Chino Porfirio.

"And now call out your name and number," Chupito is strutting
among the Specialists. "Let's go, let's go, right away."

"One, Rita!"

"Two, Penelope!"

"Three, Coca!"

"Four, Pichuza!"

"Five, Knockers!"

"Six, Lalita!"

"Seven, Sandra!"

"Eight, Maclovia!"

"Nine, Iris!"

"Ten, Peludita!"

"Hele and accounted fol, Mistel Pantoja," Chino Porfirio bows.

"It's knocked the superstition out of her, Panta, but she's becom-
ing a fanatic," Pochita traces a cross in the air. "You know your
mother's slipping out that had us so intrigued—do you know
where she was going? To the Church of St. Augustine."

"Medical Corps report," Pantaleón Pantoja orders.

" 'The examination was carried out. All the specialists were
found to be in condition to leave on the mission,' " Freckle deci-
phers. " 'The one nicknamed Coca shows signs of hematomas on
her back and arms that perhaps will impair her work output.
Signed: Health Assistant for the SSGFRI.' "

"A lie. That degenerate hates me because I slapped him and he
wants to get even," Coca lowers her strap, exposes her shoulder,

arm, looks with hatred toward the infirmary. "I've only got a few scratches my cat gave me, Mr. Pantoja."

"Well, anyway, it's better this way, baby," Panta shrugs under the sheets. "If with age she turns to religion, better if it's the true one and not barbaric beliefs."

"A cat named Juanito Marcano and he's identical to Jorge Mistral," Knockers whispers in Rita's ear.

"Oh, you'd want him even if it was only for the National Holidays," Coca zigzags like a viper. "Pig tits."

"A fine of ten soles to Coca and Knockers for talking in line," Mr. Pantoja stays calm, takes out a pencil, a notebook. "If you think you're in condition to leave with the convoy, you can, Coca, since the Health Service authorizes you to, so don't get hysterical. And now, today's work schedule."

"Three convoys. Two of forty-eight hours and one that returns this evening," Chuchupe emerges from behind the formation. "I already drew lots, Mr. Pantoja. One convoy of three girls to the encampment at Puerto América on the Morona River."

"Who commands it and who forms it?" Pantaleón Pantoja moistens the point of his pencil with his lips and takes notes.

"I am commanding it and Coca, Pichuza and Sandra are going with me," Freckle indicates. "Crazy is already nursing the *Delilah* so we can leave in ten minutes."

"Make sure Crazy behaves and doesn't pull his usual stunts, Mr. Pan-Pan," Sandra points to the hydroplane rocking on the river and to the little figure mounted on it. "Remember if I kill myself you're the one who loses. I've left you my daughters as an inheritance. And I've got six."

"Ten soles for Sandra, for the same reason as the others," Pantaleón Pantoja raises his index finger, writes. "Take your convoy to the dock, Freckle. Have a good trip, and work with spirit and conviction, girls."

"Convoy to Puerto América, march," Freckle orders. "Grab your suitcases. And now to the *Delilah,* on the double."

"Convoys two and three are leaving on the *Eve* within the hour," from Chuchupe. "In the second, Iris, Peludita, Penelope and Lalita. I'm leading it, to the Bolognesi Garrison on the Mazán River."

"And what if the little cadet is born a freak from so much fright over the little crucified boy?" Pochita screws up her face. "What a horrible tragedy that'd be, Panta."

"And the thild go with me upstleam to Camp Yavalí," Chino Porfirio slices the air with his hand. "Letuln Thulsday noon, Mistel Pantoja."

"Good. Get going and behave the way you're told to, you clown," Pantaleón Pantoja says goodbye to the specialists. "Chino and Chuchupe report to my office for a minute. I have to speak to you."

"Five more girls? What good news, Mr. Pantoja," Chuchupe rubs her hands together. "As soon as this convoy returns, I'll get them. There won't be any problem—there's a flood of applicants. Like I told you, we're getting famous."

"Very badly done. We shouldn't come out into the open," Pantaleón Pantoja points to the security motto that says: "Closed lips give no tips." "I'd prefer it if you brought me about ten candidates so I can choose the five best ones. Four, really, because for the other I've thought of—"

"Of Olguita the Blazilian!" Chino Porfirio traces breasts, hips, legs. "Blilliant idea, Mistel Pan-Pan. That statue give us fame. I letuln flom tlip and light away look fol hel myself."

"Go look for her right now and bring her to me at once," Pantaleón Pantoja blushes; his voice changes. "Before Snotnose enlists her for his brothels. You still have an hour, Chino."

"Hey, what a rush, Mr. Pantoja," Chuchupe oozes marmalade, sugar, meringue. "How I'd like to see that pretty face of Olguita's again."

"Calm down, sweetie, don't think about that anymore," Panta is absorbed, cuts a piece of cardboard, paints it, hangs it. "From now on, it is expressly forbidden to speak of the crucified boy and those crazy people of the Ark in this house. And so you don't forget, either, Mama, I'm going to hang a security motto."

"Delighted to see you again, Mr. Pantoja," the Brazilian devours him with her eyes, wiggles, perfumes the air, chirps. "So this is the famous Pantiland. Really, I'd heard so much about it and I couldn't imagine what it'd be like."

"The famous what?" Pantaleón Pantoja pushes his head forward, brings up a chair. "Please sit down."

"Pantiland, that's what people call this," the Brazilian spreads her arms, shows her shaved armpits, laughs. "Not only here in Iquitos, but everywhere. I heard of Pantiland in Manaos. What a funny name—does it come from Disneyland?"

"I'm afraid it probably comes from Panta," Mr. Pantoja looks her up and down, side to side, smiles at her, grows serious, smiles again, perspires. "But you're Peruvian and not Brazilian, aren't you? At least in the way you speak."

"I was born here. They gave me that name because I lived in Manaos," the Brazilian sits down, hikes her skirt, takes out her compact, powders her nose, the dimples in her cheeks. "But you see, everybody goes back to the country where he was born—just like in the song."

"It'd be better if you took that motto out of here, son," Mother Leonor covers her eyes. "Having to read 'Speaking of the martyr prohibited' makes Pochita and me talk about nothing else the whole blessed day. What ideas you have, Panta!"

"And what do they say about Pantiland?" Pantaleón Pantoja drums on the desk, rocks in his chair, doesn't know what to do with his hand. "What have you heard back there?"

"You can't believe people, they exaggerate a lot," the Brazilian crosses her legs, arms, acts coy, winks, moistens her lips while she talks. "Just imagine, in Manaos they said it was a city several blocks wide with armed guards."

"Well, don't be deceived, we're just beginning," Pantaleón Pantoja is smiling, showing himself to be friendly, sociable, talkative. "I can tell you for now we already have a boat and a hydroplane. But I don't like that international publicity at all."

"They said there was work for everyone, with fabulous conditions," The Brazilian raises and lowers her shoulders, plays with her fingers, flutters her eyelashes, sways her neck. shakes her hair. "That's why I got excited and took the boat. I left my eight girl friends in a very good house in Manaos packing their bags to come to Pantiland. They're going to wear the same outfit I am."

"If it doesn't bother you, I'll request you to call this place the

logistics center instead of Pantiland," Mr. Pantoja struggles to look serious, confident and functional. "Did Porfirio explain to you why I had you come?"

"He gave me an idea," the Brazilian wrinkles her nose, flutters her eyelashes, lowers her eyelids, her pupils glow. "Is it true there's the possibility of work for me?"

"Yes, we're going to expand the Service," Pantaleón Pantoja is swelling with pride, looking at a chart with graphs. "We began with four, then we increased to six, to eight, to ten, and now there'll be fifteen specialists. Who knows—someday we'll be what they say."

"I'm very pleased. I'd been thinking of going back to Manaos because I saw things were getting sticky here," the Brazilian bites her lips, wipes her mouth, checks her fingernails, flicks a speck of dust off her skirt. "I thought I hadn't made a good impression on you that day we met at Aladdin Panduro's Lamp."

"You're wrong. You made a very good impression, a very good one," Pantaleón Pantoja is arranging pencils, notebooks, opening and closing desk drawers, coughing. "I would've hired you sooner, but there was no room in the budget."

"And is it possible to know the salary and the duties, Mr. Pantoja?" The Brazilian cranes her neck, makes a bouquet of her hands, warbles.

"Three convoys a week, two by air and one by boat," enumerates Pantaleón Pantoja. "And a minimum of ten services per convoy."

"Convoys are the trips to the barracks?" the Brazilian is astonished, claps her hands, lets out a laugh, winks mischievously, exaggerates. "And services must be . . . Oh, how funny!"

"Now, let me explain one thing to you, Alicia," Mother Leonor kisses the small picture of the child martyr. "Yes, they performed an unspeakable horror. But deep down, it was fear, not evil. They were terrified by so much rain and they thought that with the sacrifice God would postpone the end of the world. They didn't want to hurt him. They thought they were sending him straight to Heaven. Haven't you seen how they've erected altars to him in all the Arks the police are uncovering?"

"As for your percentage, it's fifty percent of what is deducted

100

from the noncommissioned officers' and soldiers' pay," Pantaleón Pantoja writes on a piece of paper, hands it to her, making the details clear. "The other fifty percent goes back into upkeep. And now, though I know it's not necessary with you, because what you're worth is—er—obvious, I have to comply with regulations. Please take off your dress for a second."

"Oh, how embarrassing," the Brazilian puts on a mournful face, stands up, takes a few steps like a fashion model, makes another face. "It's my time of the month, Mr. Pantoja, it came just yesterday. Does it matter if you go in through the back door, just this once? They love to in Brazil—they even like it better."

"I only want to look at you, to give you the O.K.," Pantaleón Pantoja stands rigid, grows pale, raises his eyebrows, speaks clearly. "It's the physical that everyone has to pass. Your imagination's overheated."

"Oh, well, I was wondering where we were going to do it, since there isn't even a rug here," the Brazilian gives a little stamp on the floorboards, smiles with relief, undresses, folds her clothes, poses. "Look O.K. to you? I'm a little thin, but I'll get my weight back in a week. Think I'll be a hit with the boys?"

"Without the slightest doubt," Pantaleón Pantoja looks, admits, trembles, clears his throat. "You'll be more successful than our star, Knockers. O.K., approved. You can get dressed now."

"And not only that, Mother Leonor," Alicia examines the picture, crosses herself. "Just imagine, in addition to pictures and prayer cards, statues of the little child martyr have also begun to show up. And they say that instead of decreasing, there are more 'brothers' and 'sisters' now than before."

"What are you doing here?" Pantaleón Pantoja leaps out of his chair, takes long steps to the top of the stairs, motions furiously. "Who gave you permission to come in here? Don't you know that when I'm administering an examination it's absolutely forbidden to come up to the command post?"

"A man named Sinchi is looking for you, Mr. Pantoja," Sinforoso Caiguas stammers, stands there mouth agape.

"It's urgent and very important, Mr. Pantoja," Palomino Rioalto is staring, hypnotized.

"Get out of here, the two of you," Pantaleón Pantoja obstructs

their view with his body, bangs on the railing, stretches out his arm. "Let him wait. Out of here—it's forbidden to look."

"Bah, don't worry. It doesn't matter to me. This doesn't get used up," The Brazilian is putting on her slip, blouse, skirt. "So you're named Panta? Now I understand the business about Pantiland. What people don't think of!"

"My Christian name is Pantaleón, like my father and my grandfather before him, two distinguished military men," Mr. Pantoja is stirred, comes closer to the Brazilian, stretches two fingers toward the buttons on her blouse. "Here, let me help you."

"Couldn't you raise my cut to seventy percent?" the Brazilian purrs, walks back until she's pressed up against him, breathes in his face, searches with her hand and squeezes. "The house is making a good acquisition. I'll show you when my period is over. Be understanding, Panta—you won't regret it."

"Let go, let go—don't grab me there!" Pantaleón Pantoja gives a little jump, gets excited, ashamed, irritated. "I have to warn you about two things: you can't address me informally, only formally, like all the specialists. And no liberties with me."

"But if I made your pants puff up, it was to do you a favor, not to offend you," the Brazilian is distressed, feels sad, is surprised. "Excuse me, Mr. Pantoja. I swear to you I'll never do it again."

"Considering that you're a first-class addition to the Service, and as a very special exception, I'll give you sixty percent," Pantaleón Pantoja repents, accompanies her to the stairs. "And also because you came from so far away. But don't breathe a word of this or you'll create a terrible mess for me with your co-workers."

"Not a word, Mr. Pantoja. It'll be our little secret. Thanks a lot," the Brazilian recovers her smile, charms, flirtatious manner, goes down the steps. "I'll be leaving now. I can see you have a visitor. When no one can hear us, can I call you Mr. Pantita? It's cuter than Pantaleón or Pantoja. Bye-bye—see you later."

"Of course what they did seems horrible to me, Pochita," Mother Leonor raises the fly swatter, waits a few seconds, strikes and watches the corpse fall to the floor. "But if you knew them the way I do, you'd realize they're not naturally evil. Ignorant, yes, not perverted. I've visited them in their homes and talked with them: shoemakers, carpenters, bricklayers. Most of them don't even

102

know how to read. Since becoming 'brothers,' they don't get drunk anymore or cheat on their wives or eat meat or rice."

"Delighted, glad to meet you, gimme five," Sinchi makes a Japanese bow, crosses the command post like an emperor, sucks on his cigar and exhales smoke. "At your service, anything I can do for you."

"Good morning," Pantaleón Pantoja sniffs the air, becomes embarrassed, has a coughing fit. "Have a seat. How can I help you?"

"That knockout of a woman I met at the door left me cockeyed," Sinchi points to the stairs, whistles, gets enthusiastic, smokes. "Jesus, they told me Pantiland was a paradise of women and I see it's true. What pretty flowers grow in your garden, Mr. Pantoja."

"I have a lot of work to do and I can't waste my time, so get to the point," Pantaleón Pantoja grumbles, grabs a notebook and tries to disperse the cloud that envelops him. "As for this business of Pantiland, I'm letting you know in advance that it doesn't please me. I don't have a sense of humor."

"I didn't make up the name, the people's imagination did," Sinchi opens his arms and speaks as if he were before a roaring multitude: "The imagination of Loreto—always so sharp and spicy, so ingenious. Don't take it so hard, Mr. Pantoja. You always have to be responsive to popular creations."

"You're scaring me, Mother Leonor," Pochita touches her belly. "Even though you've left the Ark, at heart you're still a 'sister.' How fondly you talk about them. I hope you never think of crucifying our little cadet."

"Don't you have a program on Radio Amazon?" Pantaleón coughs, chokes, dries his tearing eyes. "At six in the evening?"

"That's me! You have before you the very famous *Voice of Sinchi* in person," Sinchi deepens his voice, clutches an invisible mike, declaims. "Terrorizer of corrupt officials, scourge of venial judges, whirlwind against injustice, the voice that takes and transmits the pulse of the people over the airwaves."

"Yes, I heard your program once. Quite popular, isn't it?" Pantaleón Pantoja stands up, moves away searching for fresh air, breathes deeply. "I'm very honored by your visit. What can I do for you?"

"I'm a man of my time, without prejudices, progressive, so I've

103

come to lend you a hand," Sinchi stands up, goes after him, shrouds him in smoke, holds out his limp fingers toward him. "Besides, I like you, Mr. Pantoja, and I know we can be good friends. I believe in friendship at first sight and my nose for these things never fails me. I want to help you."

"I appreciate that," Pantaleón Pantoja lets his hand be shaken, his shoulders be patted; he resigns himself to going back to his desk, to continue coughing. "But really, I don't need your help. At least not at the moment."

"That's what you think, you candid and innocent man," taking in the entire space with a gesture, Sinchi is scandalized, half-seriously, half-jokingly. "In this erotic enclosure you live far from the madding crowd and apparently you are not aware of how things really are. You don't know what they're saying out in the street, the dangers that surround you."

"I have very little time, sir," Pantaleón Pantoja checks the time, grows impatient. "Either explain to me what you want right now or do me the favor of leaving."

"If you don't demand that she apologize to me, I'm never going to set foot in this house again," Mother Leonor threatens, cries, locks herself in her room, does not want to eat. "Crucify my future grandson! Do you think I'm going to put up with such nastiness, no matter how nervous she is about her pregnancy?"

"I am subjected to irresistible pressures," Sinchi crushes the cigar in the ashtray, shreds it, is upset. "Housewives, fathers of families, schools, cultural institutions, churches of every hue and color, even witches and drug addicts. I'm human, my resistance has its limits."

"What poppycock is this? What are you talking about?" Pantaleón Pantoja is smiling, seeing the last little cloud of smoke disappear. "I don't understand one word of it. Be more explicit and get to the heart of the matter quickly."

"The city wants Pantiland to sink into ignominy and you to go bankrupt," Sinchi smilingly synthesizes. "Didn't you know that Iquitos is a city with a corrupt heart but with a puritan façade? The Special Service is a scandal that only a progressive and modern person like myself can accept. The rest of the city is horrified over

104

this mess and, speaking plainly, they want it destroyed."

"For me to be destroyed?" Pantaleón Pantoja grows very serious. "Me? The Special Service to be destroyed?"

"There's nothing in the Amazon built solidly enough that *The Voice of Sinchi* can't blow it down," Sinchi snorts, waving his fingertips in the air, puffing himself up. "Modesty to one side, if I take aim, the Special Service won't last one week and you'll have to leave Iquitos on the double. It's sad but true, my friend."

"You mean you've come to threaten me?" Pantaleón Pantoja sits up straight.

"Nothing like that—just the opposite," Sinchi lunges at specters, clutches at his heart like a tenor, counts imaginary money. "Up until now I've resisted the pressures on me because of my combative spirit and because it's a question of principle. But from now on, since I, too, have to live, and one can't live off thin air, I'll do it for minimal compensation. Doesn't that seem fair to you?"

"You mean you've come to blackmail me?" Pantaleón Pantoja stands up, his face falls, he upsets the wastepaper basket, runs to the top of the stairs.

"To help you, friend. Just ask and you'll see the cyclonic force of my broadcasts," Sinchi puffs out his chest, stands, walks, gestures. "They overthrow judges, police officers, marriages. Whatever I attack falls apart. For a few miserable cents I'm prepared to defend on the radio both the Special Service and the brain behind it. To fight the war for you, Mr. Pantoja."

"Let that old witch who doesn't understand jokes apologize to me," Pochita smashes cups, throws herself face down on the bed, scratches Panta, sobs. "Between the two of you, you're going to make me lose the baby because of these blow-ups. Do you think I said it seriously, you half-wit? It was just a fib—I was joking."

"Sinforoso! Palomino!" Pantaleón Pantoja is clapping, shouting. "Attendant!"

"What's wrong with you? Don't get upset, calm down," Sinchi stays quiet, lowers his voice, looks around him with alarm. "You don't have to answer me right away. Ask around, check on who I am and we'll talk next week."

"Get this scoundrel out of here and throw him in the river,"

105

Pantaleón Pantoja orders the men who come running to the top of the stairway. "And don't ever let him enter the logistics center again."

"Listen here, don't cut your own throat, don't be irresponsible, I'm a superman in Iquitos," Sinchi waves his arms, shoves, defends himself, slips, backs off, disappears, is soaked. "Let go of me! What does this mean? Listen, you're going to regret this, Pantoja, I came to help you. I'm your frien-n-n-n-nd."

"Sure, he's a big phony, but even the rocks listen to his program," Lieutenant Bacacorzo leafs through a magazine left lying on a table in Lucho's Bar. "I hope that dunking in the Itaya doesn't make problems for you, Captain."

"I prefer those problems to giving in to his dirty blackmail," Captain Pantoja is intrigued by a caption asking *Do You Know Who Yacuruna Is and What He Does?* "I've sent a dispatch to Tiger Collazos and I'm sure he'll understand. But really, something else is bothering me, Bacacorzo."

"The ten thousand services, Captain?" He manages to read between Lieutenant Bacacorzo's fingers: *An angel or demon of the waters, who causes cyclones and floods.* "Did they go up to fifteen thousand with the summer heat?"

"Gossip," *He rides on the back of alligators or on the skins of giant water snakes,* says an illustration that Captain Pantoja is bending over. "There's really so much gossip? Here in Iquitos? About the Service, about me?"

"Last night I dreamed the same thing again, Panta," Pochita touches her temple. "They crucified you and me on the same cross, one on each side. And Mother Leonor came and stabbed us with a spear, me in the belly and you in your little dickie. Isn't that a crazy dream, sweetie?"

"Naturally, you're the most famous man in town," *He wears tortoise shells for shoes,* assures a sentence interrupted by Lieutenant Bacacorzo's elbow. "The man most hated by women, most admired by men. And Pantiland, begging your pardon, is the hub of every conversation. But since you don't see anyone and live only for the Special Service, what does it matter to you?"

"For me it's no problem, but it is for my family," *And at night he sleeps protected by curtains made of butterfly wings,* Captain

106

Pantoja manages to read at last. "My wife is very sensitive and if she discovers this in her present condition, it'll have a tremendous effect on her. And I'm not even mentioning my mother."

"As for the gossip"—Lieutenant Bacacorzo throws the magazine on the floor, turns, recalls—"I have to tell you something very amusing. Scavino received a committee of leading citizens from Nauta, headed by the mayor. They came to bring him a petition, ha ha."

"We consider it an offensive privilege that the Special Service belongs exclusively to the army barracks and the naval bases," Mayor Paiva Runhuí pulls down his glasses, looks at his companions, adopts a solemn posture and reads. "We demand that senior citizens with military service from these neglected Amazonian towns have the right to utilize that Service and at the same reduced rates as the soldiers."

"That Service exists only in your corrupt imaginations, my friends," General Scavino interrupts them, looks at them kindly with paternal affection. "How can you even think of asking for a meeting about such nonsense? If the press finds out about this petition, you won't have your job for long, Mayor Runhuí."

"We are setting a bad example for the civilians, bringing temptation to towns that live in biblical purity," Father Beltrán suddenly changes his expression. "I hope that when they read this petition, the faces of those strategists in Lima burn with shame."

"Listen to this and you'll be bowled over, Tiger," General Scavino is squeezing the telephone, reading the petition angrily. "The news has already begun to circulate everywhere. Look at what these old guys in Nauta are asking for. The scandal's coming down on our heads, just like I kept warning you it would."

"What figures you come up with on your fingers?" Lieutenant Bacacorzo raises the piece of chicken and takes a bite. "Like Scavino says, you people in logistics always end up with your mathematical craziness."

"Damn these idiots. Before they were protesting because the troops were throwing themselves at their women, and now they're complaining because they don't have women to throw themselves at," Tiger Collazos plays with some blotting paper. "There's no way to keep them happy. What they like is to protest.

107

Throw them out on the street and don't accept such dumb-assed requests, Scavino."

"Horror of horrors," Captain Pantoja hangs the napkin on his chest, dresses the salad with oil and vinegar, brandishes his fork and eats. "If they extended the Service to civilians, keeping in mind the male population of the Amazon, the demand would rise from ten thousand to a million monthly services at least."

"We'd have to import specialists from abroad," Lieutenant Bacacorzo finishes off the remains of the meat, leaves the bone perfectly clean, drinks some beer, wipes his mouth and his hands and dreams. "The whole jungle would be converted into one big brothel, and you, in your little office on the Itaya, would be timing that flood of semen with a million stopwatches. Admit that you'd like that, Captain."

"You can't guess what I saw, Pochita," Alicia puts the basket in the pantry, takes out a package and offers it to Pochita. "In the bakery owned by Abdón Laguna, who's a 'brother,' they've started to make bread of the martyr of Moronacocha. They call them boy loaves and people are buying them by the bushel. I brought you one. Look."

"I asked you for ten and you bring me twenty," Pantaleón Pantoja looks over the banister at the straight, curly, brunette, red, chestnut heads. "You think I'm going to spend the whole day examining candidates, Chuchupe?"

"It's not my fault," Chuchupe goes down the stairs holding onto the railing. "Word got around that there were four openings and women from all the districts started coming out of the walls. They even came from San Juan de Munich and Tamshiyaco. What do you want, Mr. Pantoja? All the girls in Iquitos want to work for us."

"The truth is I don't understand it," Pantaleón Pantoja goes down the stairs behind her, looking at her plump back, gelatinous buttocks, tuberous calves. "They don't earn much here and there's too much work. What's in it for them? That nice guy Porfirio?"

"The security, Mr. Pantoja," with her head Chuchupe points toward the multicolored dresses, the groups that buzz like swarms of bees. "There's no security on the streets. One good day for the 'washerwomen' is followed by three bad ones. They never have any vacation and there's no rest on Sunday."

108

"And Snotnose is a slave driver in his brothels," Freckle silences them with a whistle and indicates that they're getting near. "He starves them to death, treats them bad and at the first sign of burning they're sent home. He doesn't know what consideration or humanity mean."

"Here it's different," Chuchupe sweetens, puts her hands in her pockets. "There are always clients, it's an eight-hour workday and they love the way you've got everything so organized. Don't you see they even put up with the fines without complaining?"

"Certainly the first day it made me a little apprehensive," Mother Leonor slices, puts on butter, marmalade, takes a bite and chews. "But what can you do—boy bread is the best in Iquitos. Don't you think so, son?"

"Good, we're going to choose these four," decides Pantaleón Pantoja. "What are you waiting for, Chino—get them lined up."

"Sepalate a little, gils, so you look bettel," Chino Porfirio takes hold of arms, pushes backs, makes them come forward, go backward, move to the side, arranges, measures. "Little dwalfs in flont and giants in leal."

"Here they are, Mr. Pantoja," Freckle jumps from side to side, demands silence, sets an example of seriousness, lines them up. "In formation, as ordered. Let's go, girls. Now, left face—show your pretty profiles."

"Should come up one by one to youl office fol naked exams?" Chino Porfirio comes up and whispers into his ear.

"Impossible. It'd put me behind for the whole morning," Pantaleón Pantoja looks at his watch, reflects, cheers up, takes a step forward and faces them. "I'm going to make a group inspection to save time. All of you, listen carefully: if any of you have objections to undressing in public, get out of line and I'll see you separately. Nobody? So much the better."

"All the men outside," Chuchupe opens the door to the pier, rouses them, pushes them, returns. "Hurry up, lazybones, didn't you hear? Sinforoso, Palomino, nurse, Chino. You too, Chupón. Shut that door, Pichuza."

"Off with your skirts, blouses, bras, please," Pantaleón Pantoja puts his hands behind his back and walks very gravely, scrutinizing, weighing, comparing. "You can keep your shoes on, those who

109

are wearing shoes. Now, half turn in place. Exactly. Now, let's see. A redhead—you. A brunette—you. An Oriental—you. A mulatto —you. All right, vacancies filled. The others, leave your addresses with Chuchupe. Maybe there'll be another opening soon. Until next time, thanks."

"The chosen women be here tomorrow at nine on the dot, for the medical examination," Chuchupe notes down streets and numbers, accompanies them to the exit, says goodbye. "Remember, girls, wash behind the ears."

"Now, let's see, let's see. This is served very hot, because if it isn't, it isn't as good," Mother Leonor distributes the bowls of steaming soup. "The famous soup of Loreto. I finally decided to make it. How did it come out, Pocha?"

"What good taste you showed in choosing them, Mr. Pan-Pan," the Brazilian smiles with maliciousness, throws off sparks as she looks, croons. "All colors and flavors. Satisfy my curiosity: aren't you afraid that seeing so much nudity, you're going to get used to it someday and won't feel anything for women? They say it happens to some doctors."

"It's very good, Mother Leonor," Pochita tests the temperature with the tip of her tongue, sips a spoonful. "It's very similar to what we call fish head soup on the coast."

"Are you trying to pull my leg, Brazilian?" Pantaleón Pantoja knits his brow. "I warn you that being a serious man is not the same as being a fool, no mistake about it."

"The difference is that all the fish in this soup are from the Amazon, and not the Pacific Ocean," Mother Leonor fills the bowls again. *"Paiche, caribe* and *gamitana.* My, how tasty it is."

"It's you who are mistaken. I'm not pulling your leg, only making a joke," the Brazilian lowers her eyelashes, grinds her hips, heaves her breasts, changes her tone. "Why don't you let me be your friend? I hardly open my mouth to you and you get muleheaded, Mr. Pan-Pan. Be real careful. Remember, I'm like a crab —I love to go against the current. If you keep dumping on me so much, I'm going to fall in love with you."

"Uf, how hot it makes you!" Pochita fans herself with the napkin, takes her pulse. "Hand me the electric fan, Panta. I'm suffocating."

"That heat isn't from the soup but from our little cadet," Panta touches her abdomen, strokes her cheek. "He must be yawning, stretching. Hey, maybe it'll be tonight. A good date: March fourteenth."

"I hope it's not before Sunday," Pochita is looking at the calendar. "So Chichi gets here first. I'd like her here for the birth."

"According to my calculations, you're still not ready," Mother Leonor perspires, moves her congested face close to the humming blades. "You've got at least a week to go."

"That's right, Mother, haven't you looked at the chart in my room? It should be between today and Sunday," Panta sucks the fish bones, wipes the plate with a piece of bread, drinks some water. "Did you follow the doctor's orders? Did you take a little walk today? With your constant companion Alicia?"

"Yes, we went as far as The Favorite to have an ice cream," Pochita is breathing hard. "But listen, really, do you know what all this stuff about Pantiland is about?"

"About what?" Pantita's hands, eyes, face are immobilized. "What did you say, sweetheart?"

"Something dirty, it seems to me," Pochita sighs, getting the breeze from the electric fan. "A few men were making off-color jokes in The Favorite about the women from—can you believe it, how funny—Pantiland. As if it came from Panta!"

"A-a-chooo, hmmmmmmm, pshhhh," Pantita chokes, sneezes, coughs, his eyes tearing.

"Take a little water," Mother Leonor feels his forehead, hands him a handkerchief, raises his arms. "This happens to you because you eat too fast, I'm always telling you. Come on, a few slaps on the back, another sip of water."

6

SSGFRI

Instructions for Utilization Centers

The Special Service for Garrisons, Frontier and Related Installations permits the circulation of these instructions, which, if strictly applied, will enable your unit to rationally and fruitfully take advantage of the SSGFRI and for this organization to complete its mission with efficacy and speed.

1. As soon as he is alerted by the SSGFRI to the convoy's arrival, the head of the unit will prepare the specialists' locations, which should combine the following characteristics: roofed; not adjoining; provided with curtains, which protect from indiscreet viewing and assure dim light or darkness, as well as with oil lamps or electric lights supplied with red lampshades or covered with cloth or paper of said color if service is nocturnal. Each location will be equipped with: cot and straw or rubber mattress, covered with oilcloth or impermeable canvas and sheet; chair, bench or nail on which to hang clothing; chamber pot or receptacle that can serve as one, such as pail or large can; washbasin with its respective supply of clean water; a piece of soap; a towel; a roll of toilet paper; an irrigator with hose and nozzle. It is suggested that some feminine, aesthetic complement be added, such as a bouquet of flowers, an etching or an artistic drawing, to stamp the location with an attractive atmosphere. Although it is advisable for the unit to have the locations ready for the arrival of the specialists, the officer in charge may consult with the chief of convoy, who will

112

offer him all the necessary assistance with the arrangement of the locations.

2. The officer in charge will take every measure to assure that the convoy remains in his unit only for the time strictly necessary for the completion of its functions and that it does not prolong its stay without reason. From the time of its arrival until its departure, the members of the convoy must remain within the unit area. In no case whatsoever is it permitted for the specialists to have any contact with civilian elements in the neighboring localities or to fraternize with the noncommissioned officers and soldiers within the unit area beyond the service period. Before and after said period the specialists will remain quartered in their locations and may not share mess with the troops nor converse with the soldiers nor visit the fortress installations. So that the convoy's presence may pass unperceived by the civilian element in the vicinity, it is advised that the entry of any outside person into the unit area be prohibited during the specialists' stay in same. The unit is obligated to provide free lodging and three meals (breakfast, lunch and dinner) to all members of the convoy.

3. It is advised that the coming of the convoy not be announced to the noncommissioned officers and soldiers until its actual arrival, since experience has shown that if the news is communicated beforehand an anxiety and nervousness spreads through the troops which demonstrably prejudices the completion of their duties. As soon as the convoy arrives, the head of the unit will establish a list of users, comprised of noncommissioned officers and soldiers, all of whom are to be authorized to request candidacy. Once the list of candidates is known, he will proceed to eliminate from the list those who suffer from any kind of infectious/contagious diseases and most especially those of a venereal sort (gonorrhea, chancres) and those infested with mites, bedbugs, lice, crabs and other types of body vermin. It is advised that candidates be made to pass a medical examination.

4. Once the list is drawn up, the users will be made aware of the specialists present and will be ordered to state their preferences. Since, judging from experience, spontaneous selection never allows an equitable distribution of users among specialists,

113

the head of the unit will employ the method he thinks best (drawing lots, merits and demerits according to service files) to divide users into equal groups for each specialist, keeping in mind that each specialist has the obligation to guarantee a minimum of ten services in each unit. In exceptional cases, where the number of users surpasses that figure, the principle of equity and symmetry will be eliminated, and a greater number of users will be assigned to the most requested or least fatigued specialist in the convoy.

5. Once the groups are established, proceed to the drawing by lots of the order of entry for each user to the location. Controllers will be installed at the doors of same. The maximum time per service is twenty minutes. In exceptional cases, in those units where the number of users does not come up to the specialists' minimum work figure (ten), the time per service may be extended to thirty minutes, but no longer in any case whatsoever. In the preliminary instructions, users should be informed that the service will be of the type considered normal, the specialist not being obliged to satisfy any demand of a strange or aberrant nature, unnatural fantasies, perversions or fetishistic whim. No user will be permitted to repeat the service either with the same or a different specialist.

6. With the purpose of distracting and preparing users while they find themselves waiting their turn to enter the location, the chief of convoy will distribute to them adequate printed material of a photographic and literary nature, which, when the user enters the specialist's location, must be returned to the controllers in the same condition in which it was received. The destruction or damaging of photos and texts will be punishable by fines and loss of future service from the SSGFRI.

7. The SSGFRI will always strive to have the convoys arrive at the utilization centers so that services can be realized at the most convenient hours (late afternoon or night)—that is, when the daytime turns of duty are finished—but if that is not possible for reasons of time or distance, the head of the unit will allow the services to take place during the day and will not detain the convoy while waiting for darkness.

8. Once the services are terminated, the head of the unit will send to the SSGFRI a carefully verified statistical report with the

following data: (a) the exact number of users serviced by each specialist; (b) name and surname of each user with the number of his service file and the debit ticket corresponding to the deduction from his pay check; (c) a brief report on the behavior of convoy members (chief of convoy, specialists, transport personnel) during their stay in the unit; and (d) constructive criticism and suggestions for the improvement of the SSGFRI.

[Signed]
CAPT. (QUARTERMASTER) PANTALEÓN PANTOJA, PA

Approved by Gen. Felipe Collazos
Chief of Administration, Supply and Logistics of the Army

Statistical Report

Lagunas, 2 September 1957
Capt. Alberto J. Mendoza, PA, is pleased to submit to the SSGFRI the following report on the passage of Convoy No. 16 through the Lagunas Encampment (Huallaga River) under his command:
Convoy No. 16 arrived at the Lagunas Encampment on Thursday, 1 September, at 1500 hours, proceeding from Iquitos on the river transport *Eve,* and departed at 1900 hours of the same day in the direction of the Puerto Arturo Encampment (on the same Huallaga River). Madame Leonor Curinchila (Chuchupe) was in charge of the convoy composed of the specialists Dulce María, Lunita, Pichuza, Barbara, Penelope and Rita. In accordance with instructions, the 83 users were divided into six groups (five of fourteen men and one of thirteen), which were serviced by the aforementioned specialists within the time limit prescribed by regulations and to their total satisfaction. In view of the fact that the woman least requested by the troops was Dulce María, she was assigned the group of only thirteen men. Attached is the list of the 83 users with given name, surname, number of service file and ticket of deduction from payroll. Deportment of convoy while quartered in Lagunas was proper. Only one incident occurred: upon arrival of

115

the transport, Reinaldino Chumbe Quisque recognized his maternal half-sister (the so-called Lunita) among the Special Service and proceeded to insult her and to administer corporal punishment to her, fortunately of mild consequences, before being restrained by the military police. Chumbe Quisque was denied servicing, and locked in the guardhouse with six days of hard labor for bad character and conduct, but was later granted amnesty from the second part of his punishment on appeal by his half-sister, Lunita, and the other specialists. The undersigned permits himself to suggest to the SSGFRI, an organization whose work all the noncommissioned officers and soldiers praise, that it study the possibility of increasing its services to the subofficers—since they have repeatedly requested this—and of creating a special corps of first-class specialists for single officers or for those with families living far from the region where they serve.

[Signed]
CAPT. ALBERTO J. MENDOZA, PA

S S G F R I

Dispatch Number Fifteen

GENERAL SUBJECT: Special Service for Garrisons, Frontier and
Related Installations
SPECIFIC SUBJECT: Anniversary and review of the first year of
service and the Hymn of the Special Service
CLASSIFICATION: Top Secret
PLACE AND DATE: Iquitos, 16 August 1957

The undersigned, Capt. (Quartermaster) Pantaleón Pantoja, PA, Chief of the Special Service for Garrisons, Frontier and Related Installations, respectfully presents himself to General Felipe Collazos, Chief of Administration, Supply and Logistics of the Army, salutes him and reports:

1. (a) With the purpose of celebrating the first anniversary of the SSGFRI on the fourth of this month, the undersigned took the

liberty of offering to the male and female personnel of this organization at the bar on the Itaya River a simple luncheon for comrades which, so as not to put too great a strain on the slender budget of the Service, was prepared by a volunteer group of specialists under the supervision of our chief of personnel, Madame Leonor Curinchila (a.k.a. Chuchupe). (b) That in the course of the banquet not only did they healthily fraternize with pleasure and good humor while sampling the delicacies of Amazon cuisine—the menu consisted of the celebrated soup of this region *(inchic capi)*, chicken and rice, coconut ice cream and, as a beverage, beer—but, at the same time, the commemoration was taken advantage of to make a halt on the road to review what the Service had achieved during its first year of existence and to exchange evaluations, suggestions and constructive criticism, always with a view to the better accomplishment of the task the Army has entrusted to us.

2. (a) In summary, the review of this first year of the SSGFRI —synthesized by the undersigned in the presence of his collaborators in a brief address during the dessert course of the banquet— registered a total of 62,160 services offered by the Service to the noncommissioned officers and soldiers of our frontier units and to the sailors of the Amazon naval bases, a figure that, although far below the demand, constitutes a modest success for the Service: said figures prove that, in every instance, the SSGFRI *utilized its operative power for its maximum yield*—the highest ambition of every productive enterprise—as can be deduced by breaking down the total of 62,160 services into its component sums. (b) That, in effect, during the first two months, when the SSGFRI could hardly rely on four specialists, the volume of services reached 4,320, which converts into an average of 540 monthly services per specialist; that is to say, twenty daily, a figure that (Headquarters will remember Dispatch Number One sent by the undersigned) corresponds to the maximum efficiency of the specialists. (c) That in the fourth and fifth months, when the corps of specialists was comprised of six members, the services rose to 6,480, which likewise yields a mean figure of twenty daily services per work unit. (d) That the fifth, sixth and seventh months represent 13,560 services, or a constant daily average of twenty for each of the eight specialists who constituted the personnel of the

117

SSGFRI. (e) That in the eighth, ninth and tenth months, the rate remained exactly the same—a maximum level of efficiency—since the 16,200 services of this trimester also tabulate as an average of twenty for the ten women of the SSGFRI, just as in these last two months the 21,600 services realized indicate, once again, that the twenty specialists on whom we currently rely have known how to maintain this high average without any variation. (f) That the undersigned permitted himself to conclude his commemorative speech by congratulating the personnel of the SSGFRI for their good conduct and regularity in their work and by exhorting them to double their efforts to attain higher levels of production in the future—quantitative as much as qualitative.

3. (a) That as a friendly gesture after the final toast to the SSGFRI, the specialists sang for the undersigned a little musical work they had secretly composed for the occasion and which they proposed be adopted as the Hymn of the Service. (b) That after the Hymn had been performed several times with real enthusiasm by all the specialists, the undersigned acceded to said request, a measure he hopes will be ratified by headquarters, keeping in mind the advantage of stimulating enterprises that, like this one, denote interest and love of the personnel for the organization of which they form a part, foment the fraternal spirit indispensable for the realization of group labor and reveal high morale, youthful spirit and even an element of ingenuity and mischievousness, which, in small doses, of course, never go too far in adding a little spice to the completed mission.

4. (a) That following are the lyrics of the aforementioned composition, which should be sung to the first verse of the tune known everywhere as "The Mexican Hat Dance":

HYMN OF THE SPECIAL SERVICE

Always serving and serving and serving
In the Army all over the Country,
Always serving and serving and serving
With devotion and pride for a fee.

All we want is to keep our men smiling,

Come along let us join in the serving;
All the soldiers and officers pleasing
That's our duty: to love and beguile.

Always serving and serving and serving
In the Army all over our Country,
Always serving and serving and serving
With devotion and pride for a fee.

For our Land it is dutiful service
In the airplane and boat to be going
With Chino, Chuchupe, Chupito
No more quarreling, diseases or lice.

Always serving and serving and serving
In the Army all over our Country
Always serving and serving and serving
With devotion and pride for a fee.

On the cots, in the dirt or the grasses
Of the campsites and the field grounds deploying
When our Captain says "Now, girls, start serving!"
Ticket-holders get serviced in mass.

Always serving and serving and serving
In the Army all over the Country
Always serving and serving and serving
With devotion and pride for a fee.

Crossing jungles and rivers and ditches
Not a leopard or puma could scare us
'Cause we serve for our Country's great honor
Making love and not war to get rich.

Always serving and serving and serving
In the Army all over our Country
Always serving and serving and serving
With devotion and pride for a fee.

So it's time for us all to be parting,
Get on board the *Delilah* and *Eve* now;

119

No more time for just talking and playing
Time to work, time to serve, time to start.

Always serving and serving and serving
In the Army all over our Country
Always serving and serving and serving
With devotion and pride for a fee.

Now goodbye and goodbye and goodbye,
Chinito, Chuchupe and Chupón;
Now farewell and farewell and farewell
To our dear Captain Pantaleón.

God bless you.
[Signed]
CAPT. (QUARTERMASTER) PANTALEÓN PANTOJA, PA

cc: Gen. Roger Scavino, Commander in Chief of Region V
(Amazon)

NOTE: *Communicate to Capt. Pantoja that the Department of Administration, Supply and Logistics of the Army only provisionally ratifies his decision to recognize the "Hymn of the Special Service" conceived by the female personnel of the SSGFRI, since it would have preferred said lyrics to be set to the music of some song rich in national folklore, instead of a foreign melody like "The Mexican Hat Dance." This suggestion should be taken into consideration in the future.*

[*Signed*]
GEN. FELIPE COLLAZOS
Chief of Administration, Supply and Logistics

Decoded radio message from Second Lt. Alberto Santana, PA,
Chief of the Horcones Post (on the Napo River), received
at the Vargas Guerra Military Encampment at Iquitos
and transmitted to addressee
(cc: Command of Region V, Amazon)

I request the following message be communicated to Capt. (Quartermaster) Pantaleón Pantoja, PA, Chief of the Special Service for Garrisons, Frontier and Related Installations:

1. In my name and in that of the subofficers, noncommissioned officers and soldiers of the Horcones Post, I wish to extend to you our most sincere congratulations on the birth of your daughter Gladys, as well as our wishes for the newborn offspring's happiness and success. The reason for the tardiness of these congratulations is our having learned only yesterday of the blessed event with the arrival in Horcones of Convoy No. 11 of the SSGFRI.

2. At the same time, in my name and in that of all the soldiers under my command, I convey to you our most fraternal solidarity as well as our rejection and firm condemnation of the treacherous insinuations and vicious suggestions that for some time now have been made against the Special Service on *The Voice of Sinchi* program over Radio Amazon, which program, in proof of our indignation, will no longer be heard in the Horcones Post. The program *Music and Songs of Yesteryear* on National Radio is now broadcast to the troops over the loudspeaker.

Gratefully,
SECOND LT. ALBERTO SANTANA, PA
Chief, Horcones Post (Napo River)

Communiqué from the Chief of the Borja Garrison, Col. Peter Casahuanqui, PA, to the Special Service for Garrisons, Frontier and Related Installations

Borja, 1 October 1957

Col. Peter Casahuanqui, PA, Chief of the Borja Garrison, regrets having to communicate to the SSGFRI that during the quartering in this unit of Convoy No. 25, led by the individual nicknamed Freckle and comprised of Coca, Peludita, Flor and Maclovia, a quartering that had to be prolonged for eight days due to the inclemency of the weather, which prevented the hydroplane *Delilah* from taking off from the Marañón River, several incidents

121

have been recorded that are detailed below:

1. With the purpose of preventing the specialists from having extra-regulatory contact with the troops after servicing (executed with normalcy on the day of the convoy's arrival), they were all quartered in the subofficers' room, duly outfitted for this purpose. Thanks to a lucky tip-off, the command was informed that the pilot of the *Delilah,* alias Crazy, was preparing an illegal transaction, since he had proposed to the subofficers of Borja an exchange of money for the services of the above-mentioned specialists. Taken by surprise in full maneuvers during the night, three subofficers of the unit received rigorous punishment, the individual nick-named Crazy was kept locked in the jail until the convoy's depar-ture and the specialists were reprimanded.

2. Despite the strict vigilance imposed around the area where the convoy was concentrated, the joint flight of specialist Maclovia and the chief of the guard charged with the convoy's protection, First Sgt. Teófilo Gualino, was recorded, on the third day of the convoy's quartering in the Borja Garrison. The necessary arrange-ments were immediately made for the pursuit and capture of the fugitives, who, it was discovered, had fled, taking illegal possession of a glider belonging to the garrison. Subsequent to two (2) days of intense search, the fugitives were found in the town of Santa María de Nieva, where they had received protection and shelter in a clandestine refuge of the Brothers of the Ark after a crossing of the Marañón rapids that could be considered miraculous if the weather and the raging river are taken into account (through the divine intercession of the boy martyr of Moronacocha, according to the couple's naïve belief). The refuge of the fanatics of the Ark was reported to the police, who proceeded to spread a dragnet, unfortunately without success since the "brothers" and "sisters" managed to hide on the mountain. The deserters from Borja, on the other hand, were detained, but the pursuit group under the command of Second Lt. Camilo Bohorquez Rojas easily subdued them. On the basis of documents confiscated from the prisoners, it was then confirmed that in the morning of that same day they had been married before the lieutenant governor of Santa María de Nieva in a civil ceremony and before the chaplain of the mis-sion in a religious ceremony. First Sgt. Teófilo Gualino has been

122

stripped of his rank, reduced to private, punished with one hundred twenty (120) days in jail on bread and water, and his reprehensible conduct entered into his service file with the censure: "Very serious offense." As for the specialist Maclovia, she is returned to the logistics center so that the SSGFRI may impose whatever sanction it thinks proper.

God bless you.
[Signed]
> COL. PETER CASAHUANQUI, PA
> Chief, Borja Garrison (Marañón River)

<div align="right">Iquitos, 12 October 1957</div>

My friend Pantoja:

Patience, like everything that is human, has its limits. I don't want to insinuate that you are abusing mine, but any impartial observer would say that you are trampling on it. How else can you characterize the stony silence accorded all the friendly oral messages I've sent to you these last weeks through your employees Freckle, Chuchupe and Chino Porfirio? The matter is sadly simple: you have to understand and to learn once and for all to distinguish between those who are your friends and those who aren't, otherwise, Mr. Pantoja—and pardon me for saying it—your flourishing business will come tumbling down. The entire city demands that I assail you and what all decent people in Iquitos consider an unprecedented scandal with no extenuating circumstances. You already know that I am a man of my times, prepared to see, to do and to know everything before I die, and capable, for the sake of progress, of accepting that in this beautiful land of Loreto, where I first saw the light of day, an industry such as yours is able to flourish. But even I, broad-minded as I am, cannot help but understand those who are shocked, who cross themselves and cry out to Heaven. At the beginning it was only four, Pantoja, my friend, but now twenty? thirty? fifty? And you bring and send these sinners by air and water throughout the Amazon. Be aware that people have gotten it into their heads that your business should be closed down. Families can't sleep in peace, knowing that such an abscess

123

of wantonness and vice is at such a short distance from their homes, in full view of their youngest daughters, and surely you have noticed that the great entertainment of all the children in Iquitos is going down to the Itaya to see the boat and the hydroplane with their multicolored cargo come and go. Just yesterday Father José María, the director of the College of St. Augustine, that little old man who's as saintly as he is wise, commented on it to me, with tears in his eyes.

Accept the reality: the life and death of your millionaire business are in my hands. Until now I have resisted the pressures and I have limited myself, from time to time, to placating the citizenry's anger somewhat, to launching discreet warnings; but if you persist in your lack of understanding and obstinacy, and if, before the end of the month, what is due me is not in my hands, there will be for your enterprise, as well as for its boss and the brains behind it, nothing less than a fight to the finish with neither piety nor compassion, and both of you will suffer the fatal consequences.

I would have liked to discuss these and many other things in a friendly way with you, Mr. Pantoja. But I distrust your character, its intemperance, those crude manners of yours; and in addition, with a smile on my lips let me tell you that two forced dunkings in the filthy waters of the Itaya are the most that this servant of yours can take as a joke and still pardon: I shall answer to the third like a man, despite the fact that I do not like violence.

Yesterday, quite late, I saw you, friend Pantoja, walking down González Vigil Avenue, very close to the old folks' home. I was going to approach to greet you, but I noted that you were so well accompanied and experiencing such a tender moment that I didn't do it, since I know how to be discreet and understanding. It pleased me very much to observe the pretty lady whom you held by the waist and who was giving you those affectionate nibbles on the ear. But it turns out that she is not your charming wife, I muttered under my breath. Instead, she's that jewel of a woman imported from Manaos by this industrious enterpriser, the lady with such a glorious past. You have exquisite taste, Mr. Pantoja, and be aware that we, the men of this city, all envy you, because the Brazilian is the most tempting and desired morsel to have set foot in Iquitos. Lucky you, and the soldiers too. Did you walk to

124

see the waterfall on beautiful Lake Morona, to swear eternal love on the cliff where the boy martyr was crucified, as has become the custom for the sweethearts of this place?

A cordial handshake from you-know-who.

<div align="right">XXX</div>

S S G F R I

<div align="right">Dispatch Number Eighteen</div>

GENERAL SUBJECT: Special Service for Garrisons, Frontier and Related Installations
SPECIFIC SUBJECT: Incidents occurring to Convoy No. 25 in Borja, 22–30 September 1957
CLASSIFICATION: Top Secret
PLACE AND DATE: Iquitos, 6 October 1957

The undersigned, Capt. (Quartermaster) Pantaleón Pantoja, PA, Chief of the Special Service for Garrisons, Frontier and Related Installations, respectfully presents himself to Gen. Felipe Collazos, Chief of Administration, Supply and Logistics of the Army, salutes him and reports:

1. With respect to the serious incidents registered at the Borja Garrison, to which the attached report by Col. Peter Casahuanqui, PA, refers, the SSGFRI has carried out a thorough investigation, which has allowed the following facts to be established:

(a) During the eight days in which Convoy No. 25 was quartered in Borja (22–30 September), the weather in that region left absolutely nothing to be desired: the sun shone, it did not rain even once, the waters of the Marañón River were very calm—according to the attached meteorological reports of the Peruvian Air Force and the Peruvian Navy.

(b) The statements from all members of Convoy No. 25 coincide in categorically asserting that their stay in Borja was due to the fact that the *Delilah*'s propeller was maliciously removed by unknown hands in order to prevent the plane's departure and to detain the convoy in Borja, since on the eighth day the propeller reappeared

<div align="center">125</div>

mounted on the apparatus in the same mysterious manner.

(c) At the same time, all members of Convoy No. 25 coincide in asserting that during their compulsory stopover of eight days in Borja, Specialists Coca, Peludita, Flor and Maclovia (the latter only while she was in the garrison, of course) were induced to grant daily and repeated services to all officers and subofficers of the unit, against SSGFRI regulations, which exclude high-ranking and intermediate authorities from its benefits, and without said services being financially compensated.

(d) The pilot of the *Delilah* declares that the reason for his confinement to the Borja jail was, exclusively, his having attempted to prevent the specialists from offering their services *ad honorem* and against regulations when they were so demanded, which services, according to approximate calculations of the women themselves, amount to the escalated figure of 247.

(e) The undersigned wants to make it clear that he is not communicating the findings of this investigation with the thought of contradicting the testimony of Col. Peter Casahuanqui, PA, an outstanding Army chief whom he admires and respects, but rather as a mere contribution intended to amplify the report of said chief in order that the whole truth may shine forth.

2. On the other hand, he has the honor of making known that the investigation conducted by the SSGFRI into the flight and subsequent marriage of Specialist Maclovia to former First Sgt. Teófilo Gualino coincides mathematically with the version contained in Col. Peter Casahuanqui's report, the former averring only that former First Sgt. Gualino and the woman took possession of a garrison launch as a loan, because the river was the only means of leaving Borja, and that it was their firm intention to return it on the first possible occasion. Specialist Maclovia has been expelled from the SSGFRI, without compensation and without a letter of recommendation on account of her irresponsible conduct.

3. The undersigned allowed himself to make the observation to headquarters that the origin of these incidents, like the majority of those that have been recorded in spite of the efforts of the SSGFRI and the officers in charge of the utilization centers, is the Service's dramatic lack of funds. Notwithstanding the dedication

and the good will of all the collaborators in the SSGFRI, the corps of twenty (20) specialists (nineteen at present, since the said Maclovia has still not yet been replaced) is totally insufficient to cover the exorbitant demand of the utilization centers, which we are unable to take care of as we would like, except, if the expression will be excused, with so many drops in the bucket, and this rationing causes anxiety, feelings of frustration and, at times, precipitate and regrettable actions. Once again, the undersigned permits himself to urge his superiors to take a vigorous and bold step by allowing the SSGFRI to increase its operational corps from twenty (20) to thirty (30) specialists, which would signify an important advance in pursuance of the still distant satisfaction of what science has called the "virile plenitude" of our soldiers in the Amazon.

God bless you.
[Signed]
CAPT. (QUARTERMASTER) PANTALEÓN PANTOJA, PA

Encl: Report of Col. Peter Casahuanqui, PA, Chief, Borja Garrison (Marañón River), and two (2) meteorological reports from the PAF and the PN

NOTE: *Transmit the above report from Capt. Pantoja to Gen. Roger Scavino, Commander in Chief of Region V, (Amazon) with the following instructions:*

1. Carry out an immediate and detailed investigation of what took place with Convoy No. 25 of the SSGFRI at the Borja Garrison between 22 and 30 September and severely punish those who are found to be responsible; and

2. Accede to the request of Captain Pantoja and provide the necessary funds to increase its operational corps from twenty to thirty specialists.

[*Signed*]
GEN. FELIPE COLLAZOS
Chief of Administration, Supply and Logistics
Lima, 10 October 1957

Confidential communiqué from Rear Adm. Pedro G. Carrillo, PN,
Chief of the River Forces of the Amazon, to Gen. Roger Scavino,
PA, Commander in Chief of Region V (Amazon)

Santa Clotilde Base, 2 October 1957

FOR YOUR CONSIDERATION:

I have the honor of informing you that expressions of surprise
and dissatisfaction in regard to the Hymn of the Special Service
have reached me from the different bases that the Navy has spread
throughout the Amazon Basin—as many from sailors as from their
officers. The men who wear the spotless uniform of the Navy
regret that the author of the lyrics of said Hymn has not found it
necessary to mention, even once, the Peruvian Navy and its sail-
ors, as if this institution were not also a supporter of the Service,
to which (is it necessary to remind you?) we contributed with a
transport boat and its respective crew as well as with an equitable
percentage of the maintenance costs, having paid until the pre-
sent with flawless punctuality the fees that have been set for us for
the required services.

Convinced that this omission is exclusively owing to careless-
ness and chance and that there was no intention to offend the
Navy nor to foment among the sailors a feeling of being passed
over by their comrades in the Army, I am sending this com-
muniqué to you, along with my greetings and the petition to
remedy, if it is in your hands, the omission of which I inform
you, since although minor and banal, it could be the cause of
irritation and touchiness that should never trouble the relations
between the sister institutions.

God bless you.
[Signed]
REAR ADM. PEDRO G. CARRILLO, PN
Chief of the River Forces of the Amazon

NOTE: *Inform Capt. Pantoja of the content of the preceding com-
muniqué, reprimand him for the inexcusable lack of tact dis-*

128

played by the SSGFRI in the matter in question and order him to give due and quick satisfaction to Rear Adm. Pedro G. Carrillo and to his comrades in the national Navy.

[*Signed*]

GEN. ROGER SCAVINO
Commander in Chief of Region V (Amazon)
Iquitos, 4 October 1957

Requena, 20two Oktobor, 1950seven

Braive Sinshi:

Herd yor program aginst injustis on Amazon Radeeo witch all of us hear hurd and we aplawd you, cause the salors of Santa Ysabelita Base bring there hores hear from Iquitos in a wale of a bote named *Eve* and they take here baths with purfumed water an dont let nobuddy tutch them and they get rid of them with out us, the progreshive yooth of Requena, doin nuthin to them. Is that fare Braive Sinshi? We alreddy formed a comity of men from the town, with our own mayor Teófilo Morey at the hed, to protest to the cheef of Santa Ysabelita Base but that coword deenyed evrything saying how Im gona permit you bois of Requena to marry the speshalists if the speshalists dont eggsist, this hairitick swaring on the boy mardir. As if we dont have ises or eers, Sinshi, what dya think? Why salors yes and us no? Dont we have prix? Tell em this on yor program Braive Sinshi makem shake an nock em ded.

Yor lisners,

ARTIDORO SOMA
NEPUMUCENO QUILCA
CAIFÁS SANCHO

With this ledder we sent you a gif of a pairit that has a gold beek like you Sinshi.

129

GENERAL SUBJECT: Special Service for Garrisons, Frontier and
Related Installations
SPECIFIC SUBJECT: Explanations of the intentions and confusion in
the Hymn of the Special Service
CLASSIFICATION: Top Secret
PLACE AND DATE: Iquitos, 16 October 1957

The undersigned, Capt. (Quartermaster) Pantaleón Pantoja, PA,
Chief of the Special Service for Garrisons, Frontier and Related
Installations, respectfully presents himself to Rear Adm. Pedro G.
Carrillo, PN, Chief of the River Forces of the Amazon, salutes him
and reports:

1. (a) That he profoundly deplores the unpardonable careless-
ness by which the lyrics of the Hymn of the Special Service do not
make explicit mention of our nation's glorious Navy and of the
valiant sailors who belong to it. (b) That not as a justification, but
merely as an informative quotient, he wishes to inform you that
this hymn was not commissioned by the leadership of the SSGFRI,
but instead was a spontaneous creation of its personnel and that
it was adopted in an unpremeditated and somewhat hasty man-
ner, without submitting it to previous critical evaluation of its form
and content. (c) That in any case, if not in its lyrics, then in the
spirit of said Hymn, as in the minds and in the hearts of those of
us who labor in the SSGFRI, are always present the Navy bases and
their sailors, for whom all of us in the Service profess the greatest
love and the highest respect.

2. That we have proceeded to correct the shortcomings of the
Hymn by enriching it with the following changes:

(a) The chorus or refrain, sung five times between the stanzas,
will be sung three times (first, third and fifth in its original form,
that is:

Always serving and serving and serving
In the Army all over our Country,
Always serving and serving and serving
With devotion and pride for a fee.

The second and fourth times, the chorus or refrain will be sung
with its second line revised in this way:

Always serving and serving and serving
In the Navy all over our Country
Always serving and serving and serving
With devotion and pride for a fee.

(*b*) The first stanza of the Hymn will definitely be modified,
striking the third line, which said: "And our sergeants and our
corporals" and replacing it in the following manner:

All we want is to keep our men smiling,
Come along let us join in the serving;
All the sailors and officers pleasing
That's our duty: to love and beguile.

God bless you.
[Signed]
⌐ Capt.(Quartermaster) Pantaleón Pantoja, PA

cc: Gen. Felipe Collazos, Chief of Administration, Supply and Log-
istics of the Army, Gen. Roger Scavino, Commander in Chief
of Region V (Amazon)

Statistical Report

Col. Máximo Dávila, PA, is pleased to submit to the SSGFRI the
following condensed report of the visit that its Convoy No. 32
made to the Barranca Garrison on the Marañón River:

DATE OF THE VISIT OF CONVOY NO. 32: 3 November 1957
MEANS OF TRANSPORT AND PERSONNEL: The boat *Eve.* Chief of
convoy: Chino Porfirio. Specialists: Coca, Knockers, Lolita,

Sandra, Iris, Juana, Loreta, Brazilian, Roberta and Eduviges
LENGTH OF STAY IN GARRISON: Six (6) hours, from 1400 to 2000 hours

NUMBER OF USERS AND DISTRIBUTION OF SERVICES: One hundred ninety-two (192) users, divided and serviced in the following way: a group of ten (10) men, assigned to the Brazilian (despite her being the most aspired to by the men in the regiment, the SSGFRI's order to assign to this specialist only the minimum number of users was obeyed); a group of twenty-two (22) men, assigned to Specialist Knockers (because she was the second most popular with the regiment) and eight groups of twenty (20) men each, assigned to the remaining specialists. This distribution was effected after the unforeseen cancellation that is explained below. Because it was necessary for the *Eve* to weigh anchor before dusk due to the quickness with which night falls at this time of year in Barranca, the users' maximum stay in the location was reduced from twenty to fifteen minutes, so that the entire operation could be ended before sundown, which was happily achieved.

EVALUATION: The services were fully agreeable to the users, some of whom only lamented the cut in time due to the reason stated above, and the conduct of Convoy No. 32 was completely proper, as has been that of all the convoys of the SSGFRI that we have had the pleasure of receiving in the Barranca Garrison.

UNFORESEEN OCCURRENCES: Traveling in Convoy No. 32, a stowaway deceitfully dressed as a woman was discovered by this unit's Health Service clinic. When handed over to the MP and interrogated, this individual turned out to be Adrián Antúnez (a.k.a. Chameleon), the same man, it was later disclosed, who is the protector and pimp of the specialist named Knockers. The stowaway confessed to having been brought aboard the *Eve* by the woman he protects and to having obtained by threats the consent of the chief of convoy and the silence of the other specialists in order to carry out his wild intention. Disguised in women's clothes, he lied to the crew, saying that he was a new specialist named Adriana. The hoax was discovered when, upon arriving in Barranca, the supposed Adriana

132

invented an illness in front of his first client, Pvt. Rogelio Simonsa, so as not to offer service in the proper place, proposing instead to execute it in a sodomite or unnatural way. Beginning to have his suspicions, Pvt. Simonsa reported the incident and the false Adriana was forcibly examined by the male nurse of the guard, his real sex being made clear. The stowaway at first insisted that he had thought up this pantomime to control more closely the earnings of specialist Knockers (of which he received 75 percent) since he suspected that she was giving him doctored-up figures in order to reduce his share. But later, in the face of his interrogators' incredulity, he confessed that having been a passive invert for many years, his true intention had been to practice his vice with the troops in order to show himself that he was more than able to take the place of a woman in her duties as a specialist. All of which was corroborated by Knockers, the woman he lives with. Because it is not within the jurisdiction of this unit to make a decision in this matter, the individual Adrián Antúnez (a.k.a. Chameleon) is being returned handcuffed and in custody on the *Eve* to the logistics center, so that the command of the SSGFRI may adopt the most convenient measures.

RECOMMENDATION: That the possibility be studied of sending the convoys of the SSGFRI to the utilization centers more frequently, because of the good effect the services have on the troops.

[Signed]
COL. MÁXIMO DÁVILA, PA
Chief, Barranca Garrison (Marañón River)

Herewith: List of users with name, surname, number of service file and discount ticket and stowaway Adrián Antúnez (a.k.a. Chameleon)

Iquitos, 1 November 1957

Worthy Missis Pantoja:
Many times I've gone up to your door to knock, but, repenting,

133

every time I've gone back to my cousin Rosita's house, crying, because hasn't your husband threatened us saying you'll go to hell before you come close to my house. But I'm desperate and already living in hell, Missis, take pity on me today, which is the day of our beloved dead ones. From here I'm going straight to the church of Pachana to pray for all your dead loved ones, Missis Pantoja, I know how to be good, I know who you are, I've seen how pretty your little girl is, with such a saintly face like the boy martyr of Moronacocha. I'll tell you when your little daughter was born we were all so happy in Pantiland, we threw a party for your husband and we got him drunk so he'd be happier with the baby, she must be like a little angel with a pure soul come from heaven we said to ourselves. So it must be, I just know it, my heart whispers it to me. You know me, once you saw me about a year or more ago, that "washerwoman" who you had come into your house by mistake, thinking I was going to wash your clothes. That was me, Missis. Help me, be good to poor Maclovia, I'm dying of hunger and poor Teófilo there in Borja, they've got him a prisoner in jail, on bread and water he tells me in a letter that one of his friends brought me, the poor guy, his only sin is loving me, do something for me, I'll be thankful till the day I die. How then do you want me to live, Missis, if your husband kicked me out of Pantiland? Saying that I had behaved myself badly up there in Borja, that I had put the idea in Teófilo's head to escape with me. It wasn't me, it was him, he told me, let's run off to Nieva, that he pardoned me for being a whore, that he'd seen me arrive in Borja and his heart told him: "The woman you've been looking for your whole life just appeared."

I have a roof over my head thanks to the kind-heartedness of my cousin Rosita, but she's poor too and can't keep me, Missis, she's writing you this letter for me because I don't know how. Have pity on me and God will reward you in heaven and the same for your little daughter, I've seen her being taken for a walk and I've thought her an angel child, what eyes. I have to go back to Pantiland, talk to your husband so he'll pardon me and hire me again. Haven't I always been a good worker? What trouble have I given him since I'm with him? None, only this one, only one little one in a year isn't so much. Don't I have the right to love a man?

134

Doesn't he drool when the Brazilian does her tricks for him? Watch out, Missis, that woman is bad, she lived in Manaos and the whores there are bandits, she must be putting something in your husband's food to keep him bewitched and right in the palm of her hand. Besides two men have already killed themselves over her, a saintly gringo, they say, and the other one a student. Isn't Mister Pan-Pan already getting what he wants? Be careful, that woman can take him away from you and you'd suffer, Missis. I'll pray it doesn't happen to you.

Talk to him, plead with him, Missis Pantoja. They're going to keep my Teófilo a prisoner for many months and I want to go see him, because, what's funny, in the nights I cry in my sleep thinking about him. Before God, he's my husband, Missis, an old priest there in Nieva married us. And in the Ark there they nailed up a chicken as a token of love and fidelity. He wasn't a "brother," but me yes, ever since Brother Francisco came to Iquitos. God bless him, I went to hear him and he converted me. I converted Teófilo, and he became a "brother" when he saw how the "brothers" helped us there in Nieva. Those poor people, for giving us food and lending us a hammock they had to go to the mountain, leaving their houses and their animals and everything they had. Is it fair to chase good people who believe in God and do good like that?

How am I going to see Teófilo if I don't have money for the boat? And where am I going to work? Snotnose is very spiteful, he doesn't want to see me because I left him to work in Pantiland. I don't want to be a "washerwoman" again, the work's killing, on top of that there's the police, who take away everything you earn. There's no place to go, Missis. Kiss him and use all kinds of tricks, like us women know how, you'll make him forgive me and I'll come on my knees to kiss your feet. I think about my Teófilo there in Borja and I want to kill myself, to stab a palm thorn into my heart like the savages in the tribes to end their pain, but my cousin Rosita doesn't let me and besides I know that neither God our Father or Brother Francisco, his steward on Earth, would pardon me for it, they love all creatures, they even love a whore. Have pity on me and make him hire me again, I'll never make him angry again, I swear it by your daughter, I'm going to pray for her till I get hoarse, Missis. My name's Maclovia, he already knows it.

Well then, thank you so much, Missis Pantoja, may God repay you, I kiss your feet and your little daughter's, with all my devotion,

<div align="center">MACLOVIA</div>

<div align="center">Request for a discharge from the Army from
Commander Godofredo Beltrán Calila, Chief of the
Corps of Military Chaplains of Region V (Amazon)</div>

Brig. Gen. Roger Scavino
Commander in Chief of Region V (Amazon)
(Delivered by hand)

Dear General:

I am performing the painful duty of requesting through your intercession my immediate discharge from the Peruvian Army, in whose ranks I have had the honor of serving these past eighteen years; that is, since the year when I was ordained a priest, and during which I have attained, I would like to think on the basis of my merits, the rank of commander. At the same time, I am performing the very sad moral imperative of returning to the Army, through you, my immediate superior, the three decorations and the four honorable citations with which, throughout my years of service in the victimized and disregarded Corps of Military Chaplains (CMC), the armed forces have wanted to encourage my efforts and at the same time render gratitude.

I feel an obligation to state clearly and in precise detail that the reason for my separation from this institution and from these medals and citations is the sinister existence, as a semi-clandestine organization of our Army, of the so-called Special Service for Garrisons, Frontier and Related Installations, a euphemistic term that in reality embraces an active and growing traffic in prostitutes between Iquitos and the military camps and the naval bases of the Amazon. Neither as a priest nor as a soldier am I able to accept that the Army of Bolognesi and of Alfonso Ugarte, which has crowned the history of Peru with notable deeds and celebrated heroes, has descended to the shameful extreme of nourishing mer-

136

cenary love in its bosom, subsidizing it with its own budget, and placing its logistical force and its quartermaster's office at its service. I want only to remind you of the contrasting paradox in the fact that during eighteen years of insistent pleas and efforts I have not succeeded in having the Army create a mobile corps of priests with the purpose of periodically carrying the sacraments of confession and of communion to the soldiers at isolated garrisons where there is no chaplain—which are in the majority—and the fact that after scarcely one year and a half of existence the aforementioned Special Service presently has at its disposal a hydroplane, a boat, a truck and very modern communications equipment to distribute throughout the entire vastness of our jungle sin, lasciviousness and, undoubtedly, syphilis.

Finally, I would like to observe that this singular Service appears and prospers just when, in the Amazon, the Catholic faith, the official faith of Peru and of her armed forces, is threatened by a superstitious plague, which under the name of the Brotherhood of the Ark devastates towns and villages, wins over initiates day after day among the ignorant and naïve and extends its grotesque cult of the child bestially sacrificed in Moronacocha everywhere, including, as has been verified, the barracks in the jungle. I do not need to remind you, my General, that scarcely two months ago, in the San Bartolomé Post on the Ucayali River, a group of fanatic recruits, secretly organized into an Ark, attempted the live crucifixion of an Indian to ward off a storm, which had to be prevented at gunpoint by the unit's officers. And it is at this time, when the Corps of Military Chaplains is resolutely fighting this blasphemous scourge and homicide in the bosom of the Amazon regiments, that headquarters thinks it opportune to authorize and promote the functioning of a service that weakens morality and relaxes the mores of the troops. That our Army should foment prostitution and itself assume the degrading function of procuring is a symptom of decadence far too serious for me to remain indifferent. If the ethical decay takes hold in the backbone of our nation, which is the armed forces, then the gangrene can spread itself at any moment throughout the sacred organism of the Nation. This modest soldier priest does not want to be an accomplice, either by commission or omission, to such a terrible process.

With a military salute,
[Signed]

COMMANDER GODOFREDO BELTRÁN CALILA, CMC
Chief, Corps of Military Chaplains of Region V (Amazon)

NOTE: *Transmit the present request to the Ministry of War and to staff headquarters with the recommendation that:*

1. The request for discharge by Commander Beltrán Calila, CMC, be accepted due to its irrevocable nature;

2. That he be mildly admonished for the somewhat intemperate terms in which he has expressed his request; and

3. That he be thanked for service he has rendered.

[Signed]

GEN. ROGER SCAVINO
Commander in Chief of Region V (Amazon)

7

Broadcast of The Voice of Sinchi, *Radio Amazon,*
9 February 1958

And with the Movado clock that adorns the wall of our studio
striking exactly six o'clock, Radio Amazon is pleased to present to
its listening audience the most widely heard program on the air:

[*Bars of the waltz "La Contamanina" rise, fall and continue in the
background.*]

THE VOICE OF SINCHI!

[*Bars of the waltz "La Contamanina" rise, fall and continue in the
background.*]

A half hour of commentary, reviews, anecdotes, information—
all in the interest of Truth and Justice. The voice that takes and
transmits over the airwaves the pulse of the people in the
Peruvian Amazon. A lively and down-to-earth human program,
written and broadcast by that well-known journalist Germán
Láudano Rosales—*The Voice of Sinchi!*

[*Bars of the waltz "La Contamanina" rise, fall and are cut completely.*]

And a very good afternoon to you, my dear and distinguished
listeners. Here I am once again on Radio Amazon, the first station
of western Peru, to bring to the man of the cosmopolitan center
and to the woman of the distant tribe taking its first steps along
the road to civilization, to the prosperous businessman and to the

humble farmer of the isolated backwaters—that is, to all those fighting and working for progress in our unconquerable Amazon —thirty minutes of friendship, amusement, confidential revelations and important debates, sensational reports and history-making news from Iquitos, the beacon of Peruvian character raised aloft in the vast verdure of our jungle. But before continuing, my dear listeners, some commercial announcements.

[Recorded and taped commercials: 60 seconds.]

And, to start off, as we do every day, our section "A Little Bit of Culture." We will never tire of repeating it, listeners: we need to raise our intellectual and spiritual levels, to deepen our knowledge, especially of what concerns our surroundings, our native soil, the city that shelters us. Let's learn its secrets, the lives and deeds of those who have given it their names, the history of the houses we inhabit, many of which have been the cradle of great leaders or the scene of never-fading episodes that are the pride of our region. Let's learn about all this because penetrating a little into our people and into our city in this way, we'll love our Fatherland and our compatriots even more.

Today we are going to tell you the history of one of the most famous mansions in Iquitos. I'm referring—you've already guessed it—to the very famous House of Iron, as it is popularly called, which stands—so original, so different and graceful—in our Army Plaza and currently houses the noble and distinguished Iquitos Social Club. *The Voice of Sinchi* asks: How many people of Loreto know who built this House of Iron that surprises and delights strangers when they set foot on the fertile soil of Iquitos? How many knew that this beautiful metal house was designed by one of the most celebrated architects and builders of Europe and of the world? How many knew, before this afternoon, that this house came from the creative mind of the brilliant Frenchman who at the beginning of this century erected in the City of Light, Paris, the universally famous tower that bears his name? The Eiffel Tower! Yes, dear listeners, you heard right: the House of Iron on the Army Plaza is the work of the daring and very renowned French inventor Eiffel, and thus it is a historical monument of the first order—

140

in our country or in any part of the world. Does this mean that the famous Eiffel himself was once in sultry Iquitos? No, he never was here. How can we explain, then, that this great work of his gleams in our beloved city? That is what Sinchi is going to reveal in the section "A Little Bit of Culture" on his program. . . .

[*A few arpeggios.*]

It was during the years of the rubber boom when the great pioneers of Loreto, the same men who plowed the dense growth of the Amazon, from north to south and from east to west, in search of the coveted rubber, competed sportingly, for the benefit of our city, in seeing who could construct his house with the most artistic and costly materials of the period. And so there came into being residences of marble, with building stones, glazed tile façades and elaborate balconies, that beautify the streets of Iquitos and bring to mind the Golden Years of the Amazon and show how the poet of our Motherland was right when he said "any past time was better." Well, then, among those pioneers, who were all great rubber barons and adventurers, was the millionaire and great citizen of Loreto Anselmo del Aguila, who, like many of his equals, was in the habit of taking trips to Europe to satisfy his restless spirit and his thirst for culture. And here we have our native of Iquitos, Don Anselmo del Aguila, during a raw European winter—can you imagine how that citizen of Loreto must have shivered?—arriving in a German city and lodging in a little hotel that powerfully called itself to his attention and delighted him with its great comfort, with the daring of its lines and its very original beauty, since it was completely constructed out of iron. What did our home-grown del Aguila do then? Neither timid nor lazy and with that fervor for his own region that distinguishes the people of our land, he said to himself: This great architectural work should be in my city; Iquitos deserves it and needs it for its elegance and excellence. And without more ado, the prodigal man from Loreto bought the little German hotel built by the great Eiffel, paying for it what they asked without haggling over one cent. He had it dismantled, shipped and brought to Iquitos, down to the last nut and bolt. The first prefabricated house in history, my dear listeners! It was reas-

141

sembled here with great care and under the loving supervision of del Aguila himself. Now you know the reason for the presence of this curious and unequaled artistic work in Iquitos.

As a final anecdote, I should add that in his kind gesture and his noble desire to enrich the urban heritage of his land, Don Anselmo del Aguila also acted somewhat recklessly in not considering that the material of the house he bought was very suitable for the polar cold of enlightened Europe, but something very different took place in the case of Iquitos, where a metal mansion, in the temperatures we know, can constitute a serious problem. Inevitably, that is what happened. The most expensive house in Iquitos proved to be uninhabitable because the sun converted it into a cauldron, and people couldn't touch the walls without blistering their hands. There was nothing else for del Aguila to do but to sell the house to a friend, the rubber planter Ambrosio Morales, who thought he was capable of putting up with the hellish atmosphere of the House of Iron, but he also failed. And so the owner changed year after year, until the ideal solution was hit upon: to convert it into the Iquitos Social Club, an institution that is uninhabited during the day, when the House of Iron is throwing off flames, and that is brightened by the presence of our most gracious ladies and our most distinguished gentlemen in the afternoons and evenings, hours when the coolness makes it inviting and temperate. But keeping in mind its illustrious progenitor, Sinchi thinks that the House of Iron should be expropriated by the city and converted into a museum or something similar, dedicated to the golden years of rubber, when our valuable black gold turned Loreto into the economic capital of the country. And with this, kind listeners, we come to the close of our first section: "A Little Bit of Culture"!

[*A few arpeggios. Commercials on record and tape: 60 seconds. A few arpeggios.*]

And now our "Commentary of the Day." Before anything else, dear listeners, since the topic I must touch upon tonight (very much against my will and because I am forced to by my duty as an honest journalist, as a citizen of Loreto, as a Catholic and as father of a family) is extremely grave and may offend your ears, I urge you to send your younger daughters and sons away from your

142

radios because, with the frankness that characterizes me and has made *The Voice of Sinchi* the citadel of truth defended by every arm in the Amazon, I won't have any choice but to refer to crude facts and to call things by their proper names, as I have always been known to do. And I shall do so with the energy and serenity of someone who knows he speaks with the backing of his people and is echoing the silent but upright thoughts of the majority.

[*A few arpeggios.*]

On numerous occasions, and with delicacy so as not to offend anyone, because that is not our desire, we have alluded on this program to an activity that is a cause of scandal and indignation to all decent and proper people, who live and think morally, and who are in the vast majority in this city. And we had not wanted to attack this shameful activity directly and head on because we naïvely trusted—we confess it freely—that the individual responsible for this outrage might reconsider, might understand once and for all the magnitude of the moral and material damage he was inflicting on Iquitos in his desire for immoderate profit, in his mercantile zeal that respects no barrier nor stops to consider how he achieves his ends, which are to hoard, to fill his coffers, even though it might be by the forbidden means of concupiscence and corruption—his own and others'. Some time ago, meeting face to face with the lack of comprehension among the simple people, and displaying our physical rectitude over these very airwaves, we conducted a civilizing campaign directed toward putting an end to the custom of whipping children in order to purify them after Holy Saturday. And with our own little grain of sand, I think we've contributed something to eradicating in the Amazon this wicked custom that made our children cry so much and left some of them psychologically incapacitated. On other occasions we have crusaded against the superstitious mange that, under the disguise of the Brotherhood of the Ark, infects the Amazon and sprinkles the jungle with innocent little animals crucified by fault of the foolishness and ignorance of one portion of our populace, by the false messiahs and pseudo Christs abusing these qualities in order to fill their own pockets and satisfy their own sick instincts for popularity, for subduing and controlling masses and for anti-Christian

143

sadism. And we have done this without backing down from the threat of being crucified ourselves in the Army Plaza here in Iquitos, as is prophesied for us in the cowardly anonymous letters, full of spelling errors, that we receive daily from those brave types who throw rocks and then hide their hands behind their backs, who dare to insult but not to show their faces. Just the day before yesterday, on the doorstep of our home as we were preparing to go out and earn our daily bread by the sweat of our brow, we stumbled on a crucified kitten—a barbarous and bloody warning. But these Herods of our time are wrong if they think they can silence Sinchi with the fear of intimidation. We will continue to combat the demented fanaticism and religious crimes of that sect over these airwaves, and to hope that the authorities capture the so-called Brother Francisco, that Antichrist of the Amazon, whom we hope soon to see rotting in jail as the conscious and perverse perpetrator of the infanticide in Moronacocha, of the several frustrated attempts at assassination by crucifixion that have been recorded during the past months in different jungle settlements fanaticized by the Ark, and of the abominable crucifixion of the old man Arévalo Benzas at the hands of these outlaw "brothers" that took place last week in the missionary town of Santa María de Nieva.

[*A few arpeggios.*]

Today, with the same steadfastness and taking all the necessary risks, *The Voice of Sinchi* asks: How long are we going to continue tolerating in our beloved city, my distinguished listeners, that shameful spectacle which is the existence of the improperly named Special Service, more commonly known as Pantiland, in ridiculous homage to its founder? *The Voice of Sinchi* asks: How long, fathers and mothers of families in refined Loreto, are we going to continue suffering the anguish of shielding our innocent and inexperienced, our ignorant children from the danger they run in being exposed, as though it were some carnival or circus, to the traffic of courtesans, of shameless women—of *prostitutes,* to stop speaking in euphemisms—who brazenly come and go from that den of iniquity erected at the gates of our city by the unlawful and unprincipled individual answering to the name of Pantaleón

Pantoja? *The Voice of Sinchi* asks: What powerful and murky interests protect this person so that, during two long years, he has been able to direct with complete impunity a business as illicit as it is prosperous, as offensive as it is opulent, right under the noses of all honest citizens? Threats do not frighten us; no one can bribe us; nothing will obstruct our crusade for progress, morality, culture and Peruvian patriotism in the Amazon. The time has come to confront the monster and, just as St. George dealt with the dragon, to chop off its head in a single blow. We want no such carbuncle in Iquitos. All our faces drop with shame and we live in constant torment and nightmare with the continuance of that industrial complex of harlots presided over, like a modern-day Babylonian sultan, by the regrettably well-known Mr. Pantoja, who never wavers in his lust for wealth and exploitation, in offending and dishonoring the most sacred institutions—such as the family, the Church and the barracks of the men who defend our territorial integrity and the sovereignty of our Homeland.

[*A few arpeggios. Commercials on record and tape: 30 seconds. A few arpeggios.*]

This is not just the history of yesterday or even of the day before yesterday. This has been going on for no less than one and one-half years—for eighteen months—during the course of which, incredulous and stupefied, we have seen licentious Pantiland grow and spread. We are not talking for the sake of talking: we've investigated, examined, checked everything to the point of exhaustion, and now *The Voice of Sinchi* is in the position to reveal, in an exclusive first for you, listener friends, the shocking truth. A truth that shakes the walls of houses and brings on fainting fits. *The Voice of Sinchi* asks: How many women—if that honorable title can be given to those who dishonorably deal in their own bodies—do you imagine work at present for the gigantic harem of Mr. Pantaleón Pantoja? A full forty. Not one more and not one less. We even know their names. Forty harlots constitute the female population of this brothel on wheels, which, putting all the technology of the electronic age at the service of unmentionable pleasures, mobilizes its human merchandise in boats and hydroplanes throughout the Amazon.

No other industry in this progressive city, which has always distinguished itself by the push of its businessmen, can count on the technical resources of Pantiland. And if you don't think so, here's proof, irrefutable facts: is it or is it not true that the improperly named Special Service has at its disposal its own telephone line; a Dodge pickup truck with license plate number "Loreto 78–256"; a radio transmitter-receiver, with its own antenna, that would make any station in Iquitos pale with envy; a Catalina 37 hydroplane that of course bears the name of a biblical courtesan, *Delilah;* a two-hundred-ton boat cynically named the *Eve;* and the most coveted and in-demand commodities of this whole region on the Itaya River, such as, for example, air conditioning, which very few of the honorable offices in Iquitos have? Who is this fortunate Mr. Pantoja, this Peruvian Farouk, who in only a year and a half has managed to build such a formidable empire? It is a secret to no one that the long tentacles of this powerful organization, whose center of operations is Pantiland, are stretched throughout the Amazon in every direction, carrying its whorish flock . . . *to where,* dear listeners? *To where,* respectable listeners? *Into the barracks of the Homeland.* Yes, ladies and gentlemen, this is the hand-over-fist moneymaking business of the Pharaonic Mr. Pantoja: to convert the jungle garrisons and encampments, the frontier bases and installations, into little Sodoms and Gomorrahs, thanks to his flying and floating brothels. Just as you hear it—exactly as I'm telling you —there is not a syllable of exaggeration in my words; and if I'm distorting the truth, let Mr. Pantoja come here and prove me wrong. Democratically, I'll grant him all the time he needs on my program—tomorrow or the day after tomorrow or whenever he wants—to contradict Sinchi if Sinchi is lying. But he won't come. Of course he won't come, because he knows better than anyone else that I am telling the truth and nothing but the overpowering truth.

But you haven't heard everything, dear listeners. There are still other matters, even more serious, if that's possible. Without restraints and without scruples, this individual, this Emperor of Vice, not content to bring sexual commerce into the barracks of the Homeland, into the temples of Peruvianhood—in what sort of artifact do you think he mobilizes his concubines? What sort of

146

hydroplane is that apparatus painted in red and green and im-
properly called the *Delilah,* which we've seen so many times, our
hearts filled with anger, plowing the diaphanous sky of Iquitos? I
dare Mr. Pantoja to come here and say in front of this microphone
that the hydroplane *Delilah* is not the same Catalina 37 hydro-
plane in which, on a glorious day for the Peruvian Air Force,
March 3, 1929, Lieutenant Luis Pedraza Romero, of such fond
memory in our city, flew nonstop between Iquitos and Yurimaguas
for the first time, filling all the citizens of Loreto with joy and
enthusiasm for progress with the feat he accomplished. Yes, ladies
and gentlemen, truth is bitter but deceit is worse. Mr. Pantoja
iniquitously tramples and denigrates a historic national monu-
ment, sacred to all Peruvians, utilizing it as a means of transporta-
tion for his traveling teams of whores. *The Voice of Sinchi* asks:
Are the military authorities of the Amazon and the country as a
whole aware of this national sacrilege? Has this Peruvicide been
reflected on by the chiefs of the Peruvian Air Force and, princi-
pally, by the high command of Air Battalion No. 42 (Amazon), who
are called upon to be the jealous guardians of the airship in which
Lieutenant Pedraza completed his memorable deed? We refuse to
believe it. We know our military and aviation chiefs, we know how
honorable they are, the self-sacrificing tasks they perform. We
believe and we want to believe that Mr. Pantoja has mocked their
vigilant attention, that he has made them the victims of some base
maneuver to perpetrate a horror of this kind, which is to convert,
by the art of meretricious magic, a historical monument into a
mobile brothel. Because if it weren't so and if, instead of being
deceived and surprised by the Great Pimp of the Amazon, there
had been some sort of collusion between these authorities and
him, then, dear listeners, it would be enough to make you cry. It
would be, listener friends, enough to make you never believe in
anyone and never respect anything ever again. But it must not and
cannot be so. And that sink of iniquity must shut its doors and the
Caliph of Pantiland must be expelled from Iquitos and from the
Amazon region with his entire caravan of odalisques sold at auc-
tion, because we, the citizens of Loreto, who are wholesome and
plain, hard-working and proper people, do not want or need them
here.

147

[A few arpeggios. Commercials on record and tape: 60 seconds. A few arpeggios.]

And now, listener friends, we move on to our section "Sinchi on the Street: Interviews and Reports." We're not going to drop the section at hand. We don't want the Czar of Pantiland to rest on his whorish laurels. You know Sinchi, respectable listeners, and you know that when he undertakes a campaign for justice, for truth, for culture or for the morality of Iquitos, he does not stop working until he achieves his goal, which is to contribute to the progress of the Amazon—even if it is only by putting a little wood on the fire. So then tonight, as a vivid and direct complement to the evil we have denounced on our own "Commentary of the Day," as living, dramatic and warmly human testimony, *The Voice of Sinchi* is going to offer you two exclusive tapes, obtained with difficulty and danger, which in themselves denounce the shady Pantiland and the character of the person who created and builds his fortune by means of it; and who, carried away by his pecuniary greed, does not hesitate to sacrifice what is most sacred for a man —namely, his reputation, his family, his honorable wife and his little daughter. Dreadful in their naked and loathsome truth, these are two testimonies that Sinchi puts into your ears, my dear listeners, so that you may recognize the daily traffic of carnal love at immoral Pantiland in all its innermost, Machiavellian mechanisms.

[*A few arpeggios.*]

Here, seated before us with an embarrassed expression because of her lack of familiarity with the microphone, we have a woman who is still young and good-looking. Her name is Maclovia. Her last name is unimportant, and besides, she prefers it not to be known, since, very humanely, she does not want her family to identify her and to suffer, knowing her real life, which is, or—excuse me—has been, was, up until now, *prostitution*. Let no one throw the first stone; let no one tear his hair. Our listeners know very well that a woman, no matter how far she has fallen, can always redeem herself, if she is given the opportunities, and the moral help to do it, if friendly hands are extended to her. The first thing for returning to the decent life is to want to. Maclovia, as you are going to

148

hear for yourself in a few moments, wants to. She was a "washer-woman." "Washerwoman" in quotation marks, of course. Undoubtedly it was because of hunger, by necessity, because of the fatality of life that she practiced that tragic profession: to go offering herself to the highest bidder through the streets of Iquitos. But later—and this is the part that interests us—she worked in vicious Pantiland. And for that reason she will be able to reveal to us what lies hidden under that circus name. Life's misfortunes pushed Maclovia toward that den of iniquity so that a Mr. X might exploit her and make his greasy profits out of her woman's dignity. But it's better for her to tell us everything herself, with the simplicity of a humble woman who was not given the opportunity to study and to become cultured, but only to acquire vast experience through life's harsh treatment. Come a little closer, Maclovia, and speak right here. Without fear and without shame. Truth neither offends nor kills. The mike is yours, Maclovia.

[*A few arpeggios.*]

Thanks, Sinchi. Look, that part about my last name's not so much for my family. The truth is, except for my cousin Rosita, I don't have any relatives, at least close ones. My mother died before I worked in what you talked about, my father drowned on a trip to the Madre de Dios and my only little brother went up into the mountains five years ago so's he wouldn't have to be in the Army and I'm still waiting for him to come back. It's more because —I don't know how to tell you, Sinchi—Maclovia only goes with the job, it's not my name either, just the opposite. My real name goes with everything else, for example with my friendships. And you've brung me here only to talk about this, right? It's like I was two women, each doing different things and each with a different name. That's what I've gotten used to. I know I'm not explaining it real good. What? How? Oh, sure, I'm getting off the point. O.K., now I'll talk about that, Sinchi.

Yeah, well, before I entered Pantiland I was a "washerwoman," like you said, and later I was in Snotnose's place. Some people think "washerwomen" coin money and live the good life. A lie this big, Sinchi. It's fucking work, real exhausting, walking all day long, your feet get this swollen, and lotsa times for nothing at all, just

to go home with your hair done up, without raising one customer. And on top of that your pimp bugs you because you haven't even brung cigarettes. You'll say what's a pimp for, then? Because if you don't got one, you feel unprotected, and besides, Sinchi, who likes to live alone, without a man? Yeah, I got off the subject again. Now I'm talking about that. It was so you'd know why, when suddenly the word got around they were giving contracts in Pantiland with fixed salaries, Sundays off and even travel, well, the "washerwomen" went crazy. It was the lottery, Sinchi, don't you understand? Guaranteed work, without going looking for customers because there were enough to give away, and on top of that, treated with all respect. Well, it seemed like a dream to us. There was a stampede for the Itaya River. But though we all went flying, there were only contracts for a few of us and there was a crowd of cunts —Oh, excuse me! And besides, with Chuchupe the boss there, there was no way to get in. Mr. Pantoja listened to all her advice and she always picked the ones who'd worked in her house in Nanay. Like with the ones from the competition, Snotnose's prostitutes—she kept them waiting around and gave them all kinds of trouble and collected some huge commissions from them. And with the "washerwomen" she was even worse. She demoralized us, telling Mr. Pantoja she didn't like the ones who came off the street, like little bitches, but the ones who worked in some known house. She meant Casa Chuchupe, for sure. Bitch, she blocked my way for at least four months. More rumors, vacancies on the Itaya, I flew down and each time I went I was banging my head against that mountain, Chuchupe. So I went to Snotnose's place, not his old brothel, but the one he bought from Chuchupe, in Nanay. But I'd only been there a couple of months when there was another opening in Pantiland. I ran down and Mr. Pan-Pan stood looking at me during the examination and he said you've got presence, girl, get in that line. And he chose me for my good body. So I got into Pantiland, Sinchi. I remember clear as day the first time I went to the Itaya, already under contract, for the physical exam. I was as happy as the day of my First Communion, I swear. Mr. Pantoja made a speech to me and the four girls who came in with me. He made us cry, I'm telling you, saying now you've got another rank, you're specialists and not whores, you've got a mission

150

to fill, you serve the Homeland, you work with the armed forces and I don't know how many other things. He speaks beautiful as you, Sinchi, and one time, I remember, you made Sandra, Peludita and me cry. We were going in the *Eve* along the Marañón River and you started talking over the radio about little orphans in the Children's Home, and our eyes filled up. . . .

Thank you, Maclovia, for what you say about us. It moves us to know that we reach all groups and that *The Voice of Sinchi* is able to strike deep chords in the individuals most hardened by life's circumstances. What you tell me is a great reward, and it's worth more, for us, than all the ingratitude we meet with. So, Maclovia, that was how you fell into the nets of the Pimp of Pantiland. What happened then? . . .

Believe me, Sinchi, I was happy. I spent the days traveling, getting to know the barracks, the bases, the encampments all over the jungle, me who up till then had never gone up in a plane. The first time they got me on the *Delilah* it scared me, tickles in my belly, shivers, I got nauseous. But later just the opposite, I loved it, they'd call for "Volunteers for an aerial convoy!" and always "Me, Mr. Pantoja, me, right here!" Now, getting back to what I was saying earlier, let me tell you one thing, Sinchi. Your programs are so beautiful, you do those great crusades, like the one for orphans, that nobody can understand why you're attacking the Brothers of the Ark, why you're slandering them and insulting them all the time. How unfair, Sinchi. We only want good to reign and for God to be pleased. What? Yeah, I'll talk about that now. Excuse me, but I had to say it to you for the sake of public opinion. So then we'd go to the barracks and the soldiers would receive us like queens. If it was up to them, we'd of spent our whole lives there, making the duty more bearable. They'd organize hikes for us, they'd loan us boats to go on the river with, they'd invite us to barbecues. Treatment like you seldom see in this business, Sinchi. And besides, the peace of knowing the work's legal, not living in fear of the police, of pigs jumping you and taking away in one minute what you earned in a month. What security working with the soldiers, feeling yourself protected by the Army—isn't that right? Who was going to make trouble for us? Even the pimps went around meek as mice. They'd think twice before raising a hand,

151

out of fear we'd go complain to the soldiers and they'd put 'em in the cooler. How many of us were there? In my time, twenty. Not now; there're forty, all of 'em happy they're in Paradise. Even the officers were dying to take care of us, Sinchi, can you picture it? Yeah, it was a pleasure. Oh, God, it makes me miserable when I think how I left Pantiland out of plain dumbness.

The truth is it was my fault. Mr. Pantoja kicked me out 'cause on a trip to Borja I ran away and married a sergeant. That was a few months ago, like centuries to me. Maybe it's a sin to get married? One of the bad things about being a specialist, they don't take married women. Mr. Pantoja says there's an incompatibility. That seems really unfair to me. Now I have to tell you it was bad news I got married, Sinchi, 'cause Teófilo turned out half crazy. But better not speak bad about him since he's a prisoner, and he'll be one for so many years. They even say they might shoot him and the other "brothers." Think they'll do that? Look, I've hardly seen my poor husband four or five times; it'd be enough to make you laugh if it wasn't such a big tragedy. And to think I made him a "brother." He'd never even started to think about the Ark, or about Brother Francisco or salvation by the crosses, until he met me. I talked to him about the Ark, I made him see it was something with good people, something for the good of your fellow man and not all the evil things the dummies were saying it was—the things you repeat, Sinchi. But what ended up convincing him was meeting the "brothers" of Santa María de Nieva; they helped us a lot when we ran away. They gave us food, loaned us money, opened up their hearts and their homes to us, Sinchi. And later, when Teófilo was a prisoner on the post, they went to see him, they brought him food every day. Right there they were teaching him truths. But I never would've dreamed he'd give himself so strongly to religion. Just imagine, when he got out of the guardhouse, me searching high and low for money to go join him in Borja, he was another man. He greeted me saying I can't touch you ever again, I'm going to be an apostle. That if I wanted to we could live together, but only as "brother" and "sister"; the apostles have to be pure. But that'd be a misery for both of us and it'd be better for each to go his own way, since they were so different, and he'd chosen sainthood. In a nutshell, you see, Sinchi, I was left without

152

Pantiland and without a husband. And I hardly got back to Iquitos when I heard they'd nailed up Don Arévalo Benzas there in Santa María de Nieva and Teófilo organized the whole thing. Oh, Sinchi, what an impression it made on me! I knew that nice old man, he was head of the town's Ark, he helped us most and gave us a lot of advice. I don't believe that story in the newspapers, the one you're repeating too, that Teófilo had him crucified to get to be head of the Ark in Santa María de Nieva. My husband had become a saint, Sinchi, he wanted to become an apostle. What the "brothers" confessed has to be true—I'm sure the old man felt he was dying, and called them and begged them to nail him to the cross so he could end up like Christ, and they did it to please him. Poor Teófilo, I hope they don't shoot him; I'd feel responsible. Don't you see I got him mixed up in this mess, Sinchi? Who'd've thought he'd end up like this, with religion so deep in his blood? Yeah, I'll talk about that right now.

So like I was telling you, Mr. Pantoja never forgave me for running away with poor Teófilo. He hasn't let me come back to Pantiland, no matter how much I begged him, and I guess now, after what I've told you, that's the end of it forever. But you gotta live, right, Sinchi? 'Cause another of Mr. Pan-Pan's taboos is talking about Pantiland. To nobody, not to family or friends, and if they ask you, deny it exists. Isn't that another crazy thing? As if even the rocks in Iquitos didn't know what Pantiland is and who the specialists are. But what d'ya want, Sinchi? Each to his own craziness, and Mr. Pantoja has more than enough of that. No, it's not true what you said once, that he runs Pantiland with a whip, like a slave driver. You have to be fair. He's got everything so well organized—another craziness of his is order. All of us used to say this seems like a barracks, not a brothel. He makes us line up in formation, call roll, you have to be still and silent when he speaks. The only things we didn't have were reveille and they didn't make us march, thank God. But really, that craziness was funny and we put up with it because in everything else he was a fair and good person. Only when he flipped, fell in love—he got hung up on the Brazilian—the unfair favoritism started; for example, he made them give her the only private cabin on the *Eve* for the trips. She has him under her thumb, I swear to you. Listen, are you going

153

to put this on too? You better erase it, I don't want any trouble with the Brazilian—she's half witch and might give me the evil eye. Besides, she's already got a pair of corpses behind her, don't forget. Erase what I said about her and Mr. Pantoja. When all's said and done, every guy's got the right to fall head over heels in love with whoever pleases him most, and the same for every woman too, don't you think? I think Mr. Pantoja would've forgiven me my running away with Teófilo if I hadn't written that letter to his wife —and I didn't even write it, I dictated it to my cousin Rosita, the teacher. I really put my foot in my mouth and that's why I got into trouble, Sinchi, I put the knife in my own back. What d'ya want —I was desperate, dying of hunger, I would've done anything to get Mr. Pan-Pan to put me under contract again. And I wanted to help Teófilo too; they had him starving in a jail in Borja. It's true Rosita warned me: "You're doing a crazy thing, Maclovia." But at the last minute it didn't look that way to me. It occurred to me I could touch his wife's heartstrings, that she'd sympathize, she'd speak to her husband and Mr. Pantoja would let me in again. It's the only time I saw him so furious; he looked like he was going to kill me. Fool that I was, thinking his wife would've interceded, that it'd already be smoothed over, I went to see him in Pantiland, sure he was going to tell me I forgive you, a fine, a physical examination and you're in again. The only thing he didn't do, Sinchi, was take out a gun. He even said filthy things to me, him who's not used to using bad words. His eyes were red, he was losing his voice, foaming at the mouth. That I'd destroyed his marriage, that I had stabbed his wife in the heart, that his mother had passed out. I had to leave Pantiland running 'cause I thought he was going to beat me. But poor him, too—right, Sinchi? His wife didn't know nothin' about nothin'. Mr. Pan-Pan's story came out in the open with my letter. Boy, did I put my foot in my mouth, but I'm no fortuneteller —how could I think his wife was so innocent she didn't know what her husband was up to to bring home the bacon. There're simple people in this world, aren't there? It seems his wife left him and took their little girl to Lima. Look at what a row broke out on my account. And so here I am again a "washerwoman." Snotnose didn't want me back 'cause I left him to go to Pantiland. He's laid down this law so's he won't be left by the women in his houses: the

woman who goes to work for Mr. Pan-Pan never returns again to Snotnose's brothels. So here I am again like at the beginning, walking up and down, not even able to pay a pimp. Everything'd be O.K. if on top of everything I hadn't gotten varicose veins. Look at my legs—did you ever see anything more swollen, Sinchi? And in spite of the heat I have to go around with thick stockings on so they don't see my veins standing out; if I didn't, I'd never pick up a customer. Well, I don't know what else to tell you, Sinchi, that's my story. . . .

Well, then, very good, Maclovia, that's right. On behalf of the listeners to *The Voice of Sinchi,* over Radio Amazon, who, we're sure, understand your tragedy and pity your bad luck, we thank you for your frankness and spontaneity. We are very grateful to you for your testimony denouncing the scabrous activities of the Bluebeard of the Itaya River, even though we may not agree with you that all your calamities come from having left Pantiland. We think that the lurid Mr. Pantoja did you great service when he let you go, giving you—of course, without intending to—the opportunity to rehabilitate yourself and to return to an honorable and normal life, which we hope you desire and achieve soon. Good afternoon, Maclovia.

[*A few arpeggios. Commercials on record and tape: 30 seconds. A few arpeggios.*]

The last words of this unfortunate woman whose testimony we have just brought to your ears, dear listeners—I'm referring to ex-specialist Maclovia—have dramatically put a finger on the sore spot of a tragic and painful matter which she pictures better than a photograph or a Technicolor movie—the peculiarities of the person who displays on his record the black deed of having created in Iquitos the most unsuspected and populous house of ill repute in the country and perhaps in all Latin America. Because, in fact, it is established and credible that Mr. Pantaleón Pantoja has a family, or better said, that he had one, and that he has been leading a double life, submerged on the one hand in the pestilential swamp of sexual commerce, and on the other, feigning a dignified and respectable home life under the protection of the ignorance in which he kept loved ones—his wife and their little

daughter—concerning his real and filthy activities. But one day the light of truth entered his unhappy home and his wife's ignorance gave way to shock, to shame, and with every justification, to anger. Then, with dignity, with all the nobility of a mother offended, of a wife deceived in her most sacred honor, this upright lady determined to abandon that hearth tainted by scandal. At Lieutenant Bergerí Airport in Iquitos, in order to bear witness to her pain and to accompany her right to the stairway leading up to the modern Faucett seaplane that would carry her off through the air of our beloved city, *The Voice of Sinchi* was *THERE!*

[*A few arpeggios, sound of airplane engine that rises, falls and remains as a background sound.*]

"Good afternoon, madam. You're Mrs. Pantoja, aren't you? Delighted to meet you."

"Yes, I am. Who are you? And what's that you have in your hand? Gladys, child, be quiet, you're ruining my nerves. Alicia, give the baby her pacifier and see if that will quiet her."

"*The Voice of Sinchi*, from Radio Amazon, at your service, madam. Will you allow me to steal a few seconds of your precious time for a very short interview?"

"An interview? Me? But about what?"

"About your husband, madam. About the illustrious and renowned Pantaleón Pantoja."

"Go and interview *him*, sir. I don't want to know anything about that person or his reputation, which makes me laugh, or about this loathsome city I hope I never see again, not even in a painting. Please, do me one little favor. Get away from here, sir—don't you see you could step on the baby?"

"I understand your pain, madam, and our listeners understand it, and you should know that you can count on all our sympathy. We know that only your suffering could drive you to refer in this offensive way to the Pearl of the Amazon, which hasn't done anything to you. Rather, it's your husband who's doing this area so much harm."

"Forgive me, Alicita, I know you're from Loreto, but I swear to you I've suffered so much in this city that I hate it with all my heart and I'll never come back, you'll have to come see me in Chiclayo.

156

Look, my eyes are filling up with tears again in front of everybody. Oh, Alicia, how embarrassing!"

"Don't cry, Pochita dear, don't cry, be strong. And me, idiot that I am, I didn't even bring a handkerchief along. Give me—hand me little Gladys, I'll take her for you."

"Allow me to offer you my handkerchief, madam. Here, please, I beg you. Don't be ashamed of crying. Weeping is to a lady what dew is to flowers, Mrs. Pantoja."

"But what are you still here for? Alicia, isn't this guy annoying? Didn't I tell you I wasn't going to give any information about my husband? And what's more, he won't be my husband for much longer. I swear to you, Alicia, once I get to Lima I'm going to see a lawyer and I'll start divorce proceedings. We'll see if they don't give me custody of little Gladys, with the filthy mess that miserable man is making here."

"It was exactly about that that we dared hope for a statement, however brief, from you, Mrs. Pantoja. Because you are not unaware, apparently, of the irregular business that—"

"Get out of here, get out of here once and for all if you don't want me to call the police. I'm getting fed up with you. I'm warning you, I'm in no mood to put up with rudeness right now."

"You better not insult him, Pochita. If he attacks you on his program, what are the people going to say? More nasty talk. Please, sir, understand her: she's humiliated, she's leaving Iquitos, she doesn't feel up to talking on radio about her difficulties. You must understand."

"Of course we understand that, my dear lady. We are aware that Mrs. Pantoja has gotten ready to leave due to the uncommendable activities to which Mr. Pantoja dedicates himself in this city and which have deserved the citizens' energetic censure. We—"

"Oh, how embarrassing, Alicia. If everybody's found out, if everybody except me knew it, what a fool I am, what a dumbbell! I hate that louse, how could he have done this to me? I'll never speak to him again, I promise you; I won't let him see little Gladys so he can't smear her."

"Pocha, calm down. Look, they're already calling you, your plane's leaving. What a shame you're going, Pochita. But you're right, dear, that man has behaved so bad he doesn't deserve to live

157

with you. Little Gladys, sweetie, give your Aunt Alicia a kissy-kissy."

"I'll write you once I get there, Alicia. Thanks so much for everything. I don't know what I'd have done without you, crying on your shoulder these awful weeks. Remember: you're not going to say anything to Panta or to Mother Leonor for two or three hours, so they don't call by radio and make the plane turn back. *Ciao,* Alicia, bye-bye."

"Have a good trip, Mrs. Pantoja. Depart with the best wishes of our listeners and with our generous understanding of your tragedy, which is also, in a way, the tragedy of all of us and of our beloved city."

[*A few arpeggios. Commercials on record and tape: 30 seconds. A few arpeggios.*]

And in view of the fact that the Movado clock in our studio indicates that it's already 6:30 P.M., we must close our show with this impressive radio document that makes clear how the master of Pantiland has not hesitated in his dismal odyssey to bring pain and grief to his own family, in the same way he is bringing them to our land, whose only crime has been to welcome him and show him hospitality. And a very good afternoon, dear listeners. You have been listening to . . .

[*Bars of the waltz "La Contamanina" rise, fall and continue in the background.*]

THE VOICE OF SINCHI!

[*Bars of the waltz "La Contamanina" rise, fall and continue in the background.*]

A half hour of commentary, reviews, anecdotes, information—all in the interests of Truth and Justice. The voice that takes and transmits over the airwaves the pulse of the people in the Peruvian Amazon. A lively and down-to-earth human program, written and broadcast by that well-known journalist Germán Láudano Rosales—*The Voice of Sinchi*—which is broadcast daily, Monday through Saturday, between 6 and 6:30 P.M. over Radio Amazon, the first radio station of western Peru.

Night of February 13–14, 1958

The gong resounds, the echo hangs quivering in the air and Pantaleón Pantoja thinks: She's gone, she's left you, she's taken your little daughter away. Rigid and somber, he is in the command post, his hands resting on the banister. He tries to forget Pochita and Gladys, he fights back his tears. Now, in addition, he's overwhelmed by terror. The gong has sounded again and he thinks: Again, all over again, the damned parade, doubles from that dream again. He is perspiring, trembling, his heart aches for those summers when he could run to bury his face in Mother Leonor's skirts. He thinks: She's left you, you won't see your daughter grow up, they'll never return. But *getting up his courage,* he pulls himself together and concentrates on the spectacle.

At first glance, there's no reason to be alarmed. The patio of the logistics center has been expanded sufficiently to serve as a coliseum or a stadium, but except for its magnified proportions, it is identical to its old self: over there are the partitions covered with posters containing mottoes, proverbs and instructions, the beams painted with the symbolic red and green colors, the hammocks, the little cubicles containing the specialists' lockers, the white screen of the Health Service and the two wooden doors with the fallen crossbar. No one here. But this familiar and uninhabited landscape does not calm Pantaleón Pantoja. His distrust grows and a tenacious buzzing bothers his ears. He is stiff, frightened, expectant, and repeats to himself: "Poor Pochita, poor Gladys, poor Pantita." Elastic and resonating, the sound of the gong makes him jump in his seat: It is going to start. He calls up all his will power, his sense of the ridiculous; he secretly prays to Santa Rosa of Lima for help and to the boy martyr of Moronacocha so he won't get up, run down the staircase in leaps and bounds and leave the logistics center *like a soul carried away by the devil.*

The door to the pier has just been opened (gently) and Pantaleón Pantoja makes out shadowy silhouettes, standing at atten-

taleón Pantoja makes out shadowy silhouettes, standing at attention, waiting for the order to enter the logistics center. The dream twins, the dream twins, he thinks, *with his hair standing on end,* feeling his body beginning to go cold from bottom to top: his feet, his ankles, his knees. But the parade has already begun and nothing justifies his panic. It is only a matter of five soldiers, who are advancing, Indian file, from the door toward the command post, each one pulling a chain, at the end of which trots, leaps, struggles . . . what? Seized by an anxiety that soaks his hands and makes his teeth clatter, Pantaleón Pantoja stretches his head forward, sharpens his gaze, scrutinizes intently: they are little dogs. A sigh of relief inflates and deflates his chest: *his soul returns to his body.* There is nothing to fear; his suspicion was silly; they are not death knells but different types of *man's best friend.* The soldiers have come closer, but they still remain far from the command post. Now Pantaleón Pantoja can distinguish them better: between one soldier and another there are several yards of light and the five little animals are lined up exactly, as for a contest. They have been noticeably bathed, clipped, brushed, combed, perfumed. Besides a collar, all of them wear around their necks red and green ribbons tied in cute little clumps of bows. The soldiers march very seriously, looking straight ahead, without hurrying or falling behind, each a short distance from the animal under his care. The dogs obediently let themselves be led. They are of different colors, shapes and sizes: dachshund, Great Dane, German shepherd, Chihuahua and wolfhound. Pantaleón Pantoja thinks: I've lost my wife and daughter, but at least what's going to happen here won't be as horrible as other times. He sees the soldiers approach him and he feels dirty, vile, wounded, and he has the impression that mange is erupting over the length and breadth of his body.

When the gong sounds again—this time the vibration is acidic and reptilian—Pantaleón Pantoja suffers a sudden fright and he shifts uncomfortably in his seat. He thinks: *Put your hand in the lion's mouth and you'll get bit.* He makes an effort and looks. His eyes leap from their sockets, his heart beats so furiously that it might explode like a plastic bag. He has grasped the banister and his fingers hurt from holding on to the wood so hard. The soldiers are already very close and he would be able to recognize their

features if he looked at them. But he only has eyes for what bumps, rolls and rattles at the end of the chains: there, where the dogs were, are huge shapes now, animated and horrible, beings that repel and fascinate him. He would like to examine them one by one, in detail, to record their harsh images before they disappear, but he cannot individualize them: his eyes jump from one to another or take them in all at once. They are enormous, half human, half monkey, with tails that lash the air, many eyes, breasts that kiss the ground, ash-colored horns, pulsating scales, hunchbacked hoofs that grate like drills in flagstone, hairy trunks, tongues and slobber adorned with flies. They have harelips, bloody scabs, noses dangling strands of mucus, feet armored with calluses, curled with ingrown toenails and bunions, and fur like thorns, among which giant lice swing and leap just like monkeys in the jungle. Pantaleón Pantoja decides *to throw his fate to the wind* and flee. Terror wrenches out his teeth, which fall onto his lap like grains of corn; they have tied his hands and feet to the banister and he will not be able to move until *they* pass in front of the command post. He is begging for someone to shoot, for someone *to blow his brains out* and finish with this torture once and for all.

But the gong has sounded again—its interminable echo vibrates along every one of his nerves—and now the first soldier is passing in slow motion in front of the command post. Tied, feverish, gagged, Pantaleón Pantoja sees: it isn't a dog or a monster. The chained figure who smiles at him impishly is a Mother Leonor into whose features have been injected, without displacing them, those of Leonor Curinchila, and to whose thin skeleton has been added —once again, thinks Pantaleón Pantoja, swallowing bile—the breasts, the buttocks, the bulges and the outjutting walk of Chuchupe. "It doesn't matter that Pocha has left, my little boy, I'll go on taking care of you," says Mother Leonor. She bows and moves away. He does not have time to reflect, since here is the second soldier: the face is that of Sinchi, as is the corpulence, the animal assurance and the microphone he carries in his hand. But the uniform and the general's stars are those of Tiger Collazos, and likewise the way of pounding his chest, of scratching his mustache, and the good-humored self-confidence of the smile and the transparent skill of giving orders. He stops for a second, just the time

161

necessary to raise the microphone to his mouth and to bellow: "Courage, Captain Pantoja: Pochita will be the star of the Special Service in Chiclayo. As for little Gladys, we'll make her the mascot of our convoys." The soldier yanks on the chain and Sinchi Collazos moves away, jumping on one foot. Now in front of him, bald, tiny in his green uniform, showing him his drawn sword, which sparkles less than his sarcastic eyes, is General Freckle Scavino. He barks: "Widow, cuckold, cocksucker! Pantaleón, queer, coward!" He moves away with a quick step, elegantly turning his head inside his collar. But already, here is Commander Beltrán with slanting eyes and a honeyed voice, admonishing and severe in his dark soutane, coldly blessing him. "In the name of the maltyl of Molonacocha, I condemn you to lemain without wife and without daughter folevel, Mistel Pantaleón." Tripping on the hem of his robe and shaken with laughter, Father Porfirio follows after the others. And here is the one who ends the parade. Pantaleón Pantoja struggles, gnaws, tries to free his hands in order to ask forgiveness, to loosen the gag to beg, but his attempts are useless and the figure with a gracious silhouette, black hair, a tawny complexion and scarlet lips is there below, haloed by an endless sadness. He thinks: I hate you, Brazilian. Hurt, the little figure smiles and her voice fills with melancholy: "Panta, you don't know your Pochita anymore?" She takes a half turn and moves away, dragged by the recruit, who yanks on the chain with force. He feels drunk with solitude, rage and fear while the gong beats deafeningly in his ears.

162

8

"Wake up, son, it's six o'clock already," Mother Leonor taps at the door, enters the bedroom, kisses Panta on the forehead. "Oh, you're up already."

"I've been bathed and shaved for an hour, Mother," Panta yawns, makes a gesture of boredom, buttons his shirt, bends down. "I slept very badly; those terrible nightmares again. Did you get everything ready for me?"

"I've packed clothes for three days," Mother Leonor assures, leaves, returns, dragging a suitcase, shows all the clothing arranged. "Will it be enough for you?"

"More than enough; I won't stay longer than two," Panta is putting on a little jockey cap, is looking at himself in the mirror. "I'm going to Huallaga, to Mendoza's, an old school buddy. We went to Chorrillos Military Academy together. Centuries since I've seen him."

"Well, up till now I didn't want to give it any importance, because it didn't seem to have any," General Scavino is reading telegrams, consulting officers, studying files, attending meetings, speaking by radio. "The police asked us for help months ago; they can't cope with so much fanaticism. Sure, of course, from the Ark. Did you get the reports? This business is getting ugly. Two new attempts at crucifixion this week. In Puerto América and in Dos de Mayo. No, Tiger, they haven't nabbed them."

"But drink your milk, Pantita," Mother Leonor is filling the cup, putting in sugar, running to the kitchen, bringing bread. "And the

163

toast I made you? I'll put a little butter and marmalade on it. Eat something, my boy, I beg you."

"Just a little coffee, that's all." Panta remains standing, takes a sip, looks at his watch, grows impatient. "I'm not hungry, Mama."

"You're going to get sick," upset, Mother Leonor smiles, insists gently, grabs him by the arm, makes him sit down. "You're not trying even a mouthful, you're just skin and bones. You're making me a nervous wreck, Panta. You don't eat, you don't sleep, you work the whole blessed day. This can't go on; you're going to get pneumonia."

"Oh, Mama, be quiet, don't be silly," Panta resigns himself, drinks the cup down in one gulp, nods his head, eats a piece of toast, wipes his mouth. "After thirty, the secret of health is fasting. I'm fine, don't worry. Here, I'll leave you a little money in case you need it."

"You're whistling 'The Mexican Hat Dance' again," Mother Leonor plugs her ears. "You don't know how I've come to hate that blasted music. It was driving Pocha crazy too. Can't you whistle anything else?"

"I was whistling? I didn't even realize it," Panta blushes, coughs, goes to his bedroom, sadly looks at a photo, lifts his suitcase, returns to the dining room. "As for Pocha, if a letter comes from her . . ."

"I don't like the Army to get mixed up in this mess," Tiger Collazos reflects, worries, vacillates, tries to catch a fly, fails. "Fighting witches and fanatics is work for priests or the police anyway. Not soldiers. Has it gotten that serious?"

"I'll take good care of it until you get back. Of course I know— don't give me stupid suggestions," Mother Leonor becomes angry, gets down on her knees, shines his shoes, brushes off his pants and shirt, touches his face. "Come here so I can bless you. Bless you, my son, and try, do what's possible. . . ."

"I know already, I know. I won't look at them, I won't say a word to them," Panta closes his eyes, clenches his fists, twists his face. "I'll give them their orders in writing and with my back to them. Don't you give me stupid suggestions either, Mama."

"What have I done to God for Him to punish me like this?" Mother Leonor sobs, raises her hands to the ceiling, becomes exas-

164

perated, taps her feet. "My son among fallen women twenty-four hours a day, and on Army orders. We're the talk of all Iquitos; on the street they point at me with their fingers."

"Calm down, Mama, don't cry, I beg you—I don't have time now," He puts his arm around her shoulders, caresses her, kisses her on the cheek. "Excuse me if I raised my voice at you. I'm a little nervous. Don't pay any attention to me."

"If your father and your grandfather were alive, they'd die of shock," Mother Leonor wipes her eyes with the hem of her skirt, points to a yellowed portrait. "They'd turn over in their graves if they saw what you've been put in charge of. In their time officers didn't stoop to such things."

"You've been repeating the same thing four times a day for the past eight months," Panta shouts, repents, lowers his voice, smiles without wanting to, explains. "I'm a military man, I have to obey orders, and until they give me something else, my duty is to do this job right. I've already told you, if you prefer I can have you sent to Lima, Mama."

"Rather surprising, yes, General," Colonel Peter Casahuanqui digs around in a bag, takes out a handful of cards and photos, makes a packet, seals it, orders dispatch this to Lima for me. "In the last uniform inspection we discovered that half the soldiers had Brother Francisco prayers or prayer cards of the boy martyr. I'm sending you some samples."

"I'm not like certain people who leave home at the first problem —don't get me wrong," Mother Leonor straightens up, shakes her index finger, adopts a belligerent posture. "I'm not one of those who decide to move out overnight without even saying goodbye, one of those who steals a daughter away from her father."

"Now don't start in on Pocha," Panta walks down the hallway, trips on a flowerpot stand, curses, rubs his ankle. "Another one of your obsessions has turned up again, Mama."

"If she hadn't stolen little Gladys from you, you wouldn't be this way," Mother Leonor opens the street door. "Maybe I can't see how you're eating yourself up alive with sorrow for your little girl, Panta? Go, leave right now."

"I can't put up with any more—quick, quick," Panta climbs the gangway of the *Eve,* goes down to the cabin, falls on the bunk,

165

murmurs. "Where I like it, there. On my throat, on my ear. Not just nibbles, but real slow bites. C'mon now."

"Glad to, Panta," the Brazilian sighs, looks at him without interest, points to the dock, draws the porthole curtain. "But at least wait till the *Eve* leaves. Subofficer Rodríguez and the sailors are getting on and off every minute. It's not for my sake but yours, sonny."

"I'm not waiting another minute," Pantaleón Pantoja tears off his shirt, drops his pants, takes off his shoes and socks, sinks down. "Close the cabin door, come here. Little pinches, little nibbles."

"Jesus, you're inexhaustible, Pantita," the Brazilian bolts the door, strips, climbs on the bunk, sways. "You alone give me more work than a regiment. What a surprise you've been to me. The first time I saw you I thought you'd never cheated on your wife."

"And it was true, but now be quiet," Pantita gasps, leans, rises, falls, enters, leaves, returns, chokes up. "I've told you I'm distracting myself, damn it. On the ear lobe, on the ear lobe."

"Know you can get TB sinking birdies so much?" the Brazilian laughs, moves, becomes bored, looks at her fingernails, stops, squats, hurries up. "It's true; lately you're skinnier than an eel. But that doesn't stop you. You're hotter every time. Yeah, I know, I'll shut up. O.K., on the ear lobe."

"Ohhhhh, at last, ohhhhh, that's good," Pantita explodes, pales, breathes, enjoys himself. "My heart's about to pop out and I'm dizzy."

"With all the reason in the world, Tiger, I don't like to get the troops involved in police matters either," General Scavino takes planes, crosses rivers in motorboats, inspects towns and encampments, demands details, sends messages. "That's why I've put up with this thing until now. But the business in Dos de Mayo is enough to upset you. Did you read Colonel Dávila's dispatch?"

"How many times a week, Pantita?" the Brazilian sits up, fills basins, washes and rinses off, dresses. "More than one specialist, that's for sure. And when there are candidates, you might as well stop counting. With the habit you've picked up of—what do you call it?—professional inspection? How shrewd you are."

"This's work, not play," Panta stretches, sits up on the bunk, gets his energy up, drags his feet into the bathroom, urinates. "Don't

laugh, it's true. Besides, you're the guilty party; you gave me the idea when I gave you your physical. It hadn't occurred to me before. Think this fooling around's easy?"

"Depends on the woman," the Brazilian throws the sheet on the floor, inspects the mattress, scrubs it with a sponge, shakes it. "With a lot of them, your birdie won't even stand up."

"Course not; I eliminate them right away," Pantaleón Pantoja lathers himself, dries off with toilet paper, pulls the chain. "The fairest way to choose the best ones. There's no fooling the birdie."

"We're leaving now, the *Eve*'s begun to shake," the Brazilian opens the porthole, moves the mattress so the sun will hit the wet part. "Come here, help me open the window, we're suffocating, when are you going to buy a fan? And now don't start feeling sorry, Pantita."

"They crucified the old woman Ignacia Curdimbre Peláez in the little square in Dos de Mayo at midnight with 214 inhabitants of the town present," Colonel Máximo Dávila dictates, revises, signs and dispatches his report. "Two policemen who attempted to dissuade the 'brothers' were given a terrible beating. According to the testimony, the old woman's agony lasted until dawn. The worst part is what follows, General, sir. The people smeared their faces and bodies with blood from the cross and they even drank it. Now they've started to worship the victim. There are prayer cards of Santa Ignacia in circulation already."

"I wasn't like this," Pantaleón Pantoja sits on the bunk, holds his head in his hands, remembers, laments. "I wasn't like this, goddamn it, I wasn't like this."

"You'd never cheated on your faithful wife and you only dropped a birdie every fifteen days," the Brazilian shakes out, washes, wrings, hangs up the sheet. "I know it all by heart, Panta. You came here and you wised up. But too much, sonny; you went to the other extreme."

"At first I blamed the climate," Pantaleón Pantoja puts on his shorts, undershirt, socks, shoes. "I thought the heat and humidity inflamed a man. But I've found out something really strange. This work's to blame for what's happening to my birdie."

"You mean being so close to temptation?" the Brazilian feels her hips, looks at her breasts, grows vain. "That you learned to cheep-

167

cheep from me? What a compliment, Panta."

"You can't understand it; even I can't understand it," Panta observes himself in the mirror, smoothes down his eyebrows, combs his hair. "It's something very mysterious, something that's never happened to anyone. A sense of the unhealthy obligation, same as a sickness. Because it's not moral but biological, Corporal."

"Or maybe you already see, Tiger, these fanatics are capable of anything," General Scavino climbs into the jeep, crosses mud holes, officiates at funerals, consoles victims, instructs officers, speaks on the telephone. "This isn't a matter of little groups. There are thousands of them. A couple of nights ago I went by the cross of the boy martyr in Moronacocha and I was astonished. There was a sea of people. Even soldiers in uniform."

"You mean you have the desire all day long because of your sense of obligation?" the Brazilian remains petrified, her mouth open, she lets out a guffaw. "Look, Panta, I've known a lot of men, I have more experience in these things than you. I assure you no one's birdie stands up just for the sake of duty."

"I'm not like everybody, that's my rotten luck. What happens to them doesn't happen to me," Pantaleón Pantoja drops the comb, loses himself in thought, thinks out loud. "As a boy I had less appetite than now. But no sooner did they give me my first assignment—rations for a regiment—than a ferocious appetite was awakened in me. I spent all day eating, reading recipes; I learned to cook. They changed my assignment and poof! goodbye, food. I started getting interested in tailoring, clothing, styles; the chief of barracks thought I was a queer. They'd put me in charge of the garrison's uniforms—get it?"

"I hope they never put you in charge of a nut house, Panta; the first thing you'd do is go crazy," the Brazilian points to the porthole. "Look at those devils, spying on us."

"Get out of here, Sandra, Viruca," Pantaleón Pantoja runs to the door, unbolts it, bellows, takes action. "A fine of fifty for each one, Freckle!"

"And what are the priests for, what do we pay chaplains for?" Tiger Collazos strides around his office, examines balance sheets, adds, subtracts, becomes indignant. "So they can scratch their

bellies? How's it possible for garrisons in the Amazon to be filling up with 'brothers,' Scavino?"

"Don't stick out your body so far, Panta," the Brazilian grabs him by the shoulders, brings him back into the cabin, closes the door. "Have you forgotten you're half naked?"

"Me forget you?" Captain Alberto Mendoza elbows aside the sailors and the soldiers, jumps aboard, opens his arms. "How could you think that, pal? Come over here and let me shake your hand. After so many years, Panta."

"What a pleasure, Alberto," Captain Pantoja claps, disembarks, shakes officers' hands, responds to the salutes of subofficers and soldiers. "You're just the same, the years haven't changed you."

"Let's have a drink at the officers' mess," Captain Mendoza grabs him by the arm, leads him across the post, pushes open a screen door, chooses a table under the fan. "Don't worry about the fucking. Everything's ready and here it always goes like clockwork. Alférez, you take charge of everything and tell us when the party's over. So while the soldiers are getting their rocks off, we can have a few beers. Great to see you again, Panta."

"Listen, Alberto, now I remember," Captain Pantoja watches through the window the specialists entering the provisions storehouse, the lines of soldiers, the controllers who are taking up their positions. "I don't know whether you know that that specialist, the one they say . . . ahh . . ."

"The Brazilian. I know; for her only ten, according to the book. Think I don't read your instructions?" Captain Mendoza feints a jab at him, orders, opens bottles, fills the glasses, makes a toast. "Beer for you, too? Two, really cold. But it's absurd, Panta. If you like that woman and their screwing her bugs you, why not give her full exemption from service? What are you the boss for if not for that?"

"No, not that," Captain Pantoja coughs, blushes, stammers, drinks. "I don't want to fail in my duty. Besides, I promise you that that specialist and I . . . really."

"All the officers know it and they like it that you've got a girlfriend," Captain Mendoza licks the foam from his mustache, lights a cigarette, drinks, asks for more beer. "But nobody gets this

system of yours. A guy can understand you're not pleased with the troops throwing themselves at your woman. So why this ridiculous formality? Ten lays are the same as a hundred, pal."

"Ten is what the regulation calls for," Captain Pantoja sees the first soldiers leaving the tents, the second and third shifts entering, swallows saliva. "How am I going to break it? I made it myself."

"Always the same, with an electronic brain; you can't," Captain Mendoza throws his head back, half closes his eyes, laughs nostalgically. "I still remember you were the only cadet in Chorrillos who'd shine his shoes to go out and muddy them up on maneuvers."

"The truth is that ever since Father Beltrán requested his discharge, the Corps of Military Chaplains has left a lot to be desired," General Scavino receives complaints, attends to recommendations, hears masses, presents trophies, mounts horses, goes bowling. "But in the last analysis, Tiger, it's a general phenomenon throughout the Amazon; the barracks couldn't be exempt from the disease. Anyway, don't worry. We're taking a firm hand in the matter. Thirty days at hard labor for carrying a prayer card of the boy martyr or of Santa Ignacia, forty-five for a photo of Brother Francisco."

"I'm in Lagunas on account of last week's incident, Alberto," Captain Pantoja sees the fourth shift leave, the fifth, the sixth entering. "Sure I read your dispatch. But it seemed serious enough to me to come and get the lay of the land."

"It wasn't worth the effort," Captain Mendoza loosens his belt, asks for a cheese sandwich, eats, drinks. "What's going on is very simple. It's a madhouse in these little towns every time a convoy of specialists approaches. The idea alone makes the spurs on all the cocks in the neighborhood get hard. And once in a while, they do some crazy things."

"To trespass on a military post is a little too crazy," Captain Pantoja sees Freckle collecting the pictures and magazines from the soldiers. "Maybe there wasn't a patrol?"

"Reinforced, like now, because it's always the same when a convoy comes," Captain Mendoza pulls him outside, shows him the fences, the sentinels with bayonets, the clusters of civilians. "Come on, let's go so you see for yourself. Get it? All the town's

stiff dicks jammed together around the camp. Look over there. See 'em? Sitting in the trees, pouring themselves outta their eyes. What d'ya want, chum? It even happened to you, who seemed out of it."

"Didn't those crazy people from the Ark have something to do with the affair?" Captain Pantoja sees the seventh shift leave, the eighth enter, the ninth, the tenth and he mutters at last. "Don't repeat the dispatch to me, Alberto, tell me what really happened."

"Eight guys from Lagunas entered the post and tried to kidnap a pair of specialists," General Scavino drums on the radio apparatus. "No, I'm not talking about the 'brothers' but the Special Service, the other jungle disaster. Do you realize where we're heading, Tiger?"

"It won't happen again, pal," Captain Mendoza pays the bill, puts on his kepi, sunglasses, lets Panta go out first. "Now, since the day before the convoy's arrival, I've doubled the patrol and placed sentries along the entire perimeter. The base gets into combat condition, so the soldiers can screw in peace. Hell, how funny it all is!"

"Calm down and lower your voice," Tiger Collazos compares reports, orders inquiries, rereads letters. "Don't get hysterical, Scavino. I know all about it, I've got Mendoza's dispatch right in front of me. The troops rescued the specialists and that was that. Well, that's no reason to commit suicide. An incident just like any other. The 'brothers' do worse things, right?"

"It's just this isn't the first incident of the kind that's occurred, Alberto," Captain Pantoja sees the Brazilian leaving a tent, sees her crossing the clearing, sees her climbing onto the *Eve*. "There's constant interference from the civilian element. In every town spouting cocks pop up when the convoy appears."

"A terrible fight broke out between soldiers and civilians over that pair of women," General Scavino receives calls, visits the jail, interrogates men under arrest, has insomnia, takes tranquilizers, writes, calls. "Did you hear correctly? Between sol-diers and ci-vilians. The kidnappers managed to get them off the post and the fight was right in the middle of town. There are four wounded men. Something really serious can happen at any moment, Tiger, on account of that damned Service."

171

"With good reason, pal," Captain Mendoza points to the onlookers, to the specialists who are leaving the tents and returning to the dock, flanked by guards. "These women look like angels fallen from heaven to these hicks who never even saw Iquitos. The soldiers are to blame too. They go telling stories in town, putting ideas in the other guys' heads. They've been ordered not to talk about it, but they don't understand."

"It annoys me this is happening now, when I'm almost ready with a project to expand the Service and give it more class," Captain Pantoja stuffs his hands into his pockets, walks crestfallen, kicking pebbles. "Something really ambitious; it's taken me a lot of days of thinking and figuring. And my plan might even solve the problem of these civilian stiff dicks, pal."

"But you'd triple the other one for me, Pantoja, the one of the priests and the pious women in Iquitos who are wearing out Scavino's patience," Tiger Collazos calls his orderly, orders him to buy cigarettes, tips him, asks for a light. "No, too much. Fifty specialists are enough. We can't recruit more, at least for the time being."

"With an operational corps of one hundred specialists and three boats sailing in a regular fashion on the rivers of the Amazon"— Captain Pantoja contemplates the preparations for the *Eve*'s departure—"no one would be able to forecast the arrival of the convoys at the utilization centers."

"You're losing your mind," General Victoria flicks a lighter and brings it close to Tiger Collazos' face. "The Army would have to give up buying weapons in order to contract more prostitutes. There's no budget can support the fantasies of that greedy climber."

"Study the plan I sent you, General, sir," Captain Pantoja types with two fingers, makes calculations, outlines synoptic tables, spends rough nights, erases, adds, insists. "We could create a system of unmethodical, irregular rotation. The convoy's arrival would always be unexpected, there'd never be occasion for incidents. Only the heads of the units would know the arrival dates."

"And to think it took so much work to make him accept the assignment of creating the Special Service," Colonel López López searches his office for an ashtray and places it next to Tiger Col-

172

lazos. "Now he's in his element. He moves among whores like a fish in water."

"That's right, the only way of effectively controlling that system would be from the air," Captain Pantoja puts memoranda into code, prepares a thermos of coffee, multiplies, divides, scratches his head, dispatches addenda. "Another plane would be needed. And at least one more officer at the quartermaster's. A second lieutenant would be enough, General, sir."

"He's got a screw loose, no doubt about it," General Scavino reads *El Oriente*, listens to *The Voice of Sinchi*, receives anonymous letters, gets to the movies late and leaves before the film is over. "If you give him his way this time and approve that project, I'm warning you I'll request my discharge, like Beltrán. Between the fanatics of the Ark and Pantoja's specialists, I'm going to be done in. I'm getting by only on my Valium, Tiger."

"I regret giving you bad news, General, sir," Colonel Augusto Valdés leaves on an expedition, invades a deserted town, curses, helps unnail, orders boys to return on a forced march. "Last night in the village of Frailecillos, two hours upriver from my garrison, they crucified the subofficer Avelino Miranda. He was on furlough, dressed as a civilian, and it's possible they didn't recognize his military rank. No, he's not dead yet but the doctors say it's a matter of hours. The entire village, thirty or forty people. Yes, they've gone into the mountains."

"Calm down, Scavino, the thing can't be that bad," General Victoria listens and makes jokes about the specialists in the Army Club, pacifying his mother about the crucifixion in the jungle. "Are those yokels really so stirred up about Pantoja's girls?"

"Stirred up, General, sir?" General Scavino takes his pulse, looks at his tongue, doodles crosses on the blotter. "This morning the bishop showed up here, with his staff of priests and nuns."

"I have the painful duty to inform you that if the so-called Special Service does not vanish, I shall excommunicate all those who work in it or make use of it," the bishop enters the office, nods, does not smile, does not sit down, wipes his ring and proffers it. "The minimal limits of decency and decorum have already been violated, General Scavino. Captain Pantoja's own mother has come to me, bewailing her tragedy."

173

"I share that judgment completely and His Eminence knows it," General Scavino rises, genuflects, kisses the ring, speaks softly, offers soft drinks, bids farewell to his visitors in the street. "If it had been up to me, that Service would never have come into being. I ask a little patience from all of you. As for Pantoja, don't mention him to me, Monsignor. What tragedy? There's no tragedy. The son of that woman who is crying over him has a large share of the blame for what is happening. At least he could have organized the thing in a mediocre, defective way. But that idiot has converted the Special Service into the most efficient unit of the armed forces."

"No way of getting around it, Panta," Captain Mendoza climbs aboard, snoops around the command bridge, looks at the compass, works the rudder. "You're the Einstein of fucking."

"Yes, naturally; I've sent several search parties to hunt down the fanatics," Colonel Augusto Valdés goes to the infirmary, cheers up the victim, stabs little flags into a map, dictates instructions, wishes good luck to the officers who are leaving. "With orders to bring me the entire village to give an explanation. It hasn't been necessary, General, sir. My men are indignant; Subofficer Avelino Miranda was always very much loved by the troops."

"Sooner or later Tiger will end up accepting my plan," Captain Pantoja shows the compartments on board the *Eve* to Captain Mendoza, the hold, the engines, spits and rubs it in with his foot. "The growth of the Service is inevitable. With three small boats, two planes, an operational corps of one hundred specialists and two adjunct officers, I'll do wonders, Alberto."

"In Chorrillos we thought your vocation was to be a computer, not an Army man," Captain Mendoza goes down the unloading ramp, returns to the post with Panta by the arm, asks have you already prepared the statistical report for me, Private? "Now I see we were wrong. Your dream is to be the Great Pimp of Peru."

"You *are* wrong. Ever since I was born I've only wanted to be a soldier, but a soldier-administrator, which is every bit as important as an artilleryman or infantryman. This is the Army right here," Captain Pantoja examines the rustic office, the kerosene lamp, the mosquito nets, the grass growing in the cracks between the floorboards, touches his chest. "You laugh and so does Baca-

corzo. I guarantee you someday you'll be surprised. We'll function throughout the country, with a flotilla of boats, buses and hundreds of specialists."

"I've put the most energetic officers at the head of the search parties," Colonel Augusto Valdés follows and directs by radio the deployment of the expedition, changes the positions of the little flags on the map, talks with the doctors. "With the anger they've got eating at them, the soldiers'll have to be restrained. Otherwise they'll lynch the fanatics on the road. As for Subofficer Miranda, it looks like he'll be saved, General. Saved, but he'll be without an arm and a little lame."

"It'll be necessary to create a new branch of the Army," Captain Mendoza receives the statistical report, rereads it, corrects it, points to his fly. "Artillery, Cavalry, Engineers Corps, Quartermaster . . . and Military Lays? Army Brothels?"

"It'll have to be a more discreet name," Captain Pantoja laughs, glimpses through the screen door the trumpeter announcing mess, the soldiers entering the wooden building. "But why not, someday? Who knows?"

"Look, the screwing is over with and there are your chicks singing 'The Mexican Hat Dance,' " Captain Mendoza points toward the *Eve*, to the whistling siren, to the specialists leaning on the rail, to Subofficer Rodríguez, who has climbed up to the command bridge. "Every time I hear your hymn, I shit from laughing so hard, pal. Going back to Iquitos right away?"

"Right away," Pantoja hugs Mendoza, climbs aboard the *Eve* in two strides, shuts the cabin door, falls on the bunk. "On my ear, on my neck, on my nipples. Scratch, nibble, bite."

"Oh, Panta, how tiresome you are," the Brazilian refuses, stamps her foot, draws the curtain, sighs looking at the ceiling, furiously throws her clothes on the floor. "Can't you see I'm tired, I just finished working? And I know already what comes later, the big jealous scene."

"Shush! Shut your beak. You know how, a little higher," Panta bends, stretches, rocks, coos, swoons, melts. "Right there, ohhh, so good."

"But I've got one thing to tell you, Panta," the Brazilian climbs up on the bunk, squats, lies down, catches fire, cools off. "I'm fed

up with you making me lose money with your kink of making them give me only ten."

"Phewww," Pantita calms down, sweats, swallows mouthfuls of air. "Can't you even keep quiet for just this minute?"

"You're to blame for me losing money and I've got to look after my interests," the Brazilian moves away, washes, dresses, opens the porthole, sticks out her head and inhales. "These things you like wear out with the years. And afterwards? All the others had twenty today, twice as many as me."

"Damn it, as if his Service didn't already mean a big enough expenditure for the quartermaster's," Colonel López López receives the telegram, reads it, shakes it. "Know what Pantoja is coming to us for now, General? To study the possibility of giving the specialists a risk bonus when they're out on convoy. It turns out they're afraid of the fanatics."

"But you get twice the percentage they do and that makes up the difference. I've proved it to you, I've made an estimate for you," Pantaleón Pantoja goes up on deck, sees Ciruca and Sandra putting cream on their faces, Freckle sleeping in a rocking chair. "How tired I am, how fast my heart's beating. Did you lose the table I made for you? Besides, have you forgotten that each month I give you fifteen percent of my wages to up your earnings?"

"I know that, Panta," the Brazilian rests her arms on the prow, looks at the trees on the shore, the dirty water, the wake of foam, the pink clouds. "But your salary is a big nothing. Don't get mad, it's the truth. And on the other hand, with that mania of yours, all the others hate me. I don't have even one friend among the girls. Even Chuchupe calls me the Captain's Pet the minute my back's turned."

"You are and it's the great shame of my life," Pantoja walks on deck, asks will we arrive in Iquitos early? Hears Subofficer Rodríguez say of course. "Don't complain so much, it isn't fair. I should be the one whining. Because of you I've broken a rule I'd respected ever since I came of age."

"See? You've begun," the Brazilian smiles at Peludita listening to the radio under an awning on the deck, at a sailor rolling a few butts. "Why aren't you more frank and instead of talking about

principles, realize you're jealous of those ten little soldiers in Lagunas."

"Do you think they'd decrease? Not at all, Tiger; they'd spread like a forest fire," General Scavino dresses like a civilian, roves among the people, reeks of onion and incense, sees the spluttering of the candles, smells the stench of the offerings. "You don't know what the anniversary of the boy martyr was like. A procession such as they've never seen in Iquitos before. The banks along the Moronacocha packed like sardines. And the lagoon the same way. There wasn't room for a launch or a boat."

"I had never failed to do my duty, curse my lot," Pantaleón Pantoja says hi to Knockers and Rita playing cards in the sunlight, leans back on a lifeboat, watches the sun set on the horizon. "I had always been the correct type, the fair type. Before you came into the picture, not even this bloodsucker scene had made me break my system."

"If you tell me you want to insult me over the ten soldiers, I'll put up with it," the Brazilian looks at her watch, makes a face, says it stopped again, winds it. "But if you keep on talking about your system you can go eat shit and I'm going down to the cabin to take a nap."

"This work and you have been the ruin of me," Pantaleón Pantoja suddenly gets upset, does not respond to the salute of the sailor talking to Pichuza, scrutinizes the river, the darkening sky. "If it wasn't for you, I wouldn't have lost my wife, my little daughter."

"How tiresome you are, Panta," the Brazilian takes him by the arm, leads him to the bunk, hands him some sandwiches, a Coca-Cola, peels him an orange, throws the rinds into the river, turns on the light. "Now comes the crying for your wife and daughter? Every time you busy yourself with me, you repent so much there's no putting up with you. Don't be such a fool, sonny."

"I need them, I miss them a lot," Panta eats, drinks, puts on his pajamas, goes to bed, his voice cracks. "The house is so empty without Pocha and without little Gladys. I'm not used to it."

"Come here, honey, c'mere, don't be a crybaby," the Brazilian keeps her slip on, lies down next to Panta, turns off the light, opens

177

her arms. "The only thing wrong with you is you're jealous of those soldiers. Get comfy. Here, let me scratch your head."

"There was even a rumor that Brother Francisco was going to appear in person," General Scavino watches the apostles in white, the faithful kneeling with their arms outstretched, the invalids, the blind, the lepers, the dwarfs, the dying who surround the cross. "Better he didn't. He was going to put us in a fix. It was impossible to order him arrested in front of twenty thousand people ready to die for him. Where the hell is he? No, there're no signs of him."

"Boat is cladle, I Pochita, you Gladys," the Brazilian sings, rocks, looks at the moon crossing the porthole and silvering the end of the bed. "What pletty baby. I sclatch yol head. I give you kisses. You want suck on titty?"

"Now it's on your head, right there. Ach, it flew away," Lieutenant Bacacorzo pushes the door to the Amazon Museum and Aquarium and lets Captain Pantoja go in front of him. "Did it bite you? I think it was a wasp."

"A little lowel, a little slowel," Pantita changes mood, becomes childish, relaxes, mellows, gets comfortable. "On my backy, on necky, on eal. Stay light thele, baby."

"Ahhh, I killed it," Lieutenant Bacacorzo slaps the tank of the marine cow or *manatí*. "Not a wasp—a horsefly. They're dangerous; people say they carry leprosy."

"I must have acidic blood because insects never bite me," Captain Pantoja walks past the crazy dolphin, the white dolphin, the red dolphin, stops in front of the carpenter ant, reads "is nocturnal, very dangerous, in one night it can destroy a small farm, they move in hundreds of thousands, when adult they sprout wings and become potbellied." "On the other hand, my poor mother, it's terrible, she walks out on the street and they eat her alive."

"Do you know these ants here eat toast with salt and bananas?" Lieutenant Bacacorzo passes his finger over the crest of a dissected iguana, over the multicolored feathers of a toucan. "You have to take care of yourself, you're very thin. You must've lost at least twenty pounds these past few months. What's wrong, Captain? Work? Worries?"

"A little of both," Captain Pantoja bends and tries vainly to catch sight of the eyes of the great, jumping and venomous black

widow spider. "When everybody tells me, it must be true. I'm going to put myself on a diet to fatten up, to regain the lost pounds."

"I regret it very much, Tiger, but I've had to order the troops to assist the police in capturing the fanatics," General Scavino receives petitions, complaints, accusations, investigates, vacillates, consults, makes a decision, informs. "Four people crucified in six months is too much. These crazy people are changing the Amazon into uncivilized territory and the time has come to use an iron hand."

"You're not taking advantage of your bachelorhood," Lieutenant Bacacorzo grasps the magnifying glass, enlarges the *huayranga* wasp, the bell wasp and the *shiro-shiro* wasp. "Instead of being happy and satisfied with the freedom you've regained, you go around gloomier than a bat."

"It's just that bachelorhood isn't much good to me," Captain Pantoja goes ahead to the big-cat section and rubs up against the stuffed black tiger, the *otorongo* or prince of the jungle, the ocelot, the puma and the spotted wildcat. "I know most men get fed up with the monotony of family life after a while and would give anything to get rid of their wives. That wouldn't have been the case with me. Truth is, it hurt me when Pocha left. And especially taking away my little girl."

"No need to say it hurt you; it shows in your face," "Young chameleons live in trees, larger ones in the water," Lieutenant Bacacorzo hears. "Well, such is life, Captain. Had any news from your wife?"

"Yes, she writes me every week. She's living with her sister Chichi back there in Chiclayo," Captain Pantoja counts the snakes, the river boa or mother of the waters, the black boa, the *mantona*, the *sachamama* or mother of the jungle. "I'm not annoyed with Pocha, I understand her very well. My assignment turned out to be very irritating to her. No decent woman would have put up with it. What're you laughing at? It's no joke, Bacacorzo."

"Excuse me, but it *is* funny," Lieutenant Bacacorzo lights a cigarette, blows the smoke between the bars of the *paucar's* cage, reads: "It imitates the song of the other birds and laughs and cries like children." "You're so picky, so strict when it comes to moral

179

questions. And with the worst reputation that can be imagined. Here in Iquitos they all think you're some terrible escaped criminal."

"Why wasn't she right to leave, ma'am—don't shut your eyes," Alicia hands the skein of wool to Mother Leonor, makes a ball, begins to knit. "Mothers put their daughters under lock and key when they see your Pantita passing by, they cross themselves and give him the horns. Realize it once and for all and pity Pocha instead."

"You think I don't know it?" Captain Pantoja entertains himself feeding the exotic fish, seeing iridescent neon tetras phosphoresce. "The Army gave me a bad deal when they entrusted this work to me."

"No one would guess you regret it, seeing you work in the Special Service with so much drive," Lieutenant Bacacorzo observes the blue tetra, the scaly window-washers and the carnivorous piranha. "Yes, I know—your sense of duty."

"The first two patrols have returned, General," Colonel Peter Casahuanqui receives the men from the expedition at the door of the barracks, congratulates them, invites them to have a beer, silences the shouting prisoners, orders them locked up in the guardhouse. "They've got half a dozen fanatics, one of them with tertian fever. They were part of the crucifixion of that old lady in Dos de Mayo. Do I keep them here, hand them over to the police, dispatch them to Iquitos?"

"Listen, you still haven't told me why you made an appointment with me in this museum, Bacacorzo," Captain Pantoja measures the *paiche* with his eye, the largest known fresh water fish in the world.

"To give you the bad news in the midst of ophidians and arachnids," Lieutenant Bacacorzo glances indifferently at the eel, the manta ray, at the turtles or water tortoises. "Scavino wants to see you urgently. He's expecting you at command headquarters at ten. Be careful, I'm warning you he's fuming."

"Only the impotent, the eunuchs, the asexual can pretend that" —*The Voice of Sinchi* rises and falls among arpeggios, declaims, becomes furious—"the brave defenders of the Homeland, who

180

sacrifice themselves by serving there on our complicated borders, live in spinsterish chastity."

"He's always fuming, at least with me," Captain Pantoja goes out on the embankment, looks at the water sparkling under the murderous sun, the motorboats and rafts coming into the port of Bethlehem. "Do you know what the tantrum is about this time?"

"About Sinchi's damned broadcast yesterday," General Scavino does not respond to his salute, does not ask him to sit down, puts on a tape and turns on the recorder. "The scoundrel didn't do anything but talk about you; he devoted the thirty minutes of his program to you. Seem like such a small thing to you, Pantoja?"

"Must our valiant soldiers resort to debilitating onanism?" *The Voice of Sinchi* questions, dances to the beat of the waltz "La Contamanina," waits for a reply, asks again, "Return to infantile self-gratification?"

"*The Voice of Sinchi?*" Captain Pantoja hears the recorder crackle, stammer, go dead, sees General Scavino shake it, hit it, try all the buttons. "Are you sure, General, sir? He attacked me again?"

"He defended you, he defended you again," General Scavino finds that the plug has come loose, mutters what a fool, connects the machine again. "And it's a thousand times worse than if he attacked you. Don't you see? This makes the Army look ridiculous and slings mud at it at the same time."

"Yes, I've followed them to the letter, General, sir," Colonel Máximo Dávila confers with the second lieutenant in charge of the quartermaster unit, reviews the provisions storehouse, draws up menus with the mess sergeant. "Only a serious problem of provisioning has come up: there are fifty detained fanatics and if I feed them, I'll have to ration the troops. I don't know what to do, General."

"I've categorically forbidden him to even mention me," Captain Pantoja sees a little yellow light go on, the reels turn, hears metallic sounds, echoes, becomes furious. "I'm at a loss for words. I promise you that—"

"Shut up and listen," General Scavino orders, folds his arms,

181

crosses his legs, looks at the tape recorder with hatred. "It's enough to make you vomit."

"The highest government officials ought to decorate Mr. Pantaleón Pantoja with the Order of the Sun," *The Voice of Sinchi* bursts forth, sparkles between Lux the Soap That Perfumes, Coca-Cola the Pause That Refreshes and Pepsodent Smiles, dramatizes and demands. "For the praiseworthy labor he carries out in procuring the satisfaction of the intimate necessities of the guardians of Peru."

"My wife heard it, and my daughters had to give her smelling salts," General Scavino turns the tape recorder off, crosses the room with his hands behind his back. "He's turning us into the laughingstock of all Iquitos with his hot-air harangues. Didn't I order you to take steps so *The Voice of Sinchi* wouldn't talk about the Special Service anymore?"

"The only way to plug up that person's mouth is to shoot him or pay him off," Pantaleón Pantoja listens to the radio, sees the specialists arranging their suitcases for going on board, Chuchupe getting on the *Delilah.* "Putting me in charge of it would make a mess; there's no other way out than greasing his palm with some cash. Go tell him to get here, Freckle, however long it takes."

"You mean you allocate part of the Special Service's budget to bribing journalists?" General Scavino looks him up and down, spreads his nostrils, wrinkles his forehead, shows his incisors. "Very interesting, Captain."

"I've got the people who crucified Subofficer Miranda here on ice," Colonel Augusto Valdés pulverizes the patrols, doubles the hours of duty, cancels leaves and passes, extenuates, infuriates his men. "Yes, he's identified most of them. Only with so much mobilization of my people after the Brothers of the Ark, I've got an unprotected border. I know there's no danger, but if some enemy wanted to attack, they'd push us back to Iquitos in a minute, General, sir."

"No, not from the budget—that's sacred," Captain Pantoja makes out a mouse running quickly across the window sill a few inches from General Scavino's head. "You have a copy of the accounting and you can check it. From my own salary. I've had to sacrifice five percent monthly of my salary to shut that blackmailer

up. I don't understand why he's done this."

"For the sake of professional scruples, for the sake of moral indignation, for the sake of human solidarity, Pantoja, my friend," Sinchi comes into the logistics center slamming the door, climbs the stairs of the command post like a gust of wind, tries to embrace Mr. Pantoja, takes off his jacket, sits on the desk, laughs, thunders, harangues. "Because I can't stand the fact that there are people, here in this city where my sainted mother brought me into the world, who scorn your work and sling mud at you all day long."

"Our agreement was very clear and you've broken it," Pantaleón Pantoja bangs a ruler against a panel, has flaming eyes and lips wet with saliva, grinds his teeth. "What the hell do you think I pay you five hundred a month for? For you to forget I exist, that the Special Service exists."

"But I'm human too, Mr. Pantoja, and I know how to assume my responsibilities," Sinchi asserts, calms him down, gestures, hears the propeller roar, sees the *Delilah* racing downriver raising two walls of water, sees it lift off, disappear into the sky. "I have feelings, drives, emotions. Wherever I go, I hear you insulted and I get worked up. I cannot allow them to slander such a gentleman. Especially since we're friends."

"I'm going to give you a very serious warning, you big cheat," Pantaleón Pantoja grabs him by the shirt, dances him backward and forward, dances him forward and backward, sees him getting frightened, reddening, trembling, lets him go. "You already know what happened last time, with your attacks against the Service. I had to hold the specialists back; they wanted to tear out your eyes and nail you up in the Army Plaza."

"I know only too well, Pantoja, my friend," Sinchi rearranges his shirt, tries to smile, regains his aplomb, his neck muscles tighten. "Do you think I didn't find out that they had nailed up my picture on the gate to Pantiland and spit at it when they came in and went out?"

"The truth is, Tiger, it's a huge problem," General Scavino imagines uprisings, artillery charges, dead and wounded, bloody newspaper headlines, discharges, verdicts, sentencings and tears. "In three weeks we've laid our hands on nearly five hundred fanatics who were hiding in the jungle. But now I don't know what

183

to do with them. It'd cause a scandal to send them to Iquitos. There'd be demonstrations; thousands of 'brothers' are walking around free. What does the general staff think?"

"But now they're happy with the compliments I pay them on my program, Mr. Pantoja," Sinchi puts on his jacket, goes as far as the banister, says goodbye to Chino Porfirio, returns to the desk, pats Mr. Pantoja's shoulders, crosses his fingers and swears. "When they see me on the street, they blow kisses at me. C'mon, Pan-Pan, my friend, let's not turn this into a tragedy. I wanted to help you. But if you prefer, *The Voice of Sinchi* will never mention you ever again."

"Because the first time you name me or speak about the Service, I'll throw all fifty specialists on top of you, and let me warn you, they all have long fingernails," Pantaleón Pantoja opens a desk drawer, takes out a revolver, loads and unloads it, spins the cylinder, takes aim at the blackboard, the telephone, the rafters. "And if they don't put an end to you, I'll finish you off myself, with one shot in the head. Understood?"

"Perfectly, Pantoja, my friend, not another word," Sinchi multiplies salutes, smiles, goodbyes, backs down the stairs, starts to run, disappears down the trail to Iquitos. "Clear as daylight. Who's Mr. Pan-Pan? No one knows him, he doesn't exist, he's never been heard of. And the Special Service? What's that, how is it eaten? Right? Sure we understand each other. Five hundred this month, like always, with Freckle?"

"No, no, surely not that," Mother Leonor whispers with Alicia, runs to the Augustine Fathers, listens to the director's secrets, comes home choking, receives Pantoja protesting. "You appeared in church with one of those harlots! And in the Church of St. Augustine, no less! Father José María has told me."

"First hear me out and try to understand, Mama," Panta tosses his cap into the clothes closet, goes to the kitchen, drinks some papaya juice with ice, wipes his mouth. "I never do it, I never show myself in the city with any of them. It was a very special situation."

"Father José María saw you two entering arm in arm, completely at ease," Mother Leonor fills the bathtub with cold water, tears the wrapping off a bar of soap, puts out clean towels. "At

184

eleven in the morning, just when all the ladies of Iquitos are going to mass."

"Because that's the hour for baptisms. It's not my fault; let me explain," Pantita takes off his sport shirt, pants, undershirt, shorts, puts on a bathrobe, slippers, enters the bathroom, disrobes, sinks into the bath water, half closes his eyes and murmurs how refreshing it is. "Knockers is one of my oldest and most able workers. I was obliged to do it."

"We can't manufacture martyrs; the ones they make are enough," Tiger Collazos checks over notebooks of newspaper clippings marked with red pencil, holds private meetings with officers from the Intelligence Service, the Police Bureau of Investigation, proposes a plan to the municipal government and executes it. "Keep them there in the barracks for a couple of weeks, on bread and water. Then scare them and let them go, Scavino. Except for ten or twelve leaders: send them to Lima."

"Knockers," Mother Leonor flutters around the bedroom, the hall, sticks her head into the bathroom, sees Panta moving his feet and splashing the floor. "Just look at the kind of people you work with, the kind you go around with. Knockers . . . Knockers! How is it possible for you to show yourself in church with that fallen woman, who, on top of everything else, has that awful name. I don't know which saint to pray to anymore. I've even gone on my knees to beg the boy martyr to take you out of this den of iniquity."

"She asked me to be her little boy's godfather and I couldn't refuse, Mama," Pantita soaps his head, face, body, rinses off in the shower, wraps himself in towels, jumps out of the bathtub, dresses himself, puts on deodorant, combs his hair. "Knockers and Chameleon made the friendly gesture of giving my name to the baby. His name's Pantaleón; I christened him myself."

"Such an honor for the family," Mother Leonor goes to the kitchen, brings a mop and rags, dries the bathroom, goes into the bedroom, hands Panta a shirt, a newly ironed pair of pants. "Since you have to do that dreadful work, at least do what you promised me. Don't walk around with them, so people won't see you."

"I know, Mama, don't be a pest, upsy-daisy, up to the ceiling, upsy-daisy," Panta gets dressed, throws dirty clothes into a ham-

185

per, smiles, moves close to Mother Leonor, hugs her, lifts her up into the air. "Oh, I forgot to show you. Look, a letter came from Pocha. She sends photos of little Gladys."

"Let's see—hand me my glasses," Mother Leonor straightens her skirt, blouse, snatches the envelope, goes over to the window. "Oh, how cute, my pretty little granddaughter, look how fat she's gotten. When are you going to give me what I ask for, Holy Christ of Bagazán? I spend my afternoons in church praying, I say novenas so you'll take us out of here, and you don't do anything."

"You've gotten so pious in Iquitos, old woman; in Chiclayo you didn't even go to mass, you only played canasta," Panta sits in a wicker rocking chair, leafs through a newspaper, solves a crossword puzzle, laughs. "I think your prayers don't work because you mix the Church up with superstition: the boy martyr, the Holy Christ of Bagazán, the Lord of Miracles, Santa Ignacia."

"Don't forget, it'll be necessary to divert people and money for the pursuit and repression of the crazy people from the Ark," Colonel López López takes planes, jeeps and launches, travels through the Amazon region, returns to Lima, makes the officers in Accounting and Finance work overtime, edits a report, appears at Tiger Collazos' office. "That means large expenses for the Army. And the Special Service is bleeding us dry; it operates at a complete loss. Aside from other problems.

"Here's Pocha's letter. There's only four lines; I'll read it to you," Panta hears music, strolls with Mother Leonor through the Army Plaza, works in his bedroom until midnight, sleeps for six hours, gets up at the crack of dawn. "They've gone to Pimentel, with Chichi, to spend the summer at the beach. She doesn't say anything about coming back, Mama."

"Starting from scratch," Tiger Collazos shoves his kepi on his head, lets General Victoria and Colonel López López go out in front of him, sits in the front seat of the car, orders the chauffeur to Rosita Ríos fast. "Yeah, sure, it's one of the possible solutions, the one Scavino would choose right away. But isn't it a little rash? I don't see the reason or the urgency for declaring the Special Service a failure. After all, the incidents it's brought on are insignificant."

"I'm not concerned with the negative things about the Special

Service, but the positive ones, Tiger," General Victoria chooses a table in the open air, sits at the head, loosens his tie, studies the menu attentively. "What's serious are its fantastic successes. As far as I'm concerned, the problem lies in the fact that, without wanting to or knowing it, we've set an infernal machine in motion. López has just traveled through all the jungle garrisons and his report is disturbing."

"I see myself with the immediate necessity of recruiting ten specialists with all speed," telegraphs Captain Pantoja. "Not to expand the Service, but to maintain the rate of work achieved up to present."

"The truth is that Pantoja's specialists have become the central concern of all the garrisons, encampments and frontier posts," Colonel López López orders shish kebab and corn on the cob to start with and marinated duck with extra chili for the second course. "I'm not exaggerating in the least, General, sir. Believe me, I could scarcely talk about anything else with the officers, subordinates and soldiers. Even the Ark crimes take second place when it comes to the specialists."

"The reason is the many patrols and groups for the search and capture of the religious murderers," Captain Pantoja puts in code. "As my superiors know, those commandos are hidden in the mountains, developing a civilian police action of the first order."

"The proof's here in this suitcase, Tiger," General Victoria decides in favor of the marinated fish and the kidneys with white rice. "Guess what these papers are. Reports on the state of air-land-river defense of our borders with Ecuador, Colombia, Brazil and Bolivia? Cold. Suggestions and plans to improve our own security and attack system in the Amazon? Cold. Studies on communications, logistics, ethnography? Cold, cold."

"The Special Service took it as its duty to have convoys of specialists travel to these commandos wherever they may be found," radios Captain Pantoja. "And we've achieved just that, thanks to the enthusiastic effort of all the personnel, without exception."

"Only requests concerning the SSGFRI, General," concludes Colonel López López. "Honey and nut pastry for dessert, and to drink, Pilsen beer, very cold. All the subordinate officers in the Amazon region have signed memos asking that they be allowed to

187

use the Special Service. Here they are in order: 172 sheets."

"For this purpose, I have created flying brigades of two or three specialists and that fragmentation of the personnel would have prevented me from continuing to ensure the regular covering of the utilization centers," telephones Captain Pantoja. "I hope I haven't overstepped my authority, General."

"And López López's poll of the officers is even more unbelievable," General Victoria pushes with a small piece of bread, accompanies each mouthful with swallows of beer, wipes his forehead with his napkin. "From captains on down, ninety-five percent of the officers also demand specialists. And from captains upward, fifty-five percent. What do you say to that, Tiger?"

"In accordance with the figures Colonel López López has communicated to me concerning his unofficial poll, I must totally modify my minimal plan to increase the SSGFRI, General, sir," Captain Pantoja winces, scribbles in notebooks, takes amphetamines in order to be at the command post at dawn, sends voluminous registered envelopes. "I beg you to consider the project I sent you null and never received. I am working night and day on a new plan. I hope to send it to you very soon."

"Because, in addition, I'm sorry to tell you that Pantoja, although he's crazy, is absolutely right, Tiger," General Victoria attacks the kidneys energetically, jokes the French are right, if you find the proper rhythm you can eat any number of dishes, eighteen, twenty. "His argument is irrefutable."

"In view of the potential doubling of the number of users, if we are going to include the subordinate officers and intermediate ranks"—Captain Pantoja discusses with Chuchupe, Freckle and Chino Porfirio, reviews the candidates, fires "washerwomen," talks to pimps, bribes madames—"I should communicate to you that the minimal plan for regular services, always at a rate below the minimum sexual drive, would require four boats of the *Eve*'s tonnage, three planes like the *Delilah* and an operational corps of 272 specialists."

"If that Service is conceded to noncommissioned officers and soldiers, why not to subordinate officers?" Colonel López López separates the onions, the bones, and finishes the marinated duck in several bites, smiles, watches a woman walk by, winks and

188

exclaims what a knockout. "And if to them, why not to the officers? Everybody raises the question. And honestly, there's no answer to it."

"Naturally, if the expansion to officers is considered, my estimates would register new variations, General, sir," Captain Pantoja visits witch doctors, takes *ayahuasca,* has hallucinations in which armies of women march across the parade grounds singing "The Mexican Hat Dance," vomits, works, exults. "I'm making a feasibility study, just in case. We'd have to create a special section, a group of exclusive specialists, of course."

"Of course," General Victoria refuses dessert, asks for coffee, takes out a bottle of saccharine, drops in two tablets, drinks the cup down in one gulp, lights a cigarette. "And if the Service is considered indispensable to the troops' biological and psychological health, it'll be necessary to increase the number of services each month. Because as you well know, Tiger, exercise builds the muscle. In this case, the demand will always exceed the supply."

"That's the way it is, General, sir," Colonel López López asks for the check, attempts to take out his wallet, hears are you crazy, you're Tiger's guests today. "Wanting to plug one hole, we've opened up a sieve and the whole quartermaster's budget's going to pour through it."

"And all our soldiers' energy," General Scavino is transferred on special assignment to Lima, visits politicians, requests hearings, advises, intrigues, arranges, returns to Iquitos.

"Christ himself couldn't put a stop to that hunger for specialists that's been awakened in the jungle, Tiger," General Victoria opens the car door, gets out first, says it's a shame not to be able to take a little nap after this lunch, orders back to the ministry. "Or, to be in style, not even the boy martyr. By the way, do you know that the cult has already reached Lima? Yesterday I discovered that my daughter-in-law has a little altar with prayer cards of the boy martyr."

"We could begin with a corps of ten specialists for officers, General, sir," Captain Pantoja talks to himself on the street, falls asleep at his desk, fantasizes, terrifies Mother Leonor with his thinness. "We'd recruit them in Lima, of course, to guarantee high quality. Do you like the initials SFO of the SSGFRI? Section For Officers

189

of the Special Service. I'll send you a detailed draft."

"Damn it, I think you're right," Tiger Collazos enters his office, ponders, opens his mail, bites a fingernail. "This shit's going too far."

9

Special edition of the daily newspaper *El Oriente*
(Iquitos, January 5, 1959), devoted
to the catastrophe in Nauta

Extraordinary report from the entire editorial staff of El
Oriente, *under the intellectual guidance of editor in chief
Joaquín Andoa, to bring to the readers of Loreto the lively,
accurate details of the tragic case of the beautiful Brazilian
—from her assault at Nauta to her burial in Iquitos—with all
the incidents that have electrified the populace*

Weeping and Surprises Accompany
Remains of Murdered Beauty

Yesterday morning at approximately 11 A.M., the mortal
remains of Olga Arellano Rosaura, known to the demi-
monde as the "Brazilian," because of her years of resi-
dence in the city of Manaos (see her biography, p. 2, cols.
3 & 4), were interred in this city's historic public cemetery
amid scenes of grief and distress from her fellow workers
and friends that moved the large crowd. Earlier, an infan-
try escort from the Vargas Guerra Military Encampment
gave the deceased military honors, in an unusual gesture
that did not fail to provoke considerable surprise, even

191

that did not fail to provoke considerable surprise, even among those most saddened by the tragic manner in which this young and misguided Loreto beauty had lost her life, a woman whom *Capt. (sic)* Pantaleón Pantoja, in his eulogy, called "an unfortunate martyr to the fulfillment of duty and a victim of man's baseness and villainy" (complete eulogy, p. 3, col. 1).

Knowing that the hapless young woman's burial was going to be celebrated yesterday morning, many curiosity seekers had congregated near the cemetery, at Alfonso Ugarte and Ramon Castilla streets, since the early hours, blocking the main entrance and the area surrounding the Monument to the Nation's War Dead. Around 10:30 A.M., those present were able to glimpse the arrival of a truck from the Vargas Guerra Military Encampment, from which descended an escort of twelve soldiers wearing helmets and Sam Browne belts and carrying rifles, under the command of Infantry Lt. Luis Bacacorzo, who posted his men on both sides of the entrance gate to the cemetery. This operation unleashed the curiosity of those present, who were unable to guess the reason for an Army escort at that time and place and under such circumstances. The mystery was to be clarified moments later. In view of the fact that the crowd of curiosity-seekers and the general public completely blocked access to the cemetery, Lt. Bacacorzo ordered the soldiers to clear the gate, which they did immediately.

At 10:45 A.M., the deluxe hearse from Iquitos' principal funeral home, Modus Vivendi, appeared, coming down Alfonso Ugarte Street completely covered with wreaths and followed by a large number of taxis and private vehicles. Only moments before, the funeral cortege, which advanced very slowly, had left the area of the Itaya River called the Special Service—commonly known as "Pantiland"—where an all-night wake for the ill-fated Olga Arellano Rosaura had been held. An impressive silence immediately spread through the area and the crowd spontaneously made way so the cortege could reach the

192

cemetery entrance. A large number of people—one hundred, according to observers' estimates—accompanied the unfortunate Olga to her final resting place, many of them—especially her fellow workers, the specialists and "washerwomen" of Iquitos—dressed in black and showing signs of grief. Notable among the members of the funeral cortege were the women employed by the institution of ill repute on the Itaya River, who understandably expressed the greatest suffering, shedding hot tears under their veils and black mantillas. An emotional and dramatic note was struck by the fact that among the specialists present in the first row were the five women who, along with the deceased "Brazilian," had undergone the grave events at Nauta in which she lost her life, including Luisa Cánepa (a.k.a. "Knockers"), who, as our readers know, suffered wounds and rather serious contusions at the hands of her assailants during the sorrowful affair (see p. 4 for a detailed summary of the ambush at Nauta and its bloody outcome). But the greatest surprise for the citizens gathered at the funeral was to see descending from the funeral hearse, dressed in the uniform of a captain in the Peruvian Army, the promoter and head of the so-called Special Service, the well-known and little esteemed Mr. Pantaleón Pantoja, whose position as an officer in the Army had been realized by no one until now—at least as far as this paper knows. Naturally, this revelation gave rise to varying comments among the public.

As the coffin was being lowered from the hearse, it became apparent that it had the cross shape, customary for dead members of the Brotherhood of the Ark. This discovery must have surprised many people, since the suspicion exists that members of this religious sect were responsible for the death of the "Brazilian"—a conjecture that has been energetically denied by the high priest of the Ark (see "Epistle to the Good Concerning the Wicked" by Brother Francisco, which we publish on p. 3, cols. 3 & 4). The coffin was lowered from the hearse and carried into the cemetery on the shoulders of Capt. Pantoja and his

collaborators in the unpopular Special Service, all of whom were dressed in strict mourning: Porfirio Wong, known as the "Chink" in the district of Bethlehem; First Subofficer Carlos Rodríguez Saravia, PN (who was commanding the boat *Eve* when the assault at Nauta occurred); Subofficer Alonso Pantinoya, PAF (a.k.a. "Crazy"), famous ex-aerial acrobatic ace; the recruits Sinforoso Caiguas and Palomino Rioalto; and the male nurse Virgilio Pacaya. The sashes of the coffin, whose top displayed an elegant and solitary orchid, were carried by the well-known Leonor Curinchila (a.k.a. "Chuchupe"), and various disciples of that center of wrongdoing on the Itaya River, such as Sandra, Viruca, Pichuza, Peludita and others, as well as the popular Juan Rivera (a.k.a. "Freckle"), who exhibited bandages and other indications of the numerous wounds he received while attempting with typical Loreto bravery to rebuff the aggression at Nauta. The coffin sashes were also held by two women of a certain age and humble origin, in conspicuous mourning, who refused to give their names or indicate what their relation to the deceased was, but whom rumor charges with being relatives of Olga Arellano Rosaura, who preferred to conceal their identity due to the uncommendable activities to which the young crucified woman had devoted her life.

The cortege was barely lined up in the manner we have described when at a signal from Capt. Pantoja, Luis Bacacorzo, in a martial voice, ordered the soldiers in his escort to "Present Arms!" which they instantly did with flair and elegance. Thus, on the shoulders of her colleagues and friends and between a double row of rifles rendering her homage, the unfortunate "Brazilian," who lost her life a short distance from where our river-sea originates, made her entrance into the public cemetery of Iquitos. The coffin was borne to the small podium, next to the Monument to the Nation's War Dead, where a plaque greets the visitor with this somber apostrophe: ENTER, PRAY, LOOK LOVINGLY AT THIS MANSION: IT MAY BE YOUR FINAL REST-

194

ING PLACE. Father Godofredo Beltrán Calila, ex-Army chaplain, now priest in charge of the Iquitos cemetery, was there, giving indications of inexplicable bad humor and annoyance, which were criticized by the crowd. The priest celebrated the funeral litany with exaggerated speed, gave no sermon whatsoever, as had been expected of him, and left the area without waiting for the conclusion of the ceremony. With the religious service over, Capt. Pantaleón Pantoja installed himself before the coffin of the unfortunate Olga Arellano Rosaura and gave the oration we reprint elsewhere in this newspaper (see p. 3, col. 1). This address brought the funeral to its climax of delicate feeling and tender emotion, with Capt. Pantoja interrupted at various moments in his speech by his own sobs, which were chorused, like sad echoes, by those of his aforementioned collaborators and the many harlots in attendance.

Immediately afterward, the coffin was again raised upon the shoulders of the same people who had carried it into the cemetery, while the others, the majority of whom were specialists and "washerwomen," took turns bearing the sashes. In this manner the cortege passed through the cemetery until it reached the southern end, where, in the Pavilion of St. Thomas, section 17, upper niche, the remains of the departed will repose. The placing of the coffin and the installation of the tablet (which reads simply, in gold letters, *Olga Arellano Rosaura, Called the Brazilian (1936–1959): Her Disconsolate Companions*) gave cause for new outpourings of sentiment and suffering over her bloody departure, many women having broken into inconsolable sobbing. The cortege disbanded after an Our Father and a Hail Mary for the eternal well-being of the defunct woman of Loreto were said. Those in attendance began to disperse toward their respective homes when a gentle rain began to fall, as if the heavens had suddenly wanted to take part in the mourning. It was twelve noon.

195

Specialist Crucified at Nauta

Considering it of interest to our readers because of its heart-rending sincerity and startling disclosures, we print below the funeral oration delivered at the burial of the murdered Olga Arellano Rosaura (a.k.a. the "Brazilian") by her friend and employer, the renowned Pantaleón Pantoja, who, to the public's surprise, since yesterday, has turned out to be a captain in the Quartermaster Unit of the Peruvian Army.

Lamented Olga Arellano Rosaura, our beloved and well-remembered Brazilian, as all of us who knew you or worked together with you in our daily business affectionately called you:

We have worn our noble uniform of an officer in the Peruvian Army in order to come and accompany you to what will be your last dwelling place on this earth because, with our head held high and with a full sense of our responsibility, it was our duty to proclaim in the eyes of the world that you had fallen as a valiant soldier in the service of your country, our beloved Peru. We have come here to demonstrate without shame and with pride that we were your friends and superiors and that we felt very honored to share with you the task that destiny had provided us, which was to serve, in a manner that was not at all easy, but rather filled with difficulties and with sacrifices (as you, our respected friend, have experienced in your flesh), our countrymen and our nation. You are an unfortunate martyr to the fulfillment of duty, a victim of the baseness and the villainy of certain men. Goaded by the demon alcohol,

196

the lowest instincts of lasciviousness or the most satanic fanaticism, the cowards who posted themselves at the Cacique Cocama Bend, on the outskirts of Nauta, in order to piratically board our river transport *Eve* by means of despicable deceit and vile lies and then with bestial brutality to satisfy their crude desires, did not know that with generous exclusivity you had consecrated that beauty of yours to the courageous soldiers of Peru.

Lamented Olga Arellano Rosaura, our well-remembered Brazilian: these soldiers, *your* soldiers, do not forget you. Right now, in the most untamed corners of our Amazon, in the streams where the anopheles mosquito is the monarch and the master, in the most distant forest clearings, there where the Peruvian Army has presented itself to demonstrate and defend our sovereignty, and there where you did not hesitate to go, never worrying about the insects, the diseases, the discomfort, but bringing the gift of your beauty and your free and contagious joy to the guardians of Peru, there are men who remember you with tears in their eyes, their chests filled with anger toward your sadistic murderers. They will never forget your kindness, your charming deviltry, and that way you had of sharing with them the rigors of military life, which, thanks to you, were always made more pleasant and tolerable for our noncommissioned officers and soldiers.

Lamented Olga Arellano Rosaura, well-remembered Brazilian, as they named you because you had lived in our sister country, to which your youthful restlessness took you, even though—we must declare it—there was not a single drop of blood in your veins nor one strand of hair on your head that was not Peruvian:

You should know that joining with the melancholy soldiers dispersed throughout the length and breadth of the Amazon, your fellow workers in the Special Service for Garrisons, Frontier and Related Installations also recall and mourn you. You were at all times a sumptuous flower enriching and perfuming the Service's logistics center on the Itaya River, whose staff always admired, respected and

197

loved you for your sense of duty, your untiring good humor, your great spirit of camaraderie and cooperation and the many other virtues with which you were blessed. In the name of them all, I want to say to you, holding back tears, that your sacrifice will not have been in vain: your still-young blood, savagely spilled, will be the sacred bond that unites us henceforward with greater strength and the example that guides us daily and stimulates us to the completion of our duty with the perfection and selflessness with which you performed it. And finally, in my own name, allow me, laying bare my heart, to thank you profoundly for so many expressions of affection and understanding, for so many intimate lessons that I shall never forget.

Lamented Olga Arellano Rosaura, our well-remembered Brazilian: *Rest in Peace!*

Chronicle of the Assault at Nauta

Blow-by-blow Account of the Crime at Cacique Cocama Bend: Its Cortege of Blood, Passion, Necrophiliac Sadism and Base Instincts

ED. NOTE: El Oriente *wants to make public its profound thanks to Police Chief Juan Amézaga Riofrío, Region V, and to the Chief Inspector, Loreto Branch, of the Police Bureau of Investigation (PBI), Federico Chumpitaz Fernández, under whose authority lies the investigation of the tragic events in Nauta, for having supplied us in the friendliest way, sacrificing many minutes of their precious time, with all the information available at the moment concerning said occurrence. We wish to emphasize the attitude of cooperation toward the free and democratic press on the part of these distinguished police chiefs, whom other department authorities should take as an example.*

The Conspiracy of Requena

As the investigation into the events at Nauta moves forward, facts are being uncovered that revise the first versions published in the printed and electronic media. Each passing minute undermines the theory according to which the assault at Nauta and the crucifixion and the death of Olga Arellano Rosaura (a.k.a. the "Brazilian") were a rite of "sacrifice and purification by blood" ordered by the Brotherhood of the Ark, a sect of which the seven suspects could have been mere instruments. As a result, the vehement campaign of our colleague Germán Láudano Rosales, on his program *The Voice of Sinchi,* defending the Brotherhood of the Ark and rejecting as false the criminals' confession to having obeyed the orders of Brother Francisco, is taking on the appearance of the truth. Sinchi's conjecture that the said confession is a tactic of the jailed men to lessen their guilt seems to be backed up by the facts. At the same time, the first interrogations that the accused have undergone in Iquitos—they arrived in this city yesterday by water from Nauta, where they had been detained since January 2—have also allowed the police and the PBI authorities to discard the other rumor that was circulating, according to which the assault at Nauta was a product of a moment's inspiration, the result of the evil influence of alcohol, and to confirm, without any room for doubt, that it was planned with great premeditation, down to its smallest and most macabre details.

Apparently it all began some two weeks before the fateful date, at a social gathering—and not a religious one, as has been said—held in the most innocent way by a group of friends from the lively town of Requena. The party must have taken place last December 14, at the home of the former mayor of the town, Teófilo Morey, on the occasion of the latter's fifty-fourth birthday. During the party, which was attended by all the accused (Artidoro Soma, 23;

199

Nepumuceno Quilca, 31; Caifás Sancho, 28; Fabio Tapayuri, 26; Fabriciano Pizango, 32; and Renán Márquez Curichimba, 22), much liquor was consumed and all the persons named above reached a state of intoxication. It was during said party that former mayor Teófilo Morey, a person very well known in Requena for his sensual appetites, his taste for good food and spirits, as well as for similar things, threw out—according to the statements of several of the codefendants—the idea of ambushing a convoy of specialists en route to some military post in order to forcibly enjoy the charms of these misguided women. (As our readers will recall, the assailants first asserted that the idea of the assault had arisen during a nighttime mass at the Requena Ark, during which seven "brothers" were chosen by lot to execute the mission determined by all those attending the ceremony—more than one hundred, according to them.) The idea was received with approval and enthusiasm by the other accused. All of them have acknowledged that the topic of the specialists arose frequently in their lives and gatherings; that they had sent written protests on several occasions to the high command of the Army, requesting authorization for said loose women to receive civilian clientele in the Amazon towns through which they passed; and that once they even formed a committee, along with other young men from Requena, to the chief of the naval base at Santa Isabel, a neighboring town, to protest the monopoly, unfair in their opinion, that the armed forces had over those expeditions of strumpets. With this background, one can understand how former mayor Teófilo Morey's suggestion, offering them the opportunity to give way to their pent-up desires, was received with rejoicing and genuine frenzy by the accused. It still has been impossible to determine whether the seven conspirators were followers of Brother Francisco and whether they frequently attended the clandestine rites of the Requena Ark, as has been said, or if this is completely false, as has been asserted by several apostles of the sect in communiqués released to the press from

their hiding places and even countersigned by Brother Francisco himself (see p. 3, cols. 3 & 4). It is said that at that same party the seven friends got around to drawing up the preliminary plans and agreed to perpetrate their twisted plot far from Requena, so as not to compromise the town's good name and to throw the authorities off their trail if there was an investigation. At the same time, they decided to make a clandestine check of the arrival dates for the next convoys of specialists to Nauta or Bagazán, whose outskirts they considered the most favorable for making their strike. Former mayor Morey offered to obtain the pertinent facts himself, thanks to the close association he had maintained, owing to his municipal post, with the officers of the Santa Isabel Base.

And setting to work without further ado, the accused perfected their plan in the course of two or three later meetings. Teófilo Morey, in fact, craftily managed to elicit from Navy First Lt. Germán Urioste the information that a river convoy of six specialists, proceeding from Iquitos, would pass through the posts of Nauta, Bagazán and Requena during the early days of January, with an arrival at the first of these points fixed for the day of the 2nd, around noon. Assembled again at the home of the former mayor, the seven individuals perfected their criminal plan, deciding to ambush the convoy on the outskirts of Nauta in order to make the victims and the police think that the perpetrators of the sexual assault were residents of that historic locality.

Apparently at this point they had conceived the idea of leaving a cross with a crucified animal as a red herring in the area near the ambush site in order to create the impression that the operation was the work of the "brothers" of the Nauta Ark. For this purpose, they equipped themselves with the necessary nails and hammers, never suspecting—so they assert—that chance was going to favor their plans horribly, offering them not an animal to crucify, but the body of a young and beautiful prostitute. The seven suspects decided to split up into two groups, each

201

giving a different explanation to family and friends for his absence from Requena. Thus, a group composed of Teófilo Morey, Artidoro Soma, Nepumuceno Quilca and Renán Márquez Curichimba left the town on December 29, in an outboard motorboat belonging to the first of those above-named, causing everyone to believe that they were headed for Lake Carahuite, where they were thinking of spending the end-of-year holidays devoting themselves to the healthy sport of fishing for shad and *gamitana*. The other group—Caifás Sancho, Fabio Tapayuri and Fabriciano Pizango—only left at dawn on January 1, in a glider belonging to the third man, assuring acquaintances that they were going hunting in the vicinity of Bagazán, where a pack of marauding jaguars had recently been discovered not far from the town.

Just as they had planned, the two groups headed downstream toward Nauta, passing that town without stopping, exactly as they had done at Bagazán, since their objective was to reach, without being seen, a point situated some three kilometers below the source of the Amazon, our great river-sea, that is, the Cacique Cocama Bend, named for the legend which tells how on days of heavy downpour there can be seen floating near the shore in this area the ghost of the famous Cocama chieftain Manuel Pacaya—the same man who at the juncture of the Marañón and Ucayali rivers pioneered in founding the progressive town of Nauta on April 30, 1840. The seven accused had selected this site in spite of the fear the above-mentioned superstition inspired in some of them, because the abundant vegetation that covers part of the riverbed was very useful to their purpose of passing unperceived. The two groups met at the Cacique Cocama Bend at dusk on January 1, camping there on low-lying ground and enjoying themselves that night in a makeshift party. Cleverly, they had set out provisioned not only with revolvers, carbines, nails and blankets for sleeping, but also with bottles of anisette and beer for each one, which enabled them to get drunk, and meanwhile, doubtlessly very excited and gar-

rulous, they grew ecstatic while thinking of the new day that would see their sick machinations and desires transformed into reality.

Piracy at Cacique Cocama Bend

From very early in the morning, the seven suspects were up in the trees, watching the waters of the Amazon. To keep a sharper eye on the river, they had provided themselves with binoculars, which were passed from hand to hand. They spent a good part of the day that way, because only at 4 P.M. did Fabio Tapayuri glimpse in the distance the red and green colors of the boat *Eve* navigating the ·yellow waters of the river-sea with its coveted cargo. The individuals immediately proceeded to execute their crafty plan. While four of them —Teófilo Morey, Fabio Tapayuri, Fabriciano Pizango and Renán Márquez Curichimba—hid the motorboat in the undergrowth along the shore and remained hidden there themselves, Artidoro Soma, Nepumuceno Quilca and Caifás Sancho climbed into the glider and went out to the center of the current in order to play their shrewd scene. Moving at a very slow speed, they approached the *Eve,* while Soma and Quilca began to wave and shout loudly, asking for help for Caifás Sancho, who they said needed urgent medical attention for a snakebite. On hearing the suspects' outcry, First Subofficer Carlos Rodríguez Saravia ordered the boat to a full stop and had them lift the sick man aboard the *Eve* (since it is provided with a small pharmacy), with the laudable purpose of giving help to the faker Caifás Sancho.

Scarcely had the three suspects managed by means of said ruse to get aboard, when they dropped their peaceful masks, took out the revolvers they had hidden on them and ordered Subofficer Rodríguez Saravia and his four men to obey their commands. While Artidoro Soma forced the group of six specialists (Luisa Cánepa, "Knockers"; Juana Barbichi Lu, "Sandra"; Eduviges Lauri, "Eduviges"; Ernesta Sipote, "Loreta"; María Carrasco Lunchu, "Flor";

203

and the unfortunate Olga Arellano Rosaura, the "Brazilian") and Juan Chupito Rivera, "Freckle," who commanded the group, to remain locked in a cabin, Nepumuceno Quilca and Caifás Sancho, with gross insults and death threats, forced the crew of the *Eve* to start up the boat and head it into the bend, where the rest of the band were lying in wait. It was in these circumstances, while the maneuver ordered by the assailants was being executed, that the quick-witted helmsman, Isidoro Ahuanari Leiva, managed to leave the deck for a moment by means of an ingenious lie (a natural bodily function) and to enter the radio post and fire out a desperate S.O.S. to the Nauta Base, which, although it did not fully understand the message, decided to send a glider with a pilot and two soldiers downstream immediately to see what was happening to the *Eve*. The boat, meanwhile, had stopped at the Cacique Cocama Bend, a strategically selected site, since owing to the abundant underbrush, the *Eve* remained half hidden and was not easily recognizable from the center of the current by the fishermen's launches and motorboats traveling our river-sea.

Cowardly Assault: Rapes and Wounds

One after the other, the steps of the criminals' Machiavellian plot were carried out with mathematical precision. Once the boat was at the Cacique Cocama Bend, the four men who had remained on land hastened to climb aboard. Along with their companions in crime, they roughly bound and gagged Subofficer Rodríguez Saravia as well as the four crewmen, who they then locked, pushing and shoving, in the ship's hold, saying hurriedly that they were there on orders from the Ark to teach a lesson on account of the sinful activities of the Special Service. Immediately, the seven pirates—who, according to the testimony of their victims, showed evidence of an advanced state of drunkenness and trembling nervousness—headed toward the cabin where they had locked up the specialists in order to satisfy their wild desires.

204

At that instant, the first bloody act occurred. Upon discovering the men's criminal intentions, the adventuresses offered strong resistance, following the example of the brave Juan Chupito Rivera ("Freckle"), who, without becoming frightened and without holding back because of his short stature or physical weakness, rushed the pirates, butting and kicking while rebuking their bad conduct; but, unfortunately, his quixotic action did not last very long, since they quickly knocked him unconscious, hitting him with their revolver butts and kicking him to the floor until they mangled his face. A similar fate was suffered by Specialist Luisa Cánepa ("Knockers"), who also showed a great deal of strength, confronting the kidnappers like a man, scratching and biting them until they hit her with such force that she lost her senses. Once the resistance of the erring women was brought under control, the pirates forced them, at the point of their revolvers and carbines, to gratify their perverted desires, for which each assailant chose a victim, a fight almost breaking out among them when they all aspired to possess the unfortunate Olga Arellano Rosaura, who, finally, was given to Teófilo Morey in consideration of his greater age.

Shooting and Rescue: Specialist Beauty Dies

Meanwhile, during the space of time that the seven individuals were conducting their violent orgy, the glider sent from the naval base at Nauta had traveled a good stretch of the river without finding signs of the *Eve*. Its crew was preparing to return when the red glow of sunset miraculously permitted recognition of the boat's red and green colors among the trees of the Cacique Cocama Bend in the distance. The glider headed immediately for a rendezvous and to the group's stupefaction was greeted with a shower of bullets, one of which wounded Pvt. Felicio Tanchiva in the thigh and lower left buttock. Having barely recovered from the shock, the soldiers returned fire. An exchange of shooting then broke out that lasted for several minutes, during which time Olga Arellano Rosaura

205

(the "Brazilian") fell mortally wounded—from shots fired by the soldiers, according to the findings of the autopsy. Seeing that they were in the weaker position, the soldiers decided to return to Nauta in search of reinforcements.

When they observed that the patrol was departing, the criminals were seized by panic over the death that had occurred and showed great confusion. The first to react, apparently, was Teófilo Morey, who exhorted his buddies to stay calm, pointing out to them that while the patrol headed for Nauta, they had time not only to flee but even to carry out their plan. It was then that someone—it has not become clear who: Morey himself, according to some, Fabio Tapayuri, according to others—suggested that they crucify the "Brazilian" instead of an animal. The criminals proceeded to execute their bloody scheme, throwing the corpse of Olga Arellano Rosaura ashore and deciding not to construct a cross but to use any tree in order to save time. They were in the midst of their macabre work when four gliders full of soldiers became visible on the horizon. The criminals fled immediately, hiding in the undergrowth. Only two of them—Nepumuceno Quilca and Renán Márquez Curichimba—were captured at that time. Climbing aboard the *Eve,* the soldiers met with a spine-tingling spectacle: terrorized and semi-naked women running around in a state of hysteria, some with signs on their faces and bodies ("Knockers") of having suffered extreme cruelty, and, a little farther on, a few steps from the shore, the beautiful body of Olga Arellano Rosaura nailed to the trunk of a tree. The shots had hit the hapless woman at the start of the skirmish, penetrating vital organs, such as the heart and brain, and instantaneously cutting short her days. The unlucky woman was taken down, covered with blankets and lifted onto the boat, in the midst of the other victims' terror and frantic weeping.

Directly after the rescue, First Subofficer Rodríguez Saravia and the crew alerted Nauta, Requena and Iquitos by radio as to what had happened, immediately mobiliz-

206

ing all the posts, naval bases and garrisons of the region in an immense search for the five fugitives. All were captured within twenty-four hours. Three of them—Teófilo Morey, Artidoro Soma and Fabio Tapayuri—were caught at nightfall on the outskirts of Nauta, which they attempted to enter surreptitiously after having traveled through many kilometers of undergrowth, ripping their clothes and lacerating their bodies. The other two—Caifás Sancho and Fabriciano Pizango—were captured in the early morning hours while going up the Ucayali in a glider stolen from the port of Nauta. One of them, Caifás Sancho, was rather seriously wounded when a bullet tore away part of his mouth.

The victims of the attack were transferred to Nauta, where Luisa Cánepa and "Freckle" received the medical attention they required, both showing a great deal of spirit and liveliness despite their injuries. The victims' first statements about the terrible experience they had just lived through were taken on the spot. Due to judicial proceedings, the corpse of the unfortunate Olga Arellano Rosaura could only be brought to Iquitos on the 4th, by air, in the hydroplane *Delilah*. Still only a *Mr.* at that time, Capt. Pantaleón Pantoja had himself transferred to Nauta in order to accompany the remains and make the preliminary investigation. The rest of the specialists returned to Iquitos by water, on the *Eve*, which had not sustained major damages during the assault, while the seven arrested men were held in Nauta for two more days and subjected to exhaustive interrogation by the authorities. Yesterday, under a heavy escort, they arrived in Iquitos on a PAF hydroplane and they are currently in the cells of the central jail on Sergeant Lores Street, where, without doubt, they will remain for some time on account of their despicable conduct.

Troubled and Scandalous Life
of Dead Specialist

She was born on April 17, 1936, in the then remote village of Nanay—the highway that joins the resort to Iquitos was not yet in existence—the daughter of Hermenegilda Arellano Rosaura and an unknown father. She was baptized May 8 of the same year in the church of Punchana with the name of Olga and her mother's two surnames. According to what people in the district who remember her say, the latter took on various jobs, such as cleaning woman at the Punchana Naval Base and at bars and restaurants in the area. She was fired from these jobs because of her taste for alcohol, which at its worst, they say, made familiar the sight of the staggering figure of "Chug-a-lug Hermes," as they nicknamed her, passing through the neighborhood in the midst of people's laughter, followed by her very young daughter, Olguita. When the child was nine or ten, a little bit of good fortune came her way. "Chug-a-lug Hermes" disappeared from Nanay, abandoning the unprotected little girl, who was charitably taken by the Seventh-Day Adventists into their little orphanage on the corner of Samanez Ocampo and Napo, where currently only the church stands. In said situation, the poor girl, who until then had been raised in filth and ignorance, like a mongrel, received her first lessons, learned to read, write and count, and led a modest but healthy and decent life, ruled by the severe moral precepts of that church. ("Those precepts can't be as sound as they make them out to be, judging by the dame's service file," commented one of our editors, with his characteristic severeness. A Catholic priest who was connected with the Army until last year, he is famous for the constant ironies of his sermons against the numerous Protestant churches housed in Iquitos and has asked us not to reveal his name.)

Drama of Young Missionary

"I remember her very well," the Adventist pastor, Rev. Abraham MacPherson, who directed the orphanage during the years in which the young Olga Arellano Rosaura stayed there has told us. "She was a happy little brown-haired girl with a quick mind and a lively spirit, who obediently followed the preachings of her guardians and teachers and from whom we expected many good things. Undoubtedly, what made her go astray was her great physical beauty, which nature endowed her with from adolescence. But then let us pray for her and take inspiration from her case to mend our own lives, instead of remembering the sad, bitter things that do no one any good and lead nowhere." Rev. MacPherson refers, in veiled terms, to an event that at the time caused a great deal of commotion in Iquitos: the sensational flight from the Seventh-Day Adventists' orphanage of the beautiful thirteen-year-old who at that time was Olguita Arellano Rosaura with one of her tutors, the young Adventist minister Richard Jay Pierce, Jr., who in those days had recently come to Iquitos from his distant land, the United States, to take up arms in his first missionary battles here. The episode ended tragically, as many readers of *El Oriente* will remember, since it was to this newspaper—already the most prestigious in Iquitos—that the tormented missionary, desperate with remorse for having succumbed to Olguita's adolescent beauty, sent his letter asking for forgiveness in the eyes of the Loreto public before putting an end to his days by hanging himself from a palm tree on the outskirts of the village of San Juan. (*El Oriente* published the complete text of his letter, in its half-English, half-Spanish, on September 20, 1949.)

Toboggan of Prostitution

After this precocious and unfortunate romantic adventure, Olga Arellano Rosaura began to slide down

209

the slope of evil habits and a loose life, to which she was unquestionably impelled by her physical beauty and her great kindness. Thus, from that time on, it was common to make out her beautiful silhouette in the night spots of Iquitos, such as the Mau Mau, The Jungle, and that now defunct den of iniquity The Flower Garden, which authorities had to close because they discovered that the above-mentioned bar, living up to its name, was a brothel where, from 4 to 7 P.M., girls from the secondary schools in Iquitos were losing their virtue. Its owner, the almost mythical Humberto Sipa (a.k.a. "Snotnose"), who spent several months in jail, has since made a successful career in that field of endeavor, as everyone knows. It would take a very long time, of course, to trace the romantic itinerary of the attractive Olguita Arellano Rosaura, to whom in those years gossip and idle talk attributed countless protectors and powerful friends, many of them married, with whom the girl did not hesitate to show herself in public. One of those unverifiable rumors asserts that Olguita was discreetly expelled from Iquitos at the end of 1952 by the then departmental prefect, Miguel Torres Salamino, because of the passionate love affair between the dissolute Olguita and the prefect's son, engineering student Miguelito Torres Saavedra, whose death in the murky waters of Quistococha Lagoon was considered a suicide by many on account of the repeated signs of desolation that the young man exhibited after his sweetheart's departure, although his family energetically denied that rumor. In any case, the restless Olguita left for the Brazilian city of Manaos, and the only thing that has been learned about the years she stayed there was that instead of correcting her conduct, she worsened it, devoting herself to a bad life in plain daylight, since she began to practice fully, in obvious places—bordellos and brothels—the age-old profession of prostitution.

Accustomed to those indecent occupations and more beautiful than ever, Olga Arellano Rosaura—to whom Loreto inventively gave the pseudonym the "Brazilian"—returned after a couple of years to her native Iquitos. Through the famous ensnarer of women in that area, Chino Porfirio, from the district of Bethlehem, she almost immediately entered the Special Service, that institution which transports women of evil ways to the frontier garrisons as if they were so many head of cattle or basic commodities. But, a little earlier, the incorrigible Olguita was the protagonist in another noisy scandal when she was taken by surprise in the last row of the Bolognesi movie house during the evening show, immorally touching and performing immodest acts with a police lieutenant, who was thereupon transferred from Loreto. There even was —our readers will remember—an attempt at aggression on the part of the officer's wife, who assaulted the "Brazilian" during a Thursday concert, the two women exchanging blows and insults on the lawn of the Army Plaza.

Thanks to her physical attributes, Olga Arellano Rosaura would soon be transformed into the star specialist of the infamous area on the Itaya River and into the *favorite friend* of the establishment's administrator and director, who, up until yesterday, we ingenuously believed to be an ordinary citizen, Mr. Pantaleón Pantoja, and who turned out to be, to the perplexity and confusion of many, nothing less than a *captain* in our Army. The close and intimate relationship that existed between the attractive dead woman and Mr. (excuse us) Capt. *on active duty* Pantoja is a secret to no one in this city: it was not rare to see this couple strolling lovey-dovey across the Plaza of 28 July or furiously embracing at sunset on the Tarapacá Embankment. An unwilling sower of tragedies, Olguita Arellano Rosaura, the seductive "Brazilian," was, sadly, the reason

for the departure from Iquitos of Capt. Pantoja's neglected wife in a deeply felt family drama that was revealed by a colleague of ours, a famous radio commentator in this city.

Tragic End

And so we come to the denouement of this life that at dusk on the second day of 1959 in the Cacique Cocama Bend, while still in full bloom, met its premature and shocking end, occasioned by traitorous shots which, perhaps bewitched by her beauty, like so many men, preferred her in their lethal path to the worthless trash of a few degenerates or fanatics. Coming to the infamous spot on the Itaya River where the Modus Vivendi Funeral Home had installed a first-class catafalque surrounded by candelabra, the many people who attended the wake for Olga Arellano Rosaura approached the coffin and admired through the transparent glass, shining intact under the funeral candles, the dark beauty of the *Brazilian!*

Exclusive Extra of *El Oriente*

Epistle to the Good Concerning the Wicked from Brother Francisco

As an "exclusive extra" we publish below a text that reached our editorial offices last night and was written in his own hand by the very renowned Brother Francisco, prophet and high priest of the Brotherhood of the Ark, who is being hunted by the police of four countries as the mastermind behind the crucifixions that for some time now have been soaking our beloved Amazon region in blood. El Oriente is in the position to guarantee the authenticity of this sensational document.

212

In the name of the Father, the Holy Ghost and the SON WHO DIED ON THE CROSS and with the permission and inspiration of the heavenly voices that await the GOOD PEOPLE, I direct myself to the public opinion of all Peru and the world in order to disprove and deny as wicked, slanderous and lacking in any truth the accusations of the WICKED PEOPLE who attempt to marry the SISTERS AND BROTHERS OF THE ARK to the violation, death and subsequent CRUCIFIXION of Miss Olga Arellano Rosaura, which sadly occurred in the Cacique Cocama Bend on the outskirts of Nauta. From my remote refuge where I bear the CROSS that the Lord in his generous and infinite wisdom has chosen as my destiny, and keeping myself far from the impious hands that cannot and will never be able to capture me or remove me from the believing, holy, GOOD people of the Sisters and the Brothers, united in divine copulation by their love for God and their hatred for wickedness, I raise my hand and, moving it powerfully from left to right and from right to left, I say, joining the shout to the gesture, NO! It is not true that the Sisters and Brothers of the Ark—whose objective is to do GOOD and to prepare themselves for rising into heaven when the Father, the Holy Ghost and the SON WHO DIED ON THE CROSS decide that this world full of EVIL and impiety should be ended in fire and water as is foretold in the GOOD book of the Bible, which will happen very soon because that is what the voices I listen to tell me, and they do not proceed from this world—have had anything to do with the crime that the WICKED committed and want to attribute to us in order to divert their guilt and make thicker and sharper our nails and rougher the WOOD of our CROSSES. None of those accused of the death of Miss Arellano has ever belonged to our BROTHERHOOD of GOOD people, neither has any of them ever attended a single one of our meetings—either in the capacity of plain spectator or in that of curiosity-seeker—which the ARKS have celebrated in the region where they have lived, that is, those in Nauta, Bagazán and Requena, as the GOOD Apostles of

213

those Arks have confirmed for me. Not one of the accused was ever seen at the meetings celebrated to offer praise to the Father, the Holy Ghost and the SON WHO DIED ON THE CROSS and to ask them for their forgiveness for their sins in order to have a cleansed soul when the FINAL MOMENT arrives. The Sisters, the Brothers, do not kill, do not rape, do not assault, do not steal and only hate the violence of the WICKED, as heaven has taught them through my lips. It will never be possible to throw in our faces even one act contrary to GOOD and it is not true that we preach crime, as is imputed to us by those who pursue us and force us to hide and to live like vicious animals in the depths of the jungles. But we pardon them because they are simple, obedient slaves in the hands of Heaven, which uses them as CROSSES that will earn for us the immortality of eternal glory. And as for our poor Olga Arellano, although she had not yet heard the word, we will henceforth incorporate her into our prayers and henceforth remember her along with our martyrs and saints who watch us, listen to us, speak to us, protect us and deservedly enjoy celestial peace up above, next to the Father, the Holy Ghost and the SON WHO DIED ON THE CROSS.

<div align="right">BROTHER FRANCISCO</div>

ED. NOTE: As a matter of fact, during the burial, prayer cards with the image of Olga Arellano Rosaura, similar to those that exist for the other crucified members of the Ark, such as the famous boy martyr of Moronacocha and Santa Ignacia, were seen circulating in the public cemetery of Iquitos.

<div align="right">*Editorial in El Oreinte, January 6, 1959*</div>

Assault on Loreto Journalist

The publication, as an exclusive extra in our edition yesterday, of the "Epistle to the Good Concerning the Wicked," which was sent to our editorial offices from his

214

secret hiding place in some spot in the jungle by Brother Francisco, leader and principal spiritual director of the "crosses" or "Brothers of the Ark," has been a pretext for our editor in chief, the well-known journalist of international reputation, Joaquín Andoa, to become the object of an unspeakable assault by police authorities of the Loreto Department and serves to swell the list of martyrs for freedom of the press. In fact, our editor in chief was summoned yesterday morning by Police Chief Juan Amézaga Riofrío, Region V (Loreto), and by the Chief Inspector, Loreto Branch, of the Police Bureau of Investigation (PBI), Federico Chumpitaz Fernández. Said authorities demanded that he reveal the manner in which the newspaper *El Oriente* had obtained the missive from Brother Francisco, a suspect pursued by the police as the *éminence grise* behind the various cases of crucifixion that have occurred in the Amazon. When our editor in chief responded, respectfully but firmly, that a journalist's sources of information constitute a professional secret and are for that reason as sacred and inviolable as revelations obtained in confession by a priest, the two police chiefs broke out into improprieties of unprecedented vulgarity against Mr. Joaquín Andoa, even threatening him with physical punishment ("We'll work you over," were their exact words) if he did not answer their questions. Since our editor in chief honorably refused to fall short of his professional ethics, he was locked up in a cell in the station house for a period of eight hours, that is, until 7 P.M., when he was released by arrangement with the departmental prefect himself. United as one man in the defense of freedom of the press, of professional secrecy and of media ethics, the entire editorial staff of *El Oriente* protests this abuse committed against an outstanding intellectual and journalist of Loreto and makes known that it has sent telegrams denouncing the act to both the National Federation of Journalists of Peru and the National Association of Journalists, our highest union organizations in the country.

215

Cacique Cocama Bend Murderers
Not to Face Military Tribunal

Iquitos, Jan. 6—A well-informed source very close to the High Command of Region V (Amazon) denied this morning the persistent rumors that have been circulating in Iquitos to the effect that the seven assailants from Nauta would be transferred to military jurisdiction to be tried in a military tribunal by means of summary proceedings. According to this source, the armed forces have not at any moment demanded that they be entrusted with the task of judging and sentencing the criminals, with the result that they will remain under the regular jurisdiction of civil justice.

Apparently the origin of the denied rumor was a request sent up to the high Army courts from Quartermaster Capt. Pantaleón Pantoja—whose functions are only too well known in this city—so that the military court's jurisdiction would require the legal investigation and punishment of those responsible for the assault at Nauta, on the basis of the argument that the boat *Eve* and its crew members belonged to the nation's navy and that the convoy of harlots formed part of a militarized organization, which would be the case of the unpopular Special Service directed by that officer. The armed forces may have rejected as "far out"—that is the term employed by our informant —Capt. Pantoja's request, indicating that when victimized by the assault, the transport boat *Eve* and its crew members were not performing any military service, but rather strictly civilian duties, and that the so-called Special Service is not nor ever can be under any circumstances a militarized institution, being only a civilian, commercial enterprise that has had incidental and merely tolerated, but never supported or officialized, relations with the

216

Army. With this in mind, the same source added, an investigation of the said Special Service that the Army general staff should have ordered will be conducted with the purpose of discovering its origin, composition, functions and benefits in order to determine its legality, and if appropriate, the liabilities and pertinent sanctions.

10

"Ah, you're up already, son," Mother Leonor spends the night frightened—in a dream a cockroach is eaten by a rat who is eaten by a lizard who is eaten by a jaguar who is crucified and whose remains are devoured by cockroaches—gets up at dawn, paces around the room in the dark, wringing her hands, and, hearing the bells chime six, she knocks at Panta's bedroom door. "What, you've put on your uniform again?"

"All Iquitos has seen me in uniform, Mama," Pantita checks how his jacket has faded and how baggy his trousers are on him, watches himself in the mirror in different poses and is overcome by melancholy. "There's no sense in going on with that lie about Mr. Pantoja."

"The Army will have to decide that, not you," Mother Leonor mixes up the kitchen keys, spills the milk, remembers she has forgotten the bread, cannot stop the tray from shaking in her hands. "Come, at least drink a little coffee. Don't leave on an empty stomach, don't be stubborn."

"O.K., but only half a cup," Panta very calmly goes to the dining room, lays his kepi and gloves on the table, sits down, drinks with little sips. "C'mon, give me a kiss. Don't put on that face, Mama, you'll give me your worries."

"I had terrible nightmares all night long," Mother Leonor throws herself on the sofa, raises her hand to her mouth, talks in a hoarse, tortured voice. "And now what's going to happen to you, Panta? What's going to become of us?"

"Nothing's going to happen," Panta takes some bills out of his

218

wallet, puts them in Mother Leonor's housecoat pocket, opens a Venetian blind, sees people going to work, the blind beggar already installed at the corner with his saucer and flute. "And besides, if it happens, I don't care."

"Heard the radio?" In the back seat of the taxi Iris changes color in amazement, hears the driver exclaim and repeats it isn't possible, what a shame, pays, gets out, goes into Pantiland slamming the door, howls. "They caught Brother Francisco! He was hiding near the Napo River, close to Mazán. I'm really worried. What'll they do with him?"

"I don't regret anything I've done," Panta sees the tombstone-maker and Alicia's husband leaving their houses, sees cars going by, young children in school uniforms with books, a little old lady selling lottery tickets, feels strange, buttons his tunic. "I've acted according to my conscience and that's a soldier's duty too. I'll face up to what's coming. Trust me, Mama."

"I always have, dear," Mother Leonor brushes him, polishes him, straightens him, opens her arms, kisses him, squeezes him, looks at the thick mustache on the old portrait. "Blind faith in you. But with this business I don't know what to think. You've gone crazy, Panta. To dress like an officer to deliver a speech at the burial of a w——! Would your father or your grandfather have done such a thing?"

"Please, Mama, don't get going on that again," Panta sees someone greeting the woman selling lottery tickets and the blind man, sees a man walking while reading the paper, a dog urinating plentifully, gives a half turn and heads toward the door. "I think I've told you it's expressly forbidden to even mention that subject again."

"Fine, I'll shut up; I *do* know how to obey superiors," Mother Leonor gives him her blessing, says goodbye to him on the sidewalk, goes back to her bedroom racked by sobs, throws herself on the bed. "May God not ask you to repent, Panta. I pray it doesn't happen, but the outrage you've committed is going to disgrace us, I'm sure."

"Well, in a certain sense, yes, at least me," Lieutenant Bacacorzo barely smiles, passes through the relatives crowded at the jail door waiting for visiting hours, shoos away a boy who is hawk-

219

ing turtles, monkeys. "I've lost the promotion I was supposed to get this year, no doubt about that. But in the last analysis, the thing's done and you can't march backwards."

"I ordered you to lead the escort, I ordered you to pay tribute to that poor woman," Captain Pantoja bends down to tie a shoe, catches sight of the slogan on the door of the Bank of the Amazon: "The jungle's money for the jungle." "All the responsibility's mine and only mine. That's what I remind General Collazos of in this letter and that's what I'm going to tell Scavino personally. You're not to blame at all, Bacacorzo: the regulations are very clear."

"They found him sleeping," Penelope sits on Sinforoso Caiguas's hammock, speaks in the center of a circle of specialists. "He'd made a little cave out of branches and leaves, he spent the day praying, he didn't eat anything the apostles brought him. Just roots and herbs. He's a saint, he's a saint."

"The truth of the matter is I shouldn't have paid attention to you," Lieutenant Bacacorzo plunges his hands into his pockets, enters the Paradise Ice Cream Shoppe, asks for coffee with milk, hears Captain Pantoja asking him isn't that the professor, the wizard? answers that's him. "Just between you and me, what you asked me to do was absolute nonsense. A person with all his marbles would have gone and told Scavino what you were trying to do, so he'd hold you back. Maybe now you'd be thanking me for it, Captain."

"Too late for tears," Captain Pantoja hears the professor advising a woman if you want your newborn not to be late in talking, you should squash kernels of corn in his mouth. "If you thought so, why the hell didn't you do it, Bacacorzo? You'd have freed me from the pangs of conscience I'm going to have if they don't give you that new stripe on my account."

"Because I haven't got all my marbles," Lieutenant Bacacorzo touches his forehead, drinks his coffee with milk, pays, listens to the professor recommending to his client and if a snake bites your little boy, you can cure him by giving him nursing bottles full of llama bile, goes out on the street. "My wife always tells me that. Now, seriously, I saw you were so moved by that specialist's death that it softened my heart."

220

"*El Oriente*'s editor in chief is killing himself saying he didn't squeal on the Brother, swearing and moaning he didn't tell a thing to the police," Coca is the last to arrive at Pantiland, announces I've got news, sits in the hammock, talks fast. "It's great; they already burned his car and almost burned his newspaper. If he doesn't get out of Iquitos, the 'brothers' will kill him. Think Mr. Andoa knew Brother Francisco's hiding place?"

"Besides, the idea of paying tribute to a whore, exactly because it was so demented, turned out so fascinating," Lieutenant Bacacorzo lets out a guffaw, walks among the peddlers and licensed stores on Lima Street, notices that the Modern Bazaar has hung up a new sign: "Merchandise Famous for Durability and Unforgettable Appearance." "I don't know what came over me; your delirium was contagious."

"There was no such delirium; it was a decision made calmly and rationally," Captain Pantoja kicks a tin can, crosses the asphalt, dodges a light truck, steps into the shade of the rose apple trees on the Army Plaza. "But that's another story. I promise you, I'll go to any lengths to keep this from hurting you, Bacacorzo."

"A good joke to tell my grandchildren, though they'll never believe me," Lieutenant Bacacorzo smiles, rests against the Heroes Monument, notices that the names are blotted out or stained from the bird droppings. "But then that's what newspapers are for. You know, I can't get used to seeing you in uniform? You look like another person to me."

"Same with me; I feel odd. Three years is a long time," Captain Pantoja turns at the Credit Bank, spits in front of the House of Iron, sees the owner of the Imperial Hotel chasing a girl. "Have you seen Scavino yet?"

"No, I haven't seen him," Lieutenant Bacacorzo looks at the shiny tiled windows at headquarters, enters the Tarapacá Embankment, stops to see a group of foreigners with cameras leaving the Tourist Hotel. "He ordered me to say I'd finished the special assignment, that's to say, my work with you. I have to report to his office Monday."

"You have four days to get up strength and prepare yourself for the storm," Captain Pantoja steps on a banana peel, observes the

flaking walls of the old College of St. Augustine, the grass that is devouring it, smashes to bits a family of ants dragging a little leaf. "So this is our last official meeting."

"I'm going to tell you a story that'll make you laugh," Lieutenant Bacacorzo lights a cigarette next to the Rotary Club Monument, discovers a few female students playing volleyball on the embankment. "Do you know what story was making the rounds for a long time among the people who caught sight of us alone and in isolated spots? That we were faggots, imagine. Hell, even that doesn't make you laugh."

"They've got him in Mazán and they've surrounded the town with soldiers," Pichuza has her ear glued to the radio, repeats in shouts what she hears, runs to the dock, points to the river. "Everybody's going to Mazán to rescue Brother Francisco. See? Look at all the launches, gliders, rafts. Look, look."

"In these years of half-secret talks, I've come to respect you a lot, Bacacorzo," Captain Pantoja puts his hand on his shoulder, sees the schoolgirls jump, hit the ball, run, feels a tickling in his ear, scratches. "You're the only friend I've made here up till now, because of this funny situation I'm in. I wanted you to know it. And also that I'm very grateful to you."

"It's mutual; I liked you from the very first minute," Lieutenant Bacacorzo consults his watch, hails a taxi, opens the door, climbs in, leaves. "And I have the impression I'm the only one who knows what you're really like. Good luck at headquarters—you're in for a rough time. Give me five, Captain."

"Come in; I've been waiting for you," General Scavino stands up, goes to meet him, does not shake hands, looks at him without hatred, without rancor, begins an electrified walk around him. "And you can imagine how impatiently. O.K., you can begin to vomit out justifications for your actions. Let's go, once and for all —get started."

"Good morning, General, sir," Captain Pantoja clicks his heels, salutes, thinks he doesn't look furious, how funny. "I request you to transmit this letter to headquarters, after you read it. In it I alone assume responsibility for what happened at the cemetery. I mean, Lieutenant Bacacorzo did not have the least—"

"Stop, don't talk to me about that individual—he turns my stom-

222

ach," General Scavino stands still for a second, raises a hand, resumes his circular pacing, his voice growing slightly angry. "I forbid you to ever mention him in my presence. I thought he was one of my trustworthy officers. He was supposed to watch over you, curb you, and he ended up being a follower of yours. But I swear to you, he's going to regret having led that escort to the whore's burial."

"He didn't do anything more than obey my orders," Captain Pantoja continues to stand at attention, speaks softly, pronounces all the syllables slowly. "I explain it in detail in this letter, General, sir. I compelled Lieutenant Bacacorzo to stage that escort in the cemetery."

"Don't start defending anyone; you're the one who needs defending," General Scavino sits down again, considers him with slow and triumphant eyes, turns over some newspapers. "I suppose you've already seen the results of your charming action. Of course, you must have read these clippings. But you still aren't familiar with these from Lima, the editorials from *La Prensa,* from *El Comercio.* Everyone is raising the roof about the Special Service."

"If you don't send me reinforcements, something very ugly could happen, Colonel, sir," Lieutenant Santana positions sentinels, orders fix your bayonets, warns the strangers one more step and I'll shoot, handles the portable radio apparatus, is frightened. "Let me transfer the nut to Iquitos. Every minute, more and more people are putting ashore and here in Mazán we're out in the open, you know that. At any moment they may try to attack the shack where I've got him."

"Don't think I'm trying to duck the responsibility for my actions, General, sir," Captain Pantoja stands at ease, feels his palms sweating, does not look at Scavino's eyes but instead at the dark blotches on his bald head, mutters. "But let me remind you that radios and newspapers had talked about the Special Service before the episode at Nauta. I haven't committed any indiscretion. My going to the cemetery didn't give the Service away. Its existence was common knowledge."

"So appearing dressed as an Army officer, in a cortege of prostitutes and pimps, is an unimportant incident," General Scavino

becomes theatrical, understanding, benevolent, even pleasant. "So paying tribute to a streetwalker as if it were a matter—"

"Of a soldier fallen in action." Captain Pantoja raises his voice, gestures, steps forward, "I'm sorry, but that is, neither more nor less, the status of Specialist Olga Arellano Rosaura."

"How dare you shout at me!" General Scavino bellows, turns red, twitches in his chair, messes up the desk, calms down instantly, "Lower that voice if you don't want me to have you arrested for insolence. Who the hell do you think you're talking to?"

"I beg you to forgive me," Captain Pantoja retreats, stands at attention, clicks his heels, lowers his eyes, whispers. "I'm very sorry, General, sir."

"Headquarters wanted to hold him there until they received instructions from Lima, but if the thing's really getting ugly in Mazán, sure, the best thing would be to bring him to Iquitos," Colonel Máximo Dávila consults with his adjunct, studies the map, signs a voucher for airplane fuel. "I agree, Santana. I'm sending you a hydroplane to take the prophet out of there. Keep a cool head and try to keep the blood from flowing into the river."

"So the idiocies in your speech—you really believe them," General Scavino regains his composure, smile, superiority, articulates syllable by syllable. "No, I'm already getting to know you better. Pantoja, you're a big cynic. You think I don't know that whore was your girlfriend? You put on that show in a moment of desperation, of sentimentality, because you were in love with her. And now, for that cunt, you come to talk to me about soldiers fallen in action."

"I swear to you that my personal feelings for that specialist did not have the least bearing on the matter," Captain Pantoja reddens, feels flames in his cheeks, stammers, digs his fingernails into his palms. "If instead of her the victim had been some other specialist, I would have proceeded in the same way. It was my duty."

"Your duty?" General Scavino screeches out with joy, stands, paces, stops in front of the window, sees that it's raining cats and dogs, that the fog hides the river. "To make a fool of the Army? To play the part of a nincompoop? To reveal that an officer is acting as a wholesale pimp? That was your obligation, Pantoja?

224

Which enemy is paying you? Because that's pure sabotage, pure fifth-column work."

"You see? What'd I bet ya? The 'brothers' saved him," Lolita claps, nails a baby frog to a cardboard cross, kneels, laughs. "I just heard it, Sinchi was telling it on the radio. They were going to put him on a plane to bring him to Lima, but the 'brothers' jumped the soldiers, rescued him and ran into the jungle. Oh, how wonderful! Long live Brother Francisco!"

"Only a couple of months ago the Army paid tribute to Dr. Pedro Andrade, who died when he was thrown from his horse, General, sir," Captain Pantoja reminds, sees the windowpanes riddled with raindrops, hears the thunder roar. "You yourself read a wonderful eulogy at the cemetery."

"Are you trying to insinuate that whores in the Special Service are in the same position as doctors assigned to the Army?" General Scavino hears a knock at the door, says come in, accepts a book an orderly hands him, shouts I don't want to be interrupted, "Pantoja, Pantoja, come down to earth."

"The specialists render the armed forces a service no less important than the assigned doctors, lawyers or priests," Captain Pantoja sees the lightning snake through the leaden clouds, waits and hears the thunder in the sky, "Begging your pardon, General, but that's the way it is and I can prove it to you."

"At least Father Beltrán isn't here to listen to this," General Scavino collapses onto a sofa, leafs through the book, throws it into the wastepaper basket, looks at Captain Pantoja, half disturbed and half fearful. "You would have knocked him cold with what you just said."

"All our noncommissioned officers and soldiers serve better, are more efficient and disciplined, and tolerate life in the jungle better since the Special Service has been in existence, General, sir," Captain Pantoja thinks Tuesday little Gladys will be two years old, becomes emotional, grieves, sighs. "All the studies and surveys we've made prove it. And as for the women who carry out this work with true self-denial, what they do has never been acknowledged."

"Then you really believe those nasty lies," General Scavino sud-

denly becomes nervous, walks from one wall to another, talks to himself while making faces. "You really think the Army should be grateful to those whores for deigning to fuck with the troops."

"I most firmly believe it, General, sir," Captain Pantoja sees the torrents of water sweeping down the deserted street, washing the roofs, windows and walls, sees that even the most robust trees are swaying like pieces of paper. "I work with them, I'm a witness to what they do. Step by step, I follow their difficult, compulsory, poorly paid and, as has been seen, dangerous work. After what happened at Nauta, the Army had the duty to render them a small homage. Their morale had to be raised somehow."

"I can't get angry, I'm so amazed," General Scavino touches his ears, forehead, bald head, shakes his head, shrugs his shoulders, has a victimized face. "It doesn't so much make me angry. I have the feeling I'm dreaming, Pantoja. You make me feel that everything's unreal, a nightmare, that I've turned into an idiot, that I don't understand anything that's happening."

"Were there shots, deaths?" Knockers is terrified, clasps her hands, prays, gathers the specialists together, asks them to console her. "Santa Ignacia, don't let anything happen to Chameleon. Yes, he's there, he went to Mazán like everybody else to see Brother Francisco. Not because he's a 'brother', he went out of curiosity."

"I assumed that this initiative wouldn't be looked upon favorably by my superiors and therefore proceeded without going through bureaucratic channels," Captain Pantoja sees the rain stop, the sky clear, the trees become very green, the street fill with people. "I know I deserve to be punished, of course. But I didn't act thinking about myself, but about the Army. Especially about the future of the Service. What happened could have caused a desertion of specialists. I had to warm their spirits, inject a little energy into them."

"The future of the Service," General Scavino deciphers, comes very close to him, observes him with commiseration and delight, speaks almost kissing his face. "So you think the Special Service still has a future? It no longer exists, Pantoja; the damned thing died. Kaput, *fini.*"

"The Special Service?" Captain Pantoja feels a sharp gust of cold air, feels the floor moving, sees the rainbow that has appeared,

wants to sit down, to close his eyes. "Already dead?"

"Don't be naïve, man," General Scavino smiles, tries to catch his eye, speaks with pleasure. "Did you think it was going to survive a scandal like this? The same day as the events at Nauta, the Navy took back its boat, the PAF its plane and Collazos and Victoria agreed it was necessary to put an end to this folly."

"I ordered them to shoot, but they didn't obey me, Colonel, sir," Lieutenant Santana shoots twice into the air, curses at his soldiers, sees the last "brothers" disappear, calls the radio operator. "There were too many fanatics, especially women. Maybe it was better; there would've been a massacre. They can't get very far. Once the reinforcements get here, I'll go out after them and nab them, you'll see."

"That order must be revoked as soon as possible," Captain Pantoja stammers without conviction, feels nauseated, leans against the desk, sees people carrying water out of their houses in buckets. "The Special Service is at its peak, three years' work is beginning to bear fruit, we're going to extend it to the subofficers and officers."

"Dead and buried forever, thank God," General Scavino rises to his feet.

"I'll present detailed studies, statistics," Captain Pantoja continues to stammer.

"It's been the only good thing to come out of that whore's murder and the scandal at the cemetery," General Scavino contemplates the city lit up by the sunlight but still dripping. "The damned Special Service was at the point of putting an end to me. But it's over with. I'll be able to walk the streets of Iquitos calmly again."

"Charts, surveys," Captain Pantoja does not make sounds, does not move his lips, notices that things are blurring. "It can't be an irrevocable decision; there's still time to rectify it."

"Mobilize the entire Amazon region if you have to, but capture that messiah for me in twenty-four hours," Tiger Collazos is reprimanded by the ministry, reprimands the Chief of Region V. "Do you want them laughing at you in Lima? What kind of officers do you have that four witches can snatch a prisoner out of your hands?"

"And I recommend that you request your discharge," General Scavino sees the first motorboats appear on the river, the smoke rise from the huts on Padre Island. "It's a friendly piece of advice. Your career is finished; you commited professional suicide with that farce in the cemetery. If you stay in the Army with that stain on your service record, you'll rot away as a captain. Hey, what's the matter? Are you crying? Tighten your belt, Pantoja."

"I'm sorry, General," Captain Pantoja blows his nose, sobs again, rubs his eyes. "Too much tension these past few days. I wasn't able to contain myself. I beg you to excuse me for this weakness."

"You should close the location on the Itaya today and hand over the keys to the quartermaster unit before noon," General Scavino signals that the interview is over, sees Pantoja snap to attention. "Leave for Lima in the Faucett plane in the morning. Collazos and Victoria will be waiting for you at the ministry at 6 P.M. so you can tell them about your exploit. And if you haven't lost your mind, follow my advice. Request your discharge and look for some job in civilian life."

"Never that, General, sir. I'll never willingly leave the Army," Captain Pantoja still does not get his voice back, still does not raise his eyes, still remains pale and ashamed. "I told you once that the Army is the most important thing in my life."

"Get going then," General Scavino condescends to shake his hand quickly, opens the door for him, stands looking at him walk away. "Before you leave, blow your nose again and wipe your eyes. Hell, no one is going to believe that I've seen an Army captain cry because they shut down a whorehouse. You're excused, Pantoja."

"With your permission, Captain, sir," Sinforoso Caiguas runs up to the command post, flourishes a hammer, a screwdriver, stands at attention, wears overalls covered with dirt. "Should I also take down the big map, the one with the little flags?"

"That too, but don't tear it," Captain Pantoja opens his desk, takes out a sheaf of papers, leafs through, tears, throws on the floor, orders. "We'll return it to the Cartography Office. Did you finish with those drawings and charts, Palomino?"

"Oh, my God, get down on your knees, weep, cross yourselves." Sandra shakes her hair, makes a cross with her arms, "He's dead, they killed him, they don't know how. It's true, it's true. They say

228

Brother Francisco's been crucified on the outskirts of Indiana village. Oh, God!"

"Yes, Captain, sir, I took them down," Palomino Rioalto jumps off a bench, lifts a loaded box, goes toward the truck parked at the door, deposits his load, returns on the double, stamps the floor. "There's still this bunch of file cards, notebooks, folders. What's to be done with this?"

"Destroy them too," Captain Pantoja turns off the light, disconnects the transmitter, wraps it in its cover, entrusts it to Chino Porfirio. "Or better still, carry this pile of garbage to the clearing and make a good bonfire. But quick, let's get going, step lively, step lively. What's the matter, Chuchupe? Crying again?"

"No, Mr. Pantoja, I promised you I won't," Chuchupe wears a flowered kerchief on her head and a white apron, is making packages, folding sheets, piling up pillows in a trunk. "But you don't know how hard it is for me to hold it in."

"The work of so many hours turned to ashes in a few seconds, Mr. Pantoja," Freckle emerges from a chaos of folding screens, boxes and suitcases, points to the flames, the smoke from the clearing. "When I think of the nights that were spent making those charts, those filing systems."

"Me too feel a gleat pain you no can imagine, Mistel Pantoja," Chino Porfirio throws a chair, a bundle of hammocks, rolled-up posters into the back. "I love this place like it was my own home, I sweal."

"Grin and bear it," Pantaleón Pantoja unplugs a lamp, packs some books, takes apart a bookshelf, loads blackboards. "That's life. Hurry up, help me take out all this, throw away what's no good. I have to turn over the depot to the quartermaster before noon. Let's see, you carry the desk."

"No, it wasn't the soldiers—it was the 'brothers' themselves," Peludita cries, hugs Iris, clutches Pichuza's hand, looks at Sandra. "The ones who were rescuing him. He asked them do it, commanded them to do it: Don't let them catch me again. Crucify me, crucify me."

"I tell you one thing, Mistel Pantoja," Chino Porfirio stoops, counts one, two, heave! and lifts. "So you know how happy I was hele. I nevel put up with bosses even fol one month. And how long

with you? Thlee yeals. And if it up to me, all my life."

"Thanks, Chino, I know," Mr. Pantoja grabs a bucket, white-washes the mottoes, sayings and warnings on the wall. "Let's see, be careful on the stairs. That's it, in small steps. I'd gotten used to this too, to all of you."

"I'm telling you, I'm not going to set foot around here for a long time, Mr. Pantoja. I'd burst into tears," Chuchupe places douches, chamber pots, towels, robes, shoes, socks in the trunk. "What dopes! It's incredible they'd think of shutting this place down in its heyday. With the beautiful plans we had."

"Man proposes and God disposes, Chuchupe—what're you going to do?" Pantoja unhooks Venetian blinds, rolls up straw mats, counts the boxes and packages in the truck, scares away the curiosity seekers surrounding the entrance to the logistics center. "Let's see, Freckle, are you strong enough to carry that file?"

"Teófilo Moley and his buddies ale to blame. If not fol them, we left in peace," Chino Porfirio tries to close the trunk, fails, makes Freckle sit on top, fastens the latch. "Damn people, they destloyed us, light, Mistel Pantoja?"

"In part, yes," Pantaleón Pantoja loops a rope around the trunk, ties knots, tightens. "But sooner or later this was going to come to an end. We had very powerful enemies within the Army itself. I see they've taken off the bandages, Freckle. You're moving your arm like new."

"One bad apple spoils the barrel," Chupito sees the veins standing out on Chino Porfirio's forehead, Mr. Pantoja's sweat. "Who's going to understand something like this? Why enemies? We were happiness to so many people, the soldiers got so glad when they saw us. They made me feel like Santa Claus when I went to the barracks."

"He chose the tree himself," Rita clasps her hands, closes her eyes, drinks the concoction, strikes her chest. "He said this one—chop it down and make the cross this size. He chose the place himself, a nice one next to the river. He told them, stand it there, it has to be here, Heaven decrees it here."

"Never a lack of envious people," Chuchupe brings in and passes around Coca-Colas, sees Sinforoso and Palomino feeding

230

the bonfire with more papers. "They couldn't swallow how well this was going, Mr. Pantoja, the progress we were making, thanks to your schemes."

"You ale a genius with these things," Chino Porfirio drinks from the bottle, belches, spits. "All the gils say so: only Blothel Flancisco above Mistel Pantoja."

"And those filing cabinets, Sinforoso?" Mr. Pantoja takes off his overalls and throws them on the fire, cleans the paint off his hands and arms with kerosene. "And the folding screen from the infirmary, Palomino? Quick, get all that up on the truck for me. C'mon, guys, step lively."

"Why don't you accept our suggestion, Mr. Pantoja?" Freckle keeps bags of toilet paper, bottles of alcohol and Mercurochrome, bandages and cotton. "Get out of the Army, where they pay you so bad for your efforts, and stay with us."

"Those benches too, Chino," Mr. Pantoja checks that nothing is left in the infirmary, rips the red cross off the medicine cabinet. "No, Freckle, I've already told you no. I'll only drop the Army when the Army drops me or when I die. The little picture too, please."

"We're going to get rich, Mr. Pantoja; don't miss your big chance," Chuchupe drags brooms, feather dusters, clothes hangers, pails. "Stay. You'll be our boss and you won't have bosses anymore. We'll obey you in everything; you'll set the commissions, the salaries, whatever seems right to you."

"Let's see, this easel between the two of us—lift, Chino!" Pantaleón Pantoja puffs, sees that the curiosity-seekers have returned, shrugs his shoulders. "I've already explained it to you, Chuchupe. I organized this at the orders of my superiors; as a business it doesn't interest me. Besides, I need to have bosses. If I didn't, I wouldn't know what to do, the world would fall out from under my feet."

"And his saintly voice consoled those of us who were crying: don't cry, brothers, don't cry, brothers," Chameleon wipes away the tears, does not see Knockers being hugged by Monica and Penelope, kisses the ground. "I saw it all, I was there, I drank a drop of his blood and my weariness from walking hours and hours

231

up the mountain melted away. I'll never touch man or woman ever again. Oh, I feel him calling me again, I'm rising, I'm an offering."

"Don't tuln youl back on fotune," Chino Porfirio sees that the curiosity-seekers are approaching, grabs a stick, hears Mr. Pantoja say leave them alone, there's nothing left to hide. "Blinging specialists to soldiels and civilians, we'll make millions."

"We'll buy gliders, launches, and as soon as we can, a little plane, Mr. Pantoja," Freckle wails like a siren, snores like a propeller, whistles "The Mexican Hat Dance," marches and salutes. "You don't need to put up half. Chuchupe and the girls are investing their savings and that's more than enough to start with."

"If we have to, we'll go into debt, we'll ask for loans from the banks," Chuchupe takes off her apron, the kerchief on her head, her hair explodes in rollers. "All the girls agree. We won't ask for explanations from you; you do what you want. Stay and help us—don't be mean."

"With oul capital and youl blains, we build empile, Mistel Pantoja," Chino Porfirio rinses his hands, face and feet in the river. "C'mon, make up yol mind."

"It's made up and the answer's no," Pantaleón Pantoja examines the bare walls, the empty space, stacks the last useless things in the doorway. "C'mon, don't pull those long faces. If you're so enthusiastic, get the business going yourselves and I hope it goes well for you. I really hope so. I'll go back to my usual work."

"I have a lot of faith and I think the thing'll turn out good, Mr. Pantoja," Chuchupe takes a little medallion from her breast and kisses it. "I've made a vow to the boy martyr so he'll help us. But of course, nothing like if you stayed on as boss."

"And they say he didn't even cry out, didn't shed one tear, didn't feel pain or nothing," Iris carries her recently born son to the Ark, asks the apostle to baptize him, sees the boy lick up the droplets of blood his godfather spills. "He said to the men who were nailing him up, harder, brothers, don't be afraid, brothers, you're doing me a favor, brothers."

"We have to carry out that plan, Mama," Freckle throws a rock at the corrugated iron roof and sees a rooster flap its wings and fly off. "What's left for us if we don't? Go back and open a brothel in

Nanay? We'd die; it's impossible to compete with Snotnose anymore—he's got a big advantage over us."

"Another house in Nanay—go back to where we were before?" Chuchupe knocks wood, contradicts, crosses herself. "Bury ourselves in a cave again, that boring, miserable work again? Break our backs so the stool pigeons can suck all our blood? Not even when I'm dead, Chupón."

"Here we've gotten used to working on a grand scale, like up-to-date people," Freckle embraces the air, sky, city, jungle. "In the daylight, with our chins held high. For me, the best part of all this is that it always looked like doing a good deed, like giving charity, consoling a guy who's been down on his luck or curing a sick man."

"The only thing he asked for was for them to hurry: nail, nail, before the soldiers get here, I want to be up there when they come," Penelope picks up a client on the Plaza of 28 July, services him in the Hotel Requena, collects 200 soles from him, says goodbye to him. "And to the 'sisters' who were rolling around and crying, he said be happy, because up there I shall be with you, my little sisters."

"The girls say it over and over, Mr. Pantoja," Chuchupe opens the truck door, gets in, sits down. " 'He makes us feel useful, proud of our work.' "

"It really killed them when you said you wele going," Chino Porfirio puts on his shirt, gets behind the wheel, warms up the motor. "I hope we can give 'em that optimism, that spilit, in new business. It basic, light?"

"And where's the corps gone? They disappeared," Pantaleón Pantoja closes the door to the pier, fastens the crossbar, takes a final look at the logistics center. "I wanted to shake their hands, to thank them for their collaboration."

"They've gone to the House of Mori to buy you a little present," Chuchupe whispers, points to Iquitos, smiles, gets sentimental. "A silver identification bracelet with your name in gold letters, Mr. Pantoja. Don't tell them I've told you, play like you don't know anything; they want to surprise you. They'll bring it to the airport."

"Heck, what a thing to do!" Pantaleón Pantoja spins his key ring, locks the main gate, climbs into the truck. "They're going to end

up making me very sad with this kind of thing. Sinforoso, Palomino! Come out or I'm leaving you inside—we're going. Goodbye, Pantiland, so long, Itaya River. Step on it, Chino."

"And they say the same moment he died the light went out of the sky, it was only four o'clock, everything got dark, it began to rain, the people were blinded by the lightning and deafened by the thunder," Coca tends bar at the Mau Mau, travels to lumber camps in search of clients, falls in love with a knife-sharpener. "The animals on the mountain began to grunt, to bellow, and the fish came out of the water to bid farewell to Brother Francisco, who was ascending."

"I've already packed the suitcases, son," Mother Leonor shuffles bundles, packages, unmade beds, takes inventory, gives up the house. "I've only left out your pajamas, your shaving things and your toothbrush."

"Fine, Mama," Panta brings suitcases to the Faucett office, sends them ahead as unaccompanied luggage. "Were you able to speak to Pocha?"

"It was hard to, but I did," Mother Leonor telegraphs the hotel reserve rooms Pantoja family. "She sounded terrible. One good piece of news: she'll travel to Lima tomorrow with little Gladys so we can see her."

"I'll go so Panta can kiss the baby, but I warn you that your son will never be forgiven for this last dirty trick, Mother Leonor," Pochita hears radios, reads magazines, listens to gossip, feels they are pointing at her on the street, thinks she is the talk of Chiclayo. "All the newspapers here keep talking about the cemetery, and do you know what they're saying about him? Pimp. Yes, yes. *Pimp.* I'll never be on friendly terms with him again, Mother Leonor. Never ever."

"I'm happy. I want to see our little girl so bad," Panta goes through the stores on Lima Street, buys toys, a doll, bibs, an organdy dress with a sky-blue belt. "How she must've changed in a year—right, Mama?"

"She says Gladys is perfect, a little chubby, very healthy. I heard her playing over the telephone—ohhh, my pretty little granddaughter," Mother Leonor goes to the Moronacocha Ark, em-

braces the "brothers," buys medallions of the boy martyr, prayer cards of Santa Ignacia, crosses of Brother Francisco. "Pochita was very happy to learn they were taking you out of Iquitos, Panta."

"Oh, really? Well, it was logical," Panta enters the Loreto Flower Shop, chooses an orchid, takes it to the cemetery, places it in the Brazilian's niche. "But she couldn't have been as happy as you were. You've shed twenty years since I gave you the news. The only thing you haven't done is go sing and dance in the streets."

"On the other hand, you don't look at all pleased," Mother Leonor copies recipes for Amazonian dishes, buys necklaces made of seeds, fish scales, fangs, flowers made from feathers, bows and arrows with multicolored strings. "And I really don't understand, that, dear. Looks as though it makes you sad to leave that dirty work behind and be a real soldier again."

"And then the soldiers came and the bums stopped dead in their tracks when they saw him dead on the cross," Pichuza plays the lottery, catches an illness in her lung, works as a servant, begs for charity in churches. "Judases, Herods, devils. What've they done, the idiots, what've they done, the idiots, that guy from Horcones who's a lieutenant now kept saying over and over. The 'brothers' didn't even hear him: they were on their knees praying and praying, with their hands lifted up."

"It's not that it makes me sad," Pantita spends his last night in Iquitos wandering the deserted streets of Iquitos by himself and with his head down. "After all, it's three years of my life. They gave me a very difficult assignment and I executed it. Despite the difficulties, the lack of understanding, I did good work. I built something that had life, that was growing, that was useful. Now they destroy it with one blow and don't even thank me."

"You don't see how it bothers you? You've gotten used to living among prostitutes and outlaws," Mother Leonor haggles over a *shambira* hammock, decides to carry it in her hand along with her travel bag and purse. "Instead of being happy about leaving here, you're bitter."

"On the other hand, don't have any illusions," Panta calls Lieutenant Bacacorzo to say goodbye, gives his old clothing to the

blind man on the corner, reserves a taxi to pick them up at noon and take them to the airport. "I doubt very much if they'll send us anyplace better than Iquitos."

"I'll be happy anywhere so long as you don't have to do the filthy business you did here," Mother Leonor is counting the hours, the minutes, the seconds until they leave. "Even if it's to the end of the world, son."

"O.K., Mama," Panta goes to bed at dawn but doesn't shut his eyes, gets up, showers, thinks today I'll be in Lima, does not feel happy. "I'm going out for a minute to say goodbye to a friend. Want anything?"

"I saw him go out and it looked like a good time, Mother Leonor," Alicia gives her a letter for Pocha and this little gift for Gladys, accompanies her to the airport, kisses and hugs her. "Shall I take you to the cemetery quick so you can see where that w—— is buried?"

"Yes, Alicia, let's slip out," Mother Leonor powders her nose, puts on a hat, trembles with anger at the airport, gets on the plane, is frightened by the takeoff. "And afterward, come with me to St. Augustine's, to say goodbye to Father José María. You two are the only friends from this place I'm going to have fond memories of."

"His head had fallen on his heart, his eyes shut, his features had gotten real gaunt and he was very pale," Rita is taken on by Snotnose, works seven days a week, comes down with the clap twice in one year, changes pimps three times. "The rain had washed the blood from the cross, but the 'brothers' had caught that holy water in rags, buckets, dishes, they drank it and were cleansed of their sins."

"Amidst the rejoicing of some and the tears of others, hated and beloved by a divided citizenry"—Sinchi deepens his voice, uses the roaring of planes as a sound effect in the background—"today at noon the much-discussed Captain Pantoja left for Lima by air. He was accompanied by his mother and the conflicting emotions of the people of Loreto. With the proverbial courtesy of Iquitos, we limit ourselves to wishing him *bon voyage* and better behavior, Captain!"

"How embarrassing, how embarrassing," Mother Leonor sees a green sheet, thick clouds, the snowy peaks of the Andes, the sandy

236

beaches along the coast, the ocean, steep cliffs. "All the w——s of Iquitos at the airport, all of them crying, all of them hugging you. Up until the very last minute this city had to make me mad. My face is still burning. I hope I never see anyone from Iquitos ever again in my life. Listen, just think—we're about to land."

"Excuse me for bothering you again, miss," Captain Pantoja takes a taxi to the hotel, has his uniform pressed, appears at headquarters of Administration, Supply and Logistics of the Army, sits in a chair for three hours, slouches. "Are you sure I should keep on waiting? My appointment was for six and it's nine P.M. Perhaps there was some mix-up?"

"No mix-up, Captain," the young lady stops polishing her nails. "They're meeting there and have ordered you to wait. A little patience; they'll call you soon. Can I offer you another photo-novel by Corín Tellado?"

"No, thanks a lot," Captain Pantoja pages through all the magazines, reads all the newspapers, consults his watch a thousand times, is hot, cold, thirsty, feverish, hungry. "The truth is I can't read; I'm a little nervous."

"Well, it's not for nothing," the woman is making eyes at him. "What they're deciding in there is your future. I hope they don't give you a harsh punishment, Captain."

"Thanks, but it isn't just that," Captain Pantoja blushes, remembers the party where he met Pochita, the years of courtship, the arch of sabers his classmates made for him on the day of his wedding. "I'm thinking about my wife and little girl. They must have arrived a while ago, from Chiclayo. I haven't seen them in ages."

"Exactly, Colonel, sir," Lieutenant Santana crosses and recrosses the jungle, arrives at Indiana, is speechless, telephones his superiors. "Dead for a couple of days and rotting like cream of wheat. A sight to make anybody's hair stand on end. Do I let the fanatics carry him away? Bury him here? He's not in a condition to be transported anywhere. He's been here two or three days and the stench makes you vomit."

"It wouldn't bother you to give me your autograph again?" the young lady hands him a book bound in leather, a fountain pen, smiles admiringly at him. "I forgot about my cousin Charo; she collects celebrities too."

237

"Very happy to. If I've given three, what's a fourth?" Captain Pantoja writes With my respectful greetings to Charo and signs. "But I'm telling you, you're wrong, I'm no celebrity. Only singers give autographs."

"You're more famous than any performer, with the things you've done, ha ha," she takes out lipstick, makes herself up using the desk's glass top for a mirror. Nobody'd believe it, Captain, with the serious face you've got."

"Could you let me use the telephone for a moment?" Captain Pantoja looks at his watch once again, goes toward the window, sees the lampposts, the houses outlined by the mist, has a foreboding of the dampness out in the street. "I'd like to call the hotel."

"Give me the number and I'll dial it for you," she pushes a button and turns the dial. "Who do you want to speak to? Your mother?"

"It's me, Mama," Captain Pantoja grabs the receiver, talks in a very low voice, looks at the woman out of the corner of his eye. "No, they still haven't seen me. Did Pocha and the baby arrive? How's my little girl?"

"Is it true the soldiers cleared the field up to the cross with their rifle butts?" Knockers works in Bethelem, in Nanay, opens her own house on the highway to San Juan, has hordes of clients, prospers, saves. "That they chopped it down with an ax? And threw Brother Francisco, cross and all, into the river for the piranhas to eat? Tell me, Chameleon—stop praying. What'd you see?"

"Hello? Panta?" Pocha modulates her voice like a tropical singer, looks at her mother-in-law smiling happily, at little Gladys walled in by toys. "Sweetheart, how are you. Oh, Mother Leonor, I'm so thrilled, I don't know what to say to him. Gladys is right beside me. She's so pretty, Panta, you'll see her. I'm telling you, every day she looks more and more like you, Panta."

"Pocha, how are you, honey?" Panta feels his heart beating, thinks I love her, she's my wife, we'll never be separated. "A kiss to the baby and another big one for you. I'm dying to see you. I couldn't make it to the airport; forgive me."

"I know you're at the ministry; your mother explained it to me," Pochita croons, sheds a few tears, exchanges the smiles of partners in crime with Mother Leonor. "It doesn't matter that you weren't,

238

silly. What have they told you, dear, what are they going to do with you?"

"Don't know, we'll see, I'm still on tenterhooks," Panta sees shadows through the panes, regains his impatience, his fear. "Once I get out, I'll fly over there. I have to hang up, Pocha, the door's opening."

"Come in, Captain Pantoja," Colonel López López does not shake his hand, does not salute him, turns his back on him, orders.

"Good evening, Colonel," Captain Pantoja enters, bites his lip, clicks his heels, salutes. "Good evening, General. Good evening, General."

"We thought you couldn't kill a fly and it turned out you were a downright wheeler-dealer," Tiger Collazos shakes his head behind a curtain of smoke. "Do you know why you had to wait so long? We'll explain it to you right now. Do you know who just left through that door? Tell him, Colonel."

"The Secretary of War and the Chief of Staff," Colonel López López's eyes throw off sparks.

"To take the remains into Iquitos was impossible because they were already stinking and Santana and his men could have caught one helluva infection," Colonel Máximo Dávila gives the report his approval, travels to Iquitos by motorboat, has an interview with General Scavino, buys a suckling pig on his return to the garrison. "And besides, the crazy people were going to follow him, the burial was going to be monstrous. I think the river was the most sensible. I don't know what you think, General."

"Can you guess why they came?" General Victoria growls, dissolves a tablet in a glass of water, drinks, turns his nose up at it. "To rebuke the Service for the scandal at Iquitos."

"To scold us as if we were new recruits, Captain, with all our gray hairs, to yell at us." Tiger Collazos twirls his mustache, lights a cigarette with the butt of the previous one. "It's not the first time we've had the pleasure of receiving those gentlemen here. How many times, Colonel, have they bothered to come here to box our ears?"

"It's the fourth time that the Secretary of War and the Chief of Staff have honored us with a visit," Colonel López López throws cigarette butts from the ashtray into the wastepaper basket.

"And each time they appear in this office they bring us a present of a new packet of newspapers, Captain," General Victoria digs in his ears, his nose, with a blue handkerchief. "In which your praises are being sung, naturally."

"These days Captain Pantoja is one of the most popular men in Peru," Tiger Collazos grabs a clipping, points to the headline ARMY CAPTAIN PRAISES PROSTITUTION: PAYS TRIBUTE TO WHORE OF LORETO. "Where do you think this rag comes from? From Tumbes; how does that grab you?"

"It's the most widely read speech in the history of this country, no doubt about it," General Victoria turns over the newspapers on his desk, shuffles and scatters them. "The people are reciting paragraphs by heart, they make jokes about it on the street. They're even talking about you abroad."

"At last, at last, the two nightmares of the Amazon ended once and for all," General Scavino unbuttons his fly. "Pantoja silenced, the prophet dead, the specialists up in smoke, the Ark dissolving. This will be the peaceful country of the good old days once again. A little affection as a prize, Peludita."

"I very much regret having caused inconveniences to my superiors with my initiative, General, sir," Captain Pantoja does not turn a hair, does not blink, holds his breath, looks fixedly at the photograph of the President of the Republic. "That was not my intention, not in the least. I made an incorrect evaluation of the pros and cons. I recognize my responsibility. I'll accept the punishment you give me for that mistake."

"The big problem is there's no punishment serious enough for the monstrosity you felt like committing there in Iquitos," Tiger Collazos crosses his arms on his chest. "You did so much damage to the Army with that scandal, not even shooting you would be a revenge enough."

"I've turned the matter over and over in my mind and each time I'm more mixed up, Pantoja," General Victoria holds his face in his hands, looks at him maliciously, with surprise, envy, jealousy. "Be honest, tell us the truth. Why did you do such a stupid thing? Were you crazy with grief over your girlfriend's death?"

"I swear to God that my feelings for that specialist absolutely did

not influence my decision, General, sir," Captain Pantoja stands rigid, does not move his lips, counts six, eight, twelve decorations on the Supreme Commander's tunic. "What I have written in the report is the strictest truth: taking that initiative, I thought I was serving the Army."

"Giving military honors to a whore, calling her a heroine, thanking her for her service rendered to the armed forces," Tiger Collazos vomits out mouthfuls of smoke, coughs, looks at his cigarette with hatred, mutters I'm killing myself. "Don't defend us, buddy. With another favor like that one, you'd ruin us for good."

"I was in a hurry, retreating instead of fighting the last battle," Father Beltrán lays his head back in the hammock, looks at the sky and sighs. "I admit I miss the camps, the guards, the stripes. These past months I've dreamed every day about swords, about the reveille trumpet. I'm trying to get my uniform back and it looks like it might be arranged. Don't forget my balls, Peludita."

"My collaborators were profoundly affected by the death of that specialist," Captain Pantoja shifts his eyes one millimeter, makes out the map of Peru, the great green blot of the jungle. "My objective was to raise their morale, encourage them, thinking about the future. I couldn't guess that the Special Service was going to be shut down. Precisely now, when it was functioning better than ever."

"Didn't you think that Service could exist only in the most absolute secrecy?" General Victoria paces around the room, yawns, scratches his head, hears church bells, says it's very late. "You were warned time and time again that the first condition of your work was secrecy."

"The existence and functions of the Special Service were known by everyone in Iquitos, much before my initiative," Captain Pantoja keeps his feet together, his hands glued to his body, his head motionless, tries to locate Iquitos on the wall map, thinks it's that black dot. "Very much in spite of me. I took every precaution to avoid it. But in such a small city it was impossible. At the end of a few months, word had gotten around."

"Was that a reason to convert rumors into an apocalyptic truth?" Colonel López López opens the door, suggests you can

leave when you want, Anita, I'll lock up. "If you wanted to give a speech, why didn't you do it in your own name and dressed as a civilian?"

"So you all miss him a lot? Me too, we were good friends, the poor guy must be freezing to death," Lieutenant Bacacorzo lies face up. "But at least they didn't kick him out of the Army; he'd of died of sorrow. Yes, like that today. Hands on your hips, head thrown back, and keep on moving, Coca."

"On account of a mistaken evaluation of the consequences, Colonel, sir," Captain Pantoja does not not move his head, does not look out of the corner of his eye, thinks how far away all that seems. "I was tormented by the idea that what happened at Nauta would cause desertion from the Service. And it was more and more difficult to recruit specialists, at least good ones. I wanted to keep them, revive their confidence and love for the institution. I very much regret having committed that error in judgment."

"Your error has cost us a week of tantrums and bad nights," Tiger Collazos lights a new cigarette, puffs, expels smoke from his mouth and nose, has mussed hair, red and tired eyes. "Is it true that all the candidates for the Special Service passed through your hands on a personal basis?"

"It was part of the entrance examination, General, sir," Captain Pantoja blushes, becomes speechless, chokes, stutters, digs his nails, bites his tongue. "To verify aptitudes. I couldn't trust my collaborators. I had uncovered favoritism, bribes."

"I don't know how you didn't wind up with tuberculosis," Tiger Collazos holds in laughter, laughs, becomes serious, laughs again, his eyes filled with tears. "I still haven't found out if you're an angelic prick or the world's biggest cynic."

"With the Special Service gone, the Ark gone, there's no one left to defend and nobody else coughs up half what they did," Sinchi slaps his belly, turns, turns again, clucks his tongue. "There's a general conspiracy to make me die of hunger. That's the reason I'm not responding to you; it's not your lack of charm, Penelope, sweetie."

"Let's put an end to the matter once and for all," General Victoria bangs the table. "Is it true you refuse to request your discharge?"

242

"I categorically refuse, General, sir," Captain Pantoja regains his energy. "The Army is my whole life."

"We were giving you an easy out," General Victoria opens a portfolio, hands Captain Pantoja a typed sheet, waits for him to read it, keeps it. "Because we could submit you to the disciplinary board and you can already guess the sentence: dishonorable discharge, expulsion."

"We've decided not to do it, because there's been enough scandal and because of your personal background," Tiger Collazos smokes, coughs, goes to the window, opens it, spits into the street. "If you prefer to stay in the Army, O.K. You realize that with the report we've added to your service file, it's going to be a long time before you get any new stripes."

"I'll do all that's possible to rehabilitate myself, General, sir," Captain Pantoja's voice, heart, eyes rejoice. "No punishment will be worse than remorse for having caused an involuntary injury to the Army."

"O.K. Don't ever put your foot in your mouth that way again." General Victoria looks at his watch, says it's ten, I'm leaving. "We've found a new assignment for you, really far from Iquitos."

"You're leaving tomorrow morning and you won't budge from that place for at least a year, not even for twenty-four hours," Tiger Collazos puts on his jacket, tightens his tie, smooths down his hair. "If you want to stay in the Army it's indispensable that people forget about the existence of the famous Captain Pantoja. Later, when no one remembers the matter, we'll see."

"Arms tied up like this, footsies like this, your head fallen on this titty," Lieutenant Santana pants, goes, comes, decorates, ties knots, measures. "And now close your eyes and play dead, Pichuza. Just like that. Poor little specialist, oh, how awful, my little crucified girl, my pretty little 'sister' from the Ark."

"The garrison at Pomata, they need a quartermaster," Colonel López López closes the curtains, locks closets, straightens up the desks, grabs a briefcase. "Instead of the Amazon River, you'll have Lake Titicaca."

"And instead of the jungle's heat you'll have the cold of the mountains," General Victoria opens the door, lets the others go out ahead of him.

"And instead of specialists—llamas and vicuñas," Tiger Collazos puts on his kepi, turns off the light, holds out his hand. "What a strange bird you turned out to be, Pantoja. Yes, you can leave now."

"Brrrr, it's so cold, so cold," Pochita is shivering. "Where're the matches, where's the darn candle, how awful it is to live without electric lights. Wake up, Panta, it's five o'clock already. I don't know why you have to go yourself to see the soldiers' breakfast, you maniac. It's really early; I'm dying of the cold. Oh, idiot, you scratched me with that bracelet again; why don't you take it off at night? I told you, it's five o'clock already. Wake up, Panta."